Selected Stories by
SAADAT HASAN MANTO

The Dog of Tithwal

Translated from the Urdu by
Khalid Hasan and Muhammad Umar Memon

archipelago books

Library of Congress Cataloging-in-Publication Data available upon request.

Archipelago Books
232 3rd Street #A111
Brooklyn, NY 11215
www.archipelagobooks.org

Distributed by Penguin Random House
www.penguinrandomhouse.com

Cover art: Henri Cartier-Bresson
Book design by Gopa & Ted2, Inc.

This book was made possible by the New York State Council on the Arts with the support of Governor Andrew M. Cuomo and the New York State Legislature.

Funding for this book was provided by a grant from the Carl Lesnor Family Foundation.

Archipelago Books also gratefully acknowledges the generous support of the National Endowment for the Arts, Lannan Foundation, the Nimick Forbesway Foundation, and the New York City Department of Cultural Affairs.

Printed in the United States

Contents

Preface

BY VIJAY SESHADRI

WHEN, THE FAMOUS legend tells us, Kabir, the fifteenth-century poet, saint, and mystic of the Gangetic plains, died, the Hindus fought with the Muslims over his body. The Muslims wanted to bury the body in anticipation of the Day of Resurrection. The Hindus wanted to take it to Varanasi, the sacred city and Kabir's birthplace, to cremate it and relinquish the ashes to the sacred river. While the quarrel was intensifying, someone lifted the shroud covering Kabir and found that he'd vanished. In his place was a mound of flowers. A miracle. The Muslims buried half the flowers. The Hindus burned the other half.

This is an attractive story. It confirms certain ideas about India that persist to this day, among both Indians and Westerners. (I first encountered it in the nineteen-seventies, a mystical, multicultural decade, in Robert Bly's introduction to his Americanized versions of Tagore's English translations of Kabir.) It echoes the Easter-morning story nicely. It combines piety toward a person with a transcendental solution to a collective human problem. Anyone who knows the history of the medieval and modern Subcontinent could be forgiven, though, if what they heard

in it was not the harmony of the spheres but, instead, the ominous rever-
berations of communalism—the word that in South Asia denotes primar-
ily religious but also sectarian (between Sunnis and Shias, for example, or
between Sikhs and Hindus) and caste and ethnic conflict. And for anyone
who knows the stark, unyielding Partition stories of the Punjabi slash
Kashmiri slash Indian slash Bombay-wallah slash Pakistani writer Saadat
Hasan Manto (1912–1955), those echoes can become almost deafening.

It might not seem inevitable that a preface to a selection of Manto's
stories should begin by evoking the death, over five hundred years ago,
of an ecstatic devotional poet. The absence in Manto of any interest in
religion other than as a communal marker (or as in the story "God-Man,"
included in this volume, an opportunity for a variety of clerical scams)
seems to make the connection even less inevitable. There is, though an
unassailable point of comparison, one that Manto himself, a subtly sar-
donic connoisseur of paradoxes, would have appreciated. No writer in
any of the Hindustani vernaculars, and, in fact, no South Asian writer of
equivalent stature in the half-millennium since Kabir would have been
less likely, figuratively speaking, to have his body fought over by the
different communal entities than Manto.

Manto can be recognized, admired, praised—as he has been almost
from his beginnings as a writer. He can be revered—as he has been. But
he can't be embraced. He had a powerful, free-floating, impartial imagination. He could fashion characters across the entire range of available
human specimens. He had tremendous negative capability. He wrote a
dry, vocally rounded, impeccably neutral, firm, precise, and limpid Urdu
prose, which has proved to be easily accessible to translation. He had
quicksilver powers of assimilation and dissemination. His storytelling

gifts—the celerity, the smooth, masterly pacing, the controlled use of melodrama within a naturalistic frame, the instinct for dramatic tensions and for bare-bones but effective mise en scène (talents that made possible his well-compensated decade-long career in the cutting-edge media of the nineteen-thirties and -forties, as a writer of radio plays for All India Radio and a screenwriter for Bollywood)—were exemplary.

All these qualities make him wonderfully readable. But this readability has sharp edges. Is it a pleasure or a danger? Not just the darkness (in some places, the utter darkness) of so much of his material provokes this question. Given that darkness, the characteristics of Manto's supreme fictions—his laconic specificity, studied reportage, understated tone, and unwillingness to take pity on his readers by giving them at least the occasional refuge of moral judgment—make it easy to wonder if his designs on us are benign. Readers who couldn't care less about the subversive effect reading him was said to have had by the authorities of his day—he was put on trial (and acquitted) six times as a menace to society—might nevertheless feel a reluctance and unease in the face of his frankness and truth-telling. Manto's career began among the Progressive writers of the Independence era, writers strongly influenced by Marxism, who demanded literature's submission to moral outcomes. They, too, largely repudiated him. Moral rage can suffuse Manto's stories, but they have no moral outcomes.

The stories in this book are Manto's most famous. They've been culled and translated from a body of Urdu writing that is huge for any career, let alone for a career of a couple of decades (twenty-two books of short fiction, along with a novel, multiple collections of radio plays, essays, and personal sketches). There are stories here with an impressionistic interiority and ruefulness reminiscent of Chekov; stories about sex that were revolutionary for their time; stories that delicately examine the deepest privacies of consciousness, that are rich with humor, absurdity, phantasmagoria, that are self-reflexive and as much about how they are told as what they tell; stories that display a remarkably advanced feminist comprehension of women who succumb to, refuse and withstand, or triumph over male oppression and control.

Stories like these represent what might be reasonably called the normal Manto, and, even, the companionable Manto, the Manto who can be talked about in the way other artists are talked about. This Manto can be analyzed as an embodiment of literary hybridization in the aftermath of imperialism, anti-imperialism, and Independence. He can be appreciated for synthesizing influences ranging from the classical Urdu poets to Poe, Maupassant, and Gorky, and adapting them to the churning reality of India in the decades of the freedom movement. Absent the tragedy of Partition, this companionable Manto would have had a (sort of) normal career and a (sort of) normal life in cosmopolitan Bombay, his beloved adopted city, open to the sea breezes and the world, instead of being panicked into fleeing from its communal riots in the months after Independence to provincial, pious, landlocked Lahore, where he died in 1955, prematurely and impoverished, of alcohol poisoning. His deep-rooted impulses to self-sabotage and self-destruction would have been sufficiently subdued, and might even have been dissolved, by a glamorous life, an affluent life. He'd still be drinking, but far more moderately, and drinking good Scotch, not the rotgut that killed him. He would have grown old as the family man he was in his own way meant to be.

But there are other stories here, too: coldly furious allegories, fevered illustrations, parables, vignettes, sketches, some of which are shapely, some of which are bitten-off shards, perpetual fragments. These are Manto's Partition stories. They don't comprise descriptions of carnage. Instead they represent by means of ironies, indirections, and a restrained, ferociously objective orchestration of effects, humans lost in a wilderness of unspeakable violence. They are acts of imaginative courage, products of the refusal to lie, which refusal in turn becomes Manto's fatality. His reputation substantially rests on these stories, and they encircle his isolated presence in the literary landscape of mid-century South Asia. Enduring (maybe *the* enduring) artifacts of the literature of Partition, they are vehicles for impossible truths about human violence, truths that however much the evidence of history renders undeniable people other than Manto—and societies everywhere, ancient, modern, and contemporary, seeking to preserve their good opinion of themselves—repress with psychic cunning and determination. This has been especially true in India, Pakistan, and what is now Bangladesh, where the surges of mass psychosis, and the imperialist indifference shot through with spite and racial animus, that define the end of the British era gave way to a massive denial—a denial that determines and compromises national, international, and geopolitical relations in the region up to this moment. Acknowledged as he's been over the past seventy years, because of those truths Manto has never been, and never could be, the object of a cult or a following. Not only is he not embraceable, he can hardly even be approached.

This is as much the case for professional readers—scholars, critics, writers of prefaces—as it is for general ones. Critical and biographical accounts—in English, anyway, and probably even more so in other

South Asian languages—inevitably circle and approximate Manto rather than trying to get a direct fix on him. Discriminations and aesthetic judgments are made; stories are classified as successes or failures; strategies are undertaken to contain this radically disenchanted, radioactive material by asserting its crucial value to the historian of Partition, its value as a certain kind of data. Writers writing about him, baffled by the limitations of discourse itself, can seem like interlocutors at a seminar table ignoring the tiger that happens to be pacing the classroom. An indication of Manto's unique achievement is, in fact, that he makes the limitations of discourse apparent, and forces us to ask questions about the moral purpose of reading itself.

Our ordinary responses to literature tend to be loquacious, or at least talkative. We argue, admire, reject; we're eloquent or ineloquent when we like or dislike. Reading, being social, involves a rhetorical contract between reader and writer. Even the majestic darkness of "King Lear" leaves room for reader response. Manto has stories that accommodate such responses. But the towering Manto stories, irreconcilable and undeniable, don't accommodate responses. They stun us into silence, and transform the roar of Partition into a surrounding silence. This surrounding silence is one from which we want to extricate ourselves as quickly as possible; and we would, quickly, except for the fact that we can hear at the center of this silence the faint, muted sobbing of Manto's anguish, and are transfixed by it. Kabir famously said that he was neither a Hindu nor a Muslim. Manto, as pure a writer and as purely a writer as there ever was, involved in humankind to the point of his own destruction, was helplessly both, and helplessly every other kind of person, in every other place. It remains very hard for us to know what to say about such an artist.

THE DOG OF TITHWAL

Kingdom's End

THE TELEPHONE RANG. Manmohan, who was sitting beside it, picked up the receiver and spoke into it. 'Hello, this is 4457.'

A delicate female voice came from the other end. 'Sorry, wrong number.'

Manmohan hung up and returned to the book he was reading.

He had read this book nearly twenty times already, even though its last pages were moth-eaten; not because it was especially interesting, but because it was the only book in this barren office.

For the past week he had been the sole custodian of this office. Its owner, a friend of his, had gone away somewhere to arrange some credit. Since Manmohan had no place of his own, he had moved here temporarily from the streets. During this one week he had read the book nearly twenty times over.

Isolated here, he bided his time. He hated any kind of employment. Otherwise, had he wanted it, the job of director in any film company was his for the taking. But working for someone was slavery and he didn't want to be a slave. Since he was a sincere, harmless person, his friends saw to his daily needs, which were negligible: a cup of tea and a couple of pieces of toast in the morning, two *phulkas* and a little bit of gravy for lunch, and a pack of cigarettes that lasted the whole day – that's all.

Manmohan had no family or relatives. He liked solitude and was inured to hardship. He could go without food for days on end. His friends didn't know much about him, except that he had left home while still very young and had found himself an abode on the Bombay pavements for quite some time now. He only yearned for one thing in life: the love of a woman. He would say, 'If I'm lucky enough to find a woman's love, my life will change completely.'

'Even then you won't work,' his friends would say.

'Work?' He would answer with a big sigh, 'Oh, I'll become a workaholic. You'll see.'

'Well then, fall in love with someone.'

'No, I don't believe in love that is initiated by the man.'

It was almost time for lunch. Manmohan looked at the wall clock opposite him. Just then the phone rang. He picked up the receiver, 'Hello, this is 4457.'

A delicate voice asked, '4457?'

'Yes, 4457,' Manmohan confirmed.

'Who are you?' the female voice asked.

'I'm Manmohan. What can I do for you?'

When there was no answer, Manmohan asked, 'Whom do you want?'

'You,' said the voice.

'Me?' he asked, somewhat surprised.

'Yes, you. Do you have an objection?'

Manmohan was flummoxed. 'Oh no, none at all.'

The voice smiled, 'Did you say your name was Madan Mohan?'

'No. Manmohan.'

'Manmohan.'

Silence ensued. After some moments, he asked, 'You wanted to chat with me?'

'Yes,' the voice affirmed.

'Well then, chat.'

After a slight pause, the voice said, 'I don't know what to say. Why don't you start?'

'Okay,' Manmohan said, and thought for a while. 'I've already told you my name. I'm temporarily living in this office. Before, I used to sleep on the pavement, but now I sleep on the desk here.'

The voice smiled, 'Did you sleep in a canopied bed on the pavement?'

Manmohan laughed. 'Before I go any further, let me make one thing clear. I've never lied. I've been sleeping on pavements for a long time. But, for about a week now, I've had this office all to myself, and I'm having the time of my life.'

'Doing what?'

'I found a book here. The pages at the back are missing. All the same, I've read it . . . oh, about twenty times. If I ever get hold of the whole book, I'll find out what became of the hero and heroine's love.'

The voice laughed. 'You're an interesting fellow.'

'Thank you,' he said with mannered formality.

After a pause, the voice asked, 'What's your occupation?'

'Occupation?'

'I mean your work. What do you do?'

'What do I do? Nothing, really. An idle man has no work to do. I loaf around all day and sleep at night.'

'Do you like your life?'

'Give me a few moments,' Manmohan started to think. 'The truth is, I've never thought about it. Now that you've put the question to me, I'm asking myself whether I do or not.'

'So did you get an answer?'

Manmohan took some time to reply, 'No, I didn't. But since I've been living it for so long, I suppose I must like it.'

The voice laughed.

Manmohan said, 'You laugh beautifully.'

'Thank you,' the voice intoned shyly and hung up.

Manmohan stood holding the receiver for some time, smiled and returned it to its cradle. He closed up the office and went out.

Next morning at about eight o'clock, while he was still asleep on the desk, the phone rang. He yawned and took the call, 'Hello, 4457.'

'Good morning, Manmohan Sahib.'

'Good morning," he started. "Oh, you! Good morning.'

'I guess you were sleeping,' said the voice.

'Yes, I was. Since I've come over here I've become spoiled. Settling back into life on the pavement will be difficult.'

'Why?'

'A person has to get up before five in the morning there.'

He heard a laugh and asked, 'Why did you cut off the call abruptly yesterday?'

'Why did you say that I laugh beautifully?'

'What a question! If something is beautiful, shouldn't it be praised?'

'No, never.'

'You can't impose such conditions on me. I've never accepted any conditions. If you laugh, I'll certainly praise it.'

'I'll hang up.'

'You're free to do that.'

'You don't care about my displeasure?'

'First off, I don't want to displease myself. If you laugh and I don't say that it's beautiful, I'd be offending my own sense of beauty, which is very dear to me.'

There was a brief silence. Then the voice came back, 'Sorry, I was talking to the maid. So you were saying you care a lot about your sense of beauty. But tell me, is there anything you love to do?'

'What do you mean?'

'I mean . . . some hobby or work . . . or, how shall I put it, yes, is there anything you can do?'

Manmohan laughed. 'Nothing much, but I do like photography a bit.'

'That's a fine hobby.'

'Fine or not, I've never thought about it.'

'You must own an excellent camera, then?'

Manmohan laughed again. 'I don't own a camera; I borrow from friends every now and then and satisfy my urge. I have a camera in mind though. If I ever make any money, I'll buy it.'

'What camera is that?'

'Exacta. It's a reflex camera. I like it a lot.'

There was silence. Then the voice came back on. 'I was thinking about something.'

'What?'

'You haven't asked for my name or phone number.'

'I didn't feel it was necessary.'

'Why not?'

'What does it matter what your name is? And you already have my phone number. That's good enough. But if you want me to call you, then give me your name and number.'

'No, I won't.'

'That's another matter altogether! If I'm not asking you, the question of giving doesn't arise.'

'You're really a very strange man.'

There was a brief silence again.

'Thinking again?' Manmohan asked.

'Yes, but I seem to have hit a dead end.'

'Then why don't you hang up? Call some other time.'

The voice became sharp. 'You're very brusque. Please hang up, or better, I should hang up.'

Manmohan smiled and put the receiver down.

Half an hour later, after he had washed his face, changed and was about to go out, the phone rang again. He picked it up and said, '4457.'

'Is Mr Manmohan there?'

'Speaking. What can I do for you?'

'I just wanted to tell you that I'm not annoyed any more.'

'I'm happy to hear that,' he replied with good cheer.

'As I was eating breakfast it occurred to me that I shouldn't really be annoyed with you. Have you had your breakfast?'

'I was just going to go out to have some. But you called.'

'Then go home and eat some.'

'I'm not in any hurry. Besides, I don't have money on me today. I think I'll skip breakfast.'

'Hearing you say all this . . . Why do you say such things? I mean, is it because something pains you?'

Manmohan thought for a bit. 'No. Whatever pains me, I've gotten used to it.'

'Shall I send you some money?'

'If you want to. You'll be one more person added to the list of my moneymen.'

'Then I won't.'

'As you wish.'

'I'm hanging up.'

'Fine.'

Manmohan put the receiver down and went out with a smile on his lips. He returned at about ten that night, changed, lay down on the desk and started to wonder who the woman who kept phoning him might be. Her voice betrayed that she was young and there was a trill, a singsong quality in the way she laughed. It was evident from her conversation that she was educated and refined. He kept thinking about her for a long time.

Just as the clock struck eleven, the phone rang. He answered it. 'Hello!'

'Mr Manmohan.'

'Speaking. What can I do for you?'

'I rang you up so many times during the day . . . Where did you disappear?'

'I may be jobless, but I still have things to do.'

'Like what?'

'Like loafing around.'

'When did you get back?'

'About ten.'

'What are you doing now?'

'I was lying on the desk, imagining what you must look like. But all I have to go on is your voice.'

'Did you succeed?'

'No.'

'Don't try. I'm very ugly.'

'Pardon me, please hang up if you are really ugly. I loathe ugliness.'

'In that case, let's say I'm beautiful. I don't want to foster hatred.'

Neither of them spoke for a while, then Manmohan asked, 'Were you thinking?'

The voice started, 'Well, no. But I was going to ask you . . .'

'Think hard before you ask.'

The sound of a refreshing laugh came on, and then, 'Shall I sing you a song?'

'Sure.'

'Give me a minute.'

He heard her clear her throat and then start to sing the ghazal by Ghalib which begins with the line, '*Nukta-cheen hai gham-e dil* . . .'

She sang it in the entirely new style of Saigal. Her voice was soft and full of pathos. When she finished, Manmohan commended her heartily, 'Very nice! Bravo!'

'Thanks,' the voice said shyly and hung up.

As he lay on the desk, the ghazal kept reverberating in Manmohan's mind throughout the night. He got up quite early the next morning and sat in the chair, waiting for the phone to ring for a good two and a half hours. He gave up, feeling a strange bitterness in his throat. He started to pace up and down the room restlessly. Then he stretched out on the desk feeling pretty annoyed. He picked up the solitary book and began reading it all over again. The phone rang in the evening.

'Who is it?' he asked in a stiff voice.

'It's me,' the voice replied.

'Where were you all this time?' he asked, still stiffly.

'Why?' the voice quaked.

'I've been rotting here since morning. Haven't had breakfast or lunch, even though I have money.'

'I only call you when I feel like it. You . . .'

'Look here,' he cut her off, 'stop being whimsical. Fix a time to call. I can't stand waiting all day long.'

'I apologize. Starting tomorrow, I will call you in the morning and again in the evening.'

'That'll do.'

'I didn't know you were so touchy.'

Manmohan smiled, 'I'm sorry. Waiting really irritates me, and when I feel irritated, I start punishing myself.'

'Oh? How?'

'You didn't call this morning. Logically, I should have gone out. But I stayed cooped up here, fretting away all day.'

'Oh, how I wish I hadn't made this mistake,' the voice was saturated with emotion. 'I didn't call on purpose.'

'And why is that?'

'Just to find out whether you would miss my call.'

'You're very naughty,' he laughed. 'Now hang up. I've got to go eat.'

'Fine. When will you be back?'

'Say, in half an hour.'

When he returned half an hour later, she called. They chatted for quite a while. She sang him another ghazal by Ghalib and he complimented her enthusiastically. They hung up.

She began to call him every morning and evening after that and he hurriedly leaped to take her call. Sometimes they talked for hours, but he never asked for her name or phone number. In the beginning he had tried to imagine her face from the sound of her voice. Now, though, he seemed to be contented with just her voice, which was everything – her face, her body, her soul.

He smiled, 'For me, your name is your voice.'

'Which is very musical.'

'No doubt about it.'

Another day she threw a very abstruse question at him, 'Mohan, have you ever been in love with a woman?'

'No.'

'Why not?'

A sudden despondency came over him. 'This is not a question I can answer in a few words. I'll have to sift through the entire rubble of my life. And if I still can't get an answer, it would irritate me very much.'

'Then let's drop it.'

Their telephonic contact had now endured for almost a month. She called him twice every day without fail. Meanwhile, a letter arrived from his friend, the owner of the office – he had managed to get the desired credit and would be back in Bombay in a week's time. A feeling of gloom washed over Manmohan.

When she next rang him up, Manmohan said, 'My kingdom is about to end.'

'Why?'

'My friend has succeeded in getting the loan. The office will become functional very soon.'

'But one of your friends must surely have a telephone?'

'Several of them do, but I can't give you their numbers.'

'Why not?'

'I don't want anyone to hear your beautiful voice.'

'But why?'

'I'm very jealous.'

She smiled and said, 'This is going to be a big fiasco.'

'Can't be helped.'

'Well then, on your kingdom's last day I'll give you my phone number.'

'That's better.'

That feeling of gloom disappeared in an instant and he started waiting anxiously for the day when his dominion over the office would end. He again tried to imagine what she must look like. He conjured up several images. None satisfied him. Well – he told himself – it's now only a matter of a few days. Since she was willing to give her phone number, he could be reasonably sure that he would also be able to see her in person. And that thought left his mind in a daze. What a day that would be when he would see her!

The next time she called him, he said to her, 'I'm dying to see you.'

'Why?'

'You said you'll give me your phone number on the last day of my dominion here.'

'Yes, I did.'

'It's reasonable to expect that you'll also give me your address and I'll be able to see you.'

'You can see me whenever you want. Even today.'

'No, no. Not today. I want to see you in proper clothes; I mean respectable clothes. I'll ask a friend; he'll order me a new suit.'

She laughed suddenly. 'You absolutely behave like a kid. Listen, I'll give you a present when we meet.'

Manmohan became emotional. 'There could be no greater present than meeting you!'

'I've bought an Exacta camera for you.'

'Oh!'

'I'll give it to you, but on one condition: that you'll take my picture.'

He smiled. 'I'll decide about that after we meet.'

They talked for a little while longer. 'Listen,' she said, 'I won't be able to call you tomorrow or the day after.'

'Why?' he asked, feeling quite anxious.

'I'm going away with my relatives. Just for two days. You'll forgive me, won't you?'

He stayed inside the office for the rest of that day. When he woke up the next morning his body was unusually warm. Oh, it's nothing – just a slight depression brought on by the thought that she won't be calling today – he concluded. But by afternoon he was running a high temperature and his body was on fire. His eyes were burning. He lay back down on the desk. He felt terribly thirsty, which obliged him to get up repeatedly and drink from the faucet. By evening his chest felt as though it was thoroughly congested, and by the next day he was totally run down. His chest pains had become unbearable.

In his delirium he talked to his beloved's voice over the phone for hours. His condition had deteriorated badly by evening. He looked at the wall clock through blurry eyes. His ears were buzzing with strange sounds, as if countless phones were ringing all at once, and his chest was wheezing without letting up. He was engulfed in a sea of noises, so when the phone did ring, the sound failed to reach his ears. It kept ringing for a long time. He came to with a start and rushed to the phone. Holding himself steady against the wall he picked up the receiver with a trembling hand, ran his stiff tongue over his parched lips and said, 'Hello!'

'Hello, Mohan!'

'Yes, it is Mohan,' his voice faltered.

'Speak a bit louder.'

He opened his mouth to say something but the words caught in his dried-up throat.

'I returned early,' she said. 'I've been calling you for quite a while. Where were you?'

His head started to spin.

'What's happening to you?'

With great difficulty he could only say, 'My kingdom ended – today.'

Blood spilled from his mouth and trickled down his neck, leaving a long, thin streak.

'Take down my number: 50314, repeat 50314. Call me tomorrow.' She hung up.

Manmohan fell over the phone face down. Bubbles of blood began to spurt from his mouth.

Translated by Muhammad Umar Memon

For Freedom's Sake

I DO NOT REMEMBER the year but it must have been when cries of 'Inqilab Zindabad' were ringing throughout Amritsar. There was excitement in the air and a feeling of restlessness and youthful abandon. We were living through heady times. Even the fearful memories of the Jallianwala Bagh massacre had disappeared, at least on the surface. One felt intensely alive and on the threshold of something great and final.

People marched through the streets every day chanting slogans against the Raj. Hundreds were arrested for breaking the law. In fact, courting arrest had become something of a popular diversion. You were picked up in the morning and quite often released by the evening. A case would be registered, a hearing held and a short sentence awarded. You came out, shouted another slogan and were arrested again.

There was so much to live for in those days. The slightest incident sometimes led to the most violent upheaval. One man would stand on a podium in one of the city squares and call for a strike. A strike would follow. There was of course the movement to wear only Indian-spun cotton to put the Lancashire textile mills out of business. There was a boycott of all imported cloth in effect. Every street had its own bonfire.

People would walk up, take off every imported piece of clothing they were wearing and chuck it into the fire. Sometimes a woman would stand on her balcony and throw down her imported silk sari into the bonfire. The crowd would cheer.

I remember this huge bonfire the boys had lit in front of the town hall and the police headquarters, where in a wild moment my classmate Sheikhoo had taken off his silk jacket and thrown it into the flames. A big cheer had gone up because it was well known that he was the son of one of the richest men of the city, who also had the dubious distinction of being the most infamous 'toady,' as government sympathizers were popularly called. Inspired by the applause, Sheikhoo had peeled off his silk shirt and offered it to the flames too. It was only later that he remembered the gold links that had gone with it.

I don't want to make fun of my friend, because in those days I too was in the same turbulent frame of mind. I used to dream about getting hold of guns and setting up a secret terrorist organization. That my father was a government servant did not bother me. I was restless and did not even understand what I was restless about.

I was never much interested in school, but during those days I had completely gone off my books. I would spend the entire day at Jallianwala Bagh. Sitting under a tree, I would watch the windows of the houses bordering the park and dream about the girls who lived behind them. I was sure one of these days one of them would fall in love with me.

Jallianwala Bagh had become the hub of the movement of civil disobedience launched by the Congress. There were small and big tents and colourful awnings everywhere. The largest tent was the political headquarters of the city. Once or twice a week, a 'dictator' – for that was what he was called – would be nominated by the people to 'lead the struggle.' He would be ceremoniously placed in the large tent; volunteers would provide him with a ragtag guard of honour, and for the next few days he would receive delegations of young political workers, all wearing home-spun cotton. It was also the 'dictator's' duty to get donations of food and money from the city's big shopkeepers and businessmen. And so it would continue until one day the police came and picked him up.

I had a friend called Ghulam Ali. Our intimacy can be judged from the fact that we flunked our high school exams together twice. Once we had run away from home and were on our way to Bombay – from where we planned to sail for the Soviet Union – when our money ran out. After sleeping for a few nights on footpaths, we had written to our parents and promised not to do such a thing again. We were reprieved.

Shahzada Ghulam Ali, as he later came to be called, was a handsome young man, tall and fair as Kashmiris tend to be. He always walked with a certain swagger that one generally associates with 'tough guys.' Actually, he was no Shahzada – which means prince – when we were at school. However, after having become active in the civil disobedience movement and run the gamut of revolutionary speeches, public proces-sions, social intercourse with pretty female volunteer workers, garlands, slogans and patriotic songs, he had for some reason come to be known as Shahzada.

His fame spread like wildfire in the city of Amritsar. It was a small place where it did not take you long to become famous or infamous. The natives of Amritsar, though by nature critical of the general run of humanity, were rather indulgent when it came to religious and political leaders. They always seemed to have this peculiar need for fiery sermons and revolutionary speeches. Leaders had always had a long tenure in our city. The times were advantageous because the established leadership was in gaol and there were quite a few empty chairs waiting to be occupied. The movement needed people like Ghulam Ali who would be seen for a few days in Jallianwala Bagh, make a speech or two and then duly get arrested.

In those days, the German and Italian dictatorships were the new thing in Europe, which is what had perhaps inspired the Indian National Congress to designate certain party workers as 'dictators.' When Shahzada Ghulam Ali's turn came, as many as forty 'dictators' had already been put inside.

When I learnt that Ghulam Ali had been named the current 'dictator', I made my way to Jallianwala Bagh. There were volunteers outside the big tent. However, since Ghulam Ali had seen me, I was permitted to go in. A white cotton carpet had been laid on the ground and there sat Ghulam Ali, propped up against cushions. He was talking to a group of cotton-clad city shopkeepers about the vegetable trade, I think. After having got rid of them he issued a few instructions to his volunteers and turned to me. He looked too serious, which I thought was funny. When we were alone, I asked him, 'And how is our prince?'

I also realized that he had changed. To my attempt at treating the whole thing as a farce, he said, 'No, Saadat, don't make fun of it. The great honour which has been bestowed on me, I do not deserve. But from now on the movement is going to be my life.'

I promised to return in the evening as he told me that he would be making a speech. When I arrived, there was a large crowd of people around a podium they had set up for the occasion. Then I heard loud applause and there was Shahzada Ghulam Ali. He looked very handsome in his spotless white khadi outfit and his swagger seemed to add to his appeal.

He spoke for an hour or so. It was an emotional speech. Even I was overcome. There were moments when I wished nothing more than to turn into a human bomb and explode for the glory of the freedom of India.

This happened many years ago and memory always plays tricks with detail, but as I write this I can see Ghulam Ali addressing that turbulent crowd. It was not politics I was conscious of while he spoke, but youth and the promise of revolution. He had the sincere recklessness of a young man who might stop a woman on the street and say to her without any preliminaries, 'Look, I love you.'

Such were the times. I think both the British Raj and the people it ruled were still inexperienced and quite unaware of the consequences of their actions. The government, without really fully comprehending the implications, was putting people in gaol by the thousands, and those who were going to gaol were not quite sure what they were doing and what the results would be.

There was much disorder. I think you could liken the general atmosphere to a spreading fire which leaps out into the air and then just as suddenly goes out, only to ignite again. These sudden eruptions that died just as suddenly, only to burst into flame once again, had created much heat and agitation in the lacklustre, melancholy state of slavery.

As Shahzada Ghulam Ali finished speaking, the entire Jallianwala Bagh came to its feet. I stepped forward to congratulate him, but his eyes were elsewhere. My curiosity was soon satisfied. It was a girl in a white cotton sari, standing behind a flowering bush.

The next day I learnt that Shahzada Ghulam Ali was in love with the girl I had seen the previous evening. And so was she with him, and just as much. She was a Muslim, an orphan, who worked as a nurse at the local women's hospital. I think she was the first Muslim girl in Amritsar to join the Congress movement against the Raj.

Her white cotton saris, her association with the Congress and the fact that she worked in a hospital had all combined to soften that slight stiffness one finds in Muslim girls. She was not beautiful, but she was very feminine. She had acquired that hard-to-describe quality so characteristic of Hindu girls – a mixture of humility, self-assurance and the urge to worship. In her the beauty of ritualistic Muslim prayer and Hindu devotion to temple gods had been alchemized.

She worshipped Shahzada Ghulam Ali and he loved her to distraction. They had met during a protest march and fallen for each other almost immediately.

Ghulam Ali wanted to marry Nigar before his inevitable and almost eagerly awaited arrest. Why he wanted to do that I am unable to say as he could just as well have married her after his release. Gaol terms in those days varied between three months and a year. There were some who were let out after ten or fifteen days in order to make way for fresh entrants.

All that was really needed was the blessing of Babaji.

Babaji was one of the great figures of the time. He was camped at the splendid house of the richest jeweller in the city, Hari Ram. Normally, Babaji used to live in his village ashram, but whenever he came to Amritsar he would put up with Hari Ram, and the palatial residence, located outside the city, would turn into a sort of shrine, since the number of Babaji's followers was legion. You could see them standing in line, waiting to be admitted briefly to the great man's presence for what was called *darshan*, or a mere look at him. The old man would receive them sitting cross-legged on a specially constructed platform in a grove of mango trees, accepting donations and gifts for his ashram. In the evening, he would have young women volunteers sing him Hindu devotional songs.

Babaji was known for his piety and scholarship, and his followers included men and women of every faith – Hindus, Muslims, Sikhs and untouchables.

Although on the face of it Babaji had nothing to do with politics, it was an open secret that every political movement in Punjab began and ended at his behest. To the government machinery, he was an unsolved puzzle. There was always a smile on his face, which could be interpreted in a thousand ways.

The civil disobedience movement in Amritsar with its daily arrests and processions was quite clearly being conducted with Babaji's blessing, if not his direct guidance. He was in the habit of dropping hints about the tactics to be followed and the next day every major political leader in the Punjab would be wearing Babaji's wisdom as a kind of amulet around his neck.

There was a magnetic quality about him and his voice was soft, per-suasive and full of nuances. Not even the most trenchant criticism could ruffle his composure. To his enemies he was an enigma.

Babaji was a frequent visitor to Amritsar, but somehow I had never seen him. Therefore, when Ghulam Ali told me one day that he planned to call on the great man to obtain his blessing for his intended marriage to Nigar, I asked him to take me along. The next day, Ghulam Ali arranged for a tonga, and the three of us – Ghulam Ali, Nigar and I – found ourselves at Hari Ram's magnificent house.

Babaji had already had his ritualistic morning bath – *ashnan* – and his devotions were done. He now sat in the mango grove listening to a stirring patriotic song, courtesy of a young, beautiful Kashmiri Pandit girl. He sat cross-legged on a mat made from date-palm leaves, and though there were plenty of cushions around, he did not seem to want any. He was in his seventies but his skin was without a blemish. I wondered if it was the result of his famous olive oil massage every morning.

He smiled at Ghulam Ali and asked us to join him on the floor. It was obvious to me that Ghulam Ali and Nigar were less interested in the revolutionary refrain of the song, which seemed to have Babaji in a kind of trance, than their own symphony of young love. At last the girl finished, winning in the bargain Babaji's affectionate approval, indicated with a subtle nod of his head, and he turned to us.

Ghulam Ali was about to introduce Nigar and himself, but he never got an opportunity, thanks to Babaji's exceptional memory for names and faces. In his low, soothing voice he inquired, 'Prince, so you have not yet been arrested?'

'No sir,' Ghulam Ali replied, his hands folded as a mark of respect.

Playing with a pencil, which he had pulled out from somewhere, Babaji said, 'But I think you have already been arrested.' He looked meaningfully at Nigar. 'She has already arrested our prince.'

Babaji's next remark was addressed to the girl who had earlier been singing. 'These children have come to seek my blessing. Tell me, when are you going to get married, Kamal?'

Her pink face turned even pinker. 'But how can I? I am already at the ashram.'

Babaji sighed, turned to Ghulam Ali and said, 'So you two have made up your minds.'

'Yes,' they answered together. Babaji smiled.

'Decisions can sometimes be changed,' he said.

And despite the reverence-laden atmosphere, Ghulam Ali answered, 'This decision can be put off, but it can never be changed.'

Babaji closed his eyes and asked in a lawyer's voice, 'Why?'

Ghulam Ali did not hesitate. 'Because we are committed to it as we are committed to the freedom of India, and while circumstances may change the timing of that event, it is final and immutable.'

Babaji smiled. 'Nigar,' he said, 'why don't you join our ashram because Shahzada is going to gaol in a few days anyway?'

'I will,' she whispered.

Babaji changed the subject and began to ask us about political activities in Jallianwala Bagh. For the next hour or so, the conversation revolved around arrests, processions and even the price of vegetables. I did not join in these pleasantries, but I did wonder why Babaji had been so reluctant to accord his blessing to the young couple. Was he not quite sure that they were in love? Why had he asked Nigar to join the ashram? Was it to help her not to think of Ghulam Ali's incarceration or did it mean that if she joined the ashram she would not be allowed to marry?

And what was going to happen to Nigar once she was admitted to the rarefied surroundings of the ashram? Would she spend her time intoning devotional and patriotic songs for the spiritual and political enlightenment of Babaji? Would she be happy? I had seen many ashram inmates in my time. There was something lifeless and pallid about them, despite their early morning cold baths and long walks. With their pale faces, sunken eyes and ravaged bodies, they somehow always reminded me of the udders of a cow from which the last drop of milk has been squeezed out. Would the monkey eyes of these same men who stank somehow of stale grass ogle this divine one made of milk, honey, and saffron? Would these same men, with their foul-smelling breath make conversation with this fragrant creature? I couldn't see Nigar living among them, she who was so young and fresh, made up entirely, it seemed to me, of honey, milk and saffron. What did ashrams have to do with India's freedom?

I had always hated ashrams, seminaries, saints' shrines and orphanages. There was something unnatural about these places. I had often seen young boys walking in single file on the street, led by men who administered these institutions. I had visited religious seminaries and schools with their pious inmates. The older ones always wore long beards and the adolescents walked around with sparse, ugly hair sprouting out of their chins. Despite their five prayers a day, their faces never showed any trace of that inner light prayer is supposed to bring about.

Nigar was a woman, not a Muslim, Hindu, Sikh or Christian, but a woman. I simply could not see her praying like a machine every morning at the ashram. Why should she, who was herself pure as a prayer, raise her hands to heaven?

When we were about to leave, Babaji told Ghulam Ali and Nigar that they had his blessing and he would perform the marriage the next day in (where else?) Jallianwala Bagh. He arrived as promised. He was accompanied by his usual entourage of volunteers, with Hari Ram the jeweller in tow. A muchbedecked podium had been put up for the ceremony. The girls had taken charge of Nigar and she made a lovely bride. Ghulam Ali had made no special arrangements. All day long, he had been doing his usual chores, raising donations for the movement and the like. Both of them had decided to hoist the Congress flag after it was all over.

Just before Babaji's arrival, I had been telling Ghulam Ali that we must never forget what had happened in Jallianwala Bagh a few years earlier, in 1919 to be exact. There was a well in the park, which people say was full of dead bodies after General Dyer had ordered his soldiers to stop firing at the crowd. Today, I had told him, the well was used for drinking water, which was still sweet. It bore no trace of the blood which had been spilt so wantonly by the British general and his Gurkha soldiers. The flowers still bloomed and were just as beautiful as they had been on that day.

I had pointed out to Ghulam Ali a house which overlooked the park. It was said that a young girl, who was standing at her window watching the massacre, had been shot through the heart. Her blood had left a mark on the wall below. If you looked carefully, you could still perhaps see it. I remember that six months after the massacre, our teacher had taken the entire class to Jallianwala Bagh and, picking up a piece of earth from the ground, had said to us, 'Children, never forget that the blood of our martyrs is part of this earth.'

Babaji was given a military-style salute by the volunteers. He and Ghulam Ali were taken around the camp, and as the evening was falling the girls began to sing a devotional song and Babaji sat there listening to it with his eyes closed.

The song ended, and Babaji opened his eyes and said, 'Children, I am here to join these two freedom lovers in holy wedlock.' A cheer went up from the crowd. Nigar was in a sari, which bore the three colours of the flag of the Indian National Congress – saffron, green and white. The ceremony was a combination of Hindu and Muslim rituals.

Then Babaji stood up and began to speak. 'These two children will now be able to serve the nation with even greater enthusiasm. The true purpose of marriage is comradeship. What is being sanctified today will serve the cause of India's freedom. A true marriage should be free of lust and those who are able to exorcize this evil from their lives deserve our respect.'

Babaji spoke for a long time about his concept of marriage. According to him, the true bliss of marriage could only be experienced if the relationship between man and wife was something more than the physical enjoyment of each other's bodies. He did not think the sexual link was as important as it was made out to be. It was like eating. There were those who ate out of indulgence and there were those who ate to stay alive. The sanctity of marriage was more important than the gratification of the sexual instinct.

Ghulam Ali was listening to Babaji's rambling speech as if in a trance. He whispered something to Nigar as soon as Babaji had finished. Then, standing up on the podium, he said in a voice trembling with emotion, 'I have a declaration to make. As long as India does not win freedom, Nigar and I will live not as husband and wife but as friends.' He looked at his wife. 'Nigar, would you like to mother a child who would be a slave at the moment of his birth? No, you wouldn't.'

The crowd applauded again and Ghulm Ali grew passionate. He was so elated from having saved Nigar from the humiliation of mothering slave children that he strayed from the subject at hand and launched into a sermon on attaining independence. At one point, he looked at Nigar and stopped speaking. To me he looked like a drunken man who realizes too late that he has no money left in his wallet. But he recovered his composure and said to Babaji, 'Both of us need your blessing. You have our solemn word of honour that the vow made today shall be kept.'

The next morning Ghulam Ali was taken in because he had threatened to overthrow the British government and had declared publicly that he would father no children as long as India was ruled by a foreign power. He was given eight months and sent to the distant Multan gaol. He was Amritsar's fortieth 'dictator' to be imprisoned and the forty thousandth prisoner of the civil disobedience movement against the Raj.

Everybody thought that freedom was just around the corner. However, the Raj was cleverer than we were prepared to give it credit for. It let the movement come to a boil, then made a deal with the leaders, and everything simmered down.

When the workers began to come out of gaol, they realized that the atmosphere had changed. Wisely, most of them decided to resume their normal, humdrum lives. Shahzada Ghulam Ali was let out after seven months, and while it is true that the people's former passion had fizzled out, he was received by a large crowd at the Amritsar railway station from where he was taken out in a procession through the city. A number of public meetings were also held in his honour, but it was evident that the fire and fury had died out. There was a sense of fatigue among the people. It was as if they were runners in a marathon who had been told by the organizers to stop running, return to the starting point, and begin again.

Years went by, but that heady feeling never returned. In my own life, a number of small and big revolutions came and went. I went to college, but failed my exams twice. My father died and I had to run from pillar to post looking for a job. I finally found a translator's position with a third-class newspaper, but I soon became restless and left. For a time, I joined the Aligarh Muslim University, but fell ill and was sent to the more salubrious climate of Kashmir to recover. After three months there, I moved to Bombay. Disgusted with its frequent Hindu-Muslim riots, I made my way to Delhi, but found it too slow. If there was movement at all, it felt somehow effete. I preferred Bombay. What did it matter that my next-door neighbour didn't even bother to ask my name?

It was now eight years since I had left Amritsar. I had no idea what had happened to my old friend or the streets and squares of my early youth. I had never written to anyone and the fact was that I was not interested in the past or the future. I was living in the present. The past, it seemed to me, was like a sum of money you had already spent, and to think about it was like drawing up a ledger account of money you no longer had.

One afternoon – I had both time and some money – I decided to go looking for a pair of shoes. Once, while passing by the Army & Navy Store, I had noticed a small shop, which had a very attractive display window. I didn't find that shop, but I noticed another, which looked quite reasonable.

'Show me a pair of shoes with rubber soles,' I told the shop assistant.

'We don't stock them,' he replied.

Since the monsoons were expected any time, I asked him if he could sell me rubber ankle-boots.

'We don't stock those either,' he said. 'Why don't you try the store at the corner? We don't carry any items made of rubber here.'

'Why?' I asked, surprised.

'It's the boss's orders,' he answered.

As I stepped out of this strange place that did not sell rubber shoes, I saw a man carrying a small child. He was trying to buy oranges from a vendor.

'Ghulam Ali,' I screamed excitedly.

'Saadat,' he shouted, embracing me. The child didn't like it and began to cry. He went into the shop and asked the assistant with whom I had just been talking to take the child home.

'It's been years, hasn't it?' he said.

He had changed. He was no longer the cotton-clad revolutionary who used to make fiery speeches in Jallianwala Bagh. He looked like a normal, domesticated man.

My mind went back to his last speech. *Nigar, would you like to mother a child who would be a slave at birth?*

'Whose child was that?' I asked.

'Mine. I have another one who is older. How many children do you have?' he answered without hesitation.

What had happened? Had he forgotten the vow he had taken that day? Was politics no longer a part of his life? What had happened to his passion for the freedom of India? Where was that firebrand revolutionary I used to know? What had happened to Nigar? What had induced her to beget slave children? Had Ghulam Ali married a second time?

'Talk to me,' he said. 'We haven't seen each other for ages.'

I didn't know where to begin, but he didn't put me to the test.

'This shop belongs to me. I've been living in Bombay for the last two years. I'm told you are a big-time writer now. Do you remember the old days? How we ran away from home to come to Bombay? God, how time flies!'

We went into the shop. A customer who wanted a pair of tennis shoes was told that he would have to go to the shop at the corner.

'Why don't you stock them? You know I also came here looking for a pair,' I said.

Ghulam Ali's face fell. 'Let's say I just don't like those things,' he replied.

'What things?'

'Those horrible rubber things. But I'll tell you why,' he said.

The anxious look, which had clouded his handsome face suddenly, cleared. 'That life was rubbish. Believe me, Saadat, I have forgotten about those days when the demon of politics was in my head. I'm very happy. I have a wife and two children and my business is doing well.'

He took me to a room at the back of the store. The assistant had come back. Then he began to talk. I will let him tell his story.

'You know how my political life began. You also know what sort of person I was. I mean we grew up together and we were no angels. I wasn't a strong person and yet I wanted to accomplish something in my life. I swear upon God that I was prepared then, as I am prepared today, to sacrifice even my life for the freedom of India. However, after much reflection, I've come to the conclusion that both the politics of India and its political leadership are immature. There are sudden storms and then all is quiet. Storms don't come out of nowhere.

'Look, man may be good or evil, but he should remain the way God made him. You can be virtuous without having your head shaved, without donning saffron robes or covering yourself with ash. Those who advocate such things forget that these external manifestations of virtue, if that be indeed what they are, will only get lost on those who follow them. Only ritual will survive, what led to the ritual will be overlooked. Look at all the great prophets. Their teachings are no longer remembered, but we still have their legacy of crosses, holy threads and unshaven armpit hair. They tell you to kill your baser self. Well, if everyone went ahead and did it, what sort of a world would it be?

'You have no idea what hell I went through because I decided to violate human nature. I made a pledge that I would not produce children. It was made in a moment of euphoria. As time passed, I began to feel that the most vital part of my being was paralysed. What was more, it was my own doing. There were moments when I felt proud of my great vow, but they passed. As the pores of my consciousness began to open, reality seemed to want to defeat my resolve. When I met Nigar after my release, I felt that she had changed. We lived together for one year and we kept our promise to Babaji. It was hell. We were being consumed by the futility of our married life.

'The world outside had changed too. Spun cotton, tricolour flags and revolutionary slogans had lost their power. The tents had disappeared from Jallianwala Bagh. There were only holes in the ground where those grand gatherings used to take place. Politics no longer sent the blood cruising through my veins as it used to.

'I spent most of my time at home and we never spoke our minds to each other. I was afraid of touching her. I did not trust myself. One day, as we sat next to each other, I had a mad urge to take her in my arms and kiss her. I let myself go, but I stopped just in time. It was a tremendous feeling while it lasted. However, in the days that followed, I couldn't get rid of a feeling of guilt.

'There had to be a way out of this absurd situation. One day we hit upon a compromise. We would not produce children. We would take the necessary steps, but we would live as husband and wife.

'Thus began a new chapter in our lives. It was as if a blind man had been given back the sight of one eye. But our happiness did not last. We wanted our full vision restored. We felt unhappy and it seemed that everything in our lives had turned into rubber. Even my body felt blubbery and unnatural. Nigar's agony was even more evident. She wanted to be a mother and she couldn't be. Whenever a child was born in the neighbourhood, she would shut herself in a room.

'I wasn't so keen on children myself because, come to think of it, one did not really have to have them. There were millions of people in the world who seemed to be able to get by without them. I could well be one of them. However, what I could no longer stand was this clammy sensation in my hands. When I ate, it felt as if I was eating rubber. My hands always felt as if they had been soaped and then left unrinsed.

'I began to hate myself. All my sensations had atrophied except this weird, unreal sense of touch, which made everything feel like rubber. All I needed to do was peel off my terrible affliction with the help of two fingers and throw it as far as possible. But I didn't have the courage.

'I was like a drowning man who clutches at straws. And one day I found the straw I was looking for. I was reading a religious text and there it was. I almost jumped. It said, "If a man and woman are joined in wedlock, it is obligatory for them to procreate." And that day I peeled off my curse and have never looked back.'

At this moment, a servant entered the room. He was carrying a child who was holding a balloon. There was a bang and all the child was left with was a piece of string with a shrivelled piece of ugly rubber dangling at the other end.

With two fingers, Ghulam Ali carefully picked up the deflated balloon and threw it away as if it were some infinitely disgusting piece of filth.

Translated by Khalid Hasan

The Dog of Tithwal

THE SOLDIERS had been entrenched in their positions for several weeks, but there was little, if any, fighting, except for the dozen rounds they ritually exchanged every day.

The weather was extremely pleasant. The air was heavy with the scent of wild flowers and nature seemed to be following its course, quite oblivious to the soldiers hiding behind rocks and camouflaged by mountain shrubbery. The birds sang as they always had and the flowers were in bloom. Bees buzzed about lazily.

Only when a shot rang out, the birds got startled and took flight, as if a musician had struck a jarring note on his instrument. It was almost the end of September, neither hot nor cold. It seemed as if summer and winter had made their peace. In the blue skies, cotton clouds floated all day like barges on a lake.

The soldiers seemed to be getting tired of this indecisive war where nothing much ever happened. Their positions were quite impregnable. The two hills on which they were placed faced each other and were about the same height, so no one side had an advantage. Down below in the valley, a stream zigzagged furiously on its stony bed like a snake.

The air force was not involved in the combat and neither of the adversaries had heavy guns or mortars. At night, they would light huge fires and hear each other's voices echoing through the hills.

The last round of tea had just been taken. The fire had gone cold. The sky was clear and there was a chill in the air and a sharp, though not unpleasant, smell of pine cones. Most of the soldiers were already asleep, except Jamadar Harnam Singh, who was on night watch. At two o'clock, he woke up Ganda Singh to take over. Then he lay down, but sleep was as far away from his eyes as the stars in the sky. He began to hum a Punjabi folk song:

> *Bring me a pair of star-spangled shoes*
> *yes, star-spangled*
> *Harnam Singh, O darlin'*
> *should it cost you your buffalo.*

On all sides, Harnam Singh could see star-spangled shoes, scattered over the sky and twinkling softly.

> *Them star-spangled shoes I'll bring you*
> *yes, star-spangled*
> *Harnam Kaur, O darlin'*
> *should it cost me my buffalo.*

He smiled, and knowing that sleep now would not come, he woke the others. The thought of a woman had excited his mind; he wanted to make foolish conversation; conversation in which he might re-live his feeling for Harnam Kaur.

Talk did begin, but it was abrupt and disjointed. Banta Singh, who was the youngest among them, and had the best voice, sat to one side as the others chatted, yawning now and then. After a while, Banta Singh, in his mournful voice, began to sing 'Hir':

'Hir said, "the yogi lied; no one pacifies an aggrieved lover/I searched and searched, but found no one who could call back the departed. A hawk lost a crane to the crow; look, does he lament or not? Give not to those who suffer fond tales."'

Then a moment later, he sang Ranjha's reply to Hir's words:

'"That hawk that lost the crane to the crow is thankfully annihilated/He is like the fakir that gave up all his possessions, and was ruined/Be contented, feel less and God becomes your witness/Quit the world, wear the sackcloth and ashes and Sayyed Waris becomes Waris Shah."'

A deep sadness fell over them. Even the grey hills seemed to have been affected by the melancholy of the songs.

Some moments later, Corporal Harnam Singh, after hurling filthy abuse at an invisible object, lay down.

This mood was shattered by the barking of a dog. Jamadar Harnam Singh said, 'Where has this son of a bitch materialized from?'

The dog barked again. He sounded closer. There was a rustle in the bushes. Banta Singh got up to investigate and came back with an ordinary mongrel in tow. He was wagging his tail. 'I found him behind the bushes and he told me his name was Jhun Jhun,' Banta Singh announced. Everybody burst out laughing.

The dog went to Harnam Singh, who produced a cracker from his kitbag and threw it on the ground. The dog sniffed at it and was about to eat it, when Harnam Singh snatched it away . . . 'Wait, you could be a Pakistani dog.'

They laughed. Banta Singh patted the animal and said to Harnam Singh, 'Jamadar sahib, Jhun Jhun is an Indian dog.'

'Prove your identity,' Harnam Singh ordered the dog, who began to wag his tail.

'This is no proof of identity. All dogs can wag their tails,' Harnam Singh said.

'He is only a poor refugee,' Banta Singh said, playing with his tail.

Harnam Singh threw the dog a cracker, which he caught in mid-air. 'Even dogs will now have to decide if they are Indian or Pakistani,' one of the soldiers observed.

Harnam Singh produced another cracker from his kitbag. 'And all Pakistanis, including dogs, will be shot.'

A soldier shouted, 'India Zindabad! Long live India!'

The dog, who was about to munch his cracker, stopped dead in his tracks, put his tail between his legs and looked scared. Harnam Singh laughed. 'Why are you afraid of your own country? Here, Jhun Jhun, have another cracker.'

The morning broke very suddenly, as if someone had switched on a light in a dark room. It spread across the hills and valleys of Tithwal, which is what the area was called.

The war had been going on for months but nobody could be quite sure who was winning it.

Jamadar Harnam Singh surveyed the area with his binoculars. He could see smoke rising from the opposite hill, which meant that, like them, the enemy was busy preparing breakfast.

Subedar Himmat Khan of the Pakistan army gave his huge moustache a twirl and began to study the map of the Tithwal sector. Next to him sat his wireless operator, who was trying to establish contact with the platoon commander to obtain instructions. A few feet away, the soldier Bashir sat on the ground, his back against a rock and his rifle in front of him. He was humming:

Where did you spend the night, my love, my moon?
Where did you spend the night?

Enjoying himself, he began to sing more loudly, savouring the words. Suddenly he heard Subedar Himmat Khan scream, 'Where did *you* spend the night?'

But this was not addressed to Bashir. It was a dog he was shouting at. He had come to them from nowhere a few days ago, stayed in the camp quite happily and then suddenly disappeared last night. However, he had now returned like a bad coin.

Bashir smiled and began to sing to the dog. 'Where did *you* spend the night, where did you spend the night?' But he only wagged his tail. Subedar Himmat Khan threw a pebble at him. 'All he can do is wag his tail, the idiot.'

'What has he got around his neck?' Bashir asked.

One of the soldiers grabbed the dog and undid his makeshift rope collar. There was a small piece of cardboard tied to it. 'What does it say?' the soldier, who could not read, asked.

Bashir stepped forward and with some difficulty was able to decipher the writing. 'It says Jhun Jhun.'

Subedar Himmat Khan gave his famous moustache another mighty twirl and said, 'Perhaps it is a code. Does it say anything else, Bashirey?'

'Yes sir, it says it is an Indian dog.'

'What does that mean?' Subedar Himmat Khan asked.

'Perhaps it is a secret,' Bashir answered seriously.

'If there is a secret, it is in the word Jhun Jhun,' another soldier ventured in a wise guess.

'You may have something there,' Subedar Himmat Khan observed.

Dutifully, Bashir read the whole thing again. 'Jhun Jhun. This is an Indian dog.'

Subedar Himmat Khan picked up the wireless set and spoke to his platoon commander, providing him with a detailed account of the dog's sudden appearance in their position, his equally sudden disappearance the night before and his return that morning. 'What are you talking about?' the platoon commander asked.

Subedar Himmat Khan studied the map again. Then he tore up a packet of cigarettes, cut a small piece from it and gave it to Bashir. 'Now write on it in Gurmukhi, the language of those Sikhs . . .'

'What should I write?'

'Well . . .'

Bashir had an inspiration. 'Shun Shun, yes, that's right. We counter Jhun Jhun with Shun Shun.'

'Good,' Subedar Himmat Khan said approvingly. 'And add: This is a Pakistani dog.'

Subedar Himmat Khan personally threaded the piece of paper through the dog's collar and said, 'Now go join your family.'

He gave him something to eat and then said, 'Look here, my friend, no treachery. The punishment for treachery is death.'

The dog kept eating his food and wagging his tail. Then Subedar Himmat Khan turned him round to face the Indian position and said, 'Go and take this message to the enemy, but come back. These are the orders of your commander.'

The dog wagged his tail and moved down the winding hilly track that led into the valley dividing the two hills. Subedar Himmat Khan picked up his rifle and fired in the air.

The Indians were a bit puzzled, as it was somewhat early in the day for that sort of thing. Jamadar Harnam Singh, who in any case was feeling bored, shouted, 'Let's give it to them.'

The two sides exchanged fire for half an hour, which of course was a complete waste of time. Finally, Jamadar Harnam Singh ordered that enough was enough. He combed his long hair, looked at himself in the mirror and asked Banta Singh, 'Where has that dog Jhun Jhun gone?'

'Dogs can never digest butter, goes the famous saying,' Banta Singh observed philosophically.

Suddenly the soldier on lookout duty shouted, 'There he comes.'

'Who?' Jamadar Harnam Singh asked.

'What was his name? Jhun Jhun,' the soldier answered.

'What is he doing?' Harnam Singh asked.

'Just coming our way,' the soldier replied, peering through his binoculars.

Subedar Harnam Singh snatched them from him. 'That's him all right and there's something around his neck. But, wait, that's the Pakistani hill he's coming from, the motherfucker.'

He picked up his rifle, aimed and fired. The bullet hit some rocks close to where the dog was. He stopped.

Subedar Himmat Khan heard the report and looked through his binoculars. The dog had turned round and was running back. 'The brave never run away from battle. Go forward and complete your mission,' he shouted at the dog. To scare him, he fired at the same time. The bullet passed within inches of the dog, who leapt in the air, flapping his ears. Subedar Himmat Khan fired again, hitting some stones.

It soon became a game between the two soldiers, with the dog running round in circles in a state of great terror. Both Himmat Khan and Harnam Singh were laughing boisterously. The dog began to run towards Harnam Singh, who abused him loudly and fired. The bullet caught him in the leg. He yelped, turned around and began to run towards Himmat Khan, only to meet more fire, which was only meant to scare him. 'Be a brave boy. If you are injured, don't let that stand between you and your duty. Go, go, go,' the Pakistani shouted.

The dog turned. One of his legs was now quite useless. He began to drag himself towards Harnam Singh, who picked up his rifle, aimed carefully and shot him dead.

Subedar Himmat Khan sighed, 'The poor bugger has been martyred.'

Jamadar Harnam Singh ran his hand over the still-hot barrel of his rifle and muttered, 'He died a dog's death.'

Translated by Khalid Hasan

The Mice of Shah Daulah

S ALIMA WAS TWENTY-ONE when she was married. And though five years had passed, she had not had a child. Her mother and mother-in-law were very worried. Her mother, more so, for fear that her husband, Najib, would marry again. Many doctors were consulted, but none were of any help.

Salima was anxious too. Few girls do not desire a child after marriage. She consulted her mother and acted on her instructions, but to no avail.

One day a friend of hers came to see her. The friend had been declared barren and so Salima was surprised to see that she held in her arms a gem of a boy. 'Fatima,' she asked indelicately, 'how did you produce this child?'

Fatima was five years older than Salima. She smiled and said, 'This is the benevolence of Shah Daulah. A woman told me that if I wanted children, I should go to the shrine of Shah Daulah in Gujarat and make my entreaty. Say, "Hazur, the first child born to me, I will offer up in your service."' This child would be born with a very small head, she told Salima. Salima didn't like this. And when Fatima insisted that this firstborn child had to be left in the service of the shrine, she was sadder still. She thought, what mother would deprive herself of her child forever? Only a monster could abandon its child, whether his head be small, his nose flat or his eyes crossed. But Salima wanted a child so badly that she heeded her older friend's advice.

She was, in any case, native to Gujarat where Shah Daulah's shrine was. So she said to her husband, 'Fatima's insisting I go with her. Would you give me permission?' What objection could her husband have? He said, 'Go, but come back quickly.' Salima went off with Fatima.

Shah Daulah's shrine was not, as she had thought, some old, decrepit building. It was a decent place which she liked well enough. But when in one chamber she saw Shah Daulah's 'mice,' with their running noses and their feeble minds, she began to tremble. There was a young girl, in the prime of her youth, whose antics were such that she could reduce the most serious of serious people to fits of laughter. Watching her, Salima laughed to herself for an instant. Then immediately her eyes filled with tears. What will become of this girl, she thought. The shrine's caretakers will sell her to somebody who'll take her from town to town like a performing monkey; the poor wretch, she'll become somebody's source of income. Her head was very small. But Salima thought, even if her head is small, her heart can't be similarly small; that remains the same, even in madmen.

Shah Daulah's mouse had a beautiful body, rounded and proportionate in every way. But her antics were those of someone whose faculties had been decimated. Seeing her wander about, laughing like a wind-up doll, Salima felt as if she'd been made for this purpose.

And yet, despite her misgivings, Salima followed her friend Fatima's advice and prayed at Shah Daulah's shrine, swearing that if she had a child, she would hand him over.

Salima continued her medical treatment as well. After two months, she showed signs of pregnancy. She was thrilled. A boy was soon born to her, a beautiful boy. There had been a lunar eclipse during her pregnancy, and he was born with a small, not unattractive, mark on his right cheek.

When Fatima visited Salima, she said that the boy should be handed over at once to Shah Daulah saab. Salima herself had accepted this, but she had been delaying it for many days; the mother in her wouldn't allow her to go through with it; she felt as though a part of her heart was being cut out.

She had been told that the firstborn of those who asked a child of Shah Daulah would have a small head. But her son's head was quite big. Fatima said, 'This is not something you can use as an excuse. This child of yours is Shah Daulah's property. You have no right over him. If you stray from your promise, remember that a scourge will befall you, the likes of which you won't forget for a lifetime.'

So, with her heart breaking, Salima went back to Gujarat, to the shrine of Shah Daulah, and handed to its caretakers her beloved flower of a son, with the black mark on his right cheek.

She wept. Her grief was so great she became sick. For a year, she hovered between life and death. She couldn't forget her boy nor the pleasing mark on his right cheek, which she had so often kissed.

She had strange dreams. Shah Daulah, in her distressed imagination, became a large mouse gnawing, with its razor-edged teeth, at her flesh. She would shriek and implore her husband to help her. 'Look, he's eating my flesh!' she would cry.

Sometimes her fevered mind would see her son entering a mouse hole. She would be holding onto his tail, but the bigger mice had him by the snout and she couldn't pull him out.

Sometimes the very young girl, whom she'd seen in a chamber of Shah Daulah's shrine, would appear before her, and Salima would let out a laugh. Then a moment later, she would begin to cry. She would cry so much that her husband wouldn't know how to quell her tears.

Salima saw mice everywhere, in bed, in the kitchen, in the bathroom, on the sofa, in her heart. Sometimes she felt she herself was a mouse: her nose was running, she was in a chamber of Shah Daulah's shrine, carrying her tiny head on her weak shoulders, and her antics made onlookers fall over themselves with laughter. Her condition was pitiable.

Her world had been scarred like the cratered face of a dead planet.

The fever subsided, and Salima's condition stabilized. Najib was relieved. He knew the cause of his wife's illness, but he was in the grip of superstition himself and hardly conscious that he had offered up his firstborn as a sacrifice. Whatever had been done seemed right to him; in fact, he felt that the son that had been born to him was not even his, but Shah Daulah saab's. When Salima's fever, along with the storm in her mind and soul, cooled, Najib said to her, 'My darling, you must forget your son. He was meant for sacrifice.'

Salima replied in a wounded voice, 'I don't believe in any of it. All my life I will curse myself for committing a great wrong by handing over a piece of my heart to those caretakers. They cannot be his mother.'

One day, Salima disappeared to Gujarat and spent eight or nine days there, making inquiries about her son, but learned nothing of his where-abouts. She returned, depressed, and said to her husband, 'Now I won't pine for him any longer.'

Pine for him she did, but inwardly.

Remember him, she did, but deep within herself. The mark on her son's right cheek had been branded on her heart.

A year later Salima had a daughter. Her face bore a great resemblance to her firstborn's although she didn't have a mark on her right cheek. Salima called her Mujiba because she had intended to name her son Mujib.

When she was two months old, Salima sat her in her lap, and taking a little kohl, made a large beauty spot on her right cheek. Then she thought of Mujib and wept. When her tears fell on her daughter's cheeks, she wiped them with her dupatta and laughed. She wanted to try and forget her grief.

Salima had two sons thereafter. Her husband was now very pleased. Finding herself in Gujarat for a friend's wedding, she returned again to the shrine and made inquiries about her Mujib, but to no avail. She thought that perhaps he had died. And so, one Thursday, she organized a memorial for him.

The women of the neighbourhood wondered for whose death these rites were being so carefully observed. Some even questioned Salima, but she gave no reply.

In the evening she took her ten-year-old Mujiba by the hand and led her inside. She made a spot on her right cheek with kohl and kissed it profusely. She had always imagined her to be her lost Mujib, but now she gave up thinking about him. After the ceremony, the weight in Salima's heart lightened. She had made a grave for him in her imagination, on which she would place flowers.

Salima's three children were now in school. Every morning she dressed them, made them breakfast, got them ready and sent them off. When they'd gone she'd think for a moment of Mujib, and the ceremony she had performed for him. Her heart was lighter and yet she felt sometimes that the mark on Mujib's right cheek was still branded on it.

One day her three children came running in, saying, 'Ammi, we want to see the show.'

'What show?' she asked lovingly.

Her eldest daughter replied, 'Ammi, there's a man who does the show.'

Salima said, 'Go and call him, but not in the house. He should do the show outside.'

The children ran off, came back with the man and watched the show.

When it was over, Mujiba went to her mother to ask for money. Her mother took out a quarter rupee from her purse and went out onto the veranda. She had reached the door when she saw one of Shah Daulah's mice moving his head in a crazed fashion. Salima began to laugh.

There were ten or twelve children around him, laughing uncontrollably. The noise was so great that no one could hear a word.

Salima advanced with the quarter rupee in her hand, but just as she was about to give it to Shah Daulah's mouse, her hand was flung back as though struck by an electric current.

This mouse had a mark on its right cheek. Salima looked closely at him. His nose was running. Mujiba, who was standing near him, said to her mother, 'This, this mouse, Ammi, why does he look so much like me? Am I a mouse too?'

Salima took Shah Daulah's mouse by the hand and went inside. She closed the door and kissed him and said prayers for him. He was her Mujib. But his antics were so moronic that Salima couldn't help but laugh even though her heart was filled with grief.

She said to Mujib, 'My son, I am your mother.'

At this, the mouse laughed uproariously, and wiping his runny nose on his sleeve, stood with his hands open before his mother and said, 'One paisa!'

His mother opened her purse, but by then her eyes had begun to overflow with tears. She took out a hundred rupees from her purse and went out to give it to the man who had made a spectacle of Mujib. He refused, saying that he couldn't part with his means of income for such a small amount. In the end Salima got him to settle on five hundred rupees. But when she came back inside, Mujib was gone. Mujiba told her that he had run out the back door.

Salima's womb cried out for him to come back, but he'd gone, never to return.

Translated by Aatish Taseer

Ten Rupees

S HE WAS PLAYING with the little girls at the far end of the alley. Inside
the chawl, her mother hunted for her everywhere. Kishori sat waiting
in their room; someone had been told to bring him tea. Sarita's mother
now began searching for her on all three floors of the chawl. Who knew
which hole Sarita had gone and died in? She even went into the bath-
rooms, yelling, 'Sarita . . . Sarita!' But Sarita, as her mother was beginning
to realize, was not in the chawl. She was outside on the corner of the alley,
near a heap of garbage, playing with the little girls, utterly carefree.

Her mother was in a panic.

Kishori sat waiting in the room; the men he'd brought – as promised,
two rich men, with a motor car – waited in the main market, but where
had her daughter vanished to? She couldn't even use the excuse of dysentery any more; she was well now. And rich men with motor cars didn't
come every day. It was Kishori's benevolence that once or twice a month,
he managed to bring clients with motor cars. Normally he was nervous
of neighbourhoods like this, with their compound stench of paan and
stale bidis. How could he bring rich men here? But because he was smart,
Kishori never brought the men to the chawl. Instead, he brought Sarita,

bathed and clothed, to them, explaining 'these are uncertain times; the place is crawling with police spies; they've taken away nearly a hundred working girls; there's even a case against me in the courts so one has to tread very carefully.'

Sarita's mother had by now become very angry. When she came down, Ramdi was sitting at the bottom of the stairs, cutting leaves for the bidis as usual. 'Have you seen Sarita anywhere?' Sarita's mother demanded, 'God knows which hole she's gone and died in. And today of all days! Wait till I find her! I'll give her a thrashing she'll remember in every joint of her body. She's a full-grown woman, you know, and all she ever does is waste the day fooling around with kids.'

Ramdi said nothing and continued to cut the bidi leaves. But Sarita's mother wasn't really speaking to her, she was just ranting as usual as she walked past. Every few days, she would go off in search of Sarin, and repeat the same words to Ramdi.

Sarita's mother would also tell the chawl's women that she wanted Sarita to marry a clerk some day. This was why she had always impressed upon Sarita the importance of education. The municipality had opened a school nearby and Sarita's mother wondered if she should admit her daughter there. 'Sister, you know, her father had such a desire that his daughter should be educated!' At this point she would sigh, and repeat the story of her dead husband, which every woman in the chawl knew by heart. If you were to say to Ramdi, 'All right, when Sarita's father worked in the railways and the big sahib insulted him, what happened?' she would immediately reply, 'Sarita's father foamed at the mouth and said to the sahib, "I'm not your servant; I'm the government's servant. You have no right to throw your weight round here. And careful – if you insult me again, I'll rip your jaws out and shove them down your throat." Then, what? What was bound to happen happened! The sahib was livid and insulted Sarita's father again. Sarita's father came forward and delivered such a powerful blow to the sahib's neck that his hat flew off his head and landed ten paces away and he saw stars in the daytime! But the sahib was not a small man either. He retaliated by kicking Sarita's father on the back with his army boot, and with such force that his spleen burst, and there and then, by the railway lines, he fell to the floor and breathed his last. The government ran a court case against the sahib and extracted a full five hundred rupees in compensation from him for Sarita's mother. But her luck was bad. She developed a taste for the lottery, and within five months, she had squandered the money.'

This story was always ready on Sarita's mother's lips, but nobody was sure whether or not it was true. In any case, it didn't evoke any compassion for her in the chawl, perhaps because everyone there was also deserving of compassion. And no one was anyone's friend. The men, by and large, slept during the day and were awake at night as many worked the night shift at the nearby mill. They lived together, but they showed no interest in each other's lives.

In the chawl, virtually everyone knew that Sarita's mother had sent her young daughter into prostitution. But since these were people who treated each other neither well nor badly, they felt no need to expose her when she'd say, 'My daughter's an innocent, she knows nothing of this world.'

One morning, when Tukaram made an advance on Sarita, her mother began to screech and yell, 'For God's sake, why doesn't anyone control this wretched baldy? May the Lord make him blind in both the eyes with which he ogles my virgin daughter! I swear, one day, there'll be such a brawl that I'll take this darling of yours and beat his head to a pulp with the heel of my shoe. Outside, he can do whatever he wants, but in here he'd better learn to behave like a decent human being, do you hear?'

Hearing this, Tukaram's cross-eyed wife appeared, tying her dhoti as she approached. 'You wretched witch, don't you dare let one more word escape your lips! This virginal daughter of yours even makes eyes at the boys who hang around the hotel. Do you think we're all blind? You think we don't know of the clerks who come to your house? This daughter of yours, Sarita, why does she get all made up and go out? You really have some nerve, coming in here with airs of respectability. Go get lost, some-where far away, go on!'

There were many well-known stories about Tukaram's cross-eyed wife. Everyone knew that when the kerosene dealer would come with his kerosene, she would take him into her quarter and lock the door. Sarita's mother loved to draw attention to this. In a voice brimming with hatred she would repeat, 'And your lover, the kerosene oil dealer – two hours at a time, when you keep him locked up in your quarter, what are you doing? Sniffing his kerosene oil?'

The spats between Tukaram's wife and Sarita's mother never lasted long because one night Sarita's mother had caught her neighbour exchanging sweet nothings with someone in pitch darkness. And the very next night, Tukaram's wife had seen Sarita with a 'gentleman man' in a motor car. As a result, the two women had made a pact between them-selves, which is why Sarita's mother now said to Tukaram's wife, 'Have you seen Sarita anywhere?'

Tukaram wife's turned her squinting eye in the direction of the street corner, 'There, near the dump. She's playing with the manager's girls.' Then in a lower voice, she added, 'Kishori's just gone upstairs. Did you see him?'

Sarita's mother looked around her and in a still lower voice said, 'He's sitting inside. But Sarita's never to be found at such times. She doesn't think, she understands nothing, all she does is spend the day running around.' With this, Sarita's mother walked towards the dump. Sarita jumped up when she saw her mother approaching the cemented urinal; the laughter fled her eyes. Her mother grabbed her arm roughly and said, 'Come on, come into the house, come in and die. Do you have nothing better to do than play these rowdy games?' On the way in, in a softer voice, she said, 'Kishori's here. He's been waiting a long time. He's brought men with motor cars. Go on, run upstairs and get dressed. And wear that blue georgette sari of yours. Oh and listen, your hair's a terrible mess, get dressed quickly and I'll come up and comb it.'

Sarita was very happy to hear that rich men with motor cars had come for her, granted she was more interested in the motor cars than in the rich men who drove them. She loved riding in motor cars. When the car would roar down the open streets and the wind would slap her face, then everything would become a whirlwind and she would feel like a tornado tearing down empty streets.

Sarita, though fifteen, had the interests of a girl of thirteen. She didn't like spending time with grown women at all. Her entire day was taken up playing silly games with the younger girls. Their favourite pastime was to draw chalk lines on the street's black tar surface, and they remained so absorbed in this game that one might almost believe that the street's traffic depended on them drawing their crooked little lines. Sometimes

Sarita would bring out old pieces of sackcloth from her room. And she and her young friends would remain immersed for hours in the singularly monotonous business of dusting them and laying them out on the footpath to sit on.

Sarita was not beautiful. Her skin was a dusky wheatish colour; it was smooth and glistened in the humid Bombay air. Her thin lips, like sapodilla skins, also blackish, quivered faintly and there were always a few tiny trembling beads of sweat on her upper lip. She looked healthy despite living in squalor; her body was short, pleasing and well-proportioned. She gave the impression that the sheer vitality of her youth had subdued all contrary forces. Men on the streets gazed at her calves whenever her dirty skirt flew up in the wind. Youth had bestowed on them the shine of polished teak. These calves, entirely unacquainted with hair, had small marks on them that recalled orange skins with tiny, juice-filled pores, ready to erupt like fountains at the slightest pressure.

Her arms were also pleasing. The attractive roundness of her shoulders made itself apparent through the baggy, badly stitched blouse she wore. Her hair was thick and long, with the smell of coconut oil rising from it. Her plait, thick like a whip, would thump against her back. But the length of her hair made her unhappy as it got in the way of the games she played; she had invented various ways of keeping it under control.

Sarita was free of all worry and anxiety. She had enough to eat twice a day. Her mother handled all their household affairs. Every morning Sarita filled buckets of water and took them inside; every evening she filled the lamp with one paisa's worth of oil. Her hand reached habitually every evening for the cup with the money, and taking the lamp, she'd make her way downstairs.

Sarita had come to think of her visits to hotels and dimly lit places with rich men, which Kishori organized four or five times a month, as jaunts. She never gave any thought to the other aspects of these jaunts. She might even have believed that men like Kishori came to all the other girls' houses, too, and that they also went on outings with rich men. And what happened on Worli's cold benches and Juhu's wet beaches, perhaps happened to all the other girls as well. On one occasion she even said to her mother, 'Ma, Shanta's quite old now. Why not send her along with me too? The rich men who just came took me to eat eggs and Shanta loves eggs.' Sarita's mother parried the question. 'Yes, yes, some day I'll send her along with you. Let her mother return from Pune, no?' Sarita relayed the good news to Shanta the next day, when she saw her coming out of the bathroom. 'When your mother returns from Pune, everything will be all right. You're going to come with me to Worli too!' Sarita began to recount the night's activities as if she was reliving a beautiful dream. Shanta, two years younger than Sarita, felt little bells ring through her body as she listened to Sarita. Even when she'd heard all Sarita had to say, she was not satisfied. She grabbed her by the arm and said, 'Come on, let's go downstairs where we can talk.' There, near the urinal where Girdhari the merchant had laid out dirty coconut husks to dry on gunny sacks, the two girls spoke till late about subjects that made them tingle with excitement.

Now, as she changed hurriedly into her blue georgette sari behind a makeshift curtain, she was aware of the cloth tickling her skin, and her thoughts, like the fluttering of a bird's wings, returned to riding in the motor car. What would the rich men be like this time? Where would they take her? These, and other such questions, didn't enter her mind.

She worried instead that the motor car would run only for a few short minutes before their arrival at the door of some hotel. She didn't like to be confined to the four walls of hotel rooms, with their two metal beds, which were not really meant for her to fall asleep on.

She put on the georgette sari, and smoothing its creases, came and stood for a moment in front of Kishori. 'Take a look, Kishori, it's all right from the back, no?' Without waiting for a reply, she moved towards the broken wooden suitcase in which the Japanese powder and rouge were kept. She took a dusty mirror, wedged it between the window bars, and bending down, put a mixture of rouge and powder on her cheeks. When she was completely ready, she smiled and looked at Kishori, her eyes seeking appreciation.

She resembled one of those painted clay figures that appear during Diwali as the showpiece in a toy shop, with her bright blue sari, lipstick carelessly smudged on her lips, onion pink powder on her dark cheeks.

In the meantime, her mother arrived. She did Sarita's hair quickly and said, 'Listen, darling, speak nicely to the men and do whatever they ask. They are important; they've come in a motor car.' Then addressing Kishori, she said, 'Now, hurry up, take her to them. Poor fellows, I don't know how long they've been left waiting.'

In the main market, a yellow car was parked outside a long factory wall, near a small board that read, IT IS FORBIDDEN TO URINATE HERE. Inside, the three young Hyderabadi men waiting for Kishori held their handkerchiefs to their noses. They would have liked to park the car ahead somewhere, but the factory wall was long and the stench of urine drifted down its entire stretch. When the young man who sat at the wheel caught sight of Kishori at the street corner, he said to his two other friends, 'Well, brothers, he's come. It's Kishori and . . . and . . .' He fixed his gaze on the street corner. 'And . . . and . . . well, she's just a little girl! You take a look . . . that one, man . . . the one in the blue sari.'

When Kishori and Sarita approached, the two young men sitting in the back removed their hats and made room for her in the middle. Kishori reached forward, opened the door and swiftly installed Sarita in the back. Closing the door, he said to the young man at the wheel, 'Forgive me, we were delayed; she was at her friend's place. Well, so?'

Kafayat, the young man, turned around and looked at Sarita, then said to Kishori, 'All right, but listen . . .' He slid across the seat and appeared at the other window. Whispering in Kishori's ear, he said, 'She's not going to kick up a fuss, is she?'

Kishori placed his hand over his chest in reply. 'Sir! You must have faith in me.' Hearing this, the young man, took two rupees out of his pocket and handed them to Kishori. 'Go, have fun!'

Kishori waved them off and Kafayat started the engine. It was five in the evening. Bombay's bazaars were clogging with traffic from cars, buses, trams and pedestrians. Sarita was lost between the two young men. She would keep her thighs clamped tightly together, place her hands over them and start to say something, then mid-sentence, fall into silence. What she would have liked to say to the young man driving was, 'For God's sake, let it rip. I'm suffocating in here.'

For a long time, no one said anything. The young man at the wheel continued to drive and the two young Hyderabadis in the back, under their long, dark coats, suppressed their nervousness at being so close to a young girl for the first time, a young girl whom, for at least while, they could call their own and touch without fear or danger.

The young man at the wheel had been living in Bombay for the past two years and had seen many girls like Sarita, both in daylight and at night. His yellow car had hosted girls of various shades and quality and so he felt no great nervousness now. Of his two friends who had come from Hyderabad, one, who went by the name of Shahab, wanted a full tour of Bombay. And it was with this in mind that Kafayat – the young owner of the car – out of friendship, asked Kishori to organize Sarita for them. To his other friend, Anwar, Kafayat said, 'Listen, man, if there ends up being one for you too, what harm is there?' But, Anwar, who was less assertive, never overcame his shyness enough to say, 'Yes, get one for me too.'

Kafayat had never seen Sarita before – it had been a while since Kishori had brought a new girl. Despite this, Kafayat showed no interest in her, perhaps because a man can only do one thing at a time and he couldn't drive as well as turn his attention to her. Once they'd left the city and the car came onto a country road, Sarita jumped up. The car's sudden speed and the gusts of cold air that came in lifted the restraint she had put on herself until now. Bursts of electricity ran though her entire body. Her legs throbbed, her arms seemed to dance, her fingers trembled and she watched the trees race past her on both sides.

Anwar and Shahab were now at ease. Shahab, who felt he had first rights to Sarita, gently moved his arm forward, wanting to place it around her back. The movement tickled her; she jumped up and landed on Anwar with a thump. Her laughter flowed out of the windows of the yellow car and carried into the distance. When Shahab tried again to place his hand on her back, she bent double with laughter. Anwar, hidden in one corner of the car, sat in silence, his mouth dry.

Shahab's mind filled with bright colours. He said to Kafayat, 'My God, man, she's a little minx.' With this, he violently pinched Sarita's thigh. In reply, and because he was closest to her, Sarita gently twisted Anwar's ear. The car erupted in laughter.

Kafayat kept turning around even though everything was visible to him in his rearview mirror. He added to the growing commotion in the back by speeding up the car.

Sarita wished she could climb out and ride on the bonnet of the car where the flying iron fairy was. She moved forward. Shahab reached for her and to steady herself, she wrapped her arms around Kafayat's neck. Without meaning to, he kissed them. A shiver went through her entire body and she leapt into the front seat of the car and began to play with Kafayat's tie. 'What is your name?' she asked Kafayat.

'My name!' he said. 'My name is Kafayat.' With this he put a ten-rupee note in her hand. She paid no further attention to his name, but squeezed the note into her blouse, brimming with childish happiness. 'You're a very nice man. And this tie of yours is also very nice.'

In that instant, Sarita saw goodness in everything and wished that all that was bad would also turn to good . . . and . . . and . . . then it would happen . . . the motor would continue to race and everything around her would become part of the whirlwind.

She suddenly felt the urge to sing. So she stopped playing with Kafayat's tie and began, 'You taught me how to love, and stirred a sleeping heart.'

For some time, she sang the film song and then, turning to Anwar who was sitting in silence, said, 'Why are you so quiet? Say something, sing something!' With this, she jumped into the back seat again and began running her fingers through Shahab's hair. 'Come on both of you, sing.

You remember that song that Devika Rani used to sing? "I'm a sparrow in the heart's jungle, singing my little song . . ." Devika Rani is so good, isn't she?'

Then she put both her hands under her thighs and – fluttering her eyelids – said, 'Ashok Kumar and Devika Rani stood close to each other. Devika Rani would say, "I'm a sparrow in the forest, singing my little song." And Ashok Kumar would say, "Sing it then."'

Sarita began the song. 'I'm a sparrow in the forest, singing my little song.'

Shahab in a loud, coarse voice answered, 'I'll become a forest bird and sing from forest to forest.'

And all of a sudden, a duet began. Kafayat provided accompaniment on the car horn. Sarita began to clap. Her thin soprano, Shahab's coarse singing, the horn's honking, the blasts of wind and the roar of the engine, came together to form an orchestra.

Sarita was happy; Shahab was happy; Kafayat was happy, and seeing them all happy, Anwar was forced to be happy. He regretted his earlier restraint. His arms began to move. His sleeping heart had stirred and he was ready now to be a part of the boisterous happiness of the other three.

As they sang, Sarita removed Anwar's hat from his head and put it on her own. She leapt into the front seat again and gazed at herself in the small mirror to see how it looked. Had he really been wearing his hat all this time? Anwar thought.

Sarita slapped Kafayat's fat thigh and said, 'If I wear your trousers and your shirt and put on a tie like this one, will I become a pukka gentleman too?'

Hearing this, Shahab couldn't decide what he should do. He yanked

Anwar's arm, 'You've been a complete idiot.' And for a moment, Anwar believed he was right.

Kafayat asked Sarita, 'What is your name?'

'My name?' Sarita replied, slipping the hat's strap under her chin. 'My name is Sarita.'

'Sarita,' Shahab said from the back seat, 'you're not a woman, you're a livewire.'

Anwar wanted to say something too, but Sarita began to sing in a high voice.

'In love town, I'll build my house . . . forgoing all the worrrrrrld.'

And bits of that world flew around them. Sarita's hair, no longer bound by her plait, broke free and scattered like dark smoke dispersed by wind; she was happy.

Shahab was happy; Kafayat was happy and now Anwar, too, was ready to be happy. The song ended; for a few moments everyone felt that it had been raining hard and had now abruptly stopped.

'Any more songs?' Kafayat asked Sarita.

'Yes, yes,' Shahab said from the back, 'let's have one more. One that even these film people won't forget!'

Sarita began again. 'Spring came to my house. And I hit the road, a little drunkenly.'

The car also wove drunkenly. Then the road straightened and the seashore came in sight. The sun was setting and the sea wind brought a chill in the air.

The car stopped. Sarita opened the door, jumped out and began to run along the shore. Kafayat and Shahab ran behind her. In the open air, on the edge of the vast ocean, with the great palms rising up from the wet sand, Sarita didn't know what it was that she wanted. She wished she could melt into the sky; spread through the ocean; fly so high that she could see the palm canopies from above, for all the wetness of the shore to seep from the sand into her feet and then . . . and then for that same racing engine, that same speed, those blasts of wind, the car horn honking – she was very happy. The three young Hyderabadi men sat down on the wet sand and opened their beers. Sarita snatched the bottle from Kafayat's hand. 'Wait, I'll pour it.'

She poured it so that the glass filled with foam. The spectacle of it excited her. She put her finger into the brownish foam, then into her mouth. On tasting its bitterness, she made a face; Kafayat and Shahab laughed uncontrollably. Still laughing, Kafayat looked over at Anwar and saw that he was laughing too.

They went through six bottles of beer; some entered their stomachs; some turned to foam and was absorbed by the sand. Sarita continued to sing. In the sea's moist air, her dark cheeks had become wet. She felt a deep contentment. Anwar now, was happy too. He wanted the sea to turn to beer, to go diving in it and for Sarita to join him.

Sarita took two empty bottles and banged them together. They made a clatter and she laughed. Kafayat, Anwar and Shahab laughed too.

Still laughing, Sarita said to Kafayat, 'Come on, let's drive the car now.'

Everyone rose. Empty beer bottles lay strewn on the wet sand. The party ran to the car. Once again, the wind began to blast, the horn honked, and Sarita's hair scattered like dark smoke. The singing resumed.

The car ploughed through the wind. Sarita continued to sing. She sat in the back between Anwar and Shahab. Anwar's head dropped from side to side. Sarita mischievously began to comb Shahab's hair with her fingers and he fell asleep. When she turned back to Anwar, she saw that he was also fast asleep. She lifted herself from in between them and lowered herself into the front seat.

In a whisper, she said, 'I've just put both your friends to bed. Now, I'll put you to bed too.'

Kafayat smiled. 'Who'll drive the car then?'

Sarita, smiling as well, replied, 'It'll keep running.' For a long time, they spoke among themselves. The bazaar reappeared. When they drove past the wall with the small board that read, IT IS FORBIDDEN TO URINATE HERE, Sarita said, 'Just here is fine.'

The car stopped. Sarita jumped out before Kafayat was able to do or say anything. She waved and walked away. Kafayat sat with one hand on the wheel, perhaps thinking back on the day's events.

Then Sarita stopped, turned around, walked back, and from her blouse, removed the ten-rupee note and placed it next to him.

Kafayat stared at it in amazement. 'Sarita, what's this?'

'This . . . why should I take this money?' she replied and ran off, leaving Kafayat still staring at the limp note.

He turned around eventually. Anwar and Shahab, like the note itself, lay slumped in the back seat, asleep.

Translated by Aatish Taseer

The Monkey Revolt

THE ALARMING NEWS that 'monkey-ism' was on the rise was trick-
ling in from all parts of the country. The government turned a blind
eye to it at first but when it noticed that the matter was threatening to
become serious it immediately sprang into action.

It is appropriate that the reader should be told right in the beginning
what 'monkey-ism' or 'apishness' stands for. Of course we can't go into
much detail here because it's a fairly long story, but briefly, the apish
movement was set in motion by none other than the monkeys themselves
and was directed squarely against humans.

Their gripe was: 'Now, when it's an incontrovertible fact that humans
are our descendants, why do they treat us so coldly, and not just coldly
but entirely contrary to the manner of apes? They tie ropes around our
necks and make us dance to the tune of their *dugdugies* in every lane and
by-lane while they stick their hands out to beg for money . . . as though
we're humans . . . Furthermore, while it is indisputable that we're their
ancestors and that our blood flows in their veins, it is pretty dubious to
say that they have climbed the evolutionary ladder to become humans. If
there is such a thing as evolutionary stages, then why didn't we, billions

of monkeys (you may call us a minority if you like, but if a census were ever taken, we would outnumber humans by far), go through them?'

The monkeys maintained: 'Why should these evolutionary stages remain the exclusive prerogative of only certain monkeys? Evolution! Hah, it's pure hogwash. Hell, they haven't at all, if anything, they've regressed. They failed to hold on to the status that was bestowed on them; they tumbled so far down from apishness that they became humans.

'Their evolution is a sign of their downfall. We want these fallen monkeys to revert to their original apishness all over again. And we have started this movement to do just that: bring them back to the fold. We bear them no ill will or enmity; in fact, we consider them our siblings. The purpose of our movement is to compel these monkeys who strut around as humans nowadays, and who've grabbed power and influence because of our laxity, to recognize their true primary nature and return to our social habitat.'

Speeches were given publicly, out in the open, and in the privacy of homes, and sometimes even in clandestine meetings. In essence, they underscored the point that vigorous protests should be made against the tyranny and violence the monkeys had unleashed in the guise of man and that demonstrations should be staged in every part of the city, raising cries of *Down with humanity! Long live apishness!*

At first humans thought this was some kind of comedy show and had a hilarious time of it. Gradually, though, the monkeys' speeches, their irrefutable arguments and their point of view began to find a place in the hearts of some humans. As a result, those in power discovered from the reports of the secret police that several humans had become the monkeys' disciples, and, as trustworthy sources verified, thousands had renounced their humanity and returned to being apes; they had sprouted long tails and started walking on all fours.

High officials in the government dismissed this as pure nonsense. That a monkey can become human is an established fact, but how can a human become a monkey? Such reverse progression had never been seen or heard. So, after consulting their superiors, they countered the monkeys' claims by unleashing an equally relentless propaganda campaign of their own: A human can never morph into a monkey.

There was no dearth of able and resourceful personalities among the monkeys. To squash the government propaganda their savants came up with the ingenious argument that if in this time man can be transformed into woman and woman into man, why not man into monkey, which is his true form.

Still man's arguments didn't entirely fail to have an effect on the monkeys. Those humans who hadn't yet completely transformed found themselves hesitating about whether to complete the process of transformation or revert to being humans. But the monkeys' powerful rejoinder sustained them in their wavering mental and physical state.

The monkeys' propaganda secretary promptly mounted an especially vehement campaign. The one incontrovertible truth was: 'Humans have come forth from us, and only because of some regrettable deviationist streak. Can they deny that they are a distorted form of us?'

In truth, humans had no answer to this crushing argument. But they kept babbling: 'Well, no, we don't deny that we were once monkeys. But we had to toil hard and go through difficult stages to achieve our status as humans. It was our granite willpower, our protracted effort, our spiritual awakening, our thought and action, our evolutionary struggle that has brought us to this sublime and lofty state . . . a race that we won and others lost. The losers are still wallowing in their simian state. When these lower primates see us in our lofty state, they burn with jealousy. So let them stew. We'll march ahead on our evolutionary path until one day, who knows, we might even become gods.'

Quick came the answer from the apes' camp: 'Brethren, what lofty state have you reached? As we see it, you're plunging ever deeper into the depths of degradation. Evolution is something we don't deny, but just tell us, where do you stand today after climbing so many steps of the evolutionary ladder and after centuries of setting up one society after another? Your entire history is filled with warfare and carnage, murder and bloodshed, with rape and the defilement of women's honour, with ruling others and being subjugated by them.

'On the other hand, look at our – your – ancestors' history. Can you cite one such dark episode in our history? Yes, we frisk about from one branch to another, but have we ever fought over them as our property? You, you humans, have been writing story after story about us in your books – including the well-known story of how we grabbed on to one another's tails to build a bridge over the river. You too build bridges, so massive that your human brains are knocked out in astonishment. But then you blow them up. Whereas who can blow up the bridge we devised? Not a single monkey's tail has behaved treacherously to this day, nor has a single monkey's wife gotten into bed with another monkey. Our wives pluck lice from our bodies and comb our hair daily, but they don't forfeit their rights doing so; they continue to be the same as ours. You're not unaware of the way your wives idle away their time, nor are your wives unaware of how you mess around. What you imply by calling us monkeys applies more appropriately to your own selves. Conversely, "human" is an apt term for us considering the meaning you give it in describing yourselves. The plain fact is that you belong to our race. The same blood runs in our veins. No wonder if at times some resemblance should crop up and, equally, no wonder that it should result in the kind of row that has erupted between us now. We invite you to return to our fold. Come back to us, and raise the cry "Down with humanity! Long live apishness!" You'll be the better for it.'

The retort from the human side came loud and clear: 'These monkeys are shouting nonsense. They're green with envy that we've reached such glorious heights. A single story written about them under God knows what perverse influence, and that too for our children, cannot be taken as the definitive word about them. Otherwise who isn't aware of the kind of justice this monkey doled out to two cats regarding their quarrel over a piece of cheese? He weighed the piece on his scale and, little by little, gobbled it up himself.'

The monkeys rejoined: 'Scales and weights are human inventions. We don't use them at all, we don't even know how to use them. Now, if you want the truth, it was no monkey who swindled the cats out of their cheese, it was a human. There's no wonder that he would dupe the poor cats. We can show thousands of such cats whom these humans, once our brothers, are feeding lentils and cauliflower instead of their natural diet of sinews and membranes and thus, having already screwed up their own nature, are hell-bent on destroying that of others. Instead of ridiculing our sense of fairness, have a look at the institutions of justice you've created. Don't your courts ride roughshod over any notion of justice every day by sending hundreds, indeed, thousands of people who have committed no crime to the gallows? We say again, they are our brothers who have somehow gone astray. Our arms are forever open to take them back, our prayers forever for them. We wish to take no revenge.'

Gradually this amicable statement morphed and, instead, this cry rose from the monkeys' camp: 'We want to take revenge . . . for this evolution . . . for this so-called progress these monkeys have foisted on themselves and turned into humans.'

The humans took severe measures of their own. Thousands of apes were taken into custody; hundreds dragged to the courts and subsequently hanged. But the movement in support of apishness continued unabated, until, finally, the human government declared it illegal. As a result, while some apes were arrested, the rest just melted away into the trees, frustrating every attempt to apprehend them. Who had the mind or the foolhardiness to chase after them in their jungle hideouts? Some monkeys, rumour had it, settled into the trees around the bungalows of some high officials, where they were well looked after and provided every comfort. This because those officials were themselves secret partisans of apishness, but loathed embracing it openly for fear of losing their high positions.

This went on for quite some time. Arrests continued, gallows were erected in the middle of chowks, the culprits were whipped, skinned and forced to crawl on their stomachs. Numerous acts and ordinances were put into effect. Nothing worked. But the monkeys were not about to call it quits. They stubbornly stuck to their position. Now and then they organized agitations, got together and stormed humans, chewed through electric cables, snatched bread from people's hands, smashed the little dugdugies to whose beat their monkey-masters made them dance, chewed through their ropes and fled.

They secretly converted several humans over to apishness, detonated home-made bombs, spread terror and, as often, risked their lives. Though the powers had broken up their organization, still they were as relentlessly united and well organized in their dispersal as ever. When man is faced with this sort of situation, he nearly goes mad. I say this because I too am one of the humans. But the strange truth is that the monkeys appeared smugly impervious to any change. They remained what they had been all along – monkeys. Their antics lost none of the playfulness. They would swoop down and snatch from the hands of humans whatever caught their fancy. Grab a gun from someone and march on like an army cadet. Batons, tear-gas grenades, nothing stopped them. They were, one might say, as restless as mercury. If you drew a gun on them, took aim and fired, they would take a leap and, before you knew it, would be sitting comfortably on your shoulder laughing their monkey heads off. If you threw a tear-gas shell at them, they'd jump and quickly turn it towards you.

The government was thoroughly fed up with their antics. A secret intelligence service report claimed that this monkey movement, or conspiracy, or whatever, could never have been launched by the monkeys themselves. A group of influential humans, supporting apishness just for kicks, must be working behind the scenes and, on further investigation, this fact was established beyond the shadow of a doubt. This disclosure was even more upsetting for the government; some officials panicked lest they should fall into the trap of apishness and, after reaching the top of the evolutionary ladder, lapse into being apes, a state their forefathers had fought long and hard to escape.

In spite of the government's countless strategies, the rising tide of the monkey movement couldn't be stemmed. Some monkeys or other would appear on a rooftop or a steeple somewhere in the city several times during the day or night and shout through his megaphone: *Down with humanity! Down with dugdugies! Long live apism!*

One day the matter got out of hand. An audacious monkey stole into the living room of none other than the city's highest authority, opened the cigar box, picked one up, lit it and started puffing away leisurely. His Honour was furious. The monkey screeched at him. His Honour scolded and threatened. The monkey couldn't care less and leaped, landing on the sofa. The next moment he took another leap and alighted on one of the chairs, leaving His Honour with the distinct feeling that the monkey's movements were mimicking his own image in the mirror. He felt so riled up and incensed, writhing inside with anger and utter helplessness, that he finally broke down in tears.

We heard about this episode from our special sources, otherwise the next day's papers had a different story to tell: *An audacious monkey made an attempt to break into the government palace but the sentries gunned him down on the spot. After the incident, all pertinent government departments have been issued strict orders to take whatever steps necessary to quell the uprising of the monkeys.*

The chief of the secret police wasn't worried so much about the monkeys. He called together his subordinates and told them, 'These antics of the monkeys don't scare me. What I'm afraid of are the humans who have already reverted to being monkeys. I'm a man of keen intelligence. I think that if we can, as the descendants of monkeys, kick up so much trouble in the world and wreak such utter chaos, what might we do if we ever went back to being monkeys? Evolution, even when reversed, cannot but spell danger, no matter how one looks at it. So my instruction to you is this: Go and ferret out the humans who have embraced apism. If you can round them up, that will kill apism.'

Now the secret, as well as the ordinary, police intensified their efforts to apprehend the neo-monkeys who were wreaking havoc every night with one mischief after another. Several monkeys were caught and were given the 'third degree' inside the fort to make them squeal the where-abouts of the neo-monkeys. But they didn't let a word slip out of their mouths and bore the harshest torture with fortitude. They didn't relent even when their females were raped before their eyes. Exasperated, the police mowed them down and their corpses were doused with kerosene and set afire.

The next morning cyclostyled copies of a poster appeared everywhere in the city. In moving language it revealed the atrocities humans had committed and appealed to those who felt compassion to abandon their humanity and return to the fold of the monkeys, which was their original place.

Within minutes the posters were pulled down, but by then thousands of humans had already seen them, and hundreds chose to join apism. None of the countermeasures of the government worked. All the zoos, now converted into prisons, were filled with monkeys. One count put the figure of thirty thousand behind bars, but the incarcerated monkeys couldn't be happier.

The authorities were caught in a strange predicament: If they turned a blind eye to the monkeys, it was feared they would unleash a veritable revolution; if the authorities tightened their control and resorted to torture and atrocities, more and more humans would feel disgusted and turn against the government – after all, the same blood flowed in their and their ancestors' veins.

At long last, the authorities felt pressed to collectively think the matter over and devise some way that the ban on the monkey organization could be lifted. Furthermore, the monkey leaders were to be invited to a conference and asked to explain their point of view so that some step towards reconciliation might be taken.

Translated by Muhammad Umar Memon

Barren

O UR FIRST ENCOUNTER took place exactly two years ago today at Apollo Bunder. It was evening. In the distance, the last remnants of the sun had disappeared behind the waves, which resembled the folds of a thick, coarse fabric when looked at from the benches on the beach. I was sitting on the other side of the Gate of India on a bench next to where a man was getting a head massage. I was looking at the ocean, stretched out as far as the eye could see. At the furthermost point, where the sky and the sea came together, huge waves rose gradually, as if the sides of a dark-coloured carpet were being folded up.

The beach lights were all on, their reflection over the water spreading thick, quivering lines on it. Below me, along the stone wall, masts and rolled-up sails swayed gently. The sound of the waves and the voices of the sightseers permeated the atmosphere like a hum. Now and then the horn of an approaching or receding car split the air like an intrusive 'hunh!' in the middle of the telling of an absorbing tale.

Such a pleasant atmosphere calls for a smoke. I pulled out a packet of cigarettes but couldn't find any matches. God knows where I had left them. I was about to put the packet back in my pocket when I heard someone nearby say, 'Here are some matches.'

I turned around and saw a young man standing behind the bench. Bombay residents are normally pale, but this man looked frighteningly so. I thanked him. 'That's very kind of you.'

He handed me the matches. I thanked him again and said, 'Please sit down.'

'Please, light your cigarette,' he said, 'I have to go.'

He seemed to be lying; it was obvious from his tone that he was neither in a hurry nor was there any particular place where he needed to be. True, you might ask how one can tell such things from a tone. But the truth is that was precisely how I felt at the time. So I said again once more, 'What's the hurry. Have a seat,' and offered him a cigarette. 'Have one.'

He looked at the packet and said, 'Thanks, but I only smoke my own brand.'

I could have sworn that he was lying again. And again it was his tone that betrayed him. This piqued my interest and I resolved firmly that I would make him sit down beside me and smoke one of my cigarettes. I believed this wouldn't be too difficult because in just two sentences he had made it plain to me that he was deluding himself. He, in fact, *wanted* to sit down and smoke but, at the same time, he felt he should do neither. This dichotomy between yes and no was clear to me in his tone. Believe me, his very existence seemed to be suspended between being and non-being.

His face, as I've already mentioned, looked incredibly pale. Apart from that, the outlines of his nose, eyes and mouth were so faint that it seemed as if someone had drawn a portrait and then given it a wash. As

I looked at him, his lips would swell at times but then fade away like a spark buried under layers of ash. It was the same with his other features: eyes like two puddles of muddy water with sparse lashes drooping over them; black hair that had a hue resembling burnt paper and appeared dry and brittle like straw. You could make out the contours of his nose more easily, but from a distance it looked pretty flat, because, as I mentioned earlier, his features were not very distinct.

He was of average height, neither tall nor short. However, when he stood a certain way, relaxing his spine, there was a marked difference in his height. Likewise, when he would suddenly stand erect, he appeared to be much taller than his true size.

His clothes were shabby, though not grimy. His jacket sleeves were frayed at the cuffs from constant wear and tear; you could see the threads unravelling. His collar was unbuttoned and his shirt looked as though it would not survive even one more washing. Yet, despite such clothing, he was trying to present himself as a respectable man. I say 'trying' because when I had looked at him, a wave of anxiety seemed to wash over his entire being, leaving me to wonder if he wasn't really trying to keep himself hidden from my eyes.

I got up, lit a cigarette, and offered the packet to him. 'Help yourself!' The way I said it and the quickness with which I lit the match and held it out to him somehow made him forget everything. Taking a cigarette, he stuck it in his mouth and started to smoke. But then he immediately realized his mistake. He promptly removed the cigarette from his mouth, pretending to cough. 'Cavenders don't agree with me,' he said. 'They have such strong tobacco that it irritates my throat right away.'

I asked, 'So what brand do you smoke?'

He stammered, 'I . . . I actually smoke very little because Dr Arolkar has advised me not to. Otherwise I buy 555, which is pretty mild.'

The doctor he mentioned was famous throughout Bombay; he charged a fee of ten rupees per visit. The 555 brand he mentioned, as you may well know, is very expensive. He'd now lied twice in one breath, which I found difficult to digest. Still, I kept quiet, even though I would have liked nothing better than to pull off his mask, expose his lies, and shame him into apologizing to me. However, when I looked at him I realized that whatever he had said became a part of him. I didn't see the kind of blush that usually sweeps across the face of a liar. Instead, I sensed that he truly believed whatever he said. His lies were spoken with complete sincerity. He lied with such conviction that he didn't experience the slightest bit of guilt. Anyway, let's drop this. Recounting all these details will require reams of paper and I would never get around to the story itself.

After a little polite conversation that seemed to put him at ease, I offered him another cigarette and mentioned how exquisite the ocean looked. Being a storywriter, I was able to talk to him about the ocean, about Apollo Bunder and all the visitors there in such an engaging way that even after six cigarettes his throat failed to become the least bit irritated. He asked me my name. When I replied he stood up and said, 'Oh you . . . you're . . . Mr . . . I've read many of your stories . . . I didn't know it was you. I'm very pleased to have met you. Really very pleased.'

I wanted to thank him but he continued, 'In fact, I remember reading one of your stories just recently. I can't recall the title though. It's the one about the girl who's in love with a man but the fellow deceives her. There's another man in the story, the narrator, who's in love with her.

When he discovers the girl's misfortunate he tells her, "You must go on living. Turn the memory of the moments you spent engrossed in his love, when you were happy, into a foundation you can build your life on." I don't remember it word for word, but do tell me one thing: Is it possible . . . forget possible, tell me straight up whether, by any chance, you are that man. Forgive me, I shouldn't be asking such a question. I really shouldn't . . . but were you the person who had a tryst with her on the rooftop and then went downstairs to sleep in your own room, leaving her alone in the slumbering moonlight with all the passions of her youth?' Here he suddenly halted and then added, 'I really shouldn't be asking this sort of thing. After all, who opens up his heart to strangers!'

'I will tell you,' I said. 'But somehow it does seem a bit odd to be asking and telling everything when one has just met someone for the first time.'

His earlier excitement cooled suddenly. He said softly, 'You're right, but who knows whether we'll ever meet again.'

I said, 'Bombay is, of course, a very large city but we can meet again, not just once but many times. I'm an idle person, I mean short story writer . . . you'll find me here every evening, provided I'm not sick. Many young women come here to stroll and I come here to find one of them to fall in love with. Love's not a bad thing!'

'Love . . . love! . . .' He wanted to say something more but couldn't, and like a rope on fire he fell tortuously silent.

I had brought up 'love' just to be funny. And given the absolutely delightful surroundings, I would have had no regrets about actually falling in love with someone. When the waning daylight and evening shadows meet, when the rows of street lights begin glimmering in the encroaching darkness, when the air becomes slightly chilled and the feeling of romance permeates the atmosphere – a man naturally longs to be close to a woman. It is that feeling, that need, which lies hidden in our unconscious.

God knows which story he was referring to. I don't remember all of my stories, especially the romantic ones. I've known very few women in my life. The stories I wrote about women were either because of a particular need or just to indulge in mental gratification of the senses. Since they lack sincerity, I don't think much of them. I have observed women of a certain class and written a few stories about them, but those aren't romances. In any case, the story he was alluding to must be one of those mediocre romances, the kind I must have written to calm my own ardour. But – what's this? – I've started telling my own story.

So when he fell silent after uttering 'love,' I felt the urge to expand further on that subject. I began: 'Well, it just so happens that our forefathers have enumerated many kinds of love, but as far as I'm concerned, whether love is born in Multan or on the icy plains of Siberia, whether it's born in winter or summer, in the heart of a rich man or a poor man, whether it's beautiful or pious, love remains love. It doesn't change. Just as the manner of a child's birth remains basically the same, so does love's. Of course, it's an entirely different matter if Saeeda Begum gives birth in a hospital where Rajkumari gives birth in a jungle, or if a sweeper-woman stirs the feelings of love in a Ghulam Muhammad while a Natwar Lal is smitten by the love of a princess. Just as children who are born prematurely remain weak after birth, so too a love born before its time suffers from weakness. Some children are born after excruciating labour; well, so are some loves – they cause a lot of pain. Just as some women miscarry, so does love miscarry for some people. And just as sterility results in an inability to conceive a child, you will find people who turn out to be incapable of love. This doesn't necessarily mean that the desire to love has completely vanished from their hearts, or that the feeling of love has been completely smothered. No, the desire may still be there, but they lack the ability to translate that into love. Just as some women are unable to conceive because of some physical problem, these people are unable to ignite the spark of love in the hearts of others because of some spiritual handicap.'

I was finding my own harangue rather interesting, so I kept lecturing away without even looking at him. When I finally looked at him, I found him gazing off into space across the ocean, entirely lost in his own thoughts. I fell silent.

The sound of a particularly loud horn suddenly jolted him out of his reverie and he blurted out absent-mindedly, 'Yes, you're absolutely right!'

I thought of asking him, 'Absolutely right? . . . Forget that. Just tell me what I've been saying.' But I kept quiet, allowing him a chance to shake off his weighty thoughts.

He went on thinking for a while and then said, 'What you said is absolutely correct, but . . . Let's drop this topic. It . . . well, never mind.'

I liked what I'd been talking about. I wanted nothing more than to have someone go on listening to me, so I repeated, 'Well, as I was saying, some men too turn out to be barren when it comes to love. I mean they do desire to love, but are never able to fulfil that desire. I tend to think this is due to some spiritual shortcoming. What do you think?'

He turned even paler, as though he'd seen a ghost. The change came over him so suddenly that I became worried and asked, 'Is everything all right? You aren't feeling ill, are you?'

'No . . . no . . .' He sounded even more worried. 'I'm not ill or anything like that. What makes you think I am?'

I replied, 'Anyone who saw you now would assume that you're ill, extremely ill. You look frightfully pale. I think you'd better go home. Come, I'll take you there.'

'No, I'll go myself. But I'm not ill . . . I do feel a slight pain in my chest now and then. Maybe it's just . . . I'll be okay. You can continue.'

It didn't look as though he would be able to concentrate on my words so I remained silent, but when he insisted, I resumed. 'I was asking what you thought about people who are unable to love. I have no idea what they feel, what their inner thoughts are. But when I think of those barren women who, in the hope of conceiving a child, make fervent entreaties to God and, disappointed by Him, resort to spells and charms – bringing ash from cremation grounds, reciting night-long incantations that were given to them by sadhus, and making votive offerings – to gain the pearl of their desire, it occurs to me that a person who's unable to love must experience a similar ordeal. Such people truly deserve compassion. I feel more for them than I do for the blind.'

His eyes brimmed with tears. He swallowed and quickly stood up. Turning his face away he said, 'Oh, it's late. I have an important errand to run and I seem to have lost quite a bit of time talking.'

I also got up, He turned towards me and pressed my hand but spoke without looking at me, 'I really must leave now,' and walked away.

The second time I met him was again at Apollo Bunder. Although I'm not one for taking walks, back in those days Apollo Bunder had somehow become part of my daily routine. A month later, though, a longish letter from an Agra poet – which, among other things, made lewd comments about the beauties who crowded Apollo Bunder's beaches and how lucky I was to be living in Bombay – pretty much destroyed whatever interest I may have had in the place. Now, whenever someone asks me to go there, I'm reminded of that poet's letter and feel like throwing up. But I was talking about a time before that letter. Then, I used to go there every evening and sit on the bench next to the place where many people were in the habit of having masseurs give their skulls a good workout, rubbing and knocking.

Day had given way to evening, with no trace of light left anywhere. The October heat was still intense, but a breeze was now blowing. Strollers, like exhausted travellers, made up most of the crowd. Behind me cars and more cars had lined up. All the benches were taken. Two chattering men, one Gujarati, the other Parsi, had settled on the bench next to me and were blabbering away in Gujarati, each with a different accent. The Parsi's voice had only two notes, one shrill, one deep that he alternated. When they both talked rapidly at the same time, it sounded as if a parrot and a mynah were having a duel.

Getting tired of their endless chatter, I got up and was about to head towards the Taj Mahal Hotel when I saw him coming my way. I didn't know his name so I couldn't call him. But when he saw me his eyes locked on, as though he'd found what he was looking for.

There were no empty benches, so I proposed, 'It's been a long time since we last met. Let's go over to the restaurant. All the benches here are taken.'

He said a few things by way of formality and came along. We walked a bit and then sat down in the large cane chairs in the restaurant. After I had ordered tea, I offered him my tin of cigarettes. Coincidentally, I had been to Dr Arolkar just that day and he had advised me to quit smoking altogether, or, failing that, to switch to smoking better quality cigarettes, like 555. So, following the doctor's advice I had bought this tin that very evening. He stared at the tin, then at me. He started to say something but then decided against it.

I broke into a laugh. 'Don't think that I've started smoking these on your advice. Actually you might call it coincidence. Today, I too ended up going to Dr Arolkar because lately I've been feeling this pain in my chest. Anyway, he advised me to smoke these, but far fewer.'

As I said this I stole a peek at him and realized that my words had upset him, so I took Dr Arolkar's prescription out of my pocket and put it on the table. 'I can't read his handwriting but he seems to have crammed every vitamin into this one prescription.'

He glanced at the prescription, which showed Dr Arolkar's name and address embossed in black letters and also the date. His erstwhile look of agitation quickly faded. He smiled and said, 'Why do most writers suffer from vitamin deficiencies?' I replied, 'Certainly not because they don't get enough to eat. It's more likely because they work a lot and get paid a pittance.'

Meanwhile the tea had arrived and we started talking about other things.

An interval of a month, maybe a month and a half, had passed between our first and second meetings. His face now looked even paler than before and there were dark circles around his eyes. Apparently he was suffering from some spiritual crisis which troubled him constantly. Every now and then he would stop short in the middle of his sentence and, quite unconsciously, let out a sigh. Even when he tried to laugh his lips hardly seemed to move.

Seeing him in this condition, I asked abruptly, 'You look sad . . . Why is that?'

'Sad . . .' A faint smile, like one you might see on the face of a person who's dying but wants to show that he isn't afraid to die, appeared on his face. 'No, I'm not sad. Could it be that you're in a sombre mood yourself?'

He finished his tea in a single gulp and quickly got up. 'All right,' he said, 'I've got to go. I have an important matter to take care of.'

I was certain that he didn't have 'an important matter to take care of.' Yet, I let him leave without trying to stop him. Once again, I had failed to find out his name, but I did find out that something was bothering him – mentally and spiritually. He was sad, or rather sadness had completely permeated his being. But he didn't want anyone to know. He wanted to live two lives: one that was real and the other that he was busy creating every minute, every second. Both of his lives were a failure. Why? That I don't know.

It was again at Apollo Bunder that we ran into each other for a third time. This time, however, I took him to my place. Although we didn't say anything on the way, we did talk quite a bit once we reached home. The moment he entered the room a look of despair appeared on his face and lingered there for a few seconds. He quickly steadied himself and, unlike in the past, tried to appear unusually cheerful and chatty, which made me feel even sorrier for him. He seemed to be denying the reality of something as certain as death. What's even worse, he sometimes seemed to be quite satisfied with his self-deception.

As we talked away, he noticed the framed photograph on my table. Getting up and moving closer to the photograph, he asked, 'May I take a look . . . with your permission, of course?'

'By all means!'

He gave the photograph a fleeting look and then sat down. 'Quite a good-looking woman. I guess she's your . . .'

'No, no. It was a long time ago. I was attracted to her; rather, I should say I almost fell in love with her. Unfortunately, she never knew about it, and I . . . No, she was married off to . . . Anyway, this is a memento of my first love, which died even before it had a chance to be born.'

'A memento of your first love! You must have had quite a few affairs since.' He ran his tongue over his dry lips. 'I mean you must have had many loves in your life – requited and unrequited.'

I was about to set him straight and tell him that this humble man was just as barren in the matter of love as he was. But, God knows why, I held back. Instead, I lied to him for no reason at all. 'Of course! Such affairs do come along, don't they? You must have had quite a few yourself.'

He didn't say anything and fell completely silent, as though he had plunged into deep waters. After he'd been submerged in his own thoughts for a long time and his silence began to weigh on me, I said, 'Well, sir, where have you gotten lost?'

He was startled. 'I . . . Nowhere. I was just thinking about something.'

'Were you reminded of something that happened to you in the past?'

I asked. 'Stumbled on a lost dream? Some old wounds starting to hurt again?'

'Wounds? Old wounds? Well, not wounds. Just one – very deep and vicious. And I have no desire for more. One is enough.' Saying that, he got up and attempted to pace inside my room. 'Attempted' because my place was small and cluttered with chairs, a table, a cot and what all – there was really no room to pace. He could only go as far as the table and then he had to stop. This time, though, he looked at the photograph closely and said, 'How much she resembles her! Her face wasn't quite as playful though. She had big eyes, the kind which can see as well as understand.' He heaved a sigh and sat back down. 'Death is beyond comprehension, especially when it seizes someone in the prime of their youth. I believe there's another power besides God – extremely jealous and begrudging anyone's happiness. But never mind . . .'

'No, no, please go on,' I insisted, 'if you don't mind. To tell you the truth, I thought you had probably never fallen in love.'

'What made you think that? A few minutes ago you said I must have had quite a few affairs myself, didn't you?'

He looked at me with questioning eyes. 'If I haven't loved, then why this sorrow that keeps gnawing at my heart? Why this affliction? This sadness? This state of being oblivious to myself? Why am I melting away like wax day and night?'

Ostensibly he was asking me, but in fact he was asking himself.

I told him, 'I lied when I said that you must have had quite a few affairs. But you lied too, when you said you weren't sad and that nothing was bothering you. It's not easy to know what's inside another person's heart.

There could be any number of reasons for your sadness and, unless you choose to tell me yourself, I can't very well come to any conclusion, can I? That you're becoming frailer and frailer by the day is obvious. Surely you've suffered a big shock, and I do sympathize with you.'

'Sympathize!' Tears rushed to his eyes. 'I don't need sympathy. Sympathy can't bring her back, can't pull the woman I loved out of the abyss of death and return her to me. You've never loved. No, you have not. Of that I'm certain. For you are unscathed by its failure. Look at me,' he demanded, and looked down at himself. 'Do you see any spot where love hasn't left its scars? My entire existence is nothing more than the rubble of love's crumbling abode. How can I relate this tale to you? And why should I? You wouldn't understand. The words, "My mother died," are not likely to affect a stranger as much as the deceased's son. To you, indeed to anybody, my tale of love would seem commonplace. But the way it has affected me, how can anyone understand it! Only I have experienced this love and only I have borne its brunt.'

He fell silent. His throat had become dry; this was obvious from his repeated attempts to swallow.

'Did she deceive you?' I asked him. 'Or was there something else?'

'Deceive? She could never deceive. For God's sake don't use that word. She wasn't a woman, she was an angel. But woe to Death that couldn't bear to see us happy and gathered her up in its wings and took her away forever . . . Ah! You've opened my wounds. So now listen. I'll tell you part of that distressing tale. She came from a distinguished, wealthy family. When we first met, I'd already squandered away the whole of my ancestral property on a life of debauchery. Nothing remained. I left my home and went to Lucknow. Since I used to own a car, driving was the one skill I had. So I decided to become a chauffeur. My first job was at the residence of Deputy Sahib and she was his only daughter.'

He drifted off into his own thoughts and stopped talking. I remained silent. After some time he snapped out of his reverie and said, 'What was I saying?'

'That you worked for a Deputy Sahib.'

'Yes. She was the Deputy Sahib's only daughter. Every morning at nine I'd drive her, Zohra, to school. She observed purdah, but how long can one remain hidden from one's chauffeur! I was able to see her face on the very second day. She wasn't just beautiful; she had something quite special about her. She was a serious, poised young woman. The straight parting in her hair gave her an unusual aura of dignity. She . . . she . . . How do I explain to you what she was really like. I don't have words to describe her inner and outer beauty.'

He kept reciting his Zohra's accomplishments for a long time, making several attempts along the way to describe her in words, but failing repeatedly. It seemed that too many thoughts had crowded into his head. Now and then his face would light up in the middle of a sentence, only to be quickly clouded over by a gloom that left him talking in sighs. He told his story extremely slowly, as if relishing it himself. His story, which he recounted one piece at a time, went something like this:

He fell madly in love with Zohra. He spent the first few days looking for opportunities to steal a glance at her and working out all kinds of plans. But when he thought about it seriously, he recognized that he and Zohra were just too far apart. How could a chauffeur even think of falling in love with the daughter of his employer? That bitter realization clouded

his days with unrelenting sadness. One day, though, he dared to scribble
a few lines to Zohra.

*Zohra! I know I'm your servant. Your father pays me a salary of
thirty rupees a month. But . . . I'm in love with you. What shall
I do? I'm so confused.*

He stuck the scrap of paper inside one of her books. The next morning
when he drove her to school his hands shook, and many times he very
nearly lost control of the steering. But, thank God, no accident occurred.
He spent the whole day in a strange state of mind. In the evening, when
he was driving her back from school, she asked him to pull over. When
he did so, she spoke in an extremely serious tone. 'Look, Naim, don't
repeat this ever again. I haven't told my father about the letter you slipped
inside my book. But if you ever do this sort of thing again, I'll be forced
to report the matter to him. Understand? Okay, now drive on.'

After that, he tried to quit working for Deputy Sahib and to extinguish
his love for Zohra, but he didn't succeed. This tug of war went on for a
month. One day he gathered his courage and wrote her another letter.
He slipped it into her book and waited for the decree of his fate. He was
sure that he'd be dismissed from his job the very next morning, but that
didn't happen. On their way back from school that evening, Zohra once
again spoke to him and admonished him. 'If you don't care about your
own honour, at least care about mine.' She said all this with such gravity
and firmness that Naim's hopes were completely dashed. Immediately he
resolved to quit his job and leave Lucknow for good. At the end of the

month he wrote one final letter to Zohra by the dim light of his lantern. Filled with pain and anguish he told her:

Zohra! I've tried my best to act on your advice. Believe me, I have. But I cannot control my heart. This is the last time I shall ever write to you. I'll leave Lucknow by tomorrow evening so you need not say anything to your father. Your silence will decide my fate. I'll live far away from you . . . but don't think that I'll ever stop loving you. My heart will always be at your feet no matter where I live. I will always remember the days when I drove the car carefully and slowly in order to spare you any jolts. What else could I have done for you anyway?

This letter, too, he slipped into her book as soon as an opportunity presented itself. As they drove to her school in the morning, Zohra didn't say a word to him. Nor did she speak to him on their way back in the evening. He went to his room utterly dejected, packed the few belongings he had and put the bundle away in a corner. Then he sat down on his cot and, in the pale light of the lantern, thought about the precipitous gulf that separated him from Zohra.

He was very despondent, well aware of his own insignificance. After all, he was just a lowly servant! What right did he have to fall in love with his employer's daughter? But the thought occurred to him from time to time that it wasn't his fault that he'd fallen in love with her. And besides, his love was not a deception. Around midnight, as he was mulling over these thoughts, he heard a knock on the door. His heart jumped to his throat, but then he thought it must be the gardener. It was possible someone had fallen sick at his home and he'd come for help. But when he opened the door, Zohra was standing across from him – yes, Zohra – in the December chill, without even her shawl.

He was tongue-tied. He didn't know what to say. There was a deathly silence for a few moments and then, finally, her lips moved and she said in a trembling voice, 'Well, Naim, I'm here. Tell me what you'd like me to do. But before you tell me, I have a few questions of my own.'

Naim was silent.

Zohra asked, 'Do you really love me?'

Naim was hurt. His face flushed. 'Zohra,' he said, 'you're asking a question which would debase my love if I attempted to answer it. Instead, let me ask you: Don't I?'

Zohra didn't respond. After a brief silence she said, 'My father has a lot of money, but I don't have a single paisa to my name. Whatever is said to be mine is, in reality, not mine but his. Without wealth would you still love me as dearly?'

Being an overly sensitive man, Naim felt as if the question was an affront to his dignity. In a voice weighed down by sorrow, he said, 'For God's sake, Zohra, please don't ask questions whose answers are so commonplace that you can even find them in third-rate romance novels.'

Zohra stepped into the room and sat down on the cot. 'I'm yours,' she said, 'and always will be.'

She kept her word. After she and Naim moved to Delhi, married and set themselves up in a small house, the Dipty Sahib came looking for them. As Naim had already found work, he wasn't home. The Dipty Sahib scolded Zohra, accusing her of sacrificing her honour. He wanted her to leave Naim and put all that had happened behind her. He was even willing to pay Naim as much as two or three thousand rupees. But Zohra wasn't ready to leave her husband, no matter what. She said to her father, 'Daddy! I'm truly happy with Naim. You could never have found a better husband for me. We don't ask you for anything. But if you can, give us your blessing; we'll be grateful for that.'

The Dipty Sahib became very angry when he heard these words. He threatened to have Naim arrested. Zohra, however, asked him matter-of-factly, 'But Daddy! What is Naim's crime? The truth is we're both innocent. We love each other and he's my husband. This isn't a crime. And I'm no longer a minor.'

The Dipty Sahib was a shrewd man. He quickly realized that he wouldn't be able to prove Naim guilty when his own daughter was a willing partner. He left Zohra forever. Later on he tried to put pressure on Naim indirectly through other people and even tried to buy him off, but failed in that as well.

Zohra and Naim were living happily, even though Naim's salary was dreadfully small and Zohra, who'd been brought up in great comfort and luxury, now had to be content with wearing homely clothes and doing all the household chores on her own. But she was happy and found herself in a new world where she continually discovered fresh dimensions of Naim's love. She was pleased, very pleased, and so was Naim. But one day, as God had willed it, Zohra felt a severe pain in her chest and before Naim could do anything about it, she passed away, leaving his world dark forever.

It took him four hours to recount this story. He had spoken haltingly, as if relishing every word he uttered. By the time he finished, his face no longer looked pale. It was flushed, as though blood had been injected into him slowly, but his eyes had tears in them and his throat was dry.

His tale told, he got up quickly, as if in a terrible hurry, and said, 'I made a big mistake. I shouldn't have told you the story of my love. I made a terrible mistake. All this about Zohra should have remained sealed inside my heart, but . . .' His voice became hoarse. 'I'm alive and she . . . she . . .' He couldn't say anything more. He shook my hand quickly and left the room.

I never saw him again. Many times I went to Apollo Bunder with the express purpose of looking for him, but I never found him there. I did receive a letter from him six or seven months later in which he wrote:

Sir!

You will recall that I told you the story of my love at your place. It was only a story, an untrue story, for there's no Zohra, nor is there a Naim. Although I do exist, I'm not the same Naim who was in love with Zohra. One day you said there were people who were truly barren of love. I am one of them, someone who has spent his entire life merely deluding his heart. Naim's love for Zohra was a distraction and Zohra's death — I still don't understand why I killed her — it's quite possible that that too had something to do with my inner darkness.

I don't know if you believed my story to be true, but let me tell you something very strange. I, the creator of that story, believed it to be true, to be based completely on reality. I believed

*that I had really loved Zohra and she had really died. It might
surprise you even more to hear that the story became increasingly
real to me as time passed. I could clearly hear Zohra's voice,
even her laughter, ring in my ears, and I could feel her warm
breath on my body. Every little detail of the story came to life
and so, in a manner of speaking, I dug my grave with my own
hands.*

*Even if Zohra isn't fiction. I am. She's dead, so I must die
too. This letter will reach you after my death. Farewell. I will
find Zohra, I'm sure. But where? Of that I'm not so sure.*

*The only reason I've scribbled these lines to you is that you're
a writer. If you can turn all of this into a story you may be
able to sell it for seven or eight rupees, since you once said you
can make that much from a story. That will be my gift to you.
Goodbye.*

Your acquaintance,
Naim

Naim created Zohra for himself and died. I created a story for myself
and lived. It's not fair.

Translated by Muhammad Umar Memon and Moazzam Sheikh

Licence

ABU THE COACHMAN was very stylish and his coach was number one in the city. He only took regulars. He earned ten to fifteen rupees daily from them, and it was enough for him. Unlike the other coachmen, he didn't have a taste for alcohol but he had a weakness for style and fashion.

Whenever his coach passed by, its bells jingling, all eyes turned to him. 'There goes that stylish Abu. Just look at the way he's sitting. And that turban, tipped to the side like that!'

When Abu heard these words and observed the admiration in people's eyes, he'd cock his head and his horse Chinni's stride would quicken. Abu held the reins as though it were hardly necessary to hold them at all, as if Chinni didn't need his master's instructions, and would keep his stride without them. At times, it seemed as though Abu and Chinni were one, or rather that the entire coach was a single life force, and who was that force, if not Abu?

The passengers Abu didn't accept cursed him roundly. Some wished him ill, 'May the Lord break his arrogance and his coach and horse land in some river.'

In the shadows cast by Abu's thin moustache, a smile of supreme self-confidence danced. It made the other coachmen burn with envy. The sight of Abu inspired them to beg, borrow and steal so that they, too, could have coaches decorated with brass fittings. But they could not replicate his distinct style and elegance. Nor could they find such devoted clients.

One afternoon, Abu was lying in his coach under the shade of a tree dozing off, when a voice rang in his ears. Abu opened his eyes and saw a woman standing below. Abu must have looked at her only once, but her extreme youth instantly pierced his heart. She wasn't a woman, she was a girl – sixteen or seventeen; slim, but sturdy; her skin dark, but radiant. She wore silver hoops in her ears. Her hair was parted in the middle and she had a pointed nose on whose summit there was a small, bright beauty spot. She wore a long kurta, a blue skirt and a light shawl over her head.

The girl said in a childish voice, 'How much do you charge for the teshan?'

Mischief played on Abu's smiling lips. 'Nothing.'

The girl's dark face reddened. 'What will you charge for the teshan?' she repeated.

Abu let his eyes linger on her and replied, 'What can I take from you, fortunate one? Go on, get in the back.'

The girl covered her firm, already well-concealed breasts, with her trembling hands. 'What things you say!'

Abu smiled. 'Go on, get in then. I'll take whatever you give me.'

The girl thought for a moment, then stepped onto the footboard and climbed in. 'Quickly. Come on then. Take me to the teshan.'

Abu turned around. 'In a big hurry, gorgeous?'

'You . . . you . . .' The girl was about to say more, but stopped mid-sentence.

The carriage began to move, and kept moving; many streets passed below the horse's hooves. The girl sat nervously in the back. A mischievous smile danced on Abu's lips. When a considerable amount of time had passed, the girl asked in a frightened voice, 'The teshan hasn't come yet?'

Abu replied meaningfully, 'It'll come. My teshan and yours are the same.'

'What do you mean?'

Abu turned to look at her and said, 'You're not such an innocent, surely? My teshan and yours really are the same. They became one the moment Abu first set eyes on you. I swear on your life, I'm your slave; I wouldn't lie.'

The girl adjusted the shawl on her head. Her eyes showed that she understood Abu's meaning. Her face also showed that she hadn't taken his words badly. But she was mulling over this dilemma: Abu and her station might well be the same; Abu was certainly smart and dressed sharp, but was he faithful too? Should she abandon her station from which, in any case, her train had long departed, for his?

Abu's voice made her start. 'What are you thinking about, fortunate one?'

The horse was prancing along happily; the air was cold; the trees lining the street raced by; their branches swooned; there was no sound except the ringing of bells. Abu, head cocked, was fantasizing about kissing the dark beauty. After some time, he tied the horse's reins to the dashboard and with a jump, landed in the back seat next to the girl. She remained silent. Abu grabbed her hands in his. 'Put your reins in my hands!'

The girl said only two words. 'Enough now.' But Abu immediately put his arms around her. She resisted. Her heart was beating hard and fast, as if it wanted to leave her and fly away.

'I love this horse and carriage more than life,' Abu said in a soft, loving voice, 'but I swear on the eleventh pir, I'll sell it and have gold bangles made for you. I'll wear old, torn clothes myself, but I'll keep you like a princess! I swear on the one, omnipresent God that this is the first love of my life. If you're not mine, I'll cut my throat this minute in front of you!' Then suddenly, he moved away from the girl. 'I don't know what's the matter with me today. Come on, I'll take you to the teshan.'

'No,' the girl said softly, 'now you've touched me.'

Abu lowered his head. 'I'm sorry. I made a mistake.'

'And will you honour this mistake?'

There was a challenge in her voice, as if someone had said to Abu, 'Let's see if your carriage can go faster than mine.' He raised his lowered head; his eyes brightened. 'Fortunate one . . .' With this, he put his hand on his firm chest and said, 'Abu will give his life.'

The girl put forward her hand. 'Then take my hand.'

Abu held her hand firmly. 'I swear on my youth. Abu is your slave.'

The next day Abu and the girl were married. She was from Gujarat district, the daughter of a cobbler; her name was Nesti. She had come to town with her relatives. They had been waiting at the station even as Abu and she were falling in love.

They were both very happy. Abu didn't sell his horse and carriage to have gold bangles made for Nesti, but he did spend his savings on gold earrings and silk clothes for her.

His heart danced when Nesti appeared before him, her silk skirt swishing from side to side. 'I swear on the Five Pure Ones, there's no one in the world as beautiful as you.' With this, he would press her against his chest. 'You're the queen of my heart.'

The two were immersed in the pleasures of youth. They sang; they laughed; they went on walks; they swore fidelity to each other. A month passed like this when suddenly one morning the police arrested Abu. A kidnapping case was registered against him. Nesti stood by him firmly, unwaveringly protesting his innocence, but despite that, Abu was sentenced to two years' imprisonment. When the court gave its verdict, Nesti wrapped her arms around Abu. 'I'll never go to my mother and father,' she said as she wept. 'I'll sit at home and wait for you.'

Abu gently touched her stomach. 'Bless you. I've given the horse and carriage to Dino. Carry on taking the rent from him.'

Nesti's parents put great pressure on her, but she didn't go back to them. Tiring at last, they gave up on her and left her to her lot. Nesti began to live alone. Dino would give her five rupees in the evening, which was enough for her expenses. She also received the money that had accumulated during the court case.

Abu and Nesti met once a week at the jail, meetings which were always too brief for them. Whatever money Nesti saved, she spent on bringing Abu comfort in jail. At one meeting, Abu, looking at her bare ears, asked, 'Where are your earrings, Nesti?'

Nesti smiled, and looking at the guard, said, 'I must have lost them somewhere.'

'You needn't take so much care of me,' Abu said with some anger, 'I'm all right, however I am.'

Nesti said nothing. Their time was up. She left smiling, but when she reached home, she wept bitterly; she wept for hours because Abu's health was declining. In this last meeting, she could hardly recognize him. The strapping Abu was a shadow of his former self. Nesti thought his sorrow had consumed him and that their separation had caused his decline. What she didn't know was that Abu had TB and that the disease ran in his family. Abu's father had been even sturdier than Abu, but TB soon sent him to his grave. Abu's elder brother had also been a strapping young man, but the disease had caused him, while in the flower of his youth, to waste away. Abu himself was unaware of this, and taking his last breath in the prison hospital, he said to Nesti in a sorrowful voice, 'If I had known I was going to die so young, I swear on the one, omnipresent God, I wouldn't have made you my wife. I've done you a great injustice. Forgive me. And listen, my horse and carriage are my hallmark. Take care of them. Stroke Chinni on the head and tell him that Abu sends his love.'

Abu died, leaving Nesti's world desolate. But she was not a woman to be easily defeated. She withstood her sorrow. The house was deserted now. In the evenings, Dino would come and comfort her. 'Have no fear, bhabhi. No one walks ahead of God. Abu was my brother. Whatever I can do for you, with God's will, I will do.'

At first Nesti didn't understand, but when her mourning period was over, Dino said in no unclear terms that she should marry him. She wanted to kick him out of the house when she heard this, but only said, 'Dino, I don't want to remarry.'

From the next day on the amount of money Dino gave her was noticeably less. Earlier, he had given her five rupees daily without fail. But now he would sometimes give her four, sometimes three. His excuse was that business was slow. Then he began disappearing for two to three days at a time. Sometimes he said he was sick; other times he'd say some part of the carriage was broken and he couldn't take it out. He went too far one day and Nesti finally said, 'Listen, Dino, don't trouble yourself with it any more. Just hand the coach and horse over to me.'

After much hemming and hawing, Dino was forced at last to place the horse and coach back in Nesti's custody. She, in turn, gave it to Maja, a friend of Abu's. Within a few days, he proposed marriage as well. When she turned him down, his eyes changed; the warmth in them seemed to vanish. Nesti took the horse and carriage back from him and gave it to a coachman she didn't know. He really broke all boundaries, arriving completely drunk one night to give her the money, and making a grab for her as soon as he walked through the door. She let him have it and fired him at once.

For eight or ten days, the coach was in the stable, out of work, racking up costs – feed on one hand, stable rent on the other. Nesti was in a state of confusion. People were either trying to marry her or rape her or rob her. When she went outside, she was met with ugly stares. One night a neighbour jumped the wall and started making advances towards her. Nesti went half mad wondering what she should do.

Back at home, she thought 'What if I were to drive the coach myself?' When she used to go on rides with Abu, she would often drive it. She was acquainted with the routes as well. But then she thought of what people would say. Her mind came up with many rejoinders. 'What's the harm? Do women not toil and do manual labour? Here working in mines, there in offices, thousands working at home; you have to fill your stomach one way or another!'

She spent a few days thinking about it. At last she decided to do it. She was confident she could. And so, after asking for God's help, she arrived one morning at the stable. When she began harnessing the horse to the carriage, the other coachmen were stupefied; some thought it was a joke and roared with laughter. The older coachmen tried dissuading her, saying it was unseemly. But Nesti wouldn't listen. She fitted up the carriage, polished its brass tackle, and after showing the horse great affection and speaking tender words to Abu, she set out from the stable. The coachmen were stunned by Nesti's dexterity; she handled the carriage expertly.

Word spread through the town that a beautiful woman was driving a coach. It was spoken of on every street corner. People waited impatiently for the moment she when she would come down their street.

At first Nesti shied away from male passengers, but she soon shed her shyness and began earning an excellent income. Her coach was never idle, here passengers got off, there they got on. Sometimes passengers would even fight among themselves over who had stopped her first.

When the work became too much, she had to fix hours for when the coach would go out – in the mornings, from seven to twelve; in the afternoons, from two to six. This arrangement proved beneficial as she managed to get enough rest as well. Chinni was happy too, but Nesti couldn't help being aware that her clients often rode in her coach only to be near her. They would make her go aimlessly from pillar to post, sometimes cracking dirty jokes in the back. They spoke to her just to hear the sound of her voice. Sometimes she felt that though she had not sold herself, people had slyly bought her anyway. She was also aware that all the city's other coachmen thought ill of her. But she was unperturbed; her belief in herself kept her at peace.

One morning, the municipal committee men called her in and revoked her licence. Their reason was that women couldn't drive coaches. Nesti asked, 'Sir, why can't women drive coaches?'

The reply came: 'They just can't. Your licence is revoked.'

Nesti said, 'Sir, then take my horse and coach as well, but please tell me why women can't drive coaches. Women can grind mills and fill their stomachs. Women can carry rubble in baskets on their heads and make a living. Women can work in mines, sifting through pieces of coal to earn their daily bread. Why can't I drive a coach? I know nothing else. The horse and carriage were my husband's, why can't I use them? How will I make ends meet? Milord, please have mercy. Why do you stop me from hard, honest labour? What am to do? Tell me.'

The officer replied: 'Go to the bazaar and find yourself a spot. You're sure to make more that way.'

Hearing this, the real Nesti, the person within, was reduced to ashes. 'Yes sir,' she answered softly and left.

She sold the horse and carriage for whatever she could get and went straight to Abu's grave. For a moment, she stood next to it in silence. Her eyes were completely dry, like the blaze after a shower, robbing the earth of all its moisture. Her lips parted and she addressed the grave, 'Abu, your Nesti died today in the committee office.'

With this, she went away. The next day she submitted her application. She was given a licence to sell her body.

Translated by Aatish Taseer

Colder Than Ice

As Ishwar Singh entered the room, Kalwant Kaur rose from the bed and locked the door from the inside. It was past midnight. A strange and ominous silence seemed to have descended on the city.

Kalwant Kaur returned to the bed, crossed her legs and sat down in the middle. Ishwar Singh stood quietly in a corner, holding his kirpan absent-mindedly. Anxiety and confusion were writ large on his handsome face.

Kalwant Kaur, apparently dissatisfied with her defiant posture, moved to the edge and sat down, swinging her legs suggestively. Ishwar Singh still had not spoken.

Kalwant Kaur was a big woman with generous hips, fleshy thighs and unusually high breasts. Her eyes were sharp and bright and over her upper lip there was faint bluish down. Her chin suggested great strength and resolution.

Ishwar Singh had not moved from his corner. His turban, which he always kept smartly in place, was loose and his hands trembled from time to time. However, from his strapping, manly figure, it was apparent that he had just what it took to be Kalwant Kaur's lover.

More time passed. Kalwant Kaur was getting restive. 'Ishr Sian,' she said in a sharp voice.

Ishwar Singh raised his head, then turned it away, unable to deal with Kalwant Kaur's fiery gaze.

This time she screamed, 'Ishr Sian.' Then she lowered her voice and added, 'Where have you been all this time?'

Ishwar Singh moistened his parched lips and said, 'I don't know.'

Kalwant Kaur lost her temper. 'What sort of a motherfucking answer is that!'

Ishwar Singh threw his kirpan aside and slumped on the bed. He looked unwell. She stared at him and her anger seemed to have left her. Putting her hand on his forehead, she asked gently, 'Jani, what's wrong?'

'Kalwant.' He turned his gaze from the ceiling and looked at her. There was pain in his voice and it melted all of Kalwant Kaur. She bit her lower lip. 'Yes jani.'

Ishwar Singh took off his turban. He slapped her thigh and said, more to himself than to her, 'I feel strange.'

His long hair came undone and Kalwant Kaur began to run her fingers through it playfully. 'Ishr Sian, where have you been all this time?'

'In the bed of my enemy's mother,' he said jocularly. Then he pulled Kalwant Kaur towards him and began to knead her breasts with both hands. 'I swear by the Guru, there's no other woman like you.'

Flirtatiously, she pushed him aside. 'Swear over my head. Did you go to the city?'

He gathered his hair in a bun and replied, 'No.'

Kalwant Kaur was irritated. 'Yes, you did go to the city and you looted more money and you don't want to tell me about it.'

'May I not be my father's son if I lie to you,' he said.

She was silent for a while, then she exploded, 'Tell me what happened to you the last night you were here. You were lying next to me and you had made me wear all those gold ornaments you'd looted from the houses of the Muslims in the city and you were kissing me all over and then suddenly, God only knows what came over you, you put on your clothes and walked out.'

Ishwar Singh went pale. 'See how your face has fallen,' Kalwant Kaur snapped. 'Ishr Sian,' she said, emphasizing every word, 'you're not the man you were eight days ago. Something has happened.'

Ishwar Singh did not answer, but he was stung. He suddenly took Kalwant Kaur in his arms and began to hug and kiss her ferociously. 'Jani, I'm what I always was. Squeeze me tighter so that the heat in your bones cools off.'

Kalwant Kaur did not resist him, but she kept asking, 'What went wrong that night?'

'Nothing.'

'Why don't you tell me?'

'There's nothing to tell.'

'Ishr Sian, may you cremate my body with your own hands if you lie to me!'

Ishwar Singh did not reply. He dug his lips into hers. His moustache tickled her nostrils and she sneezed. They burst out laughing.

Ishwar Singh began to take off his clothes, ogling Kalwant Kaur lasciviously. 'Let's play a round of cards.'

Beads of perspiration appeared over her upper lip. She rolled her eyes coquettishly and said, 'Get lost.'

Ishwar Singh pinched her lip and she leapt aside. 'Ishr Sian, don't do that. It hurts.'

Ishwar Singh began to suck her lower lip and Kalwant Kaur melted. He took off the rest of his clothes. 'Time for a round of trumps,' he said.

Kalwant Kaur's upper lip began to quiver. He peeled her shirt off, as if he was skinning a banana. He fondled her naked body and pinched her arm. 'Kalwant, I swear by the Guru, you're not a woman, you're a delicacy,' he said between kisses.

Kalwant Kaur examined the skin he had pinched. It was red. 'You're really a brute, Ishr Sian.'

Ishwar Singh smiled through his thick moustache. 'Then let there be a lot of brutality tonight.' And he began to prove what he had said.

He bit her lower lip, nibbled at her earlobes, kneaded her breasts, slapped her glowing hip resoundingly and planted big, wet kisses on her cheeks until she began to boil.

But there was something wrong.

Ishwar Singh, despite his vigorous efforts at foreplay, could not feel the fire which leads to the final and inevitable act of love. Like a wrestler who is being had the better of, he employed every trick he knew to ignite the fire in his loins, but it eluded him. He felt cold.

Kalwant Kaur was now like an overtuned instrument. 'Ishr Sian,' she whispered languidly, 'you have shuffled me enough, it is time to produce your trump.'

Ishwar Singh felt as if the entire deck of cards had slipped from his hands on to the floor.

He laid himself against her, breathing irregularly. Drops of cold perspiration appeared on his brow. Kalwant Kaur made frantic efforts to arouse him, but in the end she gave up.

In a fury, she sprang out of bed and covered herself with a sheet. 'Ishr Sian, tell me the name of the bitch who has squeezed you dry.'

Ishwar Singh just lay there panting. 'Who was she?' Kalwant screamed.

'No one, Kalwant, no one,' he replied in a barely audible voice. Kalwant Kaur placed her hands on her hips. 'Ishr Sian, I'm going to get to the bottom of this. Swear to me on the Guru's sacred name, is there a woman?'

She did not let him speak. 'Before you swear by the Guru, don't forget who I am. I am Sardar Nihal Singh's daughter. I will cut you to pieces. Is there a woman in this?'

He nodded his head in assent, his pain obvious from his face. Like a wild and demented creature, Kalwant Kaur picked up Ishwar Singh's kirpan, unsheathed it and plunged it into his neck. Blood spluttered out of the deep gash like water out of a fountain.

Then she began to pull at his hair and scratch his face, cursing her unknown rival as she continued tearing at him.

'Let go, Kalwant, let go now,' Ishwar Singh begged.

She paused. His beard and chest were drenched in blood. 'You acted impetuously,' he said, 'but I deserved it.'

'Tell me the name of that woman of yours,' she screamed.

A thin line of blood ran into his mouth. He shivered as he felt its taste.

'Kalwant, with this kirpan I have killed six men . . . with this kirpan with which you . . .'

'Who was the bitch, I ask you?' she repeated.

Ishwar Singh's dimming eyes sparked into momentary life. 'Don't call her a bitch,' he implored.

'Who was she?' she screamed.

Ishwar Singh's voice was failing. 'I'll tell you.' He ran his hand over his throat, then looked at it, smiling wanly. 'What a motherfucking creature man is!'

'Ishr Sian, answer my question,' Kalwant Kaur said.

He began to speak, very slowly, his face coated with cold sweat.

'Kalwant, jani, you can have no idea what happened to me. When they began to loot Muslim shops and houses in the city, I joined one of the gangs. All the cash and ornaments that fell to my share, I brought back to you. There was only one thing I hid from you.'

He began to groan. His pain was becoming unbearable, but she was unconcerned. 'Go on,' she said in a merciless voice.

'The house we broke into had seven people inside, six of them men whom I killed with my kirpan one by one . . . and there was one girl . . . she was so beautiful I didn't kill her I took her away.'

She sat on the edge of the bed, listening to him.

'Kalwant jani, I can't even begin to describe to you how beautiful she was . . . I could have slashed her throat but I didn't . . . I said to myself, Ishr Sian, you gorge yourself on Kalwant Kaur every day . . . how about a mouthful of this luscious fruit!

'I thought she had gone into a faint, so I carried her over my shoulder all the way to the canal which runs outside the city . . . then I laid her down on the grass, behind some bushes and . . . first I thought I would shuffle her a bit . . . but then I decided to trump her right away.'

'What happened?' she asked.

'I threw the trump . . . but, but . . .'

His voice sank.

Kalwant Kaur shook him violently. 'What happened?'

Ishwar Singh opened his eyes. 'She was dead . . . I had carried a dead body . . . a heap of cold flesh . . . jani, give me your hand.'

Kalwant Kaur placed her hand on his. It was colder than ice.

Translated by Khalid Hasan

Toba Tek Singh

A FEW YEARS AFTER Partition, the thought occurred to the governments of Pakistan and Hindustan that, as with ordinary prisoners, an exchange of lunatics was in order. Muslim madmen in Indian asylums should be sent over to Pakistan and the Hindu and Sikh lunatics languishing in Pakistani madhouses should be handed over to Hindustan.

Whether the proposition was smart or dumb only God knows. Anyway, following the decision of some wise men, a bunch of high-level conferences were convened on either side and concluded with a date for the transfer. A thorough scrutiny was mounted. Muslim lunatics with relatives still living in Hindustan were allowed to stay there; others were shepherded to the border. In Pakistan, the question of keeping anyone didn't even arise since nearly all Hindus and Sikhs had already migrated to Hindustan. The remaining Hindu and Sikh lunatics were rounded up and brought over to the border under police escort.

Regardless of what did or didn't happen across the border, in the Lahore asylum the news of the coming exchange stirred up rather interesting speculation among the inmates. There was one Muslim lunatic who had never missed reading the newspaper *Zamindar* during the last twelve years. When a friend asked him, 'Molbi Sab, what is this thing called Pakistan?' he gave the matter prolonged, deep thought and said, 'It's a place in India where they make straight razors.'

The explanation satisfied his friend.

Likewise, one Sikh inmate asked another Sikh, 'Sardarji, why are we being sent to Hindustan? We don't know their language.'

The latter smiled. 'But I know the Hindustoras' language. They are absolute rascals – these Hindustanis. They strut around.'

One day, as he was bathing, a Muslim lunatic shouted 'Pakistan Zindabad!' so loudly that he slipped, fell to the floor and was knocked out.

There were some inmates who weren't really mad. Most of them were murderers. Their relatives had them committed after bribing the officers so that they would be spared the hangman's noose. They did seem to have some inkling of why Hindustan was partitioned and what this Pakistan was, but even they didn't understand the matter clearly. Newspapers weren't much help and the watchmen were idiots and completely illiterate; nothing definite could be gleaned from conversations with them. All they knew was that there was this man Muhammad Ali Jinnah whom everyone called Quaid-e Azam. He had made a separate country for Muslims called Pakistan. But they knew nothing about where it was located. So these inmates, whose minds hadn't fused entirely, were continually in a fix about whether they were in Pakistan or Hindustan. If they were in Hindustan, then where was Pakistan?

One inmate got so mixed up about this business of Pakistan-Hindustan, Hindustan-Pakistan that he became even crazier. One day, while sweeping the floor, he suddenly climbed a tree, perched on a limb, and for the next two hours held forth non-stop on the delicate matter of Pakistan and Hindustan. When the guards tried to coax him down, he climbed even higher. When he was threatened, he told them in no uncertain terms, 'I don't want to live in Hindustan and I don't want to live in Pakistan; I'll live here in this tree.'

Finally, when the bout of madness subsided, he decided to come down, whereupon he started hugging his Hindu and Sikh friends deliriously, crying all the while because he was overcome by the thought that they would leave him there and go to Hindustan.

A Muslim radio engineer with a Master of Science degree always kept himself aloof from other inmates and walked quietly on a particular path of the asylum's garden all day long. Suddenly, one day, he took off all his clothes, gave them to an officer and started frolicking in the garden stark naked.

A plump Muslim lunatic from Chiniot, once a very active worker for the Muslim league, used to bathe fifteen or sixteen times a day. He abruptly gave up bathing altogether. His name was Muhammad Ali, and one day he announced from his cubicle that he was Muhammad Ali Jinnah. A Sikh followed suit and declared himself Master Tara Singh. This nearly led to a bloodbath, but designating both men as highly dangerous and confining them to separate quarters averted the crisis.

A young Lahori Hindu lawyer who had lost his mind after failing in love was terribly hurt upon hearing that Amritsar had now been moved to Hindustan. His beloved was a native of that city. Although she had snubbed him, even in his madness her memory was fresh in his mind. He constantly hurled obscenities at the Hindu and Muslim leaders who had conspired to eviscerate Hindustan, making him a Pakistani and his beloved a Hindustani. When talk of the exchange began, many of the other lunatics tried to bolster his sagging spirits. They told him not to lose heart; he would be packed off to Hindustan where his love lived. But he didn't want to abandon Lahore. He was afraid he wouldn't be able to set up a successful law practice in Amritsar.

There were two Anglo-Indian inmates in the European ward. They literally went into shock hearing that the English had freed India and gone back home. For hours they secretly discussed the grave matter of their status in the asylum now that the English had left. Would the European ward be kept or liquidated? Would they get a 'real breakfast'? Or would they be obliged to force the bloody Indian chapatti down their gullets in place of the double-roti?

A Sikh inmate had arrived in the asylum fifteen years ago. He could be heard uttering strange gibberish all the time: '*Upar de gurgur de aiynks de be-dhyaana de mung de daal aaf de laaltain.*' Day or night, he never slept. The watchmen could vouch for the fact that he hadn't slept even a wink in fifteen years. Whenever he heard talk in the asylum of the coming exchange, he always listened to it intently. If someone asked him his opinion, he would answer with complete seriousness: '*Upar de gurgur de aiynks de be-dhyaana de mung de daal aaf de Pakistan government.*'

Later, though, he changed *aaf de Pakistan government* to *aaf de Toba Tek Singh government*, and started asking the other loonies where Toba Tek Singh, the place he came from, was. But no one knew whether Toba Tek Singh was in Pakistan or Hindustan. And if someone tried to explain, he inevitably got confused, thinking that Sialkot, which used to be in Hindustan, was now said to be in Pakistan. Who knew, perhaps Lahore, currently in Pakistan, would shift to Hindustan tomorrow, or maybe all of Hindustan would become Pakistan. And who could say with any surety that both Hindustan and Pakistan would not disappear altogether.

Over time this lunatic's kes had become so scraggly that it almost seemed to have disappeared. He hardly ever bathed, so the hair of his beard and head had become matted and stuck together, giving his features a frighteningly grotesque look. However, he was a harmless man. During his fifteen years in the asylum he had never had a brawl with anyone. The old staff knew that he had owned quite a bit of land in Toba Tek Singh. He had been a prosperous landowner until one day, suddenly, he went berserk. His relatives brought him to the asylum in heavy chains and had him admitted. They came to visit him once a month, inquired after him and then went back. Their visits continued for a long time, but stopped when the Pakistan–Hindustan *garbar* started.

His name was Bishan Singh, but everyone called him Toba Tek Singh. Although he had no awareness of the day or month or how many years had passed, somehow he always knew the day his relatives were expected. He would tell the officer that his 'visit' was coming that day. He would take a long bath, scrub his body vigorously with soap, oil and comb his hair, have his clothes, which he hardly ever wore, brought out and slip into them, and meet his visitors thus, looking all prim and proper. If they asked him something, he remained quiet or mumbled his incomprehensible '*Upar de gurgur de aiynks de be-dhyaana de mung de daal aaf de laaltain*' now and then.

He had a daughter who, growing a little at a time, had become a young woman in fifteen years. Bishan Singh never recognized her. As a little girl, she would cry when she saw her father, and now, as a young woman, tears still welled up in her eyes at the sight of him.

When this confusing business of Pakistan and Hindustan began, he started asking his fellow lunatics where Toba Tek Singh was located. His curiosity grew by the day when he didn't get a satisfactory answer. Now the 'visits' had also stopped. Where before he would instinctively know when his relatives were coming to see him, now that inner voice no longer intimated such a visit to him.

He fervently wished those people who talked with him with such kindness and warmth and who brought him gifts of fruits, sweets and clothes would visit him. If he were to ask them, they would surely have told him whether Toba Tek Singh was located in Pakistan or Hindustan because he thought they themselves came from Toba Tek Singh.

One lunatic called himself 'God.' One day Bishan Singh asked him about Toba Tek Singh: Was it in Pakistan or Hindustan? As usual, 'God' burst out laughing and said, 'Neither in Pakistan nor Hindustan because we haven't yet given the orders.'

Bishan Singh begged 'God' many times to give the order so the dilemma could be laid to rest, but he said he was too damn busy because he had many other orders to give first. So one day, fed up with 'God's' dilly-dallying, Bishan Singh let him have a piece of his mind: '*Upar de gurgur de aiynks de be-dhyaana de mung de daal aaf Wahe Guruji da Khalsah and Wahe Guruji ki fateh — jo bole so nihal, sat siri akaal!*' Perhaps he meant to say: You're the Muslims' God, had you been the God of the Sikhs you would surely have heard my plea.

Some days before the scheduled exchange of lunatics, a Muslim friend of Bishan Sing came to see him. He had never visited him before in all these years. Bishan Singh saw him but shrugged and started to turn back. The guards stopped him and said, 'He's coming to visit you. He's your old friend Fazl Din.'

Bishan Singh hardly glanced at the man and started to mumble something. Fazl Din drew closer and put his hand on Bishan Singh's shoulder. 'I've been thinking of visiting you for quite a while now but was pressed for time. All your relatives have safely left for Hindustan. I helped them as much as I could. Your daughter Roop Kaur. . .' He suddenly held back.

Bishan Singh looked as though he was trying to remember something and then mumbled, 'Daughter Roop Kaur.'

Fazl Din said falteringly, 'Yes . . . She . . . she's all right . . . she went with them.'

Bishan Singh remained quiet. Fazl Din continued, 'Your family asked me to keep inquiring after your well-being. Now I hear that you're also leaving for Hindustan. Give my salaams to brother Balbeer Singh and brother Vadhwa Singh . . . and, yes, to sister Amrit Kaur as well. Tell brother Balbeer Singh that Fazl Din is doing well. The two brown buffaloes they had left behind – one of them gave birth to a male calf. The other also had a calf, a female, but it died after six days . . . And if there's anything more he'd like me to do, tell him I'm always ready. And this, here, a little *morandas* for you.'

Bishan Singh took the small sack of sweets and handed it to the guard standing nearby. He then asked Fazl Din, 'Where is Toba Tek Singh?'

Fazl Din was a bit bewildered. 'Where . . . where it's always been.'

Bishan Singh asked him again, 'In Pakistan or in Hindustan?'

'In Hindustan . . . No, no, it's in Pakistan.' Fazl Din was flummoxed.

Bishan Singh left, mumbling, '*Upar de gurgur de aiynks de be-dhyaana de mung de daal aaf de Pakistan and Hindustan aaf de durfatte munh.*'

Preparations for the exchange had been completed. The list of lunatics who would be swapped had been sent over to the country receiving them and the day when the exchange would take place had been fixed.

On a blistering cold morning, lorries packed with Hindu and Sikh lunatics started out from the Lahore asylum under police escort along with the officials overseeing the exchange. At the Wagah border, the superintendents of both sides met, concluded the preliminary formalities, and the exchange began, continuing well into the night.

Getting the lunatics out of the lorries and handing them over to the officials on the other side turned out to be a gruelling job indeed. Some resisted getting out, others who were willing to come out became impossible to control because they took off in different directions. As fast as the stark naked ones were clothed, they tore the clothes right off again. One rolled out a torrent of obscenities, another broke into song. Some got into fisticuffs, while others cried their hearts out, sobbing inconsolably. The hullabaloo was deafening. The female lunatics were raising their own separate hell. And all this in a cold so punishing that it made one's teeth chatter non-stop.

The majority of lunatics were against the exchange. They couldn't understand why they were being uprooted. Those who still had some sanity left were shouting *Pakistan Zindabad!* Or *Pakistan Murdabad!* – which so enraged some Muslim and Sikh lunatics that they nearly came to blows.

When Bishan Singh's turn came and the official across the Wagah border began to enter his name in the register, he asked, 'Where is Toba Tek Singh – in Pakistan or in Hindustan?'

The official laughed. 'In Pakistan.'

Bishan Singh jumped, withdrew to one side and ran to his fellow inmates. Pakistani guards grabbed him and started pushing him towards the other side of the border. He dug his heels in, refusing to budge. 'Toba Tek Singh is here!' and then he started to spew out loudly: '*Upar de gurgur de aiynks de be-dhyaana de mung de daal aaf Toba Tek Singh and Pakistan.*'

They did their best to coax him into believing by saying, 'Look, Toba Tek Singh has now moved to Hindustan, and if it hasn't yet, it will be sent there right away,' but he stubbornly refused to accept that. When they attempted to drag him forcibly across the border, he dug in with his swollen legs with such determination on the patch of earth that lay in the middle that no force in the world could move him from it.

Since he was entirely harmless, the guards didn't force him and let him stand where he was while the rest of the exchange continued.

Just before sunrise an ear-splitting cry shot out of Bishan Singh's throat. Officials from both sides of the border rushed over to him, only to find that the man who had stood on his feet day and night for the past fifteen years was lying face down. There, behind the barbed wires, was Hindustan, and here, behind the same barbed wires was Pakistan. In between, on the thin strip of no-man's-land, lay Toba Tek Singh.

Translated by Muhammad Umar Memon

Upstairs Downstairs

My publisher refused to print this story, which made me squirm up, down, and in the middle quite a bit. The thing was that a lawsuit had been brought against it in Karachi and I was fined twenty-five rupees. To find some amends, I wanted to squeeze another twenty-five rupees out of my publisher, but he didn't give in. I fidgeted around a lot and somehow scraped together some funds to have this story published so that it might reach you. Surely you'll welcome it because you're my reader, not my publisher.

—SAADAT HASAN MANTO

HUSBAND: 'Ah, it's been ages since we've sat down like this, together and alone!'

Wife: 'Yes.'

Husband: 'Responsibilities . . . as much as I try to avoid them, there is no let-up. We're surrounded by incompetents. For the sake of the nation I can't shirk my duties . . . I have to keep working.'

Wife: 'Actually, you're far too tender-hearted, when it comes to these things. Just like me.'

Husband: 'Yes, I keep myself abreast of your social activities. When you find a minute, do let me read the speeches you have been making on several recent occasions. I would like to go through them when I find time.'

Wife: 'Very well.'

Husband: 'Yes, Begum, you recall my mentioning that business to you the other day.'

Wife: 'What business?'

Husband: 'Perhaps I did not. Yesterday, by chance I happened to find myself in our middle son's room and found him reading *Lady Chatterley's Lover.*'

Wife: 'You mean that scandalous book!'

Husband: 'Yes, Begum.'

Wife: 'What did you do?'

Husband: 'I snatched the book from him and hid it.'

Wife: 'You did the right thing.'

Husband: 'I am going to consult a doctor and ask him to suggest a different diet for him.'

Wife: 'That would be absolutely the right thing to do.'

Husband: 'And how are you feeling?'

Wife: 'Fine.'

Husband: 'I was playing with the idea of . . . requesting you today . . .'

Wife: 'Oh, you are getting too bold.'

Husband: 'And all because of your winning ways.'

Wife: 'But . . . your health?'

Husband: 'Health? . . . I feel well . . . but unless I consult the doctor, I won't make any move . . . and I should be fully satisfied about that being all right from your side.'

Wife: 'I will have a word with Miss Saldhana today.'

Husband: 'And I will speak to Dr Jalal.'

Wife: 'That's the way it should be.'

Husband: 'If Dr Jalal permits.'

Wife: 'And if Miss Saldhana has no objection . . . Do wrap your scarf around your neck carefully. It is cold outside.'

Husband: 'Thank you.'

Dr Jalal: 'Did you say yes?'

Miss Saldhana: 'Yes.'

Dr Jalal: 'So did I . . . but out of mischief.'

Miss Saldhana: 'Out of mischief, I almost said no.'

Dr Jalal: 'But then I took pity.'

Miss Saldhana: 'So did I.'

Dr Jalal: 'After one full year.'

Miss Saldhana: 'Yes, after one full year.'

Dr Jalal: 'When I said yes, his pulse quickened.'

Miss Saldhana: 'She was the same way.'

Dr Jalal: 'He said to me, the fear showing in his voice, "Doctor, it seems to me my heart is not going to keep up with me. Please take a cardiogram."'

Miss Saldhana: 'That is exactly what she said to me.'

Dr Jalal: 'I gave him an injection.'

Miss Saldhana: 'I too, except that it was simple distilled water.'

Dr Jalal: 'Water is the best thing in the world.'

Miss Saldhana: 'Jalal, if you were married to that woman?'

Dr Jalal: 'And if you were married to that man?'

⇥ 131 ⇤

Miss Saldhana: 'I would have become a nymphomaniac.'

Dr Jalal: 'And I would have met my Maker by now.'

Miss Saldhana: 'You don't say.'

Dr Jalal: 'When we examine these high society idiots, they put some funny ideas in our heads.'

Miss Saldhana: 'Today as well?'

Dr Jalal: 'Today of all days.'

Miss Saldhana: 'The trouble with these people is that these funny ideas come to them after year-long intervals.'

———

Wife: *'Lady Chatterley's Lover?* Why is that book under your pillow?'

Husband: 'I wanted to see for myself how obscene it is.'

Wife: 'Let me take a peek also.'

Husband: 'No, I will read aloud from it; you do the listening.'

Wife: 'That would be very nice.'

Husband: 'I have had our son's diet changed as recommended by the doctor after I spoke to him.'

Wife: 'I was sure you would not let this matter go unattended.'

Husband: 'I have never put off until tomorrow what I can do today.'

Wife: 'I know that . . . And what is to be done today, I am sure you will not . . .'

Husband: 'You seem to be in a very pleasant mood.'

Wife: 'All because of you.'

Husband: 'I am obliged. And now if you permit . . .'

Wife: 'Have you brushed your teeth?'

Husband: 'Yes, not only have I brushed my teeth, I have also gargled with Dettol.'

Wife: 'So have I.'

Husband: 'The two of us were made for each other.'

Wife: 'That goes without saying.'

Husband: 'I will now slowly read from this infamous book.'

Wife: 'But wait, please take my pulse.'

Husband: 'It is fast . . . feel mine.'

Wife: 'Yours is racing too.'

Husband: 'Reason?'

Wife: 'A weak heart?'

Husband: 'Has to be that . . . but Dr Jalal had said there was nothing the matter.'

Wife: 'That was what Miss Saldhana also told me.'

Husband: 'He examined me thoroughly before giving his permission.'

Wife: 'I was examined thoroughly too.'

Husband: 'Then I suppose there is no harm . . .'

Wife: 'You know better . . . but your health . . .'

Husband: 'And yours?'

Wife: 'We should exercise the greatest care before . . .'

Husband: 'Did Miss Saldhana take care of that thing?'

Wife: 'What thing? . . . Oh, yes. She took care of that.'

Husband: 'So there should be no worry on that score?'

Wife: 'None.'

Husband: 'Feel my pulse now.'

Wife: 'Feels normal and mine?'

Husband: 'Yours feels normal too.'

Wife: 'Read something out of that scandalous volume.'

Husband: 'Very well, but I can feel my heart racing.'

Wife: 'So is mine.'

Husband: 'Do we have all we need?'

Wife: 'Yes, everything.'

Husband: 'If you don't mind, could you take my temperature?'

Wife: 'There is a stopwatch around, the pulse rate should be measured.'

Husband: 'I agree.'

Wife: 'Where are the smelling salts?'

Husband: 'Should be with the other things.'

Wife: 'Yes, on the side table.'

Husband: 'I think we should raise the thermostat as well.'

Wife: 'I agree.'

Husband: 'If I am overcome by weakness, don't forget my medicine.'

Wife: 'I will try, if . . .'

Husband: 'Yes . . . but only if necessary.'

Wife: 'Read out the whole page.'

Husband: 'Get ready to listen then.'

Wife: 'You sneezed.'

Husband: 'I don't know why.'

Wife: 'Strange.'

Husband: 'I find that strange also.'

Wife: 'Oh, I know what happened. Instead of raising the thermostat, I lowered it by mistake.'

Husband: 'I am glad I sneezed. That way we found out just in time.'

Wife: 'I am sorry.'

Husband: 'Not to worry, a dozen drops of brandy will do the trick.'

Wife: 'Let me measure the brandy; you are prone to get the count wrong.'

Husband: 'You are right there . . . why don't you then?'

Wife: 'Please swallow it very slowly.'

Husband: 'Can't do it any slower.'

Wife: 'Do you feel restored?'

Husband: 'I am coming round.'

Wife: 'Take some rest.'

Husband: 'Yes, I feel that I need to rest.'

Servant: 'What is the matter with the mistress today? Haven't seen her.'

Maid: 'Not feeling well.'

Servant: 'The master is not feeling well either.'

Maid: 'We knew that would happen.'

Servant: 'Yes . . . but can't understand.'

Maid: 'What?'

Servant: 'Nature plays tricks . . . both of us should be on our deathbeds, considering . . .'

Maid: 'Don't say such things . . . let the deathbed be theirs.'

Servant: 'Their deathbed would be rather grand. I would want to move it to the tiny hovel they have put us in.'

Maid: 'Where are you going?'

Servant: 'To look for a cabinetmaker. Our bed is practically broken down.'

Maid: 'And tell him to use more hardy wood this time.'

Translated by Khalid Hasan

Ram Khilavan

I HAD JUST KILLED a bedbug and was going through some old papers in a trunk, when I discovered Saeed bhaijan's picture. I put the picture in an empty frame lying on the table and sat down to wait for the dhobi.

Every Sunday I would wait like this, because by the end of the week, my supply of clean clothes had run out. I can hardly call it supply; in those days of poverty, I had just about enough clothes to meet my own basic standards for five or six days. My marriage was being negotiated at the time and, for this reason, I had for the past two or three Sundays been going to Mahim.

The dhobi was an honest man. Despite my inability to pay him sometimes, he would return my clothes every Sunday by ten. I was worried that one of these days he would grow tired of my unpaid bills and sell my clothes in the flea market, leaving me with no clothes in which to negotiate my marriage. Which, needless to say, would have been very embarrassing.

The vile, unmistakable stench of dead bedbugs filled my room. I was wondering how to dispel it when the dhobi arrived. With a 'salaam saab', he opened his bundle and put my clean clothes on the table. As he was doing so, his gaze fell on Saeed bhaijan's photograph. Taken aback, he looked closely at the picture and emitted a strange sound from his throat, 'He, he, he, hein?'

'What's the matter, dhobi?' I asked.

The dhobi's gaze fastened on the picture. 'But this, this is barrister Saeed Salim!'

'You know him?'

The dhobi nodded his head vigorously. 'Yes, two brothers. Lived in Colaba. Saeed Salim, barrister. I used to wash his clothes.'

Saeed Hassan bhaijan and Mahmood Hassan bhaijan, before immigrating to Fiji, did in fact have a practice in Bombay for a year, but this would have been a few years ago.

I said, 'You're referring to a couple of years ago?'

The dhobi nodded vigorously again. 'When Saeed Salim, barrister left, he gave me one turban, one dhoti, one kurta. New. They were very nice people. One had a beard, this big.' He made a gesture with his hand to show the length of the beard. Then pointing to Saeed bhaijan's picture, he said, 'He was younger. He had three little runts . . . they used to like to play with me. They had a house in Colaba, a big house!'

I said, 'Dhobi, they're my brothers.'

The dhobi made that strange 'he, he, he, hein?' sound again. 'Saeed Salim, barrister?'

To lessen his surprise, I said, 'This is Saeed Hassan's picture and the one with the beard is Mahmood Hassan, the eldest.'

The dhobi stared wide-eyed at me, then surveyed the squalor of my room. It was a tiny room, destitute of even an electric light. There was one table, one chair and one sack-covered cot with a thousand bedbugs.

He couldn't believe I was barrister Saeed Salim's brother, but when I told him many stories about him, he shook his head incredulously and said, 'Saeed Salim, barrister lived in Colaba, and you in this quarter?'

I responded philosophically, 'The world has many colours, dhobi. Sun in places; shade in others. Five fingers are not alike.'

'Yes, saab. That is true.'

With this, he lifted his bundle and headed to the door. I remembered his bill. I had eight annas in my pocket, which would barely get me to Mahim and back. But just so that he knew I was not entirely without principles, I said, 'Dhobi, I hope you're keeping accounts. God knows how many washes I owe you for.'

The dhobi straightened the folds of his dhoti and said, 'Saab, I don't keep accounts. I worked for Saeed Salim, barrister for one year. Whatever he gave me, I took. I don't know how to keep accounts.'

With this he was gone, leaving me to get dressed to go to Mahim.

The talks were successful. I got married. My finances improved too. I moved from the single room in Second Pir Khan Estates where I paid nine rupees a month, to a flat on Clear Road where I could afford to pay thirty-five rupees a month. The dhobi also began to receive his payments on time.

He was pleased that my finances had improved. He said to my wife, 'Begum saab, saab's brother Saeed Salim, barrister was a very big man. He lived in Colaba. When he left, he gave me a turban, one kurta and one dhoti. Your saab will also be a big man one day.'

I had told my wife the story of the photograph and of the generosity the dhobi had shown me in my days of penury. When I could pay him, I had paid him, but he never complained once. But soon my wife began to complain that he never kept accounts. 'He's been working for me four years,' I told her, 'he's never kept accounts.'

She replied, 'Why would he keep accounts? That way he could take double and quadruple the amount of money.'

'How's that?'

'You have no idea. In a bachelor's household there are always people who know how to fleece their employer.'

Nearly every month there was a dispute between my wife and the dhobi over how he did not keep an account of the clothes washed. The poor dhobi responded with complete innocence. He said, 'Begum saab, I don't know accounts, but I know you wouldn't lie. I worked for one year in the house of Saeed Salim, barrister, who is your saab's brother. His begum saab would say, 'Dhobi, here is your money', and I would say, 'All right.''

One month, a hundred and fifty pieces of clothing went to the wash. To test the dhobi, my wife said, 'Dhobi, this month sixty items of clothing were washed.'

He said, 'All right Begum saab, you wouldn't lie.' When my wife paid him for sixty clothes, he touched the money to his forehead and headed out. My wife stopped him. 'Dhobi, wait, there weren't sixty pieces of clothing, there were a hundred and fifty. Here's the rest of your money. I was just joking.'

The dhobi only said, 'Begum saab, you wouldn't lie.'

He touched the rest of the money to his forehead, said 'salaam', and walked out.

Two years after I got married, I moved to Delhi. I stayed there for a year and a half before returning to Bombay, where I rented a flat in Mahim.

In the span of three months, we changed dhobis four times because they were quarrelsome and crooked. After every wash, there would be a scene. Sometimes the quality of the wash was intolerably wretched; other times, too few clothes were returned. We missed our old dhobi. One day when we had gone through all our dhobis, he showed up with no warning, saying, 'I saw saab in the bus. I said, "How's this?" I made inquiries in Byculla and the brander told me to inquire here in Mahim. In the flat next door, I found saab's friend and so here I am.' We were thrilled, and at least on the laundry front, a period of joy and contentment began.

A Congress government came to power and a prohibition on alcohol was imposed. English alcohol was still available, but the making and selling of Indian alcohol was completely stopped. Ninety-nine per cent of the dhobis were alcoholics. That quart or half quart of alcohol, after a day spent among soap and water, was a ritual in their lives. Our dhobi had fallen ill, then tried treating his illness with the spurious alcohol that was being made illegally and sold in secret. It made him dangerously ill, bringing him close to death.

I was incredibly busy at the time, leaving the house at six in the morning and returning at ten, ten thirty at night. But when my wife heard that the dhobi was seriously ill, she went directly to his house. With the help of a servant and the taxi driver, she put him in a taxi and took him to a doctor. The doctor, moved by the dhobi's condition, refused money for his treatment. But my wife said, 'Doctor saab, you cannot keep all the merit of this good deed for yourself.'

The doctor smiled and said, 'Fine, let's go halves,' taking only half the money for the treatment.

In time, the dhobi was cured. A few injections got rid of his stomach infection and, with strong medicine, his weakness gradually went away. In a few months, he was completely well and sent up prayers for us every time he rose or sat down, 'May God make saab like Saeed Salim barrister; may saab be able to live in Colaba; may God give him a little brood; lots and lots of money. Begum saab came to get the dhobi in a motor car; she took him to a very big doctor near the fort; may God keep Begum saab happy.'

Many years passed. The country saw many upheavals. The dhobi came and went without fail every Sunday. He was now perfectly healthy; he never forgot what we had done for him and still sent up prayers for us. He had also given up liquor. In the beginning, he missed it, but now he didn't so much as mention it. Despite an entire day spent in water, he felt no need for liquor to relieve his fatigue.

Then troubled times came; no sooner had Partition happened than Hindu–Muslim riots broke out. In daylight, and at night, Muslims in Hindu neighbourhoods, and Hindus in Muslim neighbourhoods, were being killed. My wife left for Lahore.

When the situation worsened, I said to the dhobi, 'Listen dhobi, you better stop your work now. This is a Muslim neighbourhood. You don't want to end up dead.'

The dhobi smiled, 'Saab, nobody will hurt me.'

There were many incidents of violence in our own neighbourhood, but the dhobi continued to come without fail.

One Sunday morning, I was at home reading the paper. The sports page showed the tally of cricket scores while the front page gave the numbers of Hindus and Muslims killed in the riots. I was focusing on the terrifying similarity of both scores when the dhobi arrived. I opened the copybook and checked the clothes against it. The dhobi started laughing and chatting. 'Saeed Salim, barrister was a very nice man. When he left, he gave me one turban, one dhoti and one kurta. Your begum saab was also a first-rate person. She's gone away, no? To her country? If you write her a letter, send my "salaam." She came in a motor car to my room. I had such diarrhoea but the doctor gave me an injection and I got well immediately. If you write her a letter, send my "salaam". Tell her Ram Khilavan says to write him a letter too.'

I cut him off sharply. 'Dhobi, have you started drinking again?'

He laughed, 'Drink? Where can one get drink?'

I didn't think it appropriate to say more. He wrapped the dirty clothes in a bundle and went off.

In a few days, the situation became even worse. Wire after wire began to arrive from Lahore, 'Leave everything and come at once.' I decided at the beginning of the week that I would leave on Sunday, but as it turned out, I had to prepare to leave early the following day.

The clothes were with the dhobi. I thought I might retrieve them from his place before the curfew started, so that evening I took a Victoria and went to Mahalakshmi.

There was an hour left before the curfew and there was still traffic on the streets, trams were still running. My Victoria had just reached the bridge when, all of a sudden, a great commotion broke out. People ran blindly in all directions. It was as if a bullfight had begun. When the crowd thinned, I saw many dhobis in the distance with lathis in hand, dancing. Strange, indistinct sounds rose from their throats. It was where

I was headed, but when I told the Victoria driver, he refused to take me. I paid him his fare and continued on foot. When I came near the dhobis, they saw me and fell silent.

I approached one dhobi and said, 'Where does Ram Khilavan live?' Another dhobi with a lathi in his hand reeled towards us. 'What's he asking?' he said to the dhobi I'd questioned.

'He wants to know where Ram Khilavan lives.'

The blind-drunk dhobi came close and pushed up against me. 'Who are you?'

'Me? Ram Khilavan is my dhobi.'

'Ram Khilavan is your dhobi. But which dhobi's runt are you?'

One yelled, 'A Hindu dhobi's or a Muslim dhobi's?' The crowd of dhobis, blind drunk, closed in around me with their fists up, swinging their lathis. I had to answer their question: was I Muslim or Hindu? I was terrified. They had surrounded me, so running away was not an option. There were no policemen nearby to whom I could cry out for help. Dazed with fear, I started speaking in broken sentences. 'Ram Khilavan is a Hindu . . . I'm asking where he lives . . . Where is his room . . . He's been my dhobi for ten years . . . He was very sick . . . I had him treated . . . My begum . . . My memsaab came with a motor car . . .' I got as far as that and began feeling terrible pity for myself. I was filled with shame at the depths to which men were willing to sink in order to save their lives. My wretchedness made me reckless. 'I'm Muslim,' I said.

Loud cries of 'Kill him, kill him,' rose from the crowd. The dhobi, who was soused to the eyeballs drifted to one side, and said, 'Wait. Ram Khilavan will kill him.'

I turned and looked up. Ram Khilavan stood over me, wielding a heavy cudgel in his hand. He looked in my direction and began to hurl insults at Muslims in his language. Raising the cudgel over his head, he advanced on me, swearing the whole time.

'Ram Khilavan!' I yelled authoritatively.

'Shut your mouth!' he barked, '*Ram Khilavan . . .*'

My last hope had vanished. When he was close to me, I said softly, in a parched voice, 'You don't recognize me, Ram Khilavan?'

Ram Khilavan raised his cudgel in attack. Then his eyes narrowed, widened and narrowed again. The cudgel fell from his hand. He came closer, concentrating his gaze on me and cried, 'Saab!'

He turned quickly to his companions and said, 'This is not a Muslim. This is my saab. Begum saab's saab. She came with a motor car and took me to the doctor who cured my diarrhoea.'

Ram Khilavan tried to make them understand, but they wouldn't listen. They were all drunk. Fingers were pointed this way and that. Some dhobis came over to Ram Khilavan's side and fighting broke out amongst them. I saw my chance and slipped away.

At nine the next morning my things were ready. I waited only for my ticket, which a friend had gone to buy on the black market. I was deeply unsettled. I wanted the ticket to arrive quickly so that I could go to the port to board the ship to Lahore. I felt that if there were any delay, my very flat would make me a prisoner.

There was a knock on the door. I thought the ticket had arrived. I opened the door and found the dhobi standing outside.

'Salaam, saab!'

'Salaam!'

'Can I come in?'

'Come in.'

He came in, in silence. He opened his bundle and put the clothes on the bed. He wiped his eyes with his dhoti, and in a choking voice, said, 'You're leaving, saab?'

'Yes.'

He began to cry. 'Saab, please forgive me. It's all the drink's fault . . . and . . . and these days it's available for free. The businessmen distribute it and say, "Drink and kill Muslims." Who's going to refuse free liquor? Please forgive me. I was drunk. Saeed Salim, barrister was grateful to me. He gave me one turban, one dhoti, one kurta. Begum saab saved my life. I would have died of dysentery. She came with a motor car. She took me to the doctor. She spent so much money. You're going to the new country. Please don't tell Begum saab that Ram Khilavan . . .'

His voice was lost in his throat. He swung his bundle over his shoulder and headed out. I stopped him. 'Ram Khilavan, wait . . .'

But he straightened the folds of his dhoti and hurried out.

Translated by Aatish Taseer

Mozail

TARLOCHAN LOOKED UP at the night sky for the first time in four years, only because he felt tired and listless. That was what had brought him out on the terrace of Advani Chambers to take the open air and think.

The sky was absolutely clear, cloudless, stretched over the entire city of Bombay like a huge dust-coloured tent. As far as the eye could see, there were lights. Tarlochan felt as if a lot of stars had fallen from the sky and lodged themselves in tall buildings that looked like huge trees in the dark of the night. The lights shimmered like glow-worms.

This was a new experience for Tarlochan, a new feeling, being under the open night sky. He felt that he had been imprisoned in his flat for four years and thus deprived of one of nature's great blessings. It was close to three and the breeze was light and pleasant after the heavy, mechanically stirred air of the fan under which he always slept. In the morning when he got up, he always felt as if he had been beaten up all night. But in the natural morning breeze, he felt every pore in his body happily sucking in the air's freshness. When he had come up he was restless and agitated, but now, half an hour later, he felt relaxed. He could think clearly.

He began to think of Kirpal Kaur. She and her entire family lived in a mohalla, which was predominantly and ferociously Muslim. Many houses had been set on fire there and several lives had been lost. Tarlochan would have evacuated the entire family except that a curfew had been clamped down – probably a forty-eight-hour one – and Tarlochan was helpless. There were Muslims all around, and pretty bloodthirsty Muslims they were. News was pouring in from the Punjab about atrocities being committed on Muslims by Sikhs. Any hand – easily a Muslim hand – could grab hold of the soft and delicate wrist of Kirpal Kaur and push her into the well of death.

Kirpal Kaur's mother was blind and her father was a cripple. There was a brother, who lived in Deolali, where he took care of the construction contract he had recently won.

Tarlochan was really annoyed with Kirpal's brother, Naranjan, who read about the riots every day in the newspaper. In fact, a week ago, he had been told of the rapidity and intensity with which the riots were spreading. He was warned quite plainly: 'Forget about your business for the time being. We are passing through difficult times. You should stay with your family or, better still, move to my flat. I know there isn't enough space, but these are not normal times. We'll manage somehow.'

Naranjan had merely smiled through his thick moustache. 'Yaar, you are unduly worried. I have seen many such riots here. This is not Amritsar or Lahore: it is Bombay. You have only been here four years; I have lived here for twelve, a full twelve years.' God knows what Naranjan thought Bombay was. To him it was a city which would recover from the effects of riots by itself, in case they ever were to take place. He behaved as if he had some magic formula, or a fairy-tale castle that could come to no harm. As for Tarlochan, he could see quite clearly in the cool morning air that this mohalla was not safe. He was even mentally prepared to read in the morning papers that Kirpal Kaur and her parents had been killed. He did not care much for Kirpal Kaur's crippled father or her blind mother. If they were killed and Kirpal survived, it would be good for Tarlochan. If her brother, Naranjan, was killed in Deolali, it would be even better, as the coast would be clear for Tarlochan. Naranjan was not only a hindrance in his way, but a huge, big boulder blocking his path. Whenever his name came up in a conversation with Kirpal Kaur, he would call him Khingar Singh-Punjabi for 'boulder' – instead of Naranjan Singh.

The morning breeze was stirring gently around Tarlochan's head, shorn of its long hair, religiously ordained. But his heart was full of apprehensions. Kirpal Kaur had newly entered his life. Although she was the sister of the rough and ruddy Khingar Singh, she was soft, delicate and willowy. She had grown up in the village, lived through its summers and winters, but she did not have that hard, tough, masculine quality that is common to average Sikh village girls, who have to do hard, physical work. She had delicate features as if they were still in the making and her breasts were small, still needing to fill out. She was fairer than most Sikh village girls are, fair as unblemished white cotton cloth. Her body was smooth like printed linen. She was very shy.

Tarlochan belonged to the same village but he had not lived there very long. After primary school, he had gone to the city to attend high school and never went back. High school done, he began his life at college and, although during those years he went to his village numerous times, he had never even heard of this girl called Kirpal Kaur. But that may have been because he was always in a hurry to get back to the city.

The building he lived in was called Advani Chambers and, as he stood on the balcony looking at the pre-morning sky, he thought of Mozail, the Jewish girl who had a flat here. There was a time when he was in love with her 'up to his knees', as he liked to say. Never in his thirty-five years had he felt that way about any woman.

But those college days were long in the past. Between the college campus and the terrace of the Advani Chambers lay ten years, a period full of strange incidents in Tarlochan's life: Burma, Singapore, Hong Kong, and Bombay, where he had now lived for four years. And it was the first time in those four years that he had seen the sky at night, which was not a bad sight. In its dust-coloured canopy twinkled thousands of clay lamps while a cool breeze blew his way gently.

While thinking of Kirpal Kaur, his thoughts drifted back to Mozail. He had run into Mozail the very day he had moved into a second-floor flat at Advani Chambers, which a Christian friend of his had helped him rent. His first impression of her was that she was really quite mad. Her brown hair was cut short and looked dishevelled. She wore thick, unevenly laid lipstick that sat on her lips like congealed blood. She wore a loose white dress, cut so low at the neck that you could see three-quarters of her big breasts with their faint blue veins. Her bare arms were covered with a layer of fine fuzz that gave the impression that she'd just emerged from the beauty parlour with wispy clippings of hair still sticking to her. Her lips were not as thick as they looked, but it was the plastered on crimson-red lipstick that gave them the appearance of thick beefsteaks.

Tarlochan's flat faced hers, divided by a narrow passage. When he stepped forward to go into his flat, she stepped out of hers in wooden sandals. He heard their clatter and stopped. She looked at him with her big eyes through her dishevelled hair and laughed. This made Tarlochan nervous and he pulled out his key from the pocket and moved towards his door. One of Mozail's wooden sandals slipped from her foot and came skidding across the floor towards him. Before he could recover, he was on the floor and Mozail was over him, pinning him down. Her trussed-up dress revealed two bare, strong legs which had him in a scissors-like grip. He tried to get up and, in so doing, brushed against her entire body as if soaping it. Breathless now, he apologized profusely. Mozail straightened her dress and smiled. 'These wooden sandals *ek-dum kandam*, just no good.' Then she carefully re-threaded her big toe in her sandal and walked out of the corridor.

Tarlochan was afraid it might not be easy to get to befriend her, but she became quite close to him before long. She was headstrong and she did not take Tarlochan too seriously. She would make him take her out to dinner, the cinema or Juhu beach, where she would spend the entire day with him, but whenever he tried to go beyond hugging and kissing she would tell him to lay off. She would say it in such a way that all his resolve would get entangled in his beard and moustache.

Tarlochan had never been in love before. In Lahore, Burma, Singapore, he would pick up young women and pay for the service. It would never have occurred to him that one day he would find himself plunged 'up to the knees' in love with a wild Jewish girl in Bombay. She treated him with strange indifference, although she would dress up and get ready whenever he asked her to go to the movies with him. Often they would hardly have taken their seats when she would start looking around and, if she found someone she knew, she would wave to him and go sit next to him without asking Tarlochan if he minded.

The same thing would happen in restaurants. He would order an elaborate meal and she would abruptly rise in the middle of it to join an old friend who had caught her eye. Tarlochan would get terribly jealous. And when he protested, she would stop meeting him for days on end and, when he insisted, she would pretend that she had a headache or her stomach was upset. Or she would say, 'You are a Sikh. You are incapable of understanding any subtleties.'

'Such as your lovers?' he would taunt her.

She would put her hands on her hips, spread out her legs and say, 'Yes, my lovers, but why does it burn you up?'

'We cannot carry on like this,' Tarlochan would say.

And Mozail would laugh. 'You're not only a real Sikh, you're also an idiot. In any case, who asked you to carry on with me? I have a suggestion. Go back to your Punjab and marry a Sikhni.' In the end Tarlochan would always give in because Mozail had become his weakness and he wanted to be around her all the time. Often she would humiliate him in front of some young 'Kristan' lout she had picked up that day from somewhere. He would get angry, but not for long.

This cat-and-mouse thing with Mozail continued for two years, but he was steadfast. One day when she was in one of her high and happy moods, he took her in his arms and asked,' Mozail, don't you love me?'

Mozail freed herself, sat down in a chair, gazed intently at her dress, then raised her big Jewish eyes, batted her thick eyelashes and said, 'I cannot love a Sikh.'

'You always make fun of me. You make fun of my love,' he said in an angry voice.

She got up, swung her brown head of hair from side to side and said coquettishly, 'If you shave off your beard and let down your long hair which you keep under your turban, I promise you many men will wink at you suggestively, because you're really quite handsome.'

Tarlochan felt as if his hair was on fire. He dragged Mozail towards him, squeezed her in his arms and put his bearded lips on hers.

She pushed him away. 'Phew!' she said, 'Don't bother! I already brushed my teeth this morning.'

'Mozail!' Tarlochan screamed.

She paid no attention, but took out her lipstick from the bag she always carried and began to touch up her lips which looked havoc-stricken after contact with Tarlochan's beard and moustache.

'Let me tell you something,' she said without looking up. 'You have no idea how to use your bristles properly. They would be perfect for brushing dust off my navy-blue skirt.'

She came and sat next to him and began to unpin his beard. It was true he was very good-looking, but being a practising Sikh he had never shaved a single hair off his body and, consequently, he had come to assume a look which was not natural. He respected his religion and its customs and he did not wish to change any of its ritual formalities.

'What are you doing?' he asked Mozail. By now his beard, freed of its shackles, was hanging over his chest in waves.

'You have such soft hair, so I don't think I would use it to brush my navy-blue skirt. Perhaps a nice, soft woven handbag,' she said, smiling flirtatiously.

'I have never made fun of your religion. Why do you always mock mine? It's not fair. But I have suffered these insults silently because I love you. Did you know I love you?'

'I know,' she said, letting go of his beard.

'I want to marry you,' he declared, while trying to repin his beard.

'I know,' she said with a slight shake of her head. 'In fact, I have nearly decided to marry you.'

'You don't say!' Tarlochan nearly jumped. 'I do,' she said.

He forgot his half-folded beard and embraced her passionately. 'When when?'

She pushed him aside. 'When you get rid of your hair.'

'It will be gone tomorrow,' he said without thinking.

She began to do a tap dance around the room. 'You're talking rubbish, Tarloch. I don't think you have the courage.'

'You will see,' he said defiantly.

'So I will,' she said, kissing him on the lips, followed by her usual 'Phew!'

He could hardly sleep that night. It was not a small decision. However, the next day he went out to a barber in the Fort area and had him cut his hair and shave off his beard. While this operation was in progress, he kept his eyes closed. When it was finished, he looked at his new face in the mirror. It looked good. Any girl in Bombay would have found it difficult not to take a long, second look at him.

He did not leave his flat on his first hairless day, but sent word to Mozail that he was not well and would she mind dropping in for a minute. She stopped dead in her tracks when she saw him. 'My darling Tarloch,' she cried and fell into his arms. She ran her hands over his smooth cheeks and combed his short hair with her fingers. She laughed so much that her nose began to run. She had no handkerchief and calmly she lifted her skirt and wiped it. Tarlochan blushed. 'You should wear something underneath.'

'Gives me a funny feeling. That's how it is,' she replied. 'Let's get married tomorrow,' he said.

'Of course,' she replied, rubbing his chin.

They decided to get married in Poona, where Tarlochan had many friends.

Mozail worked as a salesgirl in one of the big department stores in the Fort area. She told Tarlochan to wait for her at a taxi stand in front of the store the next day, but she never turned up. He later learnt that she had gone off with an old lover of hers who had recently bought a new car. They had moved to Deolali and were not expected to return to Bombay 'for some time.'

Tarlochan was shattered, but in a few weeks he had got over it.

And it was at this point that he had met Kirpal Kaur and fallen in love with her.

He now realized what a vulgar girl Mozail was and how totally heartless. He thanked his stars that he hadn't married her.

But there were days when he missed her. He remembered that once he had decided to buy her some gold earrings and had taken her to a jeweller's, but all she wanted was some cheap baubles. That was the way she was.

She used to lie in bed with him for hours and let him kiss and fondle her as much as he wanted, but she would never let him make love. 'You're a Sikh,' she would laugh, 'and I hate Sikhs.'

One argument they always had was over her habit of not wearing any underclothes. Once she said to him, 'You're a Sikh and I know that you wear some ridiculous shorts under your trousers because that is the Sikh religious requirement, but I think it's rubbish that religion should be kept tucked under one's trousers.'

Tarlochan looked at the gradually brightening sky.

'The hell with her,' he said loudly and decided not to think about her at all. He was worried about Kirpal Kaur and the danger which loomed over her.

A number of communal incidents had already taken place in the locality. The place was full of orthodox Muslims and, curfew or no curfew, they could easily enter her house and massacre everyone.

Since Mozail had left him, he had decided to grow his hair. His beard had flourished again, but he had come to a compromise. He would not let it grow too long. He knew a barber who could trim it so skilfully that it would not appear trimmed.

The curfew was still in force, but you could walk about in the street, as long as you did not stray too far. He decided to do so. There was a public tap in front of the building. He sat down under it and began to wash his hair and freshen up his face.

Suddenly he heard the sound of wooden sandals on the cobblestones. There were other Jewish women in that building, all of whom for some reason wore the same kind of sandals. He thought it was one of them.

But it was Mozail. She was wearing her usual loose gown under which he could see her breasts dancing. It disturbed him. He coughed to attract her attention, because he had a feeling she might just pass him by. She came towards him, examined his beard and said, 'What do we have here, a twice-born Sikh?'

She touched his beard. 'Still good enough to brush my navy-blue skirt with, except that I left it in that other place in Deolali.'

Tarlochan said nothing. She pinched his arm. 'Why don't you say something, Sardar sahib?'

He looked at her. She had lost weight. 'Have you been ill?' he asked.

'No.'

'But you look run down.'

'I am dieting. So you are once again a Sikh?' She sat down next to him, squatting on the ground.

'Yes,' he replied.

'Congratulations. Are you in love with some other girl?'

'Yes.'

'Congratulations. Does she live here, I mean, in our building?'

'No.'

'Isn't that awful?'

She pulled at his beard. 'Growing this on her bidding?'

'No.'

'Well, I promise you that if you get this beard of yours shaved off, I'll marry you. I swear.'

'Mozail,' he said, 'I have decided to marry this simple girl from my village. She is a good, observing Sikh, which is why I am growing my hair again.'

Mozail got up, swung herself in a semi-circle on her heel and said, 'If she's a good Sikh, why should she marry you? Doesn't she know that you once broke all the rules and shaved your hair off?'

'No, she doesn't. I started growing a beard the very day you left me as a gesture of revenge. I met her some time later, but the way I tie my turban, you can hardly tell that I don't have a full head of hair.' She lifted her dress to scratch her thigh. 'Damn these mosquitoes,' she said. Then she added, 'When are you getting married?'

'I don't know.' The anxiety in his voice showed.

'What are you thinking, Tarlochan?' she asked. He told her. 'You are a first-class idiot. What's the problem? Just go and get her here where she would be safe.'

'Mozail, you can't understand these things. It's not that simple. You don't really give a damn and that is why we broke up. I'm sorry,' he said.

'Sorry? Come off it, you silly idiot. What you should be thinking of now is how we can get . . . whatever her name is . . . to your flat. And here you go moaning about our affair. It could never have worked. Your problem is that you are both stupid and cautious. I like my men to be reckless. OK, forget about that, let's go and get your whatever Kaur from wherever she is.'

Tarlochan looked at her nervously. 'But there's a curfew in the area,' he said.

'There's no curfew for Mozail. Let's go,' she said, almost dragging him.

She looked at him and paused. 'What's the matter?' he asked.

'Your beard, but it's not that long. However, take that turban off, then nobody will take you for a Sikh.'

'I won't go bareheaded,' he said.

'Why not?'

'You don't understand? It is not proper for me to go to their house without my turban.'

'And why not?'

'Why don't you understand? She has never seen me except in a turban. She thinks I am a proper Sikh. I daren't let her think otherwise.'

Mozail rattled her wooden sandals on the floor. 'You are not only a first-class idiot, you are also an ass. It is a question of saving her life, whatever that Kaur of yours is called.'

Tarlochan was not going to give up. 'Mozail, you've no idea how religious she is. Once she sees me bareheaded, she'll start hating me.'

'Your love be damned. Tell me, are all Sikhs as stupid as you? On the one hand, you want to save her life and at the same time you insist on wearing your turban, and perhaps even those funny knickers you are never supposed to be without.'

'I do wear my knickers – as you call them – all the time,' he said.

'Good for you,' she said. 'But think, you're going to go to that awful area full of those bloodthirsty Muslims and their big maulanas. If you go in a turban, I promise you they will take one look at you and run a big, sharp knife across your throat.'

'I don't care, but I must wear my turban. I can risk my life, but not my love.'

'You're an ass,' she said exasperatedly. 'Tell me, if you're bombed off, what use will that Kaur be to you? I swear, you're not only a Sikh, you are an idiot of a Sikh.'

'Don't talk rot,' Tarlochan snapped.

She laughed, then she put her arms around his neck and swung her body slightly. 'Darling,' she said, 'then it will be the way you want it. Go put on your turban. I will be waiting for you in the street.'

'You should put on some clothes,' Tarlochan said. 'I'm fine the way I am,' she replied. When he joined her, she was standing in the middle of the street. Her legs apart like a man, and smoking. When he came close, she blew the smoke in his face. 'You're the most terrible human being I've ever met in my life,' Tarlochan said. 'You know we Sikhs are not allowed to smoke.'

'Let's go,' she said.

The bazaar was deserted. The curfew seemed to have affected even the usually brisk Bombay breeze. It was hardly noticeable. Some lights were on but their glow was sickly. Normally at this hour the trains would start running and shops begin to open. There was absolutely no sign of life anywhere.

Mozail walked in front of him, her clogs clicking on the pavement, shattering the silence. He almost asked her to take the stupid things off and go barefoot, but he didn't. She wouldn't have agreed.

Tarlochan felt scared, but Mozail was walking ahead of him nonchalantly, puffing merrily at her cigarette. They came to a square and were challenged by a policeman. 'Where are you going?' Tarlochan fell back, but Mozail moved towards the policeman, gave her head a playful shake and said, 'It's you! Don't you know me? I'm Mozail. I'm going to my sister's in the next street because she's sick. That man there is a doctor.'

While the policeman was still trying to make up his mind, she pulled out a packet of cigarettes from her bag and offered him one. 'Have a smoke,' she said.

The policeman took the cigarette. Mozail helped him light it with hers. He inhaled deeply. Mozail winked at him with her left eye and at Tarlochan with her right and they moved on.

Tarlochan was still very scared. He looked left and right as he walked behind her, expecting to be stabbed any moment. Suddenly she stopped. 'Tarloch dear, it is not good to be afraid. If you're afraid, then something awful always happens. That's my experience.'

He didn't reply.

They came to the street which led to the mohalla where Kirpal Kaur lived. A shop was being looted. 'Nothing to worry about,' she told him. One of the rioters who was carrying something on his head ran into Tarlochan and the object fell to the ground. The man stared at Tarlochan and he knew he was a Sikh. He slipped his hand under his shirt to pull out his knife.

Mozail came tripping over as if she were drunk and pushed him away. 'Are you mad, trying to kill your own brother? This is the man I'm going to marry.' Then she said to Tarlochan, 'Karim, pick this thing up and help put it back on his head.'

The man gave Mozail a lecherous look and touched her breasts with his elbow. 'Have a good time, sali,' he said.

They kept walking and were soon in Kirpal Kaur's mohalla. 'Which street?' she asked.

'The third on the left. That building in the corner,' he whispered.

When they came to the building, they saw a man run out of it into another across the street. After a few minutes, three men emerged from that building, and rushed into the one where Kirpal Kaur lived. Mozail stopped. 'Tarloch dear, take off your turban,' she said.

'That I'll never do,' he replied.

'Just as you please, but I hope you do notice what's going on.'

Something terrible was going on. The three men had reemerged, carrying gunny bags with blood dripping from them. Mozail had an idea. 'Look, I'm going to run across the street and go into that building. You should pretend that you're trying to catch me. But don't think. Just do it.'

Without waiting for his response, she rushed across the street and ran into Kirpal Kaur's building, with Tarlochan in hot pursuit. He was panting when he found her in the front courtyard.

'Which floor?' she asked. 'Second.'

'Let's go.' And she began to climb the stairs, her wooden sandals clattering on each step. There were large bloodstains everywhere.

They came to the second floor, walked down a narrow corridor and Tarlochan stopped in front of a door. He knocked. Then he called in a low voice, 'Mehnga Singhji, Mehnga Singhji.'

A girl's voice answered, 'Who is it?'

'Tarlochan.'

The door opened slightly. Tarlochan asked Mozail to follow him in. Mozail saw a very young and very pretty girl standing behind the door trembling. She also seemed to have a cold. Mozail said to her, 'Don't be afraid. Tarlochan has come to take you away.'

Tarlochan said, 'Ask Sardar sahib to get ready, but quickly.'

There was a shriek from the flat upstairs. 'They must have got him,' Kirpal Kaur said, her voice hoarse with terror.

'Who?' Tarlochan asked.

Kirpal Kaur was about to say something, when Mozail pushed her in a corner and said, 'Just as well they got him. Now take off your clothes.'

Kirpal Kaur was taken aback, but Mozail gave her no time to think. In one moment, she divested her of her loose shirt. The young girl frantically put her arms in front of her breasts. She was terrified. Tarlochan turned his face. Then Mozail took off the kaftan-like gown she always wore and asked Kirpal Kaur to put it on. She was now stark naked herself.

'Take her away,' she told Tarlochan. She untied the girl's hair so that it hung over her shoulders. 'Go.'

Tarlochan pushed the girl towards the door, then turned back.

Mozail stood there, shivering slightly because of the cold. 'Why don't you go?' she asked.

'What about her parents?' he said.

'They can go to hell. You take her.'

'And you?'

'Don't worry about me.'

They heard men running down the stairs. Soon they were banging at the door with their fists. Kirpal Kaur's parents were moaning in the other room. 'There's only one thing to do now. I'm going to open the door,' Mozail said.

She addressed Tarlochan, 'When I open the door, I'll rush out and run upstairs. You follow me. These men will be so flabbergasted that they will forget everything and come after us.'

'And then?' Tarlochan asked.

'Then, this one here, whatever her name is, can slip out. The way she's dressed, she'll be safe. They'll take her for a Jew.'

Mozail threw the door open and rushed out. The men had no time to react. Involuntarily, they made way for her. Tarlochan ran after her. She was storming up the stairs in her wooden sandals with Tarlochan behind her.

She slipped and came crashing down, head first. Tarlochan stopped and turned. Blood was pouring out of her mouth and nose and ears. The men who were trying to break into the flat had also gathered round her in a circle, forgetting temporarily what they were there for. They were staring at her naked, bruised body.

Tarlochan bent over her. 'Mozail, Mozail.'

She opened her eyes and smiled. Tarlochan undid his turban and covered her with it. She smiled again and winked at him. Spewing tiny red bubbles from her mouth, she said, 'Go . . . see whether my underwear is still there . . . I mean . . .'

'This is my lover. He's a bloody Muslim, but he's so crazy that I always call him a Sikh,' she said to the men.

More blood poured out of her mouth. 'Damn it!' she said.

Then she looked at Tarlochan and pushed aside the turban with which he had tried to cover her nakedness.

'Take away this rag of your religion. I don't need it.'

Her arm fell limply on her bare breasts and she said no more.

Translated by Khalid Hasan

The Return

THE SPECIAL TRAIN left Amritsar at two in the afternoon, arriving at Mughalpura, Lahore, eight hours later. Many had been killed on the way, a lot more injured and countless lost.

It was at ten o'clock the next morning when Sirajuddin regained consciousness. He was lying on bare ground, surrounded by screaming men, women and children. It did not make sense.

He lay very still, gazing at the dusty sky. He appeared not to notice the confusion or the noise. To a stranger, he might have looked like an old man in deep thought, though this was not the case. He was in shock, suspended, as it were, over a bottomless pit.

Then his eyes moved and, suddenly, caught the sun. The shock brought him back to the world of living men and women. A succession of images raced through his mind. Attack . . . fire . . . escape . . . railway station . . . night . . . Sakina. He rose abruptly and began searching through the milling crowd in the refugee camp.

He spent hours looking, all the time shouting his daughter's name . . . Sakina, Sakina . . . but she was nowhere to be found. Total confusion prevailed, with people looking for lost sons, daughters, mothers, wives. In the end Sirajuddin gave up. He sat down, away from the crowd, and tried to think clearly. Where did he part from Sakina and her mother? Then it came to him in a flash – the dead body of his wife, her stomach ripped open. It was an image that wouldn't go away. Sakina's mother was dead. That much was certain. She had died in front of his eyes. He could hear her voice: 'Leave me where I am. Take the girl away.'

The two of them had begun to run. Sakina's dupatta had slipped to the ground and he had stopped to pick it up and she had said, 'Father, leave it.'

He could feel a bulge in his pocket. It was a length of cloth. Yes, he recognized it. It was Sakina's dupatta, but where was she?

Other details were missing. Had he brought her as far as the railway station? Had she got into the carriage with him? When the rioters had stopped the train, had they taken her with them? All questions. There were no answers. He wished he could weep, but tears wouldn't come. He knew then that he needed help.

A few days later, he had a break. There were eight of them, young men armed with guns. They also had a truck. They said they brought back women and children left behind on the other side.

He gave them a description of his daughter. 'She is fair, very pretty. No, she doesn't look like me, but her mother. About seventeen. Big eyes, black hair, a mole on the left cheek. Find my daughter. May God bless you.'

The young men had said to Sirajuddin, 'If your daughter is alive we will find her.'

And they had tried. At the risk of their lives, they had driven to Amritsar, recovered many women and children and brought them back to the camp, but they had not found Sakina.

On their next trip out, they had found a girl on the roadside. They seemed to have scared her and she had started running. They had stopped the truck, jumped out and run after her. Finally, they had caught up with her in a field. She was very pretty and she had a mole on her left cheek. One of the men had said to her, 'Don't be frightened. Is your name Sakina?' Her face had gone pale, but when they told her who they were she had confessed that she was Sakina, daughter of Sirajuddin.

The young men were very kind to her. They had fed her, given her milk to drink and put her in their truck. One of them had given her his jacket so that she could cover herself. It was obvious that she was ill at ease without her dupatta, trying nervously to cover her breasts with her arms.

Many days had gone by and Sirajuddin had still not had any news of his daughter. All his time was spent running from camp to camp, looking for her. At night, he would pray for the success of the young men who were looking for his daughter. Their words would ring in his ear: 'If your daughter is alive, we will find her.' Then one day he saw them in the camp. They were about to drive away.

'Son,' he shouted after one of them, 'have you found Sakina, my daughter?'

'We will, we will,' they replied all together.

The old man again prayed for them. It made him feel better. That evening there was sudden activity in the camp. He saw four men carrying the body of a young girl found unconscious near the railway tracks. They were taking her to the camp hospital. He began to follow them.

He stood outside the hospital for some time, then went in. In one of the rooms, he found a stretcher with someone lying on it.

A light was switched on. It was a young woman with a mole on her left cheek. 'Sakina,' Sirajuddin screamed. The doctor, who had switched on the light, stared at Sirajuddin.

'I am her father,' he stammered.

The doctor looked at the prostrate body and felt for the pulse. Then he said to the old man, pointing at the window, 'Open it.' Sakina's body stirred ever so faintly on the stretcher. Her hands groped for the cord which kept her shalwar tied round her waist.

With painful slowness, she unfastened it, pulled the garment down and opened her thighs.

'She is alive. My daughter is alive,' Sirajuddin shouted with joy.

The doctor broke into a cold sweat.

Translated by Khalid Hasan

A Woman's Life

SHE'D HAD A long day and she fell asleep as soon as she hit the bed. The city sanitary inspector, whom she always called Seth, had just gone home, very drunk. His love-making had been aggressive as usual and he had left her feeling bone-weary. He would have stayed longer but for his wife who, he always said, loved him very much.

The silver coins, which she had earned, were safely tucked inside her bra. Her breasts still bore the traces of the inspector's wet kisses. Occasionally the coins would clink as she took a particularly deep breath.

Her chest had felt on fire, partly because of the pint of brandy which she had drunk followed by the homemade brew they had downed with tap water after the brandy had run out.

She was sprawled face down on her wide, wooden bed. Her bare arms, stretched out on either side, looked like the frame of a kite which has come unstuck from the paper.

It was a small room and her things were everywhere. Three or four ragged pairs of sandals lay under the bed; a mangy dog lay sleeping with his head resting on them. There were bald patches on its skin and, from a distance, one could have mistaken it for a worn doormat.

On a small shelf lay her make-up things: face powder, a single lipstick, rouge, a comb, hairpins.

Swinging from a hook in the ceiling was a cage with a green parrot. The bird was asleep, its beak tucked under one of its wings. The cage was littered with pieces of raw guava and orange peels, with some black moths and mosquitoes hovering over them. A wicker chair stood next to the bed, its back grimy with use. To its left was a small table with an antiquated His Master's Voice gramophone resting on it. On the wall were four pictures. It was her habit, after being paid, to rub the money against the picture she had of the Hindu elephant god Ganesha, for good luck, before putting it away. However, whenever Madhu was expected from Poona, she hid most of the money under her bed. This had first been suggested by Ram Lal, who knew that every visit by Madhu was like a raid on Saugandhi's savings.

One day he said to her, 'Where'd you pick up this sala? What kind of a lover boy is he? He never parts with a penny and he is back every other week having a good time at your expense. What's more, he cheats you out of your hard-earned money. Saugandhi, what is it about this sala that you find so irresistible? I've been in this business for seven years and I know you chhokris well but this one beats me, I have to admit.'

Ram Lal, who scouted around for men looking for a good time, had a range of girls worth anything from ten to a hundred rupees for the night. He said to her one day, 'Saugandhi, don't ruin your business; I warn you this scoundrel will take the shirt off your back if you don't watch out. Tell you what, keep your money hidden under your bed and the next time he is here tell him something like, "I swear on your head, Madhu, for days I haven't set eyes on so much as a penny. I haven't even eaten today. Can you get me something to eat and a cup of tea from that Iranian cafe across the street?"'

Ram Lal went on, 'Sweetheart, these are bad times. By bringing in prohibition, this sali Congress government has taken the life out of the bazaar. But how would you know? You get your drop somehow or other. As God is my witness, whenever I see an empty liquor bottle in your room, I almost want to change places with you.'

Saugandhi liked to offer advice too. She had once said to her friend Jamuna, 'Let me give you some advice. For ten rupees, you let men pluck you like a chicken. Let someone so much as touch me in the wrong place and he will come to grief. You know what happened last night? Ram Lal brought a Punjabi man at about two in the morning. When we went to bed, I put out the light. I swear to you, Jamuna, he was scared! He couldn't do anything! "Come on," I said to him. "Don't you want it? It is nearly morning." But all he wanted was for the light to be switched on. I couldn't hold back my laughter. "No light," I teased him. Then I pinched him and he jumped out of bed and the first thing he did was to put the light back on. "Are you crazy?" I screamed, then I put out the light. He was scared. I tell you, it was such fun. No light, then light again. When he heard the first tram car rattle past in the morning, he hurriedly put on his clothes and ran. The sala must have won that money in gambling. Jamuna, you are still very naive. I know how to deal with men. I have my ways.'

This was true. She had her ways, which she often told her friends about. 'If the customer is nice, the quiet type, flirt with him, talk, tease him, touch him playfully. If he has a beard, comb it with your fingers and pull out a hair or two just for fun. If he is fat, then tease him about it. But never give them enough time to do what they really want; keep them occupied and they'll leave happily and you'll be spared possible misadventure. The quiet types are always dangerous. Watch them because they are often very rough.'

Actually, Saugandhi was not as clever as she pretended. She didn't have a great number of clients either. She liked men, which was why all her clever methods would desert her when it was time to use them. It only took a few sweet words, softly cooed into her ear, to make her melt. Although she was convinced that physical relations were basically pointless, her body felt otherwise. It seemed to want to be overpowered and left exhausted.

When she was a little girl, she used to hide herself in the big wooden chest which sat in a corner of her parents' home while the other children looked for her. The fear of being caught, mixed with a sense of excitement, would make her heart beat very fast. Sometimes she wanted to spend her entire life in a box, hidden from view yet dying to be found. The last five years had been like a game of hide-and-seek. She was either seeking or being sought. When a man said to her, 'I love you, Saugandhi,' she would go weak in the knees, although she knew he was lying. Love, what a beautiful word, she would think. Oh, if only one could rub love like a balm into one's body! However, she did like four of her regulars enough to have their framed pictures hanging on her wall.

She had lived intensely in the last five years. True, she hadn't had the happiness she would have wished but she had managed. Money had never interested her much. She charged ten rupees for what she did, out of which a quarter went to Ram Lal. What she was left with was enough for her needs. In fact, when Madhu came from Poona, she spent ten to fifteen rupees on him quite happily. This was perhaps the price she paid for that certain feeling that Ram Lal had once said existed between the two of them.

He was right. There was something about Madhu that Saugandhi liked. When they met, the first thing Madhu had said to her was, 'Aren't you ashamed of selling yourself, putting a price on your body? Ten rupees you take with a quarter going to that man, Ram Lal, which leaves you with seven rupees and eight annas, doesn't it? And for that you promise to give something which you can't love. And what about me? I have come looking for something which really cannot be had. I need a woman but do you need a man? I could do with any woman but could you do with any man? There is nothing between us except this sum of ten rupees, a fourth of which will go to Ram Lal and the rest to you. But I know we like each other. Shouldn't we do something about it? Perhaps we could fulfil our separate needs that way. Now listen. I am a sergeant in the police at Poona. I'll come once a month for three or four days. You don't have to be doing anything from now on. I'll look after all your expenses. What is the rent for this kholi of yours?'

Madhu had made her feel like the police sergeant's chosen woman. He had also rearranged everything in the room. There were posters showing half-clad women that she had stuck on the wall. He had removed them without her permission and then torn them up. 'Saugandhi, my dear, I won't have these. And look at this slimy earthen pitcher of yours. It needs to be scrubbed and cleaned. And what are those smelly rags lying around? Throw them out. And look at your hair. It is matted and in need of a wash. And ... and ...'

After three hours of conversation, mostly Madhu's, Saugandhi had felt as if she had known him for many years. Never before had anyone spoken to her like that, nor made her feel that her kholi was home. The men who came to her did not even notice that her bed sheets were soiled. Nobody had ever said to her, 'I think you are catching a cold; let me run along and get you something for it.' But Madhu was different; he told her things nobody ever had and she knew she needed him.

He would come once a month from Poona and before going back he would say, 'Saugandhi, if you resume that old business of yours, you'll never see me again. Yes, about this month's household expenses, the money will be on its way as soon as I get to Poona . . . so what did you say the monthly rent for this place was?'

Madhu had never sent her any money from Poona or elsewhere and Saugandhi had continued her business as usual. They both knew it but she never said, 'What rubbish you are talking! You have never given me so much as a bum penny.' And Madhu had never asked her how she was managing to survive. They were living a pretension and they were quite happy with it. Saugandhi had argued to herself that, if one was unable to buy real gold, one might as well settle for what looked like gold.

But now she was sound asleep. She was too tired to even bother to switch off the harsh, unshaded light over her bed.

There was a knock at the door. She only heard it as a faint, faraway sound. This was followed by a succession of knocks, which woke her up. She first wiped her mouth, still sodden with the aftertaste of bad liquor, and her eyes, then looked under the bed where the dog was still asleep, its head resting on her old sandals. The parrot was also in its cage, its beak tucked under its wing. There was another impatient knock. She rose from her bed and realized that she had a splitting headache. She poured herself some water from the earthen pitcher and rinsed her mouth, then filled another glass and drank it down in one gulp. Carefully, she opened the door and whispered, 'Ram Lal?'

Ram Lal, who had almost given up, replied caustically, 'I thought you had been bitten by a snake. I have been out here for an hour. Didn't you hear me?' Then in his discreet voice he asked, 'Is anybody with you?' She told him no and let him in. 'If it is going to take me an hour getting you chhokris out of bed, I might as well change my line of work. What are you looking at me like that for? Put on that nice flower-print sari of yours and dust your face with powder, and a bit of lipstick too. Out there in a car I have a rich seth waiting for you.'

Instead, Saugandhi fell into her armchair, picked up a jar of rubbing balm from the table, eased off its lid and said, 'Ram Lal, I don't feel well.'

'Why didn't you say so right away?'

Saugandhi, who was now rubbing her forehead with the balm, replied, 'I just don't feel good; maybe I had too much to drink.'

Ram Lal's expression changed. 'Is there some left? I'd love a drop.'

Saugandhi returned the balm to the table. 'If I had saved some, I would have done something about this awful headache. Look, Ram Lal, bring that man in.'

'I can't,' Ram Lal answered. 'He is an important man. He was even reluctant to park on the street. Look, sweetheart, put on those nice clothes and off we go. You won't be sorry.'

It was the usual deal: seven rupees eight annas. Had Saugandhi not been in need of money, she would have sent Ram Lal packing. In the next kholi lived a Madrasi woman whose husband had recently died in an accident. She had a grown-up daughter and they wanted to go back to

Madras but didn't have the train fare. Saugandhi had said to her, 'Don't you worry, sister, my man is expected from Poona any day. He'll give me some money and you'll be on your way.' While Madhu was indeed expected, the money, of course, was to be earned by Saugandhi herself. So she rose reluctantly from her chair and began to change. She put on the flower-print sari and a bit of makeup, and then drank another glass of water from the pitcher.

The street was very still. The lights had been dimmed because of the war. In the distance, she could see the outline of a car. They walked up to it and stopped.

Ram Lal stepped forward and said, 'Here she is, a sweet-tempered girl, very new to the business. 'Then to her, 'Saugandhi, the Seth sahib is waiting.'

She moved closer, feeling nervous. A flashlight suddenly lit her face, blinding her. 'Ugh!' grunted the man in the car, then revved up his engine and drove off without another word.

Saugandhi had had no time to react because of the torch in her face. She hadn't been able to see the man; she had only heard him say, 'Ugh!' What did he mean by that?

Ram Lal was muttering to himself. 'You didn't like her; that's two hours of mine gone waste.' He left without speaking to her. Saugandhi was trembling, trying hard to deal with the situation. 'What did he mean by "Ugh"? That he did not like me? The son of a . . .'

The car was gone, the red glow from its fading tail-lights barely visible now. She wanted to scream, 'Come back . . . Stop . . . Come back!'

She was alone in the deserted bazaar wearing her grey flowerprint sari which fluttered in the night air.

She began to walk back slowly but then she thought of Ram Lal and the man in the car and she stopped. Ram Lal had said the Seth didn't like her; he hadn't said it was because of her looks. Well, so what? There were people she did not like. There were men who came to her that she did not care for. Only the other night she had one who was so ugly that when he was lying next to her she had felt nauseated. But she hadn't shown it.

But the man in the car? He had practically spat in her face. 'Ram Lal,' he had implied, 'from what hole have you pulled out this scented reptile? And you want ten rupees for her? For her? Ugh!'

She was angry with herself and with Ram Lal who had woken her up at two in the morning, though he had meant well. It wasn't his fault and it wasn't hers but she wanted the whole scene replayed just one more time. Slowly, very slowly, she would move towards the car, then the torchlight would be flashed in her face, followed by a grunt, and she, Saugandhi, would scratch that Seth's face with her long nails, pull him out of that car by his hair and hit him till she broke down exhausted.

Saugandhi, she said to herself, you are not ugly. While it was true that the bloom of her early youth was gone, nobody had ever said she was ugly. In fact, she was one of those women men always steal a second look at. She knew she had everything a man expects in a woman. She was young and she had a good body. She was nice to people. She couldn't remember a single man in the last five years who hadn't enjoyed himself with her. She was soft-hearted. Last year at Christmas time when she was living in the Golpitha area, this young fellow from Hyderabad who had spent the night with her had found his wallet missing in the morning. Obviously, the servant boy, who was a rogue, had nicked it and disappeared. He was extremely upset because he had come all the way to Bombay to spend his holidays and he hadn't the fare to go back. She had simply returned him the money he had given her the night before.

She wanted to go home, take a long, cool drink, lie on her bed and go to sleep. She began to walk back.

However, once she was outside her kholi, the pain and humiliation came back. She just couldn't forget what had happened. She had been called out to the street and a man had slapped her across the face. She had been looked at as if she were a sheep in a farmers' market. A torch had been shone on her face to see if she had any flesh on her or whether she was just skin and bones. And then she had been rejected.

If that man came back, she would stand in front of him, tear up her clothes and shout, 'This is what you came to buy! Well, here it is. You can have it free, but you'll never be able to reach the woman who is inside this body!'

The key was where she always kept it, inside her bra, but the lock on the door had been released. She pushed gently and it creaked on its hinges. Then it was unlatched from the inside and she went in.

She heard Madhu laugh through his thick moustache as he carefully closed the door. 'At last you have done what I've always suggested,' he said. 'Taken an early morning walk. There is nothing like that for good health. If you do it regularly, all your lassitude will disappear, also that back pain you are always going on about. Did you walk as far as the Victoria Gardens?'

Saugandhi said nothing, nor did Madhu appear to expect an answer. His remarks were generally supposed to be heard, not answered.

Madhu sat in the cane chair, which bore much oily evidence of earlier contact with his greasy hair. He swung one leg on top of the other and began to play with his moustache.

Saugandhi sat on the bed. 'I was waiting for you today,' she said.

'Waiting?' he asked, a bit puzzled. 'How did you know I was coming today?'

Saugandhi smiled. 'Because last night I dreamt about you and that woke me up but you weren't there so I went for a walk.'

'And there I was when you came back,' Madhu said happily. 'Haven't the wise said that lovers' hearts beat together? When did you dream about me?'

'A few hours ago,' Saugandhi answered.

'Ah!' said Madhu. 'And I dreamt about you not too many hours earlier. You were wearing your flower-print sari. Yes, the same one you have on now. And there was something in your hands. Yes, a little bag full of money. And you said to me, "Madhu, why do you worry so much about money? Take it. What is mine is yours." And I swear on your head, Saugandhi, the next thing I knew I was out of Poona and on my way to Bombay. There is bad news though. I am in trouble. There was this police investigation I botched up and, unless I can get twenty or thirty rupees together and bribe my inspector, I can say goodbye to my job. But never mind that. You look tired. Lie down, darling, and I'll press your feet. If you are not used to taking walks, you get tired. Now lie down and turn your feet towards me.'

Saugandhi lay down, cradling her head in her arms. Then in a voice which wasn't really hers, she asked, 'Madhu, who's this person who has put you in trouble? If you are afraid of losing your job and going to jail, just let me know. In such situations, the higher the bribe, the better off you are. Since you gave me the bad news about your job, my heart has been jumping up and down. By the way, when are you going back?'

Madhu could smell liquor in Saugandhi's breath and thought this was a good time to make his pitch. 'I must take the afternoon train. By this evening, I should slip around a hundred rupees in my inspector's pocket; on second thoughts, perhaps fifty will do.'

'Fifty,' Saugandhi said. Then she rose from the bed and stood facing the four pictures on the wall. The third was Madhu's. He was sitting in a chair, his hands on his thighs and a black curtain with painted flowers forming the background. There was a rose in his lapel and two thick books lay on a small table next to his chair. He sat there, looking very conscious of being photographed. He was staring at the camera with a pained expression.

Saugandhi began to laugh. 'Is it the picture you find so amusing?' he asked.

Saugandhi touched the first, the sanitary inspector's. 'Look at that face. Once he told me that a rani had fallen in love with him. With him!' She pulled down the frame from the wall with such violence that some of the plaster came off; then she smashed it to the floor. 'When my sweeperess Rani comes in the morning, she will take away this raja with the rest of the rubbish,' Saugandhi said. Then she began to laugh, a light laugh like the first rain of summer. Madhu managed a smile with some difficulty and followed it with a forced guffaw.

By then Saugandhi had pulled down the second picture and thrown it out of the window. 'What's this sala doing here? No one with a mug like his is allowed on this wall, is he Madhu?' she asked. Madhu laughed but the sound was unnatural.

She pulled down the fourth picture, a man in a turban, and then, as Madhu watched apprehensively, his own, throwing them out together through the window. They heard them fall on the street, the glass breaking. Madhu somehow managed to say, 'Well done! I didn't like that one of mine either.'

Saugandhi moved slowly towards him. 'You didn't like that one, yeah? Well, let me ask you, is there anything about you which you should like? This bulb of a nose of yours! This small, hairy forehead! Your swollen nostrils! Your twisted ears! And that awful breath! Your filthy, unwashed body! This oil that you coat yourself with! So you didn't like your picture, eh?'

Madhu was flinching away from her, his back against the wall. He tried to put some authority into his voice. 'Look, Saugandhi, it seems to me you have gone back to that dirty old profession of yours. I am telling you for the last time . . .'

Saugandhi mimicked him, 'If you return to that dirty old profession of yours, that'll be the end. And if I find out that another man has been in your bed, I'll drag you out by your hair and throw you out on the street. As for your monthly expenses, a money order will be on its way as soon as I return to Poona. And what is the monthly rent of this kholi of yours?'

Madhu listened in total disbelief.

Saugandhi had not finished with him yet. 'Let me tell you what it costs me every month – fifteen rupees. And you know what my own rental is? Ten rupees. Out of that two rupees and eight annas go to Ram Lal, which leaves me with seven rupees and eight annas exactly, in return for which I sleep with men. What was our relationship anyway? Nothing! Ten rupees, perhaps. Every time you came you took away what you wanted – and the money too. It used to be ten rupees; now it is fifty.' She flicked away his cap with one finger and it fell to the floor.

'Saugandhi!' Madhu yelled.

She ignored him. Then she pulled out his handkerchief from his pocket, raised it to her nose, made a face and said with disgust, 'It stinks! Look at yourself, at your filthy cap and these rags that you call clothes. They all smell! Get out!'

'Saugandhi!' Madhu screamed again.

But she screamed right back. 'You creep! Why do you come here? Am I your mother, who will give you money to spend? Or are you such a ravishing man that I'd fall in love with you? You dog, you wretch, don't you dare raise your voice at me! I am nothing to you! You miserable beggar, who do you think you are? Tell me, are you a thief or a pickpocket? What are you doing in my house at this hour anyway? Should I call the police? There may or may not be a case against you in Poona but there will be a case against you here in Bombay!'

Madhu was scared. 'What has come over you, Saugandhi?'

'Who are you to put such questions to me? Get out of here . . . this instant!' The mangy dog, who had so far slept undisturbed, suddenly woke up and began to bark at Madhu, which made Saugandhi laugh hysterically.

Madhu bent down to pick up his cap from the floor but Saugandhi shouted, 'Leave it there! As soon as you get to Poona, I'll money-order it to you.' She began to laugh again as she fell into the chair. The dog, in the meantime, had chased Madhu out of the room and down the stairs. He came back wagging his short, ugly tail and flapping his ears and sat down at Saugandhi's feet. Everything was very still and for a minute she was terrified. She also felt empty, like a train which having discharged its passengers is shunted into the yard and left there.

For a long time she sat in the chair. Then she rose, picked up her dog from the floor, put him carefully on the bed, laid herself next to him, threw an arm across his wasted body and went to sleep.

Translated by Khalid Hasan

Siraj

THERE WAS a small park facing the Nagpara police post and an Iranian teahouse next to it. Dhondoo was always to be found in this area, leaning against a lamppost, waiting for custom. He would come here around sunset and remain busy with his work until four in the morning.

Nobody knew his real name, but everyone called him Dhondoo – the one who searches and finds – which was most appropriate because his business consisted of procuring women of every type and description for his clients.

He had been in the trade for the last ten years and during this period hundreds of women had passed through his hands, women of every religion, race and temperament.

This had always been his hangout, the lamppost facing the Iranian teahouse which stood in front of the Nagpara police headquarters. The lamppost had become his trademark. Often, when I passed that way and saw the lamppost, I felt as if I was actually looking at Dhondoo, besmeared like him with betel juice and much the worse for wear.

The lamppost was tall, and so was Dhondoo. A number of power lines ran in various directions from the top of this ugly steel column into adjoining buildings, shops and even other lampposts.

The telephone department had tagged on a small terminal to the post and technicians could be seen checking it out from time to time. Sometimes I felt that Dhondoo was also a kind of terminal, attached to the lamppost to verify the sexual signals of his customers. He knew all the seths living in the area who needed their sexual wires, loose or taut, restored to perfect working condition from time to time.

He knew almost all the women in the profession. He had intimate knowledge of their bodies, since they constituted the wares he transacted, and he was familiar with their temperaments. He knew exactly which woman would please which customer. But there was one exception – Siraj. He just had not been able to get a handle on her.

Dhondoo had often said to me, 'Manto sahib, this one is off her rocker. I just cannot make her out. Never seen a chhokri like her. She is so changeable. When you think she is happy and laughing her head off, just as suddenly she bursts into tears. She simply cannot get along with anyone. Fights with every "passenger." I have told her a million times to sort herself out, but it has had absolutely no effect on her. Many times I have had to tell her to go back to wherever she first came from to Bombay. Have you seen her? She has practically nothing to wear and not a penny to her name, and yet she simply will not play ball with the men I bring her. What an obstinate, mixed-up piece of work!'

I had seen Siraj a few times. She was slim and rather pretty. Her eyes were like outsize windows in her oval face. You simply could not get away from them. When I saw her for the first time on Clare Road, I felt like saying to her eyes, 'Would you please step aside for a minute so that I can see this girl?'

She was slight and yet there was so much of her. She reminded me of a glass goblet, which had been filled to the brim with strong, under-diluted spirits, and the restlessness showed. I say strong spirits because there was something sharp and tangy about her personality. And yet I felt that in this heady mixture someone had added a bit of water to soften the fire. Her femininity was strong, despite her somewhat irate manner. Her hair was thick and her nose was aquiline. Her fingers reminded me of the sharpened pencils draughtsmen use. She gave the impression of being slightly annoyed with everything, with Dhondoo and the lamppost he always stood against, with the gifts he brought her and even with her big eyes which ran away with her face.

But these are the impressions of a storyteller. Dhondoo had his own views. One day he said to me, 'Manto sahib, guess what that sali Siraj did today? Boy, am I lucky! Had it not been for God's mercy and the fact that the Nagpara police are always kind to me, I would have found myself in the jug. And that could have been one big, blooming disaster.'

'What happened?'

'The usual. I don't know what's the matter with me. I must be off my head. It is not the first time she has got me in a spot and yet I continue to carry her along. I should just wash my hands of her. She is neither my sister nor my mother, yet I'm running around trying to get her a living. Seriously, Manto sahib, I no longer know what to do.'

We were both sitting in the Iranian teahouse, sipping tea. Dhondoo poured from his cup into the saucer and began slurping up the special mixture he always blended with coffee. 'The fact is that I feel sorry for this sali Siraj.'

'Why?'

'God knows why. I wish I did.' He finished his tea and put the cup back on the saucer, upside down. 'Did you know she is still a virgin?'

'No, I didn't, Dhondoo.'

Dhondoo felt the scepticism in my voice and he didn't like it. 'I am not lying to you, Manto sahib. She is a hundred per cent virgin. You want to bet on that?'

'How's that possible?' I asked.

'Why not? A girl like Siraj. I tell you she could stay in this profession the rest of her life and still be a virgin. The thing is she simply does not let anyone so much as touch her. I know her whole bloody history. I know that she comes from the Punjab. She used to be on Lymington Road in the private house run by that memsahib, but was thrown out because of her endless bickering with the passengers. I am surprised she lasted three months there, but that was because Madam had about twenty girls at the time. But Manto sahib, how long can people feed you? One day Madam pushed her out of the house with nothing except the clothes she was wearing. Then she moved to that other madam on Faras Road. She did not change her ways and one day she actually bit a passenger.

'She lasted no more than a couple of months there. I don't know what is wrong with her. She is full of life and nobody can cool it. From Faras Road she found her way into a hotel in Khetwari and created the usual trouble. One day the manager gave her marching orders. What can I say, Manto sahib, the sali doesn't seem to be interested in anything – clothes, food, ornaments, you name it. Doesn't bathe for months until lice start crawling over her clothes. If someone gives her hash, she smokes a couple of joints happily. Sometimes I see her standing outside a hotel, listening to music.'

'Why don't you send her back? I mean it's obvious she's not interested in the business. I'll pay her fare if you like,' I suggested.

Dhondoo didn't like it. 'Manto sahib, it's not a question of paying the sali's fare. I can do that. Won't kill me.'

'Then why don't you send her back?'

He lit a cigarette, which he had tucked above his ear, drew on it deeply, expelled twin jets of smoke from his nostrils and said, 'I don't want her to go.'

'Do you love her?' I asked.

'What are you talking about, Manto sahib!' He touched both his ears. 'I swear by the Quran that such a vile thought has never entered my head. It is just that I like her a bit.'

'Why?'

'Because she's not like the others who are only interested in money – the whole damn lot of them. This one is different. When I make a deal on her behalf, she gives the impression that she's willing. I put her in a taxi with the passenger and off they go.

'Manto sahib, passengers come for a good time. They spend money. They want to see what they are getting and like to feel it with their hands. And that's when the trouble starts. She doesn't let anyone even touch her. Starts hitting them. If it's a gentleman, he slinks away quietly. If it's the other kind, then there's hell to pay. I have to return the money and go down on my hands and knees. I swear on the Quran. And why do I do it? Only for Siraj's sake. Manto sahib, I swear on your head that because of this sali my business has been reduced by half.'

One day I decided to see Siraj without Dhondoo's good offices. She lived in a no-good locality near the Byculla station, dumping ground for garbage and other refuse. The city corporation had built a large number of tin huts here for the poor. I do not want to write here about those tall buildings which stood not too far from this dump of filth because that has nothing to do with this story. This world after all is but another name for the high and the low. I knew roughly through Dhondoo where her hut was located. I went there – feeling apologetic about the good clothes I was wearing – but then this is not a story about me.

Outside her door a goat was tethered. It bleated when I approached. An old woman hobbled out, bent over her stick. I was about to leave when, through a hole in the coarse length of tattered cloth which hung over the door and served as a curtain, I saw large eyes in an oblong face.

She had recognized me. She must have been doing something, but she came out. 'What are you doing here?' she asked.

'I wanted to meet you.'

'Come in.'

'No, I want you to come with me.'

The old woman said, 'That'll cost you ten rupees.'

I pulled out my wallet and gave her the money. 'Come,' I said to Siraj.

She looked at me with those big window-like eyes of hers. It once again occurred to me that she was pretty, but in a withdrawn, frozen kind of way, like a mummified but perfectly preserved queen.

I took her to a hotel. There she sat in front of me in her not-quite-clean clothes, staring at the world through eyes which were so big that her entire personality had become secondary to them.

I gave Siraj forty rupees.

She was quiet and, to make a pass at her, I had to drink something quickly. After four large whiskies, I put my hands on her like passengers are expected to, but she showed me no resistance. Then I did something quite lewd and was sure she would go up like a keg of gunpowder but, surprisingly, she did not react at all. She just looked at me with her big eyes. 'Get me a joint,' she said.

'Take a drink,' I suggested.

'No, I want a joint.'

I sent for one. It was easy to get. She began to drag on it like experienced hash smokers. Her eyes had somehow lost their overpowering presence. Her face looked like a ravaged city. Every line, every feature suggested devastation. But what was this devastation? Had she been ravaged before even becoming whole? Had her world been destroyed long before the foundations could be raised?

Whether she was a virgin or not, I didn't care. But I wanted to talk to her, and she did not seem interested. I wanted her to fight with me, but she was simply indifferent.

In the end, I took her home.

When Dhondoo came to learn of my secret foray, he was upset. His feelings, both as a friend and as a man of business, had been hurt. He never gave me an opportunity to explain. All he said was, 'Manto sahib, this I did not expect of you.' And he walked away.

I didn't see him the next day. I thought he was ill, but he did not appear the day after either. One week passed. Twice a day I used to go to work past Dhondoo's headquarters and whenever I saw the lamppost I thought of him.

I even went looking for Siraj one day, only to be greeted by the old woman there. When I asked her about Siraj, she smiled the million-year-old smile of the procuress and said, 'That one's gone, but I can always get you another.'

The question was: Where was she? Had she run away with Dhondoo? But that was quite impossible. They were not in love and Dhondoo was not that sort of person. He had a wife and children whom he loved. But the question was: Where had they disappeared to?

I thought that maybe Dhondoo had finally decided that Siraj should go home, a decision he had always been ambivalent about. One month passed.

Then one evening, as I was passing by the Iranian teahouse, I saw him leaning against his lamppost. When he saw me, he smiled. We went into the teahouse. I did not ask him anything. He sent for his special tea, mixed with coffee, and ordered plain tea for me. He turned around in his chair and it seemed as if he was going to make some dramatic disclosure, but all he said was, 'And how are things, Manto sahib?'

'Life goes on, Dhondoo,' I replied.

'You are right, life goes on,' he smiled. 'It's a strange world, isn't it?'

'You can say that again.'

We kept drinking tea. Dhondoo poured his into the saucer, took a sip and said, 'Manto sahib, she told me the whole story. She said to me that that friend of yours, meaning you, was crazy.'

I laughed. 'Why?'

'She told me that you took her to a hotel, gave her a lot of money and didn't do what she thought you would do.'

'That was the way it was, Dhondoo,' I said.

He laughed. 'I know. I'm sorry if I showed annoyance that day. In any case, that whole business is now over.'

'What business?'

'That Siraj business, what else?'

'What happened?'

'You remember the day you took her out? Well, she came to me later and said that she had forty rupees on her and would I take her to Lahore. I said to her, "Sali, what has come over you?" She said, "Come on Dhondoo, for my sake, take me." And Manto sahib, you know I could never say no to her. I liked her. So I said, "OK, if that's what you want."

'We bought train tickets and arrived in Lahore. She knew what hotel we were going to stay in.

'The next day she says to me, "Dhondoo, get me a burqa." I went out and got her one. And then our rounds began. She would leave in the morning and spend the entire day on the streets of Lahore in a tonga, with me keeping company. She wouldn't tell me what she was looking for.

'I said to myself, "Dhondoo, have you gone bananas? Why did you have to come with this crazy girl all the way from Bombay?"

'Then, Manto sahib, one day, she asked me to stop the tonga in the middle of the street. "Do you see that man there? Can you bring him to me? I am going to the hotel. Now."

'I was confused but I stepped down from the tonga and began to follow the man she had pointed out. Well, by the grace of God, I am a good judge of men. I began to talk to him and it did not take me long to find out that he was game for a good time.

'I said to him, "I have a very special brand of goods from Bombay." He wanted me to take him with me right away, but I said, "Not that fast, friend, show me the colour of your money." He brandished a thick wad of bank notes in my face. What I couldn't understand was why, of all the men in Lahore, Siraj had picked this one out. In any case, I said to myself, "Dhondoo, everything goes." We took a tonga to the hotel.

'I went in and told Siraj I had the man waiting outside. She said, "Bring him in but don't go away." When I brought him in and he saw her, he wanted to run away, but Siraj grabbed hold of him.'

'She grabbed hold of him?'

'That's right. She grabbed hold of the sala and said to him, "Where are you going? Why did you make me run away from home? You knew I loved you. And remember you had said to me that you loved me too. But when I left my home and my parents and my brothers and my sisters and came with you from Amritsar to Lahore and stayed in this very hotel, you abandoned me the same night. You left while I was asleep. Why did you bring me here? Why did you make me run away from home? You know, I was prepared for everything and you let me down. But I have come back and found you. I still love you. Nothing has changed."

'And Manto sahib, she threw her arms around him. That sala began to cry. He was asking her to forgive him. He was saying he had done her wrong. He had got cold feet. He was saying he would never leave her again. He kept repeating he would never leave her again. God knows what rot he was talking.

'Then Siraj asked me to leave the room. I lay on a bare cot outside and went to sleep at some point. When she woke me up, it was morning. "Dhondoo," she said, "let's go." "Where?" I asked. She said, "Let's go back to Bombay." I said, "Where is that sala?" "He is sleeping, I have covered his face with my burqa," she replied.'

Dhondoo ordered himself another cup of tea mixed with coffee. I looked up and saw Siraj enter the hotel. Her oval face was glowing, but her two big eyes looked like fallen train signals.

Translated by Khalid Hasan

The Wild Cactus

THE NAME of the town is unimportant. Let us say it was in the sub-
urbs of the city of Peshawar, not far from the frontier, where that
woman lived in a small mud house, half hidden from the dusty, unmet-
alled, forlorn road by a hedge of wild cactus.

The cactus was quite dry but it had grown with such profusion that it
had become like a curtain shielding the house from the gaze of passersby.
It is not clear if it had always been there or whether it was the woman
who had planted it.

The house was more like a hut with three small rooms, all kept very
spick and span. There wasn't much in it by way of furniture, but what
there was was nice. In the backroom was a big bed, and beside it an alcove
where an earthen lamp burned all night. It was all very orderly.

Let me now tell you about the woman who lived there with her young
daughter.

There were various stories. Some people said the young girl was not
really her daughter, but an orphan whom she had taken in and raised.
Others said she was her illegitimate child, while there were some who
believed her to be her real daughter. One does not know the truth.

I forgot to tell you the woman's name, not that it matters. It could be Sakina, Mehtab, Gulshan or something else, but let's call her Sardar for the sake of convenience.

She was in her middle years and must have been beautiful in her time. Her face had now begun to wrinkle, though she still looked years younger than she was.

Her daughter – if she was her daughter – was extremely beautiful. There was nothing about her to suggest that she was a woman of pleasure, which is what she was. Business was brisk. The girl, whom I will call Nawab, was not unhappy with her life. She had grown up in an atmosphere where no concept of marital relations existed.

When Sardar had brought Nawab her first man in the big bed in the backroom, it had seemed to her quite a natural thing to have happened to a girl who had just crossed the threshold of puberty. Since then it had become the pattern of her life and she was happy with it.

And although, according to popular definition, she was a prostitute, she had no knowledge or consciousness of sin. It simply did not exist in her world.

There was a physical sincerity about her. She used to give herself completely, without reservations, to the men who were brought to her. She had come to believe that it was a woman's duty to make love to men, tenderly and without inhibitions.

She knew almost nothing about life as it was lived in the big cities, but through her men she had come to learn something of their city habits, like the brushing of teeth in the morning, drinking a cup of tea in bed and taking a quick bath before dressing up and driving off.

Not all men were alike. Some only wanted to smoke a cigarette in the morning, while others wanted nothing but a hot cup of tea. Some were bad sleepers; others slept soundly and left at the crack of dawn.

Sardar was a woman without a worry in the world. She had faith in the ability of her daughter – or whoever she was – to look after the clients. She generally used to go to bed early herself happily drugged on opium. It was only in emergencies that she was woken up. Often customers had to be revived after they had had too much to drink. Sardar would say philosophically, 'Give him some pickled mango or make him drink a glass of salt water so that he can vomit. Then send him to sleep.'

Sardar was a careful woman. Customers were required to pay in advance. After collecting the money she would say, 'Now you two go and have a good time.'

While the money always stayed in Sardar's custody, presents, when received, were Nawab's. Many of the clients were rich and gifts of cloth, fruit and sweets were frequent.

Nawab was a happy girl. In the little three-bed mud house, life was smooth and predictable. Not long ago, an army officer had brought her a gramophone and some records which she used to play when alone. She even used to try to sing along, but she had no talent for music, not that she was aware of it. The fact was that she was aware of very little, and not interested in knowing more. She might have been ignorant, but she was happy.

What the world beyond the cactus hedge was like, she had no idea. All she knew was the rough, dusty road and the men who drove up in cars, honked once or twice to announce their arrival and when told by Sardar to park at a more discreet distance, did so, then walked into the house to join Nawab in the big bed.

The regulars numbered not more than five or six, but Sardar had arranged things with such tact that never had two visitors been known to run into each other. Since every customer had his fixed day, no problems were ever encountered.

Sardar was also careful to ensure that Nawab did not become pregnant. It was an ever-present possibility. However, two and a half years had passed without any mishap. The police were unaware of Sardar's establishment and the men were discreet.

One day, a big Dodge drove up to the house. The driver honked once and Sardar stepped out. It was no one she knew, nor did the stranger say who he was. He parked the car and walked in as if he was one of the old regulars.

Sardar was a bit confused, but Nawab greeted the stranger with a smile and took him into the backroom. When Sardar followed them in, they were sitting on the bed, next to each other, talking. One look was enough to assure her that the visitor was rich and, apart from that, handsome. 'Who showed you the way?' she asked, nevertheless.

The stranger smiled, then put his arm amorously around Nawab and said, 'This one here.' Nawab sprung up flirtatiously and said, 'Why, I never saw you in my life!' 'But I have,' the stranger answered, grinning.

Surprised, Nawab asked, 'When and where?' The stranger took her hand in his and said, 'You won't understand; ask your mother.' 'Have I met this man before?' Nawab asked Sardar like a child. By now Sardar had come to the conclusion that the tip had come from one of her regulars. 'Don't worry about it. I'll tell you later,' she said to Nawab.

Then she left the room, took some opium and lay on her bed, satisfied. The stranger did not look the kind to make trouble.

His name was Haibat Khan, the biggest landlord in the neighbouring district of Hazara. 'I want no men visiting Nawab in future,' he said to Sardar on his way to his car after a few hours. 'How's that possible, Khan sahib? Can you afford to pay for all of them?' Sardar asked, being the woman of the world she was.

Haibat Khan did not answer her. Instead, he pulled out a lot of money from his pocket and threw it on the floor. He also removed a diamond ring from his finger and slipped it on Nawab. Then he walked out hurriedly, past the cactus hedge.

Nawab did not even look at the money, but she kept gazing at the ring with the big resplendent diamond. She heard the car start and move away, leaving clouds of dust in its wake.

When she returned, Sardar had picked up the money and counted it. There were nineteen hundred rupees in bank notes. One more, and it would have been two thousand, she thought, but it didn't worry her. She put the money away, took some opium and went to bed.

Nawab was thrilled. She just couldn't take her eyes off the diamond ring. A few days passed. In between, an old client came to the house, but Sardar sent him packing, saying she anticipated a police raid and had therefore decided to discontinue business.

Sardar's logic was simple. She knew Haibat Khan was rich and money would keep coming in, as before, with the added advantage that there would be only one man to deal with. In the next few days she was able to get rid of all her old clients, one by one.

A week later, Haibat Khan made his second appearance, but he did not speak to Sardar. The two of them went to the backroom, leaving Sardar with her opium and her bed.

Haibat Khan was now a regular visitor. He was totally enamoured of Nawab. He liked her artless approach to lovemaking, untinged by the hard-baked professionalism common to prostitutes. Nor was there anything housewifely about her. She would lie in bed next to him as a child lies next to its mother, playing with her breasts, sticking his little finger in her nose and then quietly going off to sleep.

It was something entirely new to Haibat Khan. Nawab was different, she was interesting and she gave pleasure. His visits became more frequent.

Sardar was happy. She had never had so much money coming in with such regularity. Nawab, however, sometimes felt troubled. Haibat Khan always seemed to be vaguely apprehensive of something. It showed in little things. A slight shiver always seemed to run through his body when a car or bus went speeding past the house. He would jump out of bed and run out, trying to read the number plate.

One night, a passing bus startled Haibat Khan so much that he suddenly wrested himself free from her arms and sat up. Nawab was a light sleeper and woke up too. He looked terrified. She was frightened. 'What happened?' she screamed.

By now, Haibat Khan had composed himself. 'It was nothing. I think I had a nightmare,' he said. The bus had gone, though it could still be heard in the distance.

Nawab said, 'No, Khan, there is something. Whenever you hear a noise, you get into a state.'

Haibat Khan's vanity was stung. 'Don't talk rubbish,' he said sharply. 'Why should anyone be afraid of cars and buses?'

Nawab began to cry, but Haibat Khan took her in his arms and she stopped sobbing.

He was a handsome man, strong of limb and a passionate lover, who ignited the fires in Nawab's young body every time he touched her. It was really he who had initiated her into the intricacies of love-making. For the first time in her life, she was experiencing the state called love. She used to pine for him when he was gone and would play her records endlessly.

Many months went by, deepening Nawab's love for Haibat Khan, and also her anxiety. His visits had of late become somewhat erratic. He would come for a few hours, look extremely ill at ease and leave suddenly. It was clear he was under some pressure. He never seemed willing or happy to leave, but he always left.

Nawab tried to get to the truth many times, only to be given evasive answers.

One morning his Dodge drove up to the house, stopping at the usual place. Nawab was asleep but she woke up when she heard him honk the horn. She rushed out and ran into Haibat Khan at the door. He embraced her passionately, picked her up and carried her inside.

They kept talking to each other for a long time about things lovers talk about. For the first time in her life, Nawab said to him, 'Khan, bring me some gold bangles.'

Haibat Khan kissed her fleshy arms many times and said, 'You will have them tomorrow. For you I can even give my life.'

Nawab squirmed coquettishly. 'Oh no Khan, it is poor me who'll have to give her life.'

Haibat Khan kissed her and said, 'I'll return tomorrow with your gold bangles and I'll put them on you myself.'

Nawab was ecstatic. She wanted to dance with joy. Sardar watched her contentedly, then reached for her opium and went to bed.

Nawab rose the next morning, still in a state of high excitement. This is the day he will bring me my gold bangles, she said to herself, but she felt uneasy. That night she couldn't sleep.

She said to her mother, 'The Khan hasn't come. He promised and he hasn't come.' Her heart was full of foreboding.

Had he had an accident? Had he been suddenly taken ill? Had he been waylaid? She heard cars passing and thought of Haibat Khan and how these noises used to terrify him.

One week passed. The house behind the cactus hedge continued to remain without visitors. Off and on, a car would go by, leaving clouds of dust behind. In her mind, passing cars and buses were now associated with Haibat Khan. They had something to do with his absence.

One afternoon, while both women were about to take a nap after lunch, they heard a car stop outside. It honked, but it was not Haibat Khan's car. Who was it then?

Sardar went outside to make sure it was not one of the old customers, in which case she would send him on his way. It was Haibat Khan. He sat in the driver's seat but it was not his car. With him was a well-dressed, rather beautiful woman.

Haibat Khan stepped out, followed by the woman. Sardar was confused. What was this woman doing with him? Who was she? Why had he brought her here?

They entered the house without taking any notice of her. She followed them inside after a while and found all three of them sitting next to one another on the bed. There was a strange silence about everything. The woman, who was wearing heavy gold ornaments, appeared to be somewhat nervous.

Sardar stood at the door and when Haibat Khan looked up she greeted him, but he made no acknowledgement. He was in a state of great and visible agitation.

The woman said to Sardar, 'Well, we are here; why don't you get us something to eat?'

'I'll have it ready in no time, whatever you wish,' Sardar replied, suddenly the hostess.

There was something about the woman which suggested authority. 'Go to the kitchen,' she ordered Sardar. 'Get the fire going. Do you have a big cooking pot?'

'Yes.' Sardar shook her head.

'Rinse it well. I'll join you later,' she said. Then she rose from the bed and began examining the gramophone.

Apologetically, Sardar said, 'One cannot buy meat around here.'

'It'll be provided,' the woman said. 'And look, I want a big fire. Now, go and do what you have been told.'

Sardar left. The woman smiled and addressed Nawab, 'Nawab, we have brought you gold bangles.'

She opened her handbag and produced heavy, ornate gold bangles, wrapped in red tissue paper.

Nawab looked at Haibat Khan, who sat next to her, very still. 'Who is this woman, Khan?' she asked in a frightened voice.

Playing with the gold bangles, the woman said, 'Who am I? I am

Haibat Khan's sister.' Then she looked at Haibat Khan, who seemed to have suddenly shrunk. 'My name is Halakat,' she said, addressing Nawab.

Nawab could not understand what was going on, but she felt terrified.

The woman moved towards Nawab, took her hands and began to slip the gold bangles on them. Then she said to Haibat Khan, 'I want you to leave the room. Let me dress her up nicely and bring her to you.'

Haibat Khan looked mesmerized. He did not move. 'Leave the room. Didn't you hear me?' she told him sharply.

He left the room, looking at Nawab as he walked out.

The kitchen was outside the house. Sardar had got the fire going. He did not speak to her, but walked past the cactus hedge, out on the road. He looked half-demented.

A bus approached. He had an urge to flag it down, get on board and disappear. But he did no such thing. The bus sped by, coating him with dust. He tried to shout after it, but his voice seemed to have gone.

He wanted to rush back into the house where he had spent so many nights of pleasure, but his feet seemed to be embedded in the ground.

He just stood there, trying to take stock of the situation. The woman who was now in the house, he had known a long time. He used to be a friend of her husband, who was dead. He remembered their first encounter many years ago. He had gone to console her after her husband's death and had ended up being her lover. It was very sudden. She had simply commanded him to take her, as if he was a servant being asked to perform a simple task.

Haibat Khan had not been very experienced with women. When Shahina, who had told Nawab her name was Halakat, or death, had become his lover, he had felt as if he had accomplished something in his life. She was rich in her own right and now had her husband's money. However, he was not interested in that. She was the first real woman in his life and he had let her seduce him.

For a long time he stood on the road. Finally, he went back to the house. The front door was closed and Sardar was cooking something in the kitchen.

He knocked and it was opened. All he could see was blood on the floor and Shahina leaning against the wall. 'I have dressed up your Nawab for you very nicely,' she said.

'Where is she?' he asked, his throat dry with terror.

'Some of her is on the bed, but most of her is in the kitchen,' she replied.

Haibat Khan began to tremble. He could now see that there was blood on the floor and a long knife. There was someone on the bed, covered with a bloodstained sheet.

Shahina smiled. 'Do you want me to lift the sheet and show you what I have there? It is your Nawab. I have made her up with great care. But perhaps you should eat first. You must be hungry. Sardar is cooking the most delicious meat in the world. I prepared it myself.'

'What have you done?' Haibat Khan screamed.

Shahina smiled again. 'Darling, this is not the first time. My husband, like you, was also faithless. I had to kill him and then throw his severed limbs for wild birds to feast on. Since I love you, instead of you, I have—'

She did not complete the sentence, but removed the sheet from the heap on the bed. Haibat Khan fainted and fell to the floor.

When he came to, he was in a car. Shahina was driving. They seemed to be in a wild country.

Translated by Khalid Hasan

God–Man

CHAUDHRY MAUJO was sitting on a cot of coarse string-matting under the shady banyan, leisurely puffing away at his hookah. Wispy balls of smoke rose from his mouth and dissipated slowly in the stagnant air of the scorching afternoon.

Ploughing his little patch of land all morning had left him totally exhausted. The sun was unbearably hot, but there was nothing like the cool smoke of the hookah to suck away all the fatigue within seconds.

The sweat on his body had dried, and although the stagnant air was hardly any comfort for his overheated body, the cool and delicious smoke of the hookah was spiralling up to his head in indescribable waves of exhilaration.

It was nearing the time when Jaina, his daughter, would bring his repast of bread and lassi from home. She was very punctual about it, even though she didn't have a soul to help her. She'd had her mother, but Maujo had divorced her two years ago following a lengthy and particularly nasty argument.

Young Jaina was a very dutiful girl. She took good care of her father. She was diligent in finishing her work so there would be time to card cotton and prepare it for spinning, or to chat with the few girlfriends she had.

Maujo didn't own much land, but it was enough to provide for his needs. His was a very small village, tucked away in a far-flung spot with no access to the railway. There was just a dirt road that connected it to a large village quite some distance away. Twice a month Chaudhry Maujo mounted his mare and rode there to buy necessities at a couple of shops.

He used to be a happy man, blissfully free of worries, except for the thought that sometimes assailed him: He had no male offspring. At such times he contented himself by thinking that he should be happy with whatever God had willed for him. But, after his wife had gone back to her parents, his life was no longer the same. It had become unspeakably cheerless and drab. It was as if she had carried all its delicious coolness and exuberance away with her.

Maujo was a religious man, but he knew only a few fundamentals of his faith: God is One and must be worshipped; Muhammad is His Prophet and it is incumbent to follow his teaching; and the Quran is the word of God which was revealed to Muhammad. That's about it.

Ritual daily prayers and the Ramzan fast – well, these he had dispensed with. The village was far too small to afford a mosque; there were only a dozen or so houses, situated far apart. People did repeat 'Allah! Allah!' often enough in their speech and carried His fear in their hearts, but that was the extent of their devotion. Nearly every household had a copy of the Quran, but no one knew how to recite it. Everyone had placed it high up on a shelf, reverentially wrapped in its velvet sheath. It was only brought down from its sanctum when it was needed for someone to swear by it or take an oath to do something.

The maulvi was called in only when a boy or girl needed to be married. The village folk took care of the funeral prayer themselves in their own tongue, not Arabic.

Chaudhry Maujo came in especially handy on such occasions. He had a way with words. They never failed to affect the listener deeply. No one could equal his manner of eulogizing the deceased and praying for his deliverance. Just last year when the strapping son of his friend Deeno died and was laid to rest in his grave, Maujo eulogized him thus:

'Oh, what a handsome young man he was! When he spat, the spittle landed twenty yards away. No one, and I mean no one, in any villages far or near could match the sturdy projectile of his piss. And what an accomplished wrestler he was! He could wriggle out of an opponent's hold as easily as unbuttoning a shirt.'

'Deeno, yaar, this is the worst day of your life! This terrible blow will affect you for the rest of your life. Was this the time for such a robust young man to die . . . such a handsome young man? How the goldsmith's lovely and headstrong daughter Neti had cast magic spells on him to win his love, but, bravo, your boy, Deeno, remained steadfast. He never gave in to her wiles. May God present him with the loveliest houri in Heaven, and may your boy never be tempted by her. And may God shower him with his mercy and blessings! Amen!'

Several people, Deeno included, were so affected by this oratory that they started crying inconsolably, and even Maujo couldn't stop his tears from bubbling out.

Maujo didn't feel the need to send for the maulvi when the idea of divorcing his wife got hold of his mind. He'd heard from elders that repeating the word 'talaq' three times over ended the matter then and there. So he ended the matter accordingly. Next day, though, he felt very sorry and ashamed that he had committed such a heinous blunder. Such squabbles were, after all, common among husbands and wives. They didn't always end in divorce. He should have been more forgiving.

He liked his Phataan. She was no longer young, but Maujo was in love with her body. He also liked the things she talked about. Above all else, she was his Jaina's mother. But it was too late now; the arrow had already left the bow. There was no way for it to fly back. Whenever he thought about the matter, the otherwise refreshing smoke of his beloved hookah caught in his throat like something bitter.

Jaina was a beautiful girl, the very image of her mother. In the space of just two years, she had suddenly blossomed from a little girl into a stunningly beautiful young woman. Her effervescent youth was spilling out of every pore of her body. Her marriage was among Maujo's constant worries, which made him miss Phataan even more. How easily she could have taken care of everything!

Rearranging his *tehmad* and himself on the cot, Maujo took a rather long drag on his hookah and started to cough. Just then he heard a voice, '*As-salamu alaikum*, and may God's mercy and blessings be upon you!'

Maujo started and turned around to look. He saw a long-bearded elderly man in flowing lily-white clothes. He returned the greeting and wondered where the man had materialised from.

The stranger had big, commanding eyes smeared with kohl and long, flowing locks of hair. His hair and beard were a blend of grey and black, with the grey predominating, and he wore a snow-white turban. An embroidered, saffron-coloured silk sash was thrown over his shoulder and he held a thick staff with a silver ball at the top. He had a pair of delicate shoes of soft red leather on his feet.

The man's appearance inspired immediate respect in Maujo. He quickly got up and asked courteously, 'Where are you from and when did you arrive?'

The man's lips, shadowed by a moustache trimmed in the fashion recommended by Islamic custom, curved into a smile. 'Where do fakirs come from? They have no place to call home, and there is no fixed time for their arrival, or for when they leave. They go wherever God wills them to, and stop where He orders them to halt.'

The words affected Maujo deeply. He took the elder's hand in his with great reverence, kissed it, and then touched it to his eyes, saying, 'Consider Chaudhry Maujo's house your own.'

The elderly man smiled and sat down on the cot, lowering his head over his staff and wrapping his hands around the ball. 'Perhaps some good deed you did has so pleased God, eminent is His majesty, that He has sent this sinner your way.'

An overjoyed Maujo asked, 'So you have come here at His behest?'

The maulvi raised his head and said in a huff, 'Who else's? You think I came here at your command? Am I your servitor or His whom I have worshipped for a good forty years to reach my insignificant station?'

Maujo shivered. He asked in his coarse but entirely sincere way to be forgiven for his unintended lapse. 'Maulvi Sahib, we uncouth village folk, who don't even know how to offer our prayer properly, often end up making such mistakes. We are sinners. But to forgive, and have God also forgive us, behooves you.'

'Precisely. That's why I'm here,' said the maulvi, closing his big kohl-lined eyes.

Chaudhry Maujo sat on the bare ground and started massaging the maulvi's legs. Meanwhile Jaina appeared. The minute she saw the other man, she quickly pulled her veil over her head and face. His eyes still closed, the maulvi asked, 'Who is it, Chaudhry Maujo?'

'Jaina, my daughter, Maulvi Sahib.'

The maulvi looked at Jaina through his half-closed eyes and said to Maujo, 'Tell her that we are fakirs, there is no need to observe purdah before us.'

'Of course not. No purdah at all, Maulvi Sahib.' Then, looking at Jaina he said, 'He is Maulvi Sahib, among God's most favoured devotees. Remove your veil.'

Jaina lifted her veil. The maulvi looked at the girl for as long as his heart desired and told Maujo, 'Chaudhry Maujo, you've got a beautiful daughter.'

Jaina blushed.

'She takes after her mother,' Maujo said.

'Where is her mother?' The maulvi looked again at the girl's blossoming youth.

Maujo felt out of his wits. He didn't know what to say.

The maulvi asked again, 'Where is her mother?'

Flabbergasted, Maujo blurted out, 'She died.'

The maulvi, his eyes riveted on the girl, noticed her reaction and said in a thundering voice, 'You're lying!'

Maujo timidly grabbed the maulvi's feet out of contrition. 'Yes, I lied,' he said, feeling remorseful. 'Please forgive me. I'm a big liar. I divorced her, Maulvi Sahib.'

With a long 'hu-u-u-u-h' the maulvi turned his eyes away from Jaina's veil and trained them on Maujo. 'You're a big sinner! What was the poor woman's fault?'

Drowned in utter shame, Maujo said meekly, 'I'm really confused. It was just a trifling, nothing serious, but it got out of hand and ended up in divorce. I'm truly a sinner. I was regretting my action the very next day. I told myself it was a foolish thing to do, but it was already too late. It was pointless to dwell on regret.

The maulvi put his staff on Maujo's shoulder. 'The sublime and lofty God is full of mercy and grace. If He wills, he can fix what is spoiled. If He wills, He will order this lowly fakir to find a way out of this difficulty for you.'

A grateful Maujo fell on the maulvi's feet and began to cry. The maulvi again glanced at Jaina, who was also in tears. 'Come here, girl!'

His voice was so commanding that Jaina simply couldn't ignore it. She put the food and lassi aside and approached the cot. The maulvi grabbed her arm and ordered her to sit down.

When she lowered herself to the ground, he pulled her up by her arm. 'Come, sit by my side.'

Jaina drew her body together as she sat next to him. The maulvi threw his arm around her waist and pulled her closer, pressing her to his side. 'What have you brought for us to eat?' he asked.

Jaina tried to pull away a little but she found the hand on her waist quite unyielding. 'Roti, saag, and lassi,' she replied.

The maulvi squeezed her firm, slender waist. 'Okay, lay it out for us.'

Jaina got up to lay out the food. Meanwhile, the maulvi tapped the silver hilt of his staff on Maujo's shoulders a couple of times. 'Get up, Maujo, and wash our hands.'

Maujo sprang to his feet, drew water from the nearby well and, like the devoted acolyte of a holy man, washed the maulvi's hands. The girl laid out the meal on the cot.

After the maulvi had devoured all the food himself, he ordered Jaina to wash his hands. She couldn't very well refuse. After all, the maulvi's bearing and appearance and his manner of talking were so commanding.

The maulvi belched noisily and pronounced loudly, '*Al-hamdu lillah!*' He then ran his wet hands over his beard, belched a second time, and stretched out on the cot, all the while gazing at Jaina's chador that had slid down from her face. Jaina quickly gathered the pots and left. The maulvi closed his eyes and announced, 'Maujo, we're going to take a nap now.'

Maujo massaged the maulvi's legs until he dozed off and then withdrew. Going off to one side, Maujo lit a couple of cow dung cakes, gave his chillum a fresh piece of tobacco, and started smoking the hookah on an empty stomach. But he was happy. He felt that a heavy burden had been lifted off his chest somehow. In his characteristic rustic but sincere manner he thanked God, the Most High, Who had sent along His angel of mercy in the guise of Maulvi Sahib.

Initially he was of a mind to stay by the maulvi, in case he needed some service, but when the man didn't wake up for quite some time, Maujo went to his field and resumed his work. He didn't care at all that he was hungry; rather, he was beside himself with happiness because the maulvi had eaten his share of the food, which he considered a great blessing for himself.

When Maujo returned from the field before sundown it pained him to see that Maulvi Sahib was nowhere in sight. He cursed himself roundly for this negligence. Why had he left the maulvi? Why hadn't he stayed near him? Perhaps the maulvi was displeased and decided to go away. He might even have called down God's curse upon Maujo. With that thought his simple peasant's soul began to tremble with fear and tears appeared in his eyes.

Maujo looked for Maulvi Sahib everywhere but couldn't find him. No trace of him either even after it got quite dark. Maujo gave up exhausted, lamenting and cursing himself. Homeward bound, his head hung low, he saw two harried young men coming along the road. He asked what the matter was. After some hemming and hawing they blurted out the truth: They had dug up a pot of wine stashed in a dirt heap and were about to drink from it when, all of a sudden, an elderly man with the luminous face of a divine being confronted them with wrathful eyes. This was a downright unlawful act. God had forbidden the consumption of intoxicants. They were committing a sin for which there was absolutely no forgiveness. The young men were so intimidated that they couldn't utter a word and just took to their heels.

Maujo told them that that heavenly figure was in fact a man of God. Then he gave voice to his fear: all this didn't bode well for the village. No telling what calamity might descend on it now. First he'd acted discourteously by leaving the maulvi alone; now these boys had attempted to imbibe the forbidden drink.

The Chaudhry mumbled, 'Only God can save us now, my boys, only God,' and headed home.

He didn't exchange any words with Jaina, just sat down quietly on the cot and began smoking his hookah. Tumultuous thoughts were swirling around in his head. He was sure that both he and the village were in for some unspeakable calamity.

The evening meal was ready. Jaina had cooked extra for Maulvi Sahib. When he didn't come, she asked about him. Maujo replied with sorrow, 'He's gone. Why would he want to stay among us sinners!'

Jaina felt very sorry because Maulvi Sahib had promised to find a way to bring her mother home. He was gone. Who would find a way to do that now? She sat down quietly on the low wooden stool. The meal started to get cold.

A while later the deorhi came alive with the sound of movement and the two started. Maujo got up and went to the deorhi, returning moments later with Maulvi Sahib. In the dim light of the oil lamp Jaina noticed the maulvi's unsteady gait and the small earthen pot he held in his hands.

Maujo helped him to the cot. Maulvi Sahib handed the pot over to Maujo and stammered, 'God put us through the worst ordeal today. We stumbled upon two young men from your village. They had dug up a pot of wine from the earth and were about to drink. The minute they saw us they ran. Their conduct shocked us. So young and on the verge of committing such a grave sin! But then we thought: At their age one does sometimes stray from the straight path. So we entreated God, the Most High, to forgive the boys their sin. And lo, He replied . . . Do you know what he said?'

'No,' said Maujo, trembling all over.

'He said, "Do you agree to take their sin upon yourself?" I said, "I do, Sublime Lord." His voice came, "Well then, drink the whole pot yourself and we will pardon the boys."'

Maujo drifted off into the world his imagination had conjured up. His hair stood on end. 'So you drank?' he asked timidly.

The maulvi's voice trembled. 'Yes, I did. I d-d-d-drank . . . to assume their sin . . . to save them . . . to please God Almighty. There is still some left in the pot. I have to drink that too. Put it away carefully. Make sure not a drop disappears.

Maujo put the pot in a small room, tying a piece of cloth tightly over its mouth. When he returned to the courtyard he saw Maulvi Sahib making Jaina massage his head while he told her, 'If a man does something good for the sake of others, God, eminent is His glory, is very pleased with such a man. Right now, He is also very pleased with you. So am I.'

As an expression of his pleasure, he made Jaina sit next to him and kissed her forehead. She cringed and hurried to get up, but the maulvi's grip was firm. He clasped her to his chest and said to Maujo, 'Chaudhry, fate is smiling on your daughter.'

The Chaudhry was overwhelmed with gratitude. 'It is all due to your prayer . . . your kindness.'

Once again the maulvi pressed the girl to his chest. 'When God is kind, everyone else is kind too. Jaina, I'll teach you a prayer. Keep saying it and God will be kind to you.'

The maulvi got up quite late the next morning. Out of deference tinged with a feeling of awe, Maujo hadn't dared to go to work in his field and had remained beside the maulvi's cot in the courtyard. When, finally, the man's sleep broke, Maujo helped him brush his teeth with a twig and wash his hands and face. Then he brought the pot of wine over to him as ordered. The maulvi mumbled some pious words, removed the cloth from the pot, blew into it a few times, and emptied a few bowls. Now he looked at the sky, again mumbled some words, and said in a loud voice, 'Oh Lord, we will prevail in whatever test you put us to.' Addressing the Chaudhry, he said, 'Maujo, we've just been ordered to tell you, go right now and bring your wife back! We've found a way.'

Maujo was overjoyed. He hurriedly saddled his mare. Promising to return early the next day and advising Jaina to look to the maulvi's every comfort and not shrink from serving him as best as she could, he left.

Jaina got busy scrubbing the dirty dishes. The maulvi, comfortably settled on the cot, kept staring at her and drinking wine from the bowl. Eventually he pulled out a string of large beads and started to roll them through his fingers. When Jaina was finished, he said to her, 'Look here, Jaina, do your *wuẓu*.'

'I don't know how to, Maulvi Sahib,' she replied innocently.

He chided her softly. 'You don't know how to make wuzu? Tut-tut-tut. How will you face God then?' He stood up from the cot and taught her to perform wuzu, scouring every last nook and corner of the girl's body with his eyes as he went over the different acts of ritual washings with her.

This done he asked for the prayer rug. There was none. He chided her again with the same tenderness. He asked her to get a sheet instead, spread it out in an inner room of the house and then latch the main door. When she had done so, he asked her to bring the wine pot and the bowl over. She did that. He drank half a bowlful of wine, set the still half-full bowl down in front of him, closed his eyes and resumed telling his beads. Meanwhile Jaina sat quietly near him.

His remained busy with his beads for a long while. Then he opened his eyes, blew into the half-full bowl three times over and offered it to Jaina. 'Drink!'

Shaking, Jaina took the bowl with hesitant hands.

'Didn't we say drink?' the maulvi commanded in his awe-inspiring voice. 'It will rid you of all your miseries.'

Jaina quickly downed the liquid. A smile spread across the maulvi's thin lips. 'Look, we're about to start our *wazifa* again. When you see our index finger rise, it is a sign for you to fill the bowl about halfway and drink from it immediately. Understand?'

The maulvi didn't wait for her to answer; he closed his eyes and sank back into his meditation.

A terribly bitter taste exploded in Jaina's mouth; she felt as if the inside of her chest was on fire. She desperately wanted to get up and drink some cold water. But how could she? So she just sat there, enduring the stinging sensation in her throat and chest. Suddenly the maulvi's index finger rose with a snap. As if hypnotized, the obedient girl quickly filled half the bowl and drank the wine. She wanted to spit it out but she just couldn't get up.

Meanwhile, the maulvi continued rolling his beads, deep in meditation, his eyes closed in rapture. Jaina felt as if her head was spinning and she was succumbing to the relentless onslaught of drowsiness. In her semi-conscious state she saw herself in the arms of a youth with neither beard nor moustache who was taking her along to enjoy the pleasures of paradise.

When she opened her eyes, she saw herself stretched out on the coarse sheet. With her half-open, inebriated eyes she looked around herself and wondered: *When did I lie down here, and why?* Everything seemed shrouded in fog. She fought back another wave of sleep and abruptly got up. Maulvi Sahib – where was he? . . . And that paradise?

It was an empty space that confronted her. She stepped into the courtyard and found the maulvi making his wuzu. He turned around at the sound of her footsteps and smiled. Jaina withdrew to the room. She sat down on the sheet and began thinking about her mother, whom her father had gone to bring back home. There was still a whole night before they returned.

And to top it all, she was feeling quite hungry. She hadn't cooked a meal. Many thoughts were crowding into her agitated mind. After a while the maulvi appeared and said, 'I have to do a wazifa for your father. It will require an all-night vigil by some grave. I'll also pray for you.' Then he left.

He returned at the crack of dawn. His great big eyes, now bereft of their line of kohl, were bloodshot. His voice was faltering, his tread wobbly. As he entered the courtyard, he looked at Jaina with a smile, approached her and pressed her against his chest. He kissed her and plopped down on the cot. Jaina sat on a stool in a far corner and began mulling over the events of the previous evening, her recollection of which was quite hazy. She was also waiting for her father who should have been back by now. A full two years had passed since she had been separated from her mother . . . And yes, the paradise . . . that paradise . . . How was it? Was her companion Maulvi Sahib? She could vaguely remember that whoever it was didn't sport a beard; he was someone young.

'Jaina,' the maulvi said to her after some time, 'Maujo hasn't returned yet.'

She remained quiet.

'And there I was, performing the wazifa especially for his sake throughout the desolate night, sitting with bowed head by a dilapidated grave!' he told the girl. 'When will he return? Do you think he'll be able to bring your mother back?'

Her only answer: 'Perhaps he'll be here soon. He will come home. So will Mother. But I can't say anything for sure.'

Suddenly the sound of footsteps was heard. Jaina got up quickly. The moment she saw her mother she immediately wrapped her arms around her and broke into tears. When Maujo came in, he greeted the maulvi with the greatest courtesy and reverence and commanded his wife, 'Phataan, say salaam to Maulvi Sahib!'

Phataan disengaged herself from her daughter and, wiping her tears, offered salaams to the maulvi. The latter gaped at her with his red fiery eyes and said to Maujo, 'I've just returned after performing a night-long wazifa for you by a grave. God has heard me. Everything will be all right.'

Chaudhry Maujo dropped down to the floor and quickly started pressing the maulvi's calves. So overwhelmed was he by feelings of deep gratitude and reverence that he couldn't say anything to the maulvi; instead, he said to his wife tearfully, 'Come here, Phataan, you thank Maulvi Sahib for I don't know how to.'

She came and sat next to her husband. All she could say was, 'We poor folk, how can we ever thank you enough.'

The maulvi looked closely at Phataan. 'Maujo Chaudhry, he said, 'you were absolutely right. Your wife is truly beautiful. In spite of her age, she looks young. Exactly like Jaina . . . even more beautiful. We will put everything right, Phataan, for God is inclined to be merciful and giving.'

Both husband and wife sank into silence. Maujo continued pressing the maulvi's calves, while Jaina busied herself with getting the fire going in the hearth.

After a while the maulvi rose from the cot, patted Phataan's head gently and said to Maujo, 'God commands that if a man wants to remarry the wife he has divorced, he must, in punishment, have her first marry another man and seek divorce from him. Only then is it lawful for her first husband to remarry her.'

'I've heard this before, Maulvi Sahib,' Maujo said softly.

The maulvi made Maujo get up and placed his hand on his shoulder. 'I entreated God tearfully not to put your poor soul through such harsh punishment; I said that you erred without meaning to. But God answered, "How long do you expect Us to go on listening to your intercessions? If there is anything you want for yourself, well, We'll give it to you." I submitted, "My Lord, Lord of the Sea and the Earth, I don't ask anything for myself. You've already given me everything. But Maujo Chaudhry – he loves his wife dearly. . ." He proclaimed, "Well then, We want to test his love and your faith. You marry her for a day and hand her over to Maujo the next day after divorcing her. This is the best We can do for you, and that too because for the past forty years you have been unfailing in your devotion to Us.'"

An overjoyed Maujo cried out, 'I accept, Maulvi Sahib, I accept.'

He looked at his wife with a twinkle in his eyes and asked, 'So Phataan, what do you say?'

But without waiting for an answer, he blurted out again, 'We both accept.'

The maulvi closed his eyes, mumbled something, breathed over the two, and raised his eyes to the sky. 'God, the Blessed, the Most High, may we triumph over this ordeal with Your help!' Then he said to the Chaudhry, 'Well, Maujo, I'm going out now. When I return, I'd like you and Jaina to leave here and spend the night somewhere else. Come back in the morning.' And he went out.

When he returned in the evening, Jaina and Maujo were ready. He exchanged a few short words with them and started mumbling something. A little later, after a sign from him, father and daughter promptly exited the house.

The maulvi fastened the door latch and said to Phataan, 'For this one night you're my wife. Go bring the bedding and spread it out on the cot. We will sleep.'

Phataan did as commanded. The maulvi said, 'Bibi, you sit here. I'll be along shortly.'

He then went into the other room. In the light of the earthen oil he spotted his wine pitcher in a corner near the stack of pots and pans. He shook the pitcher. There was some wine left. Still standing, he impatiently gulped a few mouthfuls of the intoxicant directly from the pitcher and used the embroidered saffron-coloured silk sash that was slung across his shoulder to wipe his lips and moustache. Then he closed the door.

He re-emerged after quite some time with the bowl in hand. Phataan was sitting on the cot. He blew into the bowl three times and offered it to her. 'Come on, drink up!'

Phataan gulped down the liquid and instantly felt queasy. The maulvi tapped on her back a few times and said, 'There, okay!'

Phataan tried to feel better, and to a degree she did. The maulvi stretched out on the bed.

In the morning, when Maujo and Jaina returned, they found Phataan sleeping alone in the courtyard with no sign of the maulvi anywhere. Maybe he's gone out for a bit . . . to the fields, Maujo thought. He tried to wake Phataan. Mumbling some inarticulate sounds, she slowly opened her eyes. Then, in a clear distinct voice, she mumbled, 'Paradise! Oh, sheer paradise!' But as soon as she saw Maujo, she sat up in the bed, eyes wide open.

'Where is Maulvi Sahib?' Maujo asked.

Phataan, who still hadn't fully recovered her senses, replied, 'Maulvi Sahib? What Maulvi Sahib? Oh he, God knows where he's gone . . . Isn't he here?'

'No,' Maujo said, 'Okay, I'll go out and look for him.'

Just as he was leaving he heard Phataan's muffled scream. He turned around to look at her. She was pulling out something black from under the pillow. 'What the hell is this?' she asked, looking at the object in her hand.

'Hair,' Maujo replied.

Phataan quickly threw that tangled clump of hair down on the floor. Maujo picked it up and gave it a close look. 'It's a beard and sideburns.'

Jaina, who was standing near them, said, 'Maulvi Sahib's beard and sideburns.'

'Yes, his beard and sideburns,' affirmed her mother from the bed.

Maujo was nonplussed. 'But where is the Maulvi Sahib himself?'

Suddenly a thought came into his simple, trusting peasant mind. 'Jaina, Phataan, you don't understand. He was a godly person, full of saintly graces. He fulfilled what we most yearned for and left us this memento to remember him by.'

He reverently kissed that clump of hair, touched it to his eyes, and, handing it to Jaina, told her, 'Go, wrap it in a clean piece of cloth and put it in the big chest. God willing, it will bring blessings to our household forever.'

Once Jaina left, he sat down next to his Phataan and told her lovingly, 'I will learn to say my namaz and always pray for the saintly elder who again brought us together.'

Phataan just sat there in hushed silence.

Translated by Muhammad Umar Memon

The Assignment

BEGINNING with isolated incidents of stabbing, it had now developed into full-scale communal violence, with no holds barred. Even homemade bombs were being used.

The general view in Amritsar was that the riots could not last long. They were seen as no more than a manifestation of temporarily inflamed political passions which were bound to cool down before long. After all, these were not the first communal riots the city had known. There had been so many of them in the past. They never lasted long. The pattern was familiar. Two weeks or so of unrest and then business as usual. On the basis of experience, therefore, the people were quite justified in believing that the current troubles would also run their course in a few days. But this did not happen. They not only continued, but grew in intensity.

Muslims living in Hindu localities began to leave for safer places, and Hindus in Muslim majority areas followed suit. However, everyone saw these adjustments as strictly temporary. The atmosphere would soon be clear of this communal madness, they told themselves.

Retired judge Mian Abdul Hai was absolutely confident that things would return to normal soon, which was why he wasn't worried. He had two children, a boy of eleven and a girl of seventeen. In addition, there was an old servant who was now pushing seventy. It was a small family. When the troubles started, Mian sahib, being an extra cautious man, had stocked up on food . . . just in case. So on one count, at least, there were no worries.

His daughter, Sughra, was less sure of things. They lived in a three-storey house with a view of almost the entire city. Sughra could not help noticing that, whenever she went on the roof, there were fires raging everywhere. In the beginning, she could hear fire engines rushing past, their bells ringing, but this had now stopped. There were too many fires in too many places.

The nights had become particularly frightening. The sky was always lit by conflagrations like giants spitting out flames. Then there were the slogans which rent the air with terrifying frequency – '*Allaho Akbar*', '*Har Har Mahadev.*'

Sughra never expressed her fears to her father, because he had declared confidently that there was no cause for anxiety. Everything was going to be fine. Since he was generally always right, she had initially felt reassured.

However, when the power and water supplies were suddenly cut off, she expressed her unease to her father and suggested apologetically that, for a few days at least, they should move to Sharifpura, a Muslim locality, where many of the old residents had already moved to. Mian sahib was adamant. 'You're imagining things. Everything is going to be normal very soon.'

He was wrong. Things went from bad to worse. Before long there was not a single Muslim family to be found in Mian Abdul Hai's locality.

Then one day Mian sahib suffered a stroke and was laid up. His son, Basharat, who used to spend most of his time playing self-devised games, now stayed glued to his father's side. All the shops in the area had been permanently boarded up.

Dr Ghulam Hussain's dispensary had been shut for weeks and Sughra had noticed from the rooftop one day that the adjoining clinic of Dr Goranditta Mal was also closed. Mian sahib's condition was getting worse day by day. Sughra was almost at her wits' end. One day she took Basharat aside and said to him, 'You've got to do something. I know it's not safe to go out, but we must get some help. Our father is very ill.'

The boy went, but came back almost immediately. His face was pale with fear. He had seen a blood-drenched body lying in the street and a group of wild-looking men looting shops. Sughra took the terrified boy in her arms and said a silent prayer, thanking God for his safe return. However, she could not bear her father's suffering. His left side was now completely lifeless. His speech had been impaired and he mostly communicated through gestures, all designed to reassure Sughra that soon all would be well.

It was the month of Ramadan and only two days to Id. Mian sahib was quite confident that the troubles would be over by then. He was again wrong. A canopy of smoke hung over the city, with fires burning everywhere. At night the silence was shattered by deafening explosions. Sughra and Basharat hadn't slept for days.

Sughra in any case couldn't because of her father's deteriorating condition. Helplessly, she would look at him, then at her young, frightened brother and the seventy-year-old servant Akbar, who was useless for all practical purposes. He mostly kept to his bed, coughing and fighting for breath. One day Sughra told him angrily, 'What good are you? Do you realize how ill Mian sahib is? Perhaps you are too lazy to want to help, pretending that you are suffering from acute asthma. There was a time when servants used to sacrifice their lives for their masters.'

Sughra felt very bad afterwards. She had been unnecessarily harsh with the old man. In the evening, when she took his food to him in his small room, he was not there. Basharat looked for him all over the house, but he was nowhere to be found. The front door was unlatched. He was gone, perhaps to get some help for Mian sahib. Sughra prayed for his return, but two days passed and he hadn't come back.

It was evening and the festival of Id was now only a day away. She remembered the excitement which used to grip the family on this occasion. She remembered standing on the rooftop, peering into the sky, looking for the Id moon and praying for the clouds to clear. But how different everything was today. The sky was covered in smoke and on distant roofs one could see people looking upwards. Were they trying to catch sight of the new moon or were they watching the fires, she wondered.

She looked up and saw the thin sliver of the moon peeping through a small patch in the sky. She raised her hands in prayer, begging God to make her father well. Basharat, however, was upset that there would be no Id this year.

The night hadn't yet fallen. Sughra had moved her father's bed out of the room onto the veranda. She was sprinkling water on the floor to make it cool. Mian sahib was lying there quietly looking with vacant eyes at the sky where she had seen the moon. Sughra came and sat next to him. He motioned her to get closer. Then he raised his right arm slowly and put it on her head. Tears began to run from Sughra's eyes. Even Mian sahib looked moved. Then with great difficulty he said to her, 'God is merciful. All will be well.'

Suddenly there was a knock on the door. Sughra's heart began to beat violently. She looked at Basharat, whose face had turned white like a sheet of paper. There was another knock. Mian sahib gestured to Sughra to answer it. It must be old Akbar who had come back, she thought. She said to Basharat, 'Answer the door. I'm sure it's Akbar.' Her father shook his head, as if to signal disagreement.

'Then who can it be?' Sughra asked him.

Mian Abdul Hai tried to speak, but before he could do so Basharat came running in. He was breathless. Taking Sughra aside, he whispered, 'It's a Sikh.'

Sughra screamed, 'A Sikh! What does he want?'

'He wants me to open the door.'

Sughra took Basharat in her arms and went and sat on her father's bed, looking at him desolately.

On Mian Abdul Hai's thin, lifeless lips, a faint smile appeared. 'Go and open the door. It is Gurmukh Singh.'

'No, it's someone else,' Basharat said.

Mian sahib turned to Sughra. 'Open the door. It's him.'

Sughra rose. She knew Gurmukh Singh. Her father had once done him a favour. He had been involved in a false legal suit and Mian sahib had acquitted him. That was a long time ago, but every year, on the occasion of Id, he would come all the way from his village with a bag of sawwaiyaan. Mian sahib had told him several times, 'Sardar sahib, you really are too kind. You shouldn't inconvenience yourself every year.' But Gurmukh Singh would always reply, 'Mian sahib, God has given you everything. This is only a small gift which I bring every year in humble acknowledgement of the kindness you once showed me. Even a hundred generations of mine would not be able to repay your favour. May God keep you happy.'

Sughra was reassured. Why hadn't she thought of it in the first place? But why had Basharat said it was someone else? After all, he knew Gurmukh Singh's face from his annual visit.

Sughra went to the front door. There was another knock. Her heart missed a beat. 'Who is it?' she asked in a faint voice.

Basharat whispered to her to look through a small hole in the door.

It wasn't Gurmukh Singh, who was a very old man. This was a young fellow. He knocked again. He was holding a bag in his hand of the same kind Gurmukh Singh used to bring.

'Who are you?' she asked, a little more confident now. 'I am Sardar Gurmukh Singh's son Santokh.'

Sughra's fear had suddenly gone. 'What brings you here today?' she asked politely.

'Where is Judge sahib?' he asked. 'He is not well,' Sughra answered.

'Oh, I'm sorry,' Santokh Singh said. Then he shifted his bag from one hand to the other. 'Here is some sawwaiyaan.' Then after a pause, 'Sardarji is dead.'

'Dead!'

'Yes, a month ago, but one of the last things he said to me was, "For the last ten years, on the occasion of Id, I have always taken my small gift to Judge sahib. After I am gone, it will become your duty." I gave him my word that I would not fail him. I am here today to honour the promise I made to my father on his deathbed.'

Sughra was so moved that tears came to her eyes. She opened the door a little. The young man pushed the bag towards her. 'May God rest his soul,' she said.

'Is Judge sahib not well?' he asked. 'No.'

'What's wrong?'

'He had a stroke.'

'Had my father been alive, it would have grieved him deeply. He never forgot Judge sahib's kindness until his last breath. He used to say, "He is not a man, but a god." May God keep him under his care. Please convey my respects to him.'

He left before Sughra could make up her mind whether or not to ask him to get a doctor.

As Santokh Singh turned the corner, four men, their faces covered with their turbans, moved towards him. Two of them held burning oil torches; the others carried cans of kerosene oil and explosives. One of them asked Santokh, 'Sardarji, have you completed your assignment?'

The young man nodded.

'Should we then proceed with ours?' he asked.

'If you like,' he replied and walked away.

Translated by Khalid Hasan

Two-Nation Theory

THE FIRST TIME Mukhtar saw Sharda was from his rooftop, where he had gone to grab a kite that had landed there. It was only a glimpse. She lived in the house across the street, which was lower than theirs, and he had seen her through the open window of the bathroom where she was washing herself, pouring water on her body from a pitcher. This was a surprise. Where had this girl materialized from, because no girl lived in that house. The ones who used to had all been married off. The only female now left was Roop Kaur, with her flabby husband and their three boys.

Mukhtar picked up his kite and stole another look at the girl. She was beautiful. A shudder ran through him. The water drops on the golden down of her body were shimmering. Her complexion was light brown, but it had the glow of copper. The tiny droplets of water that sparkled on her skin were making her body melt, drop by drop, or that was how it appeared to him. He was watching her through one of the eyeholes in the low brick wall built on all four sides of the open roof. His eyes were glued to the body of this girl bathing herself. She was no more than sixteen and there were water drops on her small, round breasts, lovely to look at.

But he did not feel aroused. He just kept watching this young, beautiful, naked girl with great concentration as if she were a painting. There was a large mole in the corner of her mouth, which just sat there, soberly, as if it was unaware of its being there, but others were aware of its existence and knew that it was exactly where it ought to have been.

The golden down on her arms was studded with sparkling water drops. Her hair was not golden but light brown. Perhaps her hair had refused to go golden. Her body was full and supple but no lascivious thoughts came to him. He just kept looking at her through the eyehole. She soaped her body and he could smell its aroma spreading over her light brown, copper-hued body. The foam on her skin looked lovely. When she poured water over herself to wash it away, he felt as if she had removed her foamy covering with one calm, smooth move. When she was done, she dried herself with a towel, put on her clothes unhurriedly and, placing both hands on the window sill, stood up. She blushed. Her eyes, Mukhtar felt, had taken a dip into a lake of shyness. She closed the window shut and, involuntarily, Mukhtar laughed.

Then she threw open the window and looked towards him angrily. Mukhtar spoke, 'Please don't blame me but why were you bathing with the window open?' She said nothing, cast another angry look at him and shut the window. Four days later, Roop Kaur came to their house, accompanied by that girl. Mukhtar's mother and sister were excellent knitters. Many girls from the neighbourhood would come to them to learn how to knit and do crochet work. This girl was fond of learning how to crochet and that was why she had come. Mukhtar stepped out of his room into the courtyard, smiled and left. She drew herself together when she saw him. Mukhtar learnt that her name was Sharda and she was Roop Kaur's cousin, daughter of her uncle. She lived in the small town of Chichoki Malyaan with her poor relatives, but Roop Kaur had asked her to come live with her family. She had finished high school and she was said to be very intelligent. It had taken her no time to learn how to crochet.

Several days passed. By now Mukhtar knew that he had fallen in love with her. It had happened gradually, from the moment he had first seen her through that eyehole to this point where her thought never left his heart for a moment. It occurred to Mukhtar several times that falling in love was wrong because Sharda was a Hindu. How could a Muslim dare fall in love with a Hindu? But the fact was that he just could not bear the thought of not being in love with her. Sharda would sometimes talk to him but somewhat diffidently. The first thing that would come to her mind on seeing him would be the memory of the day he had seen her through that eyehole taking a bath naked. One day, when Mukhtar's mother and sister had gone to offer condolences at a family friend's home, Sharda walked in, carrying the small bag she always did. It was about ten in the morning and Mukhtar was stretched on a cot in the courtyard reading a newspaper. 'Where is Behanji?' she asked, referring to his sister. Mukhtar's hands began to tremble, 'She has gone out.' 'And Mataji?' Sharda asked, which was what she called his mother. Mukhtar got down from the cot. 'She . . . she has gone with her.' 'All right then,' she said, looking worried. Joining her hands in a namaste, she was about to leave when Mukhtar said, 'Sharda!' 'Yes?' She looked like someone who had just received an electric shock. Mukhtar said, 'Sit down. They will be back very soon.' 'No, I am leaving,' she replied but kept standing.

Picking up his courage, Mukhtar pulled her towards him by the wrist and kissed her on the lips. It all happened so quickly that Sharda was taken by surprise. By now both of them were trembling. 'Please forgive me,' was all Mukhtar said. Sharda kept quiet but her copper complexion turned red and her lips began to quiver as if they were complaining about having been teased. Mukhtar drew Sharda close to his chest and she did not resist. But there was a look of astonishment on her face. She seemed to be asking herself, 'What is it that has happened? What is happening? Should it have happened? Is this what happens to others as well?'

Mukhtar made her sit on the cot and asked, 'Why don't you speak Sharda?' Under her dupatta, Sharda's heart was beating fast. She did not answer him. Mukhtar felt bothered by her silence. 'Please say something Sharda, if what I have done has offended you, as God is my witness, I'll apologize. I will never even raise my eyes towards you. I would never have had the courage but I don't know what came over me. The fact is, the fact is that I am in love with you.' Sharda's lips moved as if they were trying to form the word 'love.' Mukhtar began to talk animatedly, 'I don't know if you understand the meaning of love. I don't know much about it myself. All I know is that I love you. I want to hold all of you in one hand. If you want, I can place my life in your hands. Sharda, why don't you speak?'

Sharda's eyes became dreamy. Mukhtar began to talk again. 'I saw you that day through that eyehole. I saw you and that is a sight I will not forget till judgement day. Why are you so shy? My eyes never stole your beauty. They just beheld a splendid scene. If you can bring it back, I will kiss your feet.' And he kissed one of her feet.

She trembled. Then she rose from the cot and said, her voice quivering, 'What are you doing? In our religion . . .' Mukhtar said excitedly, 'Forget religion. All is right in the religion of love.' He wanted to kiss her again but she leapt aside and, still smiling, she ran out. Mukhtar wanted to run up to the roof and jump from there into the courtyard and start dancing. Some time later, Mukhtar's mother and sister returned and so did Sharda. Mukhtar slipped away, his eyes to the ground. He did not want his secret to get out. The next day, he walked up to the rooftop. She was standing by the window, combing her hair. 'Sharda,' Mukhtar called out. She was startled. The comb fell from her hand, landing in the street. 'You are so timid; look your comb has fallen.' 'Why don't you buy me a new one then; this one has fallen into the gutter,' Sharda said. 'Now?' Mukhtar asked. 'No, no, I was only joking.' 'I was also joking. Could I have left you to buy a comb? Never.' Sharda smiled, 'How am I going to do my hair?' Mukhtar slipped his finger through the eyehole from where he was watching her. 'Use my fingers.'

Sharda laughed. Mukhtar felt that he could happily spend his entire life under the shade of that laughter. 'Sharda, by God, you laughed and I am in ecstasy. Why are you so lovely? There is no girl in the whole wide world who is as lovely. I want to smash these curtains of clay that stand between us.' Sharda laughed again. Mukhtar said, 'No one else should hear you laugh, nor even watch you when you do. Sharda, you must only laugh for me. Whenever you want to laugh, just call me. I will raise protective walls around you with my kisses.' 'You know how to talk,' Sharda said. 'Then give me a reward, just a look of love from across there. I will save that look in my eyes and I'll keep it hidden.' He noticed someone's shadow behind her and he moved away. When he returned, she was not at the window.

They came close in the days that followed and whenever they got a chance they would talk the sweet nothings that lovers do. One day, Roop

Kaur and her husband, Lala Kalu Mal, were out of the house. Mukhtar happened to be walking past when a pebble hit him. He looked up and saw Sharda. She motioned him to come up. They were completely alone and they talked intimately for a long time. Mukhtar said, 'I apologize for what I did that day. And I want to do the same thing today, but this time I won't apologize.' Then he placed his lips on Sharda's quivering lips. 'Say you are sorry,' Sharda said naughtily. 'No, those are not your lips, they are mine. Am I wrong?' Sharda lowered her eyes, 'Not only those lips, all of me is yours too.'

Mukhtar became grave. 'Look Sharda, we are standing on the top of a volcano. I assure you – and you should believe it – that no woman will ever come into my life except you. I swear that I will remain yours for the rest of my life. My love will be steadfast. Do you also make the same promise?' Sharda raised her eyes. 'My love is true.' Mukhtar threw his arms around her and squeezed her to his chest. 'Live, but only for me, for my love. By God, Sharda, if you had not returned my love, I would have killed myself. You are in my arms and I feel that every blessing of the world, every happiness, is in my lap. I am so fortunate.'

Sharda rested her head on Mukhtar's shoulder. 'You know how to talk; I cannot bring to my lips what is in my heart.' They were together for a long time, absorbed in one another. When Mukhtar left, his spirits were imbued with a new and delicious pleasure. He kept thinking all night and the next day he left for Calcutta, where his father ran a business. He returned after eight days. Sharda came for her crochet hour. They did not speak but he felt her eyes asking him, 'Where have you been all these days? Never said a word to me and left for Calcutta? What happened to those claims of love? I am not going to speak to you. Don't look at me.

What do you want to say to me now?' There was much Mukhtar wanted to say to her but they could not find themselves alone. He wanted to talk to her for a long, long time. Two days passed. But their eyes talked whenever they ran into each other. On the third day, with Roop Kaur and her husband, Lala Kalu Mal, again out of the house, Sharda called him.

She met him on the stairs and, when Mukhtar tried to embrace her, she wrested herself free and ran upstairs. She was annoyed. Mukhtar said to her, 'Sweetheart, come sit with me. I have important things to talk to you about, things which concern us both.' She sat next to him on a bed. 'Don't try to talk yourself out of it. Why did you go to Calcutta without telling me? Really, I wept so much.' Mukhtar kissed her eyes. 'That day when I went home, I kept thinking all night. After what took place that day, I had to think. We were like man and wife. I erred and you let yourself go. In one leap, we covered such vast distances. We never thought about the direction we should take. You understand, Sharda.'

She lowered her eyes. 'Yes.' 'I went to Calcutta to talk to my father and you will be happy to know that I have his blessings.' Mukhtar's eyes had lit up with joy. He took Sharda's hands in his and said, 'A weight has lifted from my heart; I can marry you now.' 'Marriage!' she said in a low voice. 'Yes, marriage.' Sharda asked, 'How can we marry?' Mukhtar smiled, 'Where is the difficulty? You become a Muslim.' Sharda was startled. 'Muslim!' Mukhtar replied calmly, 'Yes, yes, what else can it be? I know your family will be up in arms, but I have made arrangements. We will go to Calcutta. My father will do the rest. The day we arrive, he will send for a cleric who will make you a Muslim and we will get married right away.' Sharda clenched her lips, as if they were sewn up. Mukhtar looked at her.

'Why have you become quiet?' She said nothing. 'Sharda, tell me what is it?' Mukhtar asked in a worried voice.

With great difficulty, Sharda replied, 'You become a Hindu.' 'I become a Hindu?' he asked in an astonished voice. Then he laughed. 'How can I become a Hindu?' 'And how can I become a Muslim?' she asked in a low voice. 'Why can't you become a Muslim . . . I mean you love me. And Islam is the best of religions. The Hindu religion is no religion. Hindus drink cow urine; they worship idols. I mean it is all right in its place, but it cannot compare with Islam. If you become a Muslim, every-thing will fall in place.' Sharda's copper face had gone white. 'You won't become a Hindu?' Mukhtar laughed, 'Are you mad!' Sharda's face had blanched. 'You should leave. They will be coming about now.' She rose from the bed. Mukhtar couldn't understand. 'But Sharda . . .' 'No, no, please leave, go quickly or they will be here,' she said in a cold, uncaring voice. Mukhtar's throat had gone dry but with great difficulty he said, 'We love each other, Sharda why are you upset?' 'Go, go away, our Hindu religion is very bad; you Muslims are the good ones.' There was hatred in her voice. She went into the other room and shut the door. Mukhtar, his Islam tucked inside his chest, left the house.

Translated by Khalid Hasan

The Patch

WHEN A SUPPURATED boil appeared on Gopal's thigh, he was terrified.

It was summer and mangoes were in season and plentiful: in bazaars, streets, shops and even with street vendors. Wherever you looked, you saw mangoes. They came in all colours: red, yellow, green, multi-hued. Heaps upon heaps of them – and in all varieties – were on sale in the fruit and vegetable market at throwaway prices. The shortage experienced a year earlier had been more than made up for.

Outside the school, Gopal had had his fill of them at fruitseller Chootu Ram's stand. All the money he had saved during the month he had spent on those mangoes, saturated as they were with juice and honey. After school closed that day, Gopal, the taste of mangoes still in his mouth, had decided to stop by at Ganda Ram, the sweetmeat seller's, for a glass of buttermilk. He had asked him to prepare the drink but the man had refused, saying, 'Babu Gopal, settle the old account first and you can have fresh credit, not otherwise.'

Had Gopal not gorged himself on mangoes or had he had any money on him, he would have settled Ganda Ram's account there and then. He would then have paid for his glass of buttermilk which had in fact been prepared by Ganda Ram, and a piece of ice could be seen floating about in it. This sweetmeat seller had made a face and put the glass behind his back on a round iron dish. There was little Gopal could do and then, on the fourth day precisely, this big boil had appeared on his thigh. It had kept growing for the next three to four days. This had made Gopal very nervous, not quite knowing what to do. The boil itself did not bother him as much as the pain it was beginning to cause. What made things worse was that with each passing day the boil was getting redder and redder and some of the skin that covered it had begun to come off. At times Gopal felt as if under all that red there was a pot on the boil and whatever was in it wanted to burst out all in one go. So big had it become that once he felt as if one of his glass marbles had jumped out of his pocket and lodged itself in his thigh.

Gopal said nothing about the boil to anyone at home. He knew that if his father found out, all the anger that he felt over his fly-infested police station would be taken out on him. It was also possible that he might thrash him with the stick that the lawyer Girdhari Lal's assistant had brought for him from Wazirabad the other day. His mother was no less hot-tempered. Had she chosen not to punish him for eating all those mangoes, she would have boxed his ears red for having wolfed them down all by himself. The principle his mother had laid down was, 'Gopal, even if it is poison that you want to take, you should do so at home.' Gopal knew what was behind this: her wish to sample the same delights that he was enjoying.

Be that as it may, the fact was that this boil was destined to appear on Gopal's thigh and it had done so. As far as he could work it out, it was the mangoes he had eaten that had caused this boil to appear. He had made no mention of it to anyone at home, because he still remembered the dressing-down he had got from his father, Lala Prashotam Das, police inspector, as he sat under the big municipal tap wearing only a loincloth, with the water gushing over his bald head and his big belly jutting forth. He was sucking mango after mango through the filter of his moustache. A dozen mangoes lay in front of him in a pail that he had taken from a street fruitseller in return for tearing up the ticket he had earlier given him. Gopal was rubbing his father's back, peeling away layers of dirt from it. When he had dipped a clean hand into the pail to quietly pull out a mango, Lalaji had prised the tiny fruit from his hand and put it in his own mouth, along with his moustache, and said, 'How shameless! When will you learn to be respectful of your elders?'

And when with a weepy face Gopal had replied, 'Father, I too want to eat mangoes,' the Inspector sahib, chucking away the stone in an open drain that ran in the street, said, 'Gopu mangoes are just too hot for you, but if you want boils and carbuncles, then you are most welcome to them. Let it rain three or four times and then you can eat them to your heart's content. I will ask your mother to make you some buttermilk. Now get back to rubbing my back.' Gopal, having run into this roadblock, quietly resumed his assigned chore. The very thought of the mango's sour taste had made his mouth water and he kept swallowing it for a long time.

The very next day he gorged himself on those mangoes and four days later a boil appeared on his thigh. What his father had said had come true. Now, had Gopal mentioned his boil to anyone at home, he would have received a good beating, which was why he had kept quiet, while all the time thinking of some way of stopping the boil from growing any further.

One day on returning home from the police station, his father called out Gopal's mother and announced, as he handed her a packet, 'This Bombay balm is something of great value, one remedy that equals a hundred remedies. This is the time of year when boils and carbuncles are common, so all you need to be rid of them is just one single application. That's all. This is something special from Bombay, so tuck it away somewhere safe.'

Gopal was playing cricket in the courtyard with his sister, Nirmala. It just happened that, when the Inspector sahib was busy explaining to his wife something about the balm he had given her, Nirmala lobbed the ball towards him and since Gopal was trying to listen to his father the ball hit him precisely on the spot where his boil was. The pain was excruciating but he said not a word as he was used to bearing pain in silence. He had become used to being caned at school by his teacher, Hari Ram. Pain was nothing new to him. Just as the ball landed on his boil, he heard his father say, 'Just apply a little balm on the boil and all will be well in a jiffy. Like this!' As he snapped his fingers, something clicked in Gopal's mind. Now he knew how to be rid of his pain.

His mother placed the balm in her sewing basket, where Gopal knew she kept all things she considered valuable. The most carefully guarded thing in that basket was a pair of tweezers, which she used every ten or fifteen days to pull out hair over her forehead to make it appear broader than it was. The white ash she used to apply afterwards at the spots from where she had pulled out the hair was also kept in this basket. However, to be absolutely certain, Gopal lobbed the ball under the bed and while retrieving it made sure that the balm had been duly placed in the sewing basket.

In the afternoon, with Nirmala in tow, he went to the rooftop, where sacks of coal used to be stored under a rain shelter, armed with the small pair of scissors with which his father used to clip his nails, the balm and a bit of cotton cloth that his mother has saved to finish the sewing of his father's loose pyjamas. They sat down on the floor next to the sacks of coal. Nirmala produced the piece of cotton and spread it out on her thigh, over the sleek, silken surface of her shalwar. When Gopal looked at her with his dancing eyes, it seemed as if this eleven-year-old girl, who was lissome as a reed growing on a river bank, was readying herself for a great task. Her little heart, which used to beat in fear of her parents' admonitions and her dolls getting soiled, was now all aflutter with the thought that she was about to view the boil on her brother's thigh. Her ear lobes had gone red and they felt warm.

Gopal, who had not whispered a word about his boil to anyone, had told her his secret and how he had eaten all those mangoes without letting anyone know, how he had not been able to drink any buttermilk after and how this boil as big as a coin had appeared on his thigh. After he had told her his story, he said to her in a confidential voice, 'Look, Nirmala, no one at home is to know this.' A serious look appeared on Nirmala's face. 'I am not mad.' Gopal, being sure that Nirmala would keep the confidence, rolled up his trouser over one leg and showed her the boil, which she touched lightly with her finger, keeping herself at as much distance as she could. She trembled involuntarily, made a whistling noise, looked at the quite red boil and said, 'How red it is!' 'It is going to get even redder,' Gopal bragged with manly courage. 'Really?' Nirmala exclaimed with astonishment. 'This is nothing, the boil I saw on Charanji was much bigger and redder than this,' Gopal replied, while running two of his fingers across the boil. 'So, is it going to grow in size?' Nirmala asked, slipping closer. 'Who knows, it's still growing,' Gopal answered, pulling out the balm from his pocket. Nirmala was scared. 'Will this balm make it right?' Gopal uncovered the balm by peeling away the paper that covered it and shook his head affirmatively. 'One application and it will burst open.' 'Burst open!' Nirmala felt as if a balloon had just popped next to her ear. Her heart was beating fast. 'And whatever is in there will gush out,' Gopal said, dabbing his finger with balm.

Nirmala's pink complexion by now was pale like the Bombay balm. With her heart in her mouth, she asked, 'But why do these boils spring up, brother?' 'By eating things with hot properties,' Gopal replied like an expert physician. Nirmala remembered the two eggs she had eaten two months ago. She began to think. They talked some more and then they got down to the business at hand. With great delicacy, Nirmala cut a perfectly round patch of cloth. It was round like the round roti her mother baked every day. Gopal applied some balm on the round patch, spread it out and examined his boil with great care. Nirmala, bent over Gopal, was watching everything he was doing with great interest. When Gopal placed the patch on his boil, she trembled as if someone had put a piece of ice on her body. 'Will it get better now?' Nirmala asked, but half-questioningly. Gopal had not yet answered her when they heard steps, which were their mother's who was coming up to pick up some coal. Gopal and Nirmala looked at each other at the same time and, without saying a word, hid everything under the box in which their cat Sundri had used to give birth to her kittens. Then without a word, they slunk away.

When Gopal ran down the stairs, his father sent him out on a buying errand. When he returned, he ran into Nirmala on the street. He handed over the cold, sweet drink he had brought for his father to her and went over to Charanji's house. In the process, he forgot to put back the things he and Nirmala had hidden under that box when they had heard their mother walking up. He was at Charanji's quite long, playing cards. After they had had their fill, the two left the room, hand in hand. Something that made Charanji laugh highlighted an old mark on his left cheek, which reminded Gopal of his boil and the things he had hidden under the box. Wresting himself free, he ran towards home.

He studied the situation. His mother was sitting in the courtyard, while his father read out the day's news from the newspaper *Milap*. They were both laughing over something. Gopal went past them and, though they looked at him, they did not say anything. This reassured Gopal that his mother had not taken a look at her sewing basket yet. Quietly, he walked upstairs to the rooftop. He was about to step out on it when something he saw made him stop.

Nirmala was sitting next to the box. Gopal stepped back so that he could see what was up without being seen. With great concentration, Nirmala, her long, thin fingers delicately working the scissors they held, was cutting a piece of cloth into a round patch. After she was done, she applied a little balm on it, then bending her neck, she unbuttoned her shirt to uncover a protrusion on the right side of her chest, which resembled a half bubble in a faucet.

Nirmala blew on the patch and placed it on that slight protrusion.

Translated by Khalid Hasan

Mummy

H ER NAME WAS Stella Jackson, but everyone called her Mummy. A short, active woman in her middle years, whose husband had been killed in the last great war. His pension still came every month.

I had no idea how long she had lived in Poona. The fact was that she was such a fascinating character that after meeting her once, such questions somehow became irrelevant. She herself was all that mattered. To say that she was an integral part of Poona may sound like an exaggeration, but as far as I am concerned all my memories of that city are inextricably linked with her.

I am a very lazy person by nature, yet I do dream about great travels. If you hear me talking, you would think I was about to set out to conquer the Kanchenjunga peak in the Himalayas. It is another matter that once I get there I might decide not to move at all.

I can't really remember how many years I had been in Bombay when I decided one day to take my wife to Poona. Let me work it out. Our first child had been dead four years and it was another four years since I had moved to Bombay. So, actually, I had been living there for eight years, but not once had I taken the trouble to visit the famous Victoria Gardens or the museum. It was therefore quite unusual for me to get up one morning and take off for Poona. I had recently had a tiff at the film studio where I was employed as a writer. I wanted to get away – a change of scene, if you like. For one thing, Poona was not far and there were a number of my old movie friends living there.

We took a train, arrived, scampered out of the station and realized that the Parbhat Nagar suburb where we planned to stay with friends was quite far. We got into a tonga which turned out to be the slowest thing I had ever been in. I hate slowness, be it in men or animals. However, there was no alternative.

We were in no particular hurry to get to Parbhat Nagar, but I was getting impatient with the absurd conveyance we were in. I had never seen anything more ridiculous since Aligarh, which is notorious for its horse-drawn ikkas. The horse moves forward and the passengers slip backwards. Once or twice, I suggested to my wife that perhaps we should walk the rest of the way, or get hold of a better specimen of tonga, but she quite logically observed that there was nothing to choose from between one tonga and the next and, besides, the sun would be unbearable. Wives.

Another equally ridiculous-looking tonga was coming from the opposite direction. Suddenly, I heard someone shout, 'Hey Manto, you big horsie.' It was Chadda, my old friend, huddled in the back with a worn-out woman. My first reaction was regret. What had gone wrong with his aesthetic sense? Running around with a woman old enough to be his mother? I couldn't guess her age, but I noticed that despite her heavy makeup, the wrinkles on her face were visible. It was so grossly painted that it hurt the eye.

I had not seen Chadda for ages. He was one of my best friends and, had he not been with the sort of woman he was with, I would have greeted him with something equally mindless. In any case, both of us got down.

He said to the woman, 'Mummy, just a minute.' He pumped my hand vigorously, then tried to do the same to my extremely formal wife. 'Bhabi, you have performed the impossible, I mean, getting this bundle of lazy bones all the way from Bombay to Poona.'

'Where are you headed for?' I asked.

'On important business. Now, listen, don't waste time. You are going straight to my place.' He began to issue instructions to the tongawala, adding, 'Don't charge the fare. It'll be settled.'

Then he turned to me. 'There is a servant around. See you later.' Without waiting for an answer, he jumped into his tonga, where the woman whom he had called Mummy sat waiting for rum. The embarrassment I had felt earlier was gone.

His house was not far from where we had met. It looked like an old dâk bungalow. 'This is it,' the tongawala said. 'I mean Chadda sarub's house.' I could see from my wife's expression that she was not overly enthusiastic about the prospects. As a matter of fact, she had not been overly enthusiastic about coming to Poona. She was afraid that once there I would team up with my drinking friends and, since I was supposed to be having a change of scene, most of my time would be spent in what was to her highly objectionable company. I got down and asked my wife to follow me, which she did after some hesitation, as it was clear to her that my mind was made up.

It was the kind of house the army likes to requisition for a few weeks and then abandon. The walls were badly in need of paint and the rooms could only have belonged to a careless bachelor, an actor most likely, paid every two or three months – and that, too, in instalments.

I was conscious that this was no place for wives, but there was nothing to do but wait for Chadda, and then move to Parbhat Nagar, where this old friend of mine lived with his wife in more reasonable surroundings.

The servant in a way suited the place. When we arrived we found all the doors open and nobody in sight. When he finally materialized he took no notice of us, as if we had lived there for years. He came into the room and sailed past us without saying a word. I thought he was an out-of-work actor sharing the house with Chadda. However, when he came again and I asked him where the servant was to be found, he informed me gravely that he himself was the holder of that office.

We were both thirsty. When I asked him to get us a drink of water, he began looking for a glass. Finally, he produced a chipped glass mug from the bottom drawer of a cupboard and murmured, 'Only last night, sahib sent for half a dozen glasses. Now what on earth could have happened to them!'

My wife said she did not want a drink after all. He put the mug back exactly where he had unearthed it – in the bottom drawer of the cupboard – as if without this elaborate ritual the entire household would come tumbling down. Then he left the room.

While my wife took one of the armchairs, I made myself comfortable on the bed, which was probably Chadda's. We did not say anything to each other. After some time, Chadda arrived. He was alone. He seemed quite indifferent to the fact that we were his guests.

'What's what old boy,' he said. 'Let's run up to the studio for a few minutes. With you in tow, I'm sure I can pick up an advance, because this evening . . .' Then he looked at my wife. 'Bhabi, I hope you haven't made a mullah out of him.' He laughed. 'To hell with all the mullahs of the world. Come on, Manto, get moving. I am sure bhabi won't mind.'

My wife said nothing, although it wasn't difficult to guess what she was thinking. The studio was not far. After a noisy meeting with Mr Mehta the accountant, Chadda succeeded in making him cough up an advance of two hundred rupees. When we returned to the house, we found my wife sleeping in the armchair. We did not disturb her and moved into the next room, where I noticed everything was either broken or in an advanced state of disrepair. At least it gave the place a uniformity of sorts.

There was dust on everything, an essential touch to the bohemian character of Chadda's lodgings. From somewhere, he found the elusive servant, handed him a hundred rupees and said, 'Prince of Cathay, get us two bottles of third-class rum, I mean, 3-X rum and six new glasses.'

I later discovered that the servant was not only the Prince of Cathay, but the prince of practically every major country and civilization in the world. It all depended on Chadda's mood of the moment.

The Prince of Cathay left, fondling the money he had been given. Lowering himself on the bed, which had a broken spring mattress, Chadda ran his tongue over his lips in anticipation of the rum he had ordered and said, 'What's what. So you did hit Poona after all.' Then he added in a worried voice, 'But what about bhabi? I'm sure she's bloody upset.'

Chadda did not have a wife, but he was always worried about the wives of his friends. He used to say that he had remained single because he felt insecure when dealing with wives. 'When it's suggested to me that I should get married, my first reaction is always positive. Then I start thinking and in a few minutes come to the conclusion that I don't really deserve a wife. And that's how the project gets thrown into cold storage every time,' was one of his favourite explanations.

The rum arrived, and with it, the glasses. Chadda had sent for six, but the Prince of Cathay had dropped three on the way. Chadda was unconcerned. 'Praise be to the Lord that at least the bottles are unharmed,' he observed philosophically.

Then he opened the bottle hurriedly, poured the rum into virgin glasses and toasted me: 'To your arrival in Poona.' We downed our drinks in long swigs. Chadda poured more, then tiptoed into the other room to see if my wife was still asleep. She was. 'This is no good,' he announced 'Let me make some noise so that she wakes up . . . but before that let me organize some tea for her. Prince of Jamaica,' he shouted.

The Prince of Jamaica materialized at once. 'Go to Mummy's place and ask her to kindly prepare some first-class tea and have it sent over. Immediately.'

Chadda drank up, then poured himself a more civilized measure and said, 'For the time being, I am watching my drinking. The first four drinks make me very sentimental and we still have to go to Parbhat Nagar to dump bhabi.'

The tea came, set on a nice tray. Chadda lifted the lid of the teapot, smelled the brew and declared, 'Mummy is a jewel.' Then he sent for the Prince of Ethiopia and began screaming at him. When he was sure that the racket had awakened my wife, he picked up the tray daintily and told me to follow him. He put it down with an exaggerated flourish on a table and announced, 'Tea is served, madam.'

My wife did not appear too amused by Chadda's antics, but she drank two cups and said, not so ill-humouredly, 'I suppose the two of you have already had yours.'

'I must plead guilty to that charge, but we did it in the secure knowledge that we'd find forgiveness,' Chadda said.

My wife smiled, encouraging Chadda to continue. 'Actually, both of us are pigs of the purest breed who are permitted to eat every forbidden fruit on earth. It is therefore time that we took steps to move you to a holier place than this.'

My wife was not amused. She did not care for Chadda. The fact is that she did not care much for any of my friends, especially him because she thought he was always transgressing the limits of what she considered correct behaviour. I don't think it had ever occurred to Chadda how people reacted to him. He considered it a waste of time, like playing indoor games. He beamed at my wife and shouted, 'Prince of Kababistan, get us a Rolls-Royce tonga.'

The Rolls-Royce tonga came and we left for Parbhat Nagar. My friend Harish Kumar was not at home, but his wife was, which we found helpful. Chadda said, 'As melons influence melons, in the same way, wives influence wives. We are off to the studio now, but we will soon return to verify the results.'

Chadda's strategy was always simple. Create so much confusion that enemy forces get no opportunity to plan theirs. He pushed me towards the door, giving my wife no time to object. 'Operation successfully accomplished. What now? Yes, Mummy great Mummy,' Chadda declared.

I wanted to ask him who this Mummy of his was, daughter of what

Tutankhamun, but he began to speak about totally unconnected matters, leaving my question to wither on the vine.

The tonga took us back to the house which was called Saeeda Cottage. Chadda had christened it Kabida Cottage, the abode of the melancholy, as it was his theory that all its residents were in a state of advanced melancholia. Like many of his other theories, this one too was not quite consistent with the facts.

Chadda was not the only resident of Saeeda Cottage. There were others, all actors, and all working for the same film company which paid salaries every third month – in the form of advance. Almost all the inmates of the establishment were assistant directors. There were chief assistant directors, their deputies and assistants who, in turn, had their own assistants. It seemed to me that everyone was everyone's assistant and on the lookout for a financier to help him set up his own film company.

Because of the war, food rationing was in effect, but none of the Saeeda Cottage residents had a ration card. When they had money, they used to buy from the black market at exorbitant prices. They always went to the movies and, during the season, to the races. Some even tried their luck at the stock exchange, but no one had so far made a killing.

Since space was limited, even the garage was used for residential purposes. It was occupied by a family. The husband was not an assistant director, but the film company chauffeur, who kept odd hours. His wife, a good-looking young woman, was named Shireen. She had a little boy who had been collectively adopted by the residents of Saeeda Cottage.

The more liveable rooms in the cottage were occupied by Chadda and two of his friends, both actors, who had yet to make the big time. One was called Saeed, but his professional name was Ranjeet Kumar, a quiet, nice-looking man. Chadda often referred to him as the tortoise because he did everything very, very slowly.

I do not now remember the real name of the other actor, but everybody called him Gharib Nawaz. He came from a well-to-do family of the princely state of Hyderabad. He had come to Poona to get into the movies. He was paid two hundred and fifty rupees a month, but since being hired a year earlier had been paid only once – an advance against salary. The money had gone to rescue Chadda from the clutches of a very angry Pathan moneylender. There was hardly anyone in Saeeda Cottage who did not owe money to Gharib Nawaz.

Despite Chadda's theory, none of them was particularly melancholy. In fact they lived fairly happily, and even when they talked of their straitened circumstances it was in an offhand, cheerful manner.

When Chadda and I returned, we ran into Gharib Nawaz outside the front gate. Chadda pulled out some money from his pocket and gave it to him – without counting – and said, 'Four bottles of Scotch. If I've given you less, then I know you'll make up for it. If I've given you more, I know I'll get it back. Thank you.'

Gharib Nawaz smiled. 'This is Mr – one two,' he said to him, meaning me. 'Detailed discussions are not possible at this stage because he has had a few rums. But wait until the evening when the Scotch begins to flow.'

We went inside. Chadda yawned, picked up the half-empty bottle of rum, took stock of its contents and shouted for the Prince of the Cossacks. There was no answer. 'I think he is drunk,' he observed, pouring himself another drink.

Chadda's room was like an old junk shop. However, it had a window or two, through one of which I now saw Venkutrey the music director, another old friend of mine, peeping in. It was difficult to tell by looking at him what race he belonged to – whether he was Mongol, Negroid, Aryan or something completely unknown to anthropology.

While one particular feature might, for a moment, suggest certain origins, it was immediately cancelled out by another feature, pointing at entirely different possibilities. However, he was from Maharashtra. His nose, unlike that of his famous forebear, the warrior Shivaji, was flat, which he always assured people was a great help in reproducing certain notes.

'Manto seth,' he screamed when he saw me.

'The hell with seths,' Chadda said. 'Don't stand there. Come in.' Venkutrey appeared, put a bottle of rum on the table and said he was at Mummy's when he was told that one of Chadda's friends was in town. 'I was wondering who that could be. Didn't know it was sala Manto the old sinner.'

Chadda slapped his head. 'Shut your trap. You've produced a bottle of rum, that's enough.' Venkutrey picked up my empty glass and poured himself a large measure. 'Manto, this sala Chadda was telling me this morning, "Venkutrey, I want to get drunk tonight. Get some booze." Now I was broke and I was wondering where I was going to get the money.'

'You are an imbecile,' Chadda said.

'Is that so, then where do you think I managed to get this big bucket of rum from? It wasn't a gift from your father, I can tell you that.' He finished his glass. 'What did Mummy say?' Chadda asked. 'Was Polly there, and Thelma . . . and that platinum blonde?'

Chadda didn't wait for his answer. 'Manto, what a bundle of goods that one is! I had always heard of platinum blondes, but by God I had never set eyes on one, that is, until yesterday. She's lovely. Her hair is like threads of fine silver. She is great, Manto. I tell you she's great. Mummy zindabad. Mummy zindabad.' Then he said to Venkutrey, 'You bloody man, say Mummy zindabad.'

Chadda grabbed my arm. 'Manto, I think I am getting very sentimental. You know in tradition the beloved is supposed to have black hair like a rain cloud, but what we have here is an entirely different bill of fare. Her hair is like finely spun silver . . . or maybe not . . . now I don't know what platinum looks like. I have never seen the bloody thing in my life. How can I describe the colour! Just try to imagine blue steel and silver mixed together.'

'And a shot of 3-X rum,' Venkutrey suggested, knocking back his.

'Shut up,' Chadda told him. 'Manto, I am really going bananas over this girl. Oh, the colour of her hair. What are those things fish have on their bellies, or is it all over? The pomfret fish. What are those things called? Damn fish, I think snakes have them too, those tiny, shimmering things. Scales, that's right, they're called scales. In Urdu they're called "khaprey", which is a ridiculous name for something so beautiful. We have a word for them in Punjabi. I know it. Yes . . . "chanay." What a lovely word. It sounds right. It sounds just right. That's what her hair is like . . . small, brilliant, slithering snakes.'

He got up. 'To hell with small, brilliant, slithering snakes. I'm going out of my mind. I'm getting sentimental.'

'What was that?' Venkutrey asked absent-mindedly.

'Beyond your feeble powers of comprehension, my friend,' Chadda replied.

Venkutrey mixed himself another drink. 'Manto, this sala Chadda thinks I don't understand English. You know I'm matriculate. My father loved me. He sent me to . . .'

'Your father was mad. He made you the greatest musician in the world. He twisted your nose and made it flat so that you could sing flat notes. Manto, whenever he has had a couple of drinks, he starts talking about his father. Yes, he's a matriculate, but should I then tear up my BA degree?'

I drank. 'Manto,' Chadda said, 'if I fail to conquer this platinum blonde, I promise you Mr Chadda will renounce the world, go to the highest peak in the Himalayas and contemplate his navel.'

He said he was throwing a big party that night. 'Had you not hit town, that rascal Mehta would never have given me the advance. Well, tonight is the night.' He began to sing in his highly unmusical voice. Before Venkutrey could protest at this most foul murder of music, the door opened to reveal Gharib Nawaz and Ranjeet Kumar, each holding two bottles of Scotch. We poured them some rum.

It turned out that the name of this jewel was Phyllis. She worked in a hairdressing salon and was generally to be seen with a young fellow, who, everybody assured me, looked like a sissy. The entire male population of Saeeda Cottage was infatuated with her.

Gharib Nawaz had declared that morning that he might rush back to Hyderabad, sell some property, return with the proceeds and sweep her off her feet. Chadda's only plus was his good looks. Venkutrey was of the view that she would fall into his lap the moment she heard him sing. Ranjeet Kumar was in favour of a more direct approach. However, in the end, it was clear that success would depend on whom Mummy favoured.

Chadda looked at his watch. 'Let the bloody platinum blonde go to blazes. We have to be in Parbhat Nagar, because I am sure by now Mrs Manto is angry. Now, if I get a sentimental fit in her presence, you'll have to look after me.' He finished his drink and called for the Prince of Egypt, the land of mummies.

The prince appeared, rubbing his eyes as if he had just been disinterred from the earth after hundreds of years. Chadda sprinkled his face with some rum and told him to conjure up two royal Egyptian chariots.

The chariots came and soon we were on our way to Parbhat Nagar. My friend Harish Kumar was home and my wife seemed to be in a good mood. Chadda winked at him as we entered to indicate that something was on the cards for the evening.

Harish asked my wife if she'd like to come to the studio to watch him shoot a couple of scenes. She wanted to know if a musical sequence was being filmed. When told that it would be the next day, she seemed to lose interest. 'Why not tomorrow then?' Harish's wife suggested. The poor woman was sick of taking guests to the studios. She told my wife, 'You look tired. I think you should get some rest.'

Harish said it was a good idea. 'Manto, you'd better come with me to see the studio chief. He has expressed an interest in your writing a film for him.' My wife was pleased. Chadda provided the final touch to the drama. He said he was leaving as he had something important to do. We said our good-byes. When we met later on the road, Chadda shouted lustily, 'Raja Harish Chander zindabad.'

Harish did not come with us. He had to meet his girlfriend.

From the outside, Mummy's house looked like Saeeda Cottage, but the resemblance ended there. I had expected to find myself in a sort of brothel, but it was a perfectly normal, middle-class Christian household. It looked a bit younger than Mummy, perhaps because it was simple and wore no makeup. When she walked in, I felt that while everything around her had remained the same age as the day it was bought, she had moved on and grown old. She was wearing the same bright makeup.

Chadda introduced her briefly: 'This is Mummy the great.' She smiled, then admonished him gently. 'You sent for tea in such an unholy hurry that I am sure Mrs Manto could not have found it drinkable. It was all your friend Chadda's fault,' she told me.

I said the tea was great. Then she said to Chadda, 'I fixed dinner, otherwise you always get impatient at the last moment.' Chadda threw his arms around her. 'You are a jewel, Mummy. Of course we are going to eat that dinner.'

Mummy wanted to know where my wife was. When we told her that she was with friends in Parbhat Nagar, she said, 'That's awful, why didn't you bring her?'

'Because of the party tonight,' Chadda replied.

'What party? I decided to call it off the moment I saw Mrs Manto.'

'What have you done, Mummy?' Chadda exclaimed. 'And to think that we planned this entire charade just for that!'

Then on an impulse he jumped up. 'But you only thought of calling the party off. You didn't actually call it off. As such, hereby I call off your decision to call off the party. Cross your heart.' He drew a cross across Mummy's heart and shouted, 'Hip hip hurray!'

The fact was that Mummy had called off the party. I could also see that she didn't want to disappoint Chadda. She touched him on the cheek affectionately and said, 'Let me see what I can do.'

She left. Chadda's spirits rose. 'General Venkutrey, report to headquarters and arrange immediate transportation of all heavy guns to the battlefront.'

Venkutrey saluted smartly and left for Saeeda Cottage. He was back in ten minutes with the heavy guns – the four bottles of Scotch – with the servant bringing up the rear. 'Come in, come in, my Caucasian prince. The girl with hair the colour of snake scales is coming tonight. You too can try your luck.'

I was thinking about Mummy. Chadda, Gharib Nawaz and Ranjeet Kumar were like little children waiting for their mother who had gone out to buy them toys. Chadda was more confident because he was the favourite child and he knew that he would get the best toy. The others were not altogether without hope. Every situation has its own music. The one in Mummy's home had no harsh notes. Drinking seemed perfectly normal. It was like imbibing milk.

Her makeup still bothered me, however. Why did she have to paint her face like that? It was an insult to the love she showered with such generosity on Chadda, Gharib Nawaz and Venkutrey . . . and who knew how many more.

I asked Chadda, 'Why does your Mummy look so flashy?'

'Because the world likes flashy things. There are not many idiots around like you and me who wish colours to be sober and understated, music to be soft, who don't want to see youth clad in the garments of childhood and age in the mantle of youth. We who call ourselves artists are actually second-class asses, because there is nothing first class on this earth. It is either third or second class, except . . . except Phyllis. She alone is first class.'

Venkutrey poured his drink over Chadda's head. 'Snakes scales . . . you have gone mad.'

Chadda lapped it up. 'This has cooled me down.'

Venkutrey began his long, rambling story about how much his father loved him, but Chadda was having none of that.

'To hell with your entire family,' he said. 'I want to talk about Phyllis.' He looked at Gharib Nawaz and Ranjeet Kumar, who were huddled together in a corner whispering in each other's ears. 'You leaders of the great gunpowder plot, your conspiracies will never succeed. Victory in battle will kiss Chadda's feet. Isn't that so, my Prince of Wales?'

The Prince of Wales seemed more worried about the bottle of rum, which was getting emptier by the minute. Chadda laughed and poured him a hefty measure.

The lights had been switched on, and outside, evening had fallen. Then we heard Mummy on the veranda. Chadda shouted a slogan and ran out. Ranjeet Kumar and Gharib Nawaz exchanged glances, waiting for the door to open.

Mummy came in, followed by four or five Anglo-Indian girls – Polly, Dolly, Kitty, Elma, Thelma – and a young man who answered to the description that had been provided to me of Phyllis's friend.

Phyllis was the last to appear. Chadda had his arm around her. He had already declared victory. Gharib Nawaz and Ranjeet Kumar looked positively unhappy at this unsporting behaviour.

All hell broke loose. Suddenly everyone was jabbering away in

English, trying to impress the girls. Venkutrey failed his matriculation several times in a row. Soon he went into a corner with Thelma, offering free instruction in Indian classical dance.

Chadda was surrounded by a bevy of giggling girls. He was reciting dirty limericks which he knew by the hundred. Mummy was busy with her arrangements. Ranjeet Kumar sat alone, smoking cigarette after cigarette. Gharib Nawaz was asking Mummy if she needed any money.

The Scotch was brought in ceremoniously. Phyllis was offered a drink, but she shook her head. She said she did not like whisky. Even Chadda was refused. Finally, Mummy prepared a light drink, put the glass to her lips and said, 'Now be a brave girl and gulp it down.'

Chadda was so thrilled that he recited another twenty limericks. I was thinking. Man must have got bored with nakedness when he decided to don clothes, which is why sometimes he gets bored with them and reverts to his original state. The reaction to good manners is certainly bad manners.

I watched Mummy. She was surrounded by the girls and was giggling with the rest of them at Chadda's antics. She was wearing the same vulgar, tasteless makeup under which her wrinkles could be seen in high relief. She looked happy. I wondered why people thought escape to be a bad thing. Here was an act of escape. The exterior was unattractive, but the soul was beautiful. Did she need all those unguents, lotions and colouring liquids?

Polly was telling Ranjeet Kumar about her new dress, which she had picked up as a bargain and altered at home. And now it was perfectly lovely. Ranjeet Kumar was offering to buy her two new ones, although he was unlikely to get an advance in the near future. Dolly was trying to talk

Gharib Nawaz into lending her some more money. He knew perfectly well that he would never see it again, but was still trying to convince himself to the contrary.

Thelma was being tutored in the intricacies of Indian classical dance by Venkutrey, who knew that she would never make a dancer. She knew that too, but she was still listening to him with great concentration. Elma and Kitty were drinking steadily.

In this tableau it was difficult to be sure about the rights and wrongs. Was Mummy's flashiness right or a part of the situation? Who could say? In her heart there was love for everyone. Perhaps she had coloured her face, I said to myself, so that the world should not see what she was really like. Maybe she did not have the emotional strength to play mother to the whole world. She had just chosen a few.

Mummy did not know that during her absence in the kitchen, Chadda had persuaded Phyllis to take a massive drink, not on the sly, but in front of the others. Phyllis was slightly high, but only slightly. Her hair was like polished steel, waving gently from side to side like her young sinuous body.

It was midnight. Venkutrey was no longer trying to make a classical dancer out of Thelma. Now he was telling her about his father, who loved him to the point of distraction. Gharib Nawaz had forgotten that he had already lent some more money to Dolly. Ranjeet Kumar had disappeared with Polly. Elma and Kitty were sleepy.

Around the table sat Phyllis, her friend and Mummy. Chadda was no longer sentimental. He sat next to Phyllis and it was evident he was determined to take her tonight.

At some point, Phyllis's friend got up, laid himself down on the sofa and went to sleep. Gharib Nawaz and Dolly left the room. Elma and Kitty said their goodnights and went home. Venkutrey, after praising his wife's beauty one more time, cast a longing look at Phyllis, put his arm around Thelma and took her out into the garden.

Suddenly a loud argument developed between Mummy and Chadda. He was drunk, angry and foul-mouthed. He had never spoken to her like that. Phyllis had given up her feeble efforts to make peace between the two. Chadda wanted to take her to Saeeda Cottage and Mummy had told him that she would not permit that. He was screaming at her now. 'You old pimp, you have gone mad. Phyllis is mine. Ask her.'

'Chadda, my son, why don't you understand? She is young, she is very young,' Mummy said to him, but Chadda was beyond reason. For the first time it occurred to me how young Phyllis was, hardly fifteen. Her face was like a raindrop surrounded by silver clouds.

Chadda pulled Phyllis towards him, squeezed her against his chest in a passionate B-grade movie embrace. 'Chadda, leave her alone. For God's sake let her go,' Mummy screamed, but he paid no attention to her.

Then it happened. She slapped him across the face. 'Get out, get out!' she shouted.

Chadda pushed Phyllis aside, gave Mummy a furious look and walked out. I followed him.

When I arrived at Saeeda Cottage, he was lying on his bed, face down, fully clothed. We did not speak. I went to my room and slept.

I got up late the next morning. Chadda was not in his room. I washed and as I was coming out of the bathroom I heard his voice outside. 'She is unique. By God, she is great. You should pray that when you reach her age you should become like her.'

I did not want to hang around much longer. I waited for him to come back to the house, but after about half an hour I left for Parbhat Nagar.

Harish hadn't returned home. I told his wife that we had had a late night, so he had decided to sleep at Saeeda Cottage. We took our leave and on the way I told my wife about the night's incident. Her theory was that Phyllis was either related to Mummy or the old woman wanted to save her for some better client. I kept quiet.

After several weeks I had a letter from Chadda. All it said was, 'I behaved like a beast that evening. Damn me.'

I went to Poona a few months later on business. When I called at Saeeda Cottage, Chadda was out. Gharib Nawaz was playing with Shireen's son. We shook hands. I learnt from him that Chadda hadn't spoken to Mummy after that night, nor had she visited Saeeda Cottage.

She had sent Phyllis back to her parents. It turned out that she had run away from home with that young fellow. Ranjeet Kumar – who had just walked in – was confident that had Phyllis stayed on, he would have scored. Gharib Nawaz had no such illusions, but he was sorry she was gone.

They said Chadda had not been well for some time, but refused to see a doctor. As we were talking, Venkutrey rushed in. He looked very nervous. He had met Chadda on the street, found him feeling groggy and put him in a tonga to get him home, but Chadda had fainted on the way. We ran out. Chadda lay in the tonga looking very ill. We brought him in. He was unconscious.

I told Gharib Nawaz to get a doctor. He consulted Venkutrey and left. They returned a little later with Mummy. 'What has happened to my son?' she asked. 'What kind of friends are you? Why didn't you send me word?' she said.

She immediately took charge. 'Get hold of some ice and rub his forehead. Massage his feet. Fan his face.' Then she went out to get a doctor. Everyone looked relieved, as if the entire responsibility of bringing Chadda back to health was now Mummy's.

Chadda had begun to regain consciousness when Mummy returned with the doctor. The doctor examined him, then took Mummy aside. She told us there was no cause for worry. Chadda was still a bit disoriented. He saw Mummy. He took her hand in his and said, 'Mummy, you are great.'

She ran her hand gently over Chadda's burning face. 'My son, my poor son,' she said.

Tears came to Chadda's eyes. 'Don't say that. Your son is a scoundrel of the first order. Go get your husband's old service revolver and shoot him.'

'Don't talk rubbish,' she said. She rose. 'Boys, Chadda is very ill. I'm going to take him to the hospital.'

Gharib Nawaz sent for a taxi. Chadda could not understand why he was being taken to hospital, but Mummy told him that he would be more comfortable there than at home. 'It's nothing,' she said.

He was laid up for many days, with Mummy spending most of her time with him. However, he did not seem to be getting better. His skin had become sallow and he was losing strength. The doctors were of the view that he should be taken to Bombay, but Mummy said, 'No, I'm going to take him home and he's going to get well.'

I had to leave Poona, but I phoned from Bombay every other day. I had started to lose hope, but slowly, very slowly, Chadda began to come round. I had to go to Lahore for a few weeks. When I returned to Bombay there was a letter from Chadda. 'The great Mummy has reclaimed her unworthy son from the dead,' he had written. There was so much love in that line. When I told my wife, she observed icily, 'Such women are generally good at these things.'

I wrote to Chadda a few times, but he didn't answer. Later, somebody told me that Mummy had sent him to the hills to stay with friends. He was soon better – and bored – and returned to Poona. I was there that day.

He looked weak, but nothing else had changed. He talked about his illness as if he had had a minor bicycle accident. Saeeda Cottage had seen a few changes in his absence. A Bengali music director called Sen had moved in. He shared his room with Ram Singh, a young boy from Lahore who had come to Bombay, like so many others, to get into films.

Ranjeet Kumar had been picked up to play the lead in a movie. He had been promised the direction of the next one, provided the one under production did well. Chadda had finally managed to raise an advance of one thousand five hundred rupees from the studio. Gharib Nawaz had just come back from Hyderabad and the general finances of Saeeda Cottage were in good shape as a result of that. Shireen's boy had new clothes and new toys.

My friend Harish was currently trying to seduce his new leading lady, who was from Punjab. He was, however, afraid of her husband, who had a formidable moustache and looked like a wrestler. Chadda's advice to Harish had been sound: 'Don't worry about him at all. He may be a wrestler, but in the field of love he is bound to fall flat on his face. All you need to learn are a few heavyweight Punjabi swear words from me. I'll settle for one hundred rupees per lesson. You'll need them in awkward situations.'

Harish had struck a deal and, at the rate of a bottle of rum per choice Punjabi swear word, had learnt half a dozen of them. However, there had been no occasion to test his new powers. His affair was doing well without them.

Mummy's parties had been reconvened and the old crowd – Polly, Dolly, Elma, Thelma etc. – was back. Venkutrey had still not given up his efforts to induct Thelma into the mysteries of Indian classical dance. Gharib Nawaz was still lending money and Ranjeet Kumar, who was about to hit the big screen, was using his new position to ingratiate himself with the girls. Chadda's dirty limericks were still flowing.

There was only one thing missing – the girl with the platinum blonde hair, the colour of snake scales and blue steel and silver. Chadda never mentioned her. Occasionally, one would see him looking at Mummy, then lowering his eyes, recalling the events of that night. Off and on, after his fourth drink, he would say, 'Chadda, you are a damned brute.'

Mummy was still the Mummy – Polly's Mummy, Dolly's Mummy, Chadda's Mummy, Ranjeet Kumar's Mummy – still the wonderful manageress of her unique establishment. Her makeup was still flashy, and her clothes even flashier. Her wrinkles still showed, but for me they had come to assume a sacred dimension.

It was Mummy who had come to the rescue of Venkutrey's wife when she had had a miscarriage. She had taken charge of Thelma when she had caught a dangerous infection from a dance director who had promised to put her in the movies. Recently, Kitty had won five hundred rupees in a crossword puzzle competition and Mummy had persuaded her to give some of it to Gharib Nawaz, who was a bit short. 'Give it to him now and you can keep taking it back,' she had advised her.

There was only one man she didn't like: the music director Sen. She had told Chadda repeatedly, 'Don't bring him to my house. There is something about him that makes me uneasy. He doesn't fit.'

I returned to Bombay carrying with me the warmth of Mummy's parties. Her world was simple and beautiful and reassuring. Yes, there was drinking and sex and a general lack of seriousness, but one felt no emotional unease. It was like the protruding belly of a pregnant woman: a bit odd, but perfectly innocent and immediately comprehensible.

One day I read in the papers that the music director Sen had been found murdered in Saeeda Cottage. The suspect was said to be a young man named Ram Singh.

Chadda wrote me an account of the incident later.

'I was sound asleep that night. Suddenly, I felt someone slump into my bed. It was Sen. He was covered in blood. Then Ram Singh rushed into the room holding a knife. By this time, everyone was up. Ranjeet Kumar and Gharib Nawaz ran in and disarmed Ram Singh. Sen's breathing grew uneven and then stopped. "Is he dead?" Ram Singh asked. I nodded my head. "Please let go of me. I won't run away," he said calmly.

'We didn't know what to do, so we immediately sent for Mummy. She took stock of the situation in her unruffled manner and escorted Ram Singh to the police, where he made a statement confessing to the killing. The next few weeks were awful. Police, courts, lawyers, the works. There was a trial and the court acquitted Ram Singh.

'He had made the same statement under oath that he had made to the police. Mummy had said to him, "Son, speak the truth. Tell them what happened." Ram Singh had spoken the truth. He had told the court that Sen had promised to get him to sing for films, provided he would sleep with him. He had let himself be persuaded, but was always troubled by what he was doing. One day he had told Sen that if he tried to force him to perform the unnatural act again, he would kill him. And that was exactly what had happened that night. Sen had tried to force him and Ram Singh had stabbed him repeatedly with a kitchen knife.'

Chadda had written, 'In this age of untruth, the triumph of truth is astonishing.'

A party had been organized to celebrate Ram Singh's acquittal and when it was over Mummy had suggested that he should return to his parents in Lahore. Gharib Nawaz had bought him a ticket and Shireen had prepared food for him to take on the long journey. Everyone had gone to the station to see him off.

A week or so after this, I was asked by the studio to come to Poona to complete an assignment. Nothing had changed at Saeeda Cottage. It was still the way it always was. When I arrived, a minor party was in progress to celebrate the birth of another son to Shireen. Venkutrey had got hold of two tins of Glaxo baby food from somewhere, not an easy thing at the time. Suggestions were also being invited on a name for the child.

Everybody was trying to look cheerful, but I couldn't help feeling that there was something the matter with Chadda, Gharib Nawaz and Ranjeet Kumar. A vague sadness hung in the air. Was it the weather which was beginning to turn chilly or was it Sen's murder? I could not decide.

For one week I was shut up in Harish's house because I was in a hurry to complete my assignment. I was a bit surprised that Chadda hadn't come to see me all this time, nor Gharib Nawaz for that matter.

Then one afternoon Chadda burst into the house. 'This rubbish you've been writing, have you been paid something for it yet?' he asked. I told him I had received two thousand rupees only the other day and the money was in my jacket. He took out four hundred rupees and rushed out, pausing just long enough to tell me that there was a party at Mummy's house that evening and I was expected.

When I arrived, it was already in full swing. Ranjeet and Venkutrey were dancing with Polly and Thelma. Kitty was dancing with Elma, and Chadda was jumping around like a rabbit with Mummy in his arms. Everyone was quite drunk. My entrance was greeted with guffaws and cheers. Mummy, who had always maintained a certain formality with me, took hold of my hand and said, 'Kiss me, dear.'

'That's enough dancing,' Chadda announced above the din. 'I want to do some serious drinking now. Open a new bottle, my Prince of Scotland.' The prince, who was very drunk, appeared with a bottle and dropped it on the floor. 'It is only a bottle, Mummy. What about broken hearts?' Chadda said before she could scold the servant.

A chill fell over the party. A new bottle was duly produced. Chadda poured everyone a huge drink. Then he began to make a speech: 'Ladies and gentlemen, we have among us this evening this man called Manto. He thinks he's great story writer, but I think that's rubbish. He claims that he can fathom the depths of the human soul. That too is a lot of rubbish. This world is full of rubbish. I met someone yesterday after ten years and he assured me that we had met only the other week. That too is rubbish. That man was from Hyderabad. I pronounce a million curses on the Nizam of Hyderabad who has tons of gold but no Mummy.'

Someone shouted, 'Manto zindabad,' but Chadda continued with his speech. 'This is a conspiracy hatched by Manto, otherwise my instructions were clear. We should have greeted him with catcalls. I have been betrayed. But let me talk of that evening when I behaved like a beast with Mummy because of that girl with hair the colour of snake scales. Who did I think I was? Don Juan?

'Be that as it may, but it could have been done. With one kiss, I could have sucked in all her virginity with these big fat lips of mine. She was very young, very weak . . . what's the word, Manto? . . . yes, very unformed. After a night of love, she would either have carried the guilt with her the rest of her life, or she would have completely forgotten about it the next morning.

'I am glad Mummy threw me out that night. Ladies and gentlemen, now I end my speech. I've already talked lot of rubbish. Actually, I was planning a longer speech, but I can't speak any longer. I'm going to get myself a drink.'

Nobody spoke. It occurred to me that he had been heard in complete silence. Mummy also looked a bit lost. Chadda sat there nursing his drink. He was quiet. His speech seemed to have drained him out. 'What's with you?' I asked.

'I don't know – tonight the whisky is not battering in the buttocks of my brain as it always does,' he answered philosophically.

The clock struck two. Chadda, who in the meanwhile had begun a dance with Kitty, pushed her aside and said to Venkutrey, 'Sing us something, but I warn you, none of your classical mumbo-jumbo.'

Venkutrey sang a couple of songs, set to the melancholy evening raga Malkauns. The atmosphere grew even sadder.

Gharib Nawaz was so moved that his eyes became wet. 'These Hyderabadis have weak eye-bladders. You never know when they might start dripping,' Chadda observed. Gharib Nawaz wiped his eyes and took Elma on to the floor. Venkutrey put a record on. Chadda picked up Mummy and began to bounce around.

At four o'clock, Chadda suddenly said, 'That's it.' He picked up a bottle from the table, put it to his mouth and drank what was left of it. 'Let's go, Manto.'

When I tried to say goodbye to Mummy, he pulled me away. 'There are going to be no goodbyes tonight.'

When we were outside, I thought I heard Venkutrey crying. I wanted to go back, but Chadda stopped me. 'He too has a faulty eye-bladder.'

Saeeda Cottage was only a few minutes' walk. We did not speak. Before going to bed, I tried to ask Chadda about the strange party, but he said he was sleepy.

When I got up the next morning, I found Gharib Nawaz standing outside the garage wiping his eyes.

'What's the matter?' I asked him.

'Mummy's gone.'

'Where?'

'I don't know.'

Chadda was still in bed, but it seemed he hadn't slept at all. He smiled when I asked him if it was true. 'Yes, she's gone. Had to leave Poona by the morning train.'

'But why?' I asked.

'Because the authorities did not approve of her ways. Her parties were considered objectionable, outside the limits of the law. The police tried to blackmail her. They offered to leave her alone if she would do their dirty work for them. They wanted to use her as a procuress, an agent. She refused. Then they dug up an old case they had registered against her. They had her charged with moral turpitude and running a house of ill repute and they obtained court orders expelling her from Poona.

'If she was a procuress, a madam, and her presence was bad for society's health, then she should have been done away with altogether. Why, if she was a heap of filth, was she removed from Poona and ordered to be dumped elsewhere?'

He laughed bitterly. 'Manto, with her a purity has vanished from our lives. Do you remember that awful night? She cleansed me of my lust and meanness. I am sorry she's gone, but I shouldn't be sorry. She has only left Poona. She will go elsewhere and meet more young men like me and she will cleanse their souls and make them whole. I hereby bestow my Mummy on them.

'Now, let's go and look for Gharib Nawaz. He must have cried himself hoarse. As I told you, these Hyderabadis have weak eye-bladders. You never know when they might start dripping.'

I looked at Chadda. Tears were floating in his eyes like corpses in a river.

Translated by Khalid Hasan

Yazeed

T HE TUMULTUOUS EVENTS of 1947 came and flitted away like a few
bad days appearing unexpectedly in an otherwise pleasant season.
Karim Dad hadn't simply attributed the upheavals to Providence, sat
back complacently and done nothing; rather, he had faced the storm val-
iantly, like a man. He sparred with the enemy forces quite a few times,
not so much to bring them to their knees, but only to offer vigorous
resistance. He knew the enemy was far too powerful, but he also knew
that to lay down his arms would be an insult not just to himself but to
every man. This, at any rate, was how others thought of him, those who
had seen him fighting with those brutes and willingly putting his life in
harm's way. But if you asked Karim Dad whether he considered putting
down his weapons before the enemy an insult, he would think long and
hard, as though pondering a difficult mathematical question.

He didn't know how to add or subtract, any more than how to multiply
or divide. After the riots of '47 were over, people sat down to take stock
of the losses, both human and material. Karim Dad didn't involve himself
in this computation. All he knew was that the war had claimed the life of

his father Rahim Dad, whose corpse he had carried on his shoulders and laid to rest in the grave he had dug by a well with his own hands.

There had been more incidents like this in the village. Hundreds of young and old men had been butchered; several girls abducted, some brutally raped. Those who had suffered these wounds were crying as much over their own ill fate as over the exceptional ruthlessness of the enemy. But not a single tear was ever spotted in Karim Dad's eyes. He was proud of his father's gallantry. Exhausted from fighting against a pack of rioters armed with dozens of lances and hatchets, the old man's strength had given out and he had fallen. When the news of his death was brought to Karim Dad, he merely addressed his father's spirit thus: 'Look, yaar, this isn't a nice thing to do. Didn't I tell you to carry some weapon on you at all times!'

He then dug a pit by the well and interred his father's dead body. Standing by the grave, he uttered a few words by way of the Fatiha: 'Only God knows best about sins and recompense. But let me just wish you Paradise!'

The rioters had dispatched Rahim Dad – who had been not just a father but also a great friend to Karim Dad – with such fiendish cruelty, that any time people recalled his savage murder, they never failed to hurl obscenities at the murderers. At such times Karim Dad never spoke a word. Several of his flourishing grain fields had been completely laid to waste and two houses reduced to ashes, yet Karim Dad didn't spare his losses a second thought. Now and then, though, one did hear him utter this much: 'Whatever happened was due to our own failings.' When asked what those failings were, he chose to remain silent.

While the village folks were still lamenting over their dead, Karim Dad got himself married to the same blossoming Jaina he'd had his eyes on for some time. Jaina was grieving. Her brother, a strapping youth, had been killed in the riots. He had been the only person left whom she could count on for support since the death of their parents. That she also loved Karim Dad dearly was beyond doubt, but the pain of losing her brother had cast a pall over that love somewhat. Her eyes, lively and smiling before, now never seemed free of tears.

Karim Dad couldn't stand wailing and crying at all. The sight of a doleful Jaina annoyed him, but he chose not to mention it to her, thinking that, tender-hearted woman that she was, his words might hurt her feelings even more. However, one day he couldn't hold back any more. He caught up with her in the field and gave her a piece of his mind. 'Look, it's been a whole year since the dead were shrouded and buried. Even they are probably tired of all this keening and wailing over them. Let go of it, my dear. Who knows how many more deaths we're fated to see in this life. Save some tears for the future.'

Jaina took umbrage at his words, but what could she do? She was deeply in love with the man. During long bouts of solitude, she tried her best to conjure up some meaning in his words and, eventually, convinced herself that what he had said wasn't all that unreasonable after all.

The elders opposed their marriage when the proposal was run past them; however, their opposition turned out to be quite weak. Excessive mourning had sapped their energies so completely that they couldn't even hold on to oppositions that had every chance of success. And so Karim Dad got married. With the customary wedding fanfare and music, and after every ceremony was duly performed, Karim Dad brought his beloved Jaina home as his bride.

Since the rioting a year ago, the whole village had assumed something of the depressing air of a cemetery. Thus, when Karim Dad's marriage arrangements got under way with a lot of hullabaloo and excitement, a vague feeling of trepidation swept over some people. They cringed and felt as though it wasn't Karim Dad's but some malicious spirit's wedding procession that was unfolding before them. Some friends informed Karim Dad about this reaction and he laughed his head off. One day, jokingly, he mentioned it to his new bride, who instantly began quaking with alarm.

'Well,' he said to Jaina, taking hold of her wrist with its beautiful, bright bracelet, 'you can't escape. You're stuck with this ghost for the rest of your life. Even Rahman Sain's hocus-pocus can't rid you of him.'

Jaina stuck her hennaed finger between her teeth, blushed a little, and got out only this much, 'Kaimay, nothing seems to frighten you!'

Karim Dad ran the tip of his tongue over his reddish-brown moustache and smiled broadly. 'What is there to frighten anyone? Fear doesn't exist.'

By now, Jaina's grief had subsided quite a bit. She was soon to be a mother. To see her in the fullness of her blossoming youth made Karim Dad enormously happy. He would say to her, 'You were never so stunningly beautiful before, Jaina, I swear. If all this beauty is only for the sake of the baby who's coming, I'll have to fight with that little rascal, I'm telling you.'

Jaina would blush and quickly cover her big, bulging belly with her chador, which made him laugh and tease her even more. 'Why are you hiding that thief? Don't I know that all this dolling up is just for that little swine?'

At that Jaina would become serious. 'Why are you swearing at the baby? After all it's your own.'

'And Karim Dad is the biggest swine of them all,' he would say, his reddish-brown moustache quivering from the rumble of his laughter.

The 'Little' Eid came along, followed a couple of months later by the 'Big' Eid. Karim Dad celebrated both with equal fanfare and great fuss. The rioters had attacked his village twelve days before the Big Eid and his father Rahim Dad and Jaina's brother Fazl Ilahi had both been murdered in that attack. Jaina cried a lot as she remembered their killings but, realizing how Karim Dad was predisposed to put any tragedy behind him, she couldn't grieve as much as her own temperament called for.

Sometimes when she thought about it, she wondered how she could have begun to forget the most tragic incident of her life so imperceptibly. She had absolutely no memory of how her parents had died. Fazl Ilahi was six years older than her. He wasn't just a brother; he had been both father and mother to her. She was absolutely sure that it was for her sake alone that he hadn't married. And it was to save her honour that he had lost his life fighting the enemy – a fact known to the whole village. His death was truly the greatest catastrophe of her life, a veritable hell suddenly let loose upon her just twelve days before the Big Eid. Whenever she thought about that calamity now, the realization that she was drifting further away from its effects never failed to surprise her.

As the month of Muharram approached, for the first time Jaina expressed her desire to Karim Dad. She was very interested in seeing the decorated horse and the *taziyas* of Muharram. She had heard a lot about them from her girlfriends. She asked Karim Dad, 'If I'm feeling up to it, will you take me to see the Muharram horse?'

'I will, even if you aren't feeling well, and the swine too,' he replied with a smile.

She hated the word 'swine', took immediate offence to it and often lost her cool. But it was uttered with such endearing honesty that her bitterness was instantly transformed into an indescribable sweetness and she would begin to see how the word 'swine' could be filled with genuine affection and love.

The rumour of an imminent war between India and Pakistan had been circulating for quite some time. Actually, almost as soon as Pakistan was established it had been taken for granted that there would definitely be a war, but *when* was something the inhabitants of the village couldn't say with any certainty. If anyone asked Karim Dad about it, his short answer invariably was, 'It will be when it will be. What's the point of losing sleep over it?'

But whenever Jaina heard about that dreaded event, it knocked the living daylights out of her. She was a peace-loving woman by nature. Even ordinary squabbles made her terribly nervous. Besides, during the previous mayhem she'd been witness to a great deal of carnage and bloodshed. Her own brother, Fazl Ilahi, had been mowed down in one such riot. She would cringe with an unknown fear and ask, 'Kaimay, what will it be?'

Karim Dad would smile. 'How would I know? Maybe a boy, maybe a girl.'

Such a cheerful reply made her feel even more helpless. Soon she would forget all about the dreaded war, focusing all her attention on whatever else Karim Dad was saying. He was a strong, fearless man who loved Jaina very much. After buying himself a rifle, he had quickly become an expert marksman. These things kept her spirits up. But now and then, when she was by the waterfront and heard from a terrified girlfriend of the rumours about war being spread by the village folk, she would instantly go into a daze.

One day, Bakhtu the midwife came for Jaina's daily check-up and brought along the news that the Indians were about to stop the river. Jaina couldn't understand. She asked, 'About to stop the river . . . which river?'

'The one that waters our fields.'

Jaina thought for a while and then said with a smile, 'Mausi, have you gone mad? Who can stop rivers? They aren't just any old street drain.'

Rubbing Jaina's belly gently, Bakhtu replied, 'Bibi, I don't know. I'm just telling you what I heard. This information has even appeared in newspapers.'

'What information?' Jaina was still finding it hard to believe.

Feeling Jaina's stomach with her wrinkled hand, the old woman said, 'The same . . . about stopping the river.' Then she pulled Jaina's shirt down over her stomach and said with the confidence of a seasoned obstetrician, 'God willing, you'll have your baby in exactly ten days.'

When Karim Dad came home, the first thing Jaina asked him about was this rumour about the river. At first he tried to evade the question, but when she persisted, he said casually, 'Yes, I've heard something like that.'

'Like what?'

'Just that the Hindustan-wallahs will divert the waters of our rivers.'

'Why?'

'To ruin our crops,' Karim Dad replied.

The answer convinced Jaina that rivers could be stopped from flowing. With a feeling of utter despondency she merely said, 'How cruel they are.'

This time around, Karim Dad took some time to smile. 'But tell me, did Mausi Bakhtu visit you today?'

'She did,' Jaina replied half-heartedly.

'What did she say?'

'That the baby will be born exactly ten days from today.'

'Zindabad!' Karim Dad cried out boisterously.

Jaina was furious. She muttered, 'You're making merry, while only God knows what calamity awaits us.'

Karim Dad got up and left for the *chaupal*. Here, practically all the men of the village were crowding around Chaudhry Natthu asking him about this news of cutting off the water to their river. One man was roundly swearing at Pandit Nehru, another was cursing Indians without letting up, a third was persistently denying that the waters of a river could be diverted. There were also some in whose opinion what lay ahead was punishment for their own sins, best averted by collective prayer in the mosque.

Karim Dad sat quietly in a corner listening to their exchange. Chaudhry Natthu was the most effusive among those swearing at the Indians. Karim Dad was shifting so often in his seat that it gave the impression this sort of conversation was making him very nervous. The men were all saying with one voice that cutting off the water was a very nasty act indeed, the height of meanness, downright vile, a most horrid oppression, a sin, the very same conduct as Yazeed's.

Karim Dad cleared his throat a few times as if preparing to say something. When another volley of the coarsest obscenities rose to the Chaudhry's mouth, he yelled, 'Chaudhry, don't call anyone bad names!'

The swear word for doing something to the lower anatomy of the Indians' mother caught in the Chaudhry's throat. He turned around and directed a mighty strange look towards Karim Dad, who, meanwhile, had busied himself arranging his turban on his head. 'Huh . . .what did you say?'

In a soft but firm voice Karim Dad responded, 'Just that you shouldn't swear at anyone.'

The word that was caught in the Chaudhry's throat now shot out of his mouth with incredible force. He asked sharply, '*Anyone?* Who the hell are they to you?'

Now the Chaudhry addressed the folks gathered in the chaupal. 'You heard him, didn't you? He says don't rebuke anyone. Ask him: Who are they to him?'

With tremendous poise and self-control Karim Dad replied, 'Who are they to me? Well, they are my enemies.'

Something resembling raucous laughter rose from the Chaudhry's throat so loudly that the bristles of his moustache flew to either side of his lips from the force. 'You heard him. They're his enemies. So we should love them. Right, boy?'

And Karim Dad, in the manner of a deferential boy, answered, 'No, Chaudhry, I'm not asking you to love them. I only ask that they shouldn't be called bad names.'

Karim Dad's bosom buddy Miran Bakhsh, who was sitting right next to him, asked, 'Why?'

'What's the point of it, yaar? They want to make your fields barren and you think that all you need in order to get even with them is a few insults. That isn't smart, is it? Insults are the recourse of people who have run out of answers.'

'And you, do you have an answer?' asked Miran Bakhsh.

'Whether I have one or not is not the issue,' Karim Dad said after a pause. 'This matter concerns tens of thousands, indeed hundreds of thousands. A single person's answer can't stand as the answer for everyone. Such matters require a lot of deep thought and deliberation . . . to devise a solid plan of action. They cannot divert the course of the water in one day. It'll take them years. And, pray tell, is your strategy simply to hurl obscenities at them for a few minutes and let out all your rage?' He put his hand on Miran Bakhsh's shoulder and added with genuine affection, 'All I know, yaar, is that, somehow, even calling Hindustan mean, despicable, vile and tyrannical is wrong.'

'Listen to this!' Chaudhry Natthu blurted out instead of Miran Bakhsh.

However, Karim Dad continued his conversation with Miran Bakhsh. 'It's foolishness to expect mercy from the enemy. Once the battle has begun, lamenting that the enemy is using large-bore rifles while we have small-bore, that our bombs are fairly small and theirs are much larger . . . Tell me, honestly, is that any kind of complaint? Whether it's a small knife or a large knife, both can be used to kill. Am I wrong?'

It was the Chaudhry, again, who started thinking, but got discombobulated in a second. 'But the issue . . . ' he said with irritation, 'the issue is that they're stopping the water. They want to starve us to death.'

Karim Dad removed his hand from Miran Bakhsh's shoulder and spoke directly to the Chaudhry. 'Chaudhry, when you've designated someone as your enemy, why complain that he wants to kill you be means of hunger and thirst? Did you think he would send you great big pots of sumptuous pilafs and pitchers of ice-cooled fruit juice from across the border, rather than laying waste to your lush fields and crops? Did you think he would plant gardens for your enjoyment?'

The Chaudhry lost his cool. 'Damn you, what nonsense is this?'

Miran Bakhsh, too, asked Karim Dad softly, 'Yes, yaar, what nonsense is this?'

'It isn't nonsense, Miran Bakhsha,' Karim Dad attempted to reason with his friend. 'Just think a little: In a battle what wouldn't one opponent do to defeat the other. When a wrestler, all set for the bout, descends into the arena, he has every right to use whatever manoeuvres he sees fit . . ."

'Makes sense,' Miran Bakhsh agreed, shaking his shaven head.

Karim Dad smiled. 'Well then, stopping the river also makes sense. For us it's an atrocity, but for them it's entirely admissible.'

'You call it admissible?' the Chaudhry butted in. 'When your tongue is hanging out from thirst, we'll see whether such an atrocity is still admissible. When your kids are begging for a single morsel of food, will you still call it admissible?'

Karim Dad ran his tongue over his parched lips and replied, 'Yes, Chaudhry, even then. Why do you only remember that he's our enemy and conveniently forget that we're just as much his enemy? If we had it in our power, we would cut his food and water supply too. Now that the enemy is able and about to do that, we'll certainly have to think of a way to counter his move. And futile name-calling won't do that. The enemy won't send rivers of milk flowing your way, Chaudhry Natthu! If he could, he would poison every drop of your water. You call it plain inequity, plain bestiality because you don't like this way of killing. Isn't it a bit odd that even before the war has begun you're setting up conditions, as if it is a marriage contract and you have the freedom to set down your conditions? To tell the enemy, "Don't kill me by starvation and thirst, but, by all means, kill me with a gun that is of such and such bore." This, in fact, is the real *nonsense*. Think about it with a cool head.'

This was all that was needed to send the Chaudhry to the height of his irritation. 'So bring some ice and cool my head!'

'This too is my responsibility now.' Karim Dad laughed tapping Miran Bakhsh on the shoulder, and then got up and walked out of the chaupal.

Just as he was stepping inside the *deorhi* of his house, he saw Bakhtu coming out. A toothless smile appeared on her lips when she saw Karim Dad.

'Congratulations, Kaimay. You've got a boy, the very image of the moon. Now think about a nice name for him.'

'Name?' Karim Dad thought for a moment. 'Yazeed . . . that'll do, yes, Yazeed.'

Bakhtu the midwife was stunned, her face dropped, while an over-joyed Karim Dad barged into the house shouting jubilantly. Jaina was lying on the charpoy, looking paler than before, with a cotton-ball of a little baby boy beside her, sucking away at his thumb. Karim Dad looked at the baby with a mix of affection and pride. He tweaked the baby's cheek playfully with his finger and muttered, 'Oh my Yazeed!'

A shocked scream escaped from Jaina's lips, 'Yazeed?'

Looking closely at his son's face and its features, Karim Dad affirmed, 'Yes, Yazeed. That's his name.'

Jaina's voice suddenly dropped to a whisper, 'What are you saying, Kaimay – Yazeed?'

He smiled. 'So what's wrong with it? It's just a name.'

'But whose name . . . Think!' was all she could say.

Karim Dad replied in a grave tone of voice, 'It isn't necessary that he should turn out to be the same Yazeed, the one who cut off the water; this one will make it flow again.'

Translated by Muhammad Umar Memon

The New Constitution

MANGU THE TONGAWALA was considered a man of great wisdom among his friends. He had never seen the inside of a school, and in strictly academic terms was no more than a cipher, but there was nothing under the sun he did not know something about. All his fellow tongawalas at the adda, or tonga stand, were well aware he was versed in worldly matters. He was always able to satisfy their curiosity about what was going on.

Recently, when he had learnt from one of his fares about a rumour that war was about to break out in Spain, he had patted Gama Chaudhry across his broad shoulders and predicted in a statesmanlike manner, 'You will see, Chaudhry, a war is going to break out in Spain in a few days.' And when Gama Chaudhry had asked him where Spain was, Ustad Mangu had replied very soberly: 'In Vilayat, where else?'

When war finally broke out in Spain and everybody came to know of it, every hookah-smoking tonga driver at the station adda became convinced in his heart of Ustad Mangu's greatness. At that hour, Ustad Mangu was driving his tonga on the dazzling surface of the Mall, exchanging views with his fare about the latest Hindu-Muslim rioting.

That evening when he returned to the adda, his face looked visibly perturbed. He sat down with his friends, took a long drag on the hookah, removed his khaki turban and said in a worried voice, 'It is no doubt the result of a holy man's curse that Hindus and Muslims keep slashing each other up every other day. I have heard it said by my elders that Akbar Badshah once showed disrespect to a saint, who angrily cursed him in these words: "Get out of my sight! And, yes, your Hindustan will always be plagued by riots and disorder." And you can see for yourselves. Ever since the end of Akbar's raj, what else has India known but riot after riot!'

He took a deep breath, drew on his hookah reflectively and said, 'These Congressites want to win India its freedom. Well, you take my word, they will get nowhere even if they keep bashing their heads against the wall for a thousand years. At the most, the Angrez will leave, but then you will get maybe the Italywala or the Russiawala. I have heard that the Russiawala is one tough fellow. But Hindustan will always remain enslaved. Yes, I forgot to tell you that part of the saint's curse on Akbar which said that India will always be ruled by foreigners.'

Ustad Mangu had intense hatred for the British. He used to tell his friends that he hated them because they were ruling Hindustan against the will of the Indians and missed no opportunity to commit atrocities. However, the fact was that it was the gora soldiers of the cantonment who were responsible for Ustad Mangu's rather low opinion of the British. They used to treat him like some lower creation of God, even worse than a dog. Nor was Ustad Mangu overly fond of their fair complexion. He would feel nauseated at the sight of a fair and ruddy gora soldier's face. 'Their red wrinkled faces remind me of a dead body whose skin is rotting away,' he used to say.

After an argument with a drunken gora, he would remain depressed for the entire day. He would return to his adda in the evening and curse the man to his heart's content, while smoking his Marble brand cigarette or taking long drags at his hookah.

He would deliver himself of a heavyweight curse, shake his head with its loosely tied turban and say, 'Look at them, came to the door to borrow a light and the next thing you knew they owned the whole house. I am sick and tired of these offshoots of monkeys. The way they order us around, you would think we were their fathers' servants!'

But even after such outbursts, his anger would show no sign of abating. As long as a friend was keeping him company, he would keep at it. 'Look at this one, resembles a leper? Dead and rotting. I could knock him out cold with one blow, but the way he was throwing his git-pit at me, you would have thought he was going to kill me. I swear on your head, my first urge was to smash the damn fellow's skull, but then I restrained myself. I mean it would have been below my dignity to hit this wretch.' He would wipe his nose with the sleeve of his khaki uniform jacket and keep murmuring curses. 'As God is my witness, I'm sick of suffering and humouring these Lat sahibs. Every time I look at their blighted faces, my blood begins to boil in my veins. We need a new law to get rid of these people. Only that can revive us, I swear on your life.'

One day Ustad Mangu picked up two fares from district courts. He gathered from their conversation that there was going to be a new constitution for India and he felt overwhelmed with joy at the news. The two Marwaris were in town to pursue a civil suit in the local court and, while on their way home, they were discussing the new constitution, the India Act.

'It is said that from 1 April, there's going to be a new constitution. Will that change everything?'

'Not everything, but they say a lot will change. The Indians would be free.'

'What about interest?' asked one.

'Well, this needs to be inquired. Should ask some lawyer tomorrow.'

The conversation between the two Marwaris sent Ustad Mangu to seventh heaven. Normally, he was in the habit of abusing his horse for being slow and was not averse to making liberal use of the whip, but not today. Every now and then, he would look back at his two passengers, caress his moustache and loosen the horse's reins affectionately. 'Come on son, come on, show 'em how you take to the air.'

After dropping his fares, he stopped at the Anarkali shop of his friend, Dino the sweetmeat vendor. He ordered a large glass of lassi, drank it down, belched with satisfaction, took the ends of his moustache in his mouth, sucked at them and said in a loud voice, 'The hell with 'em all!'

When he returned to the adda in the evening, contrary to routine, no one that he knew was around. A storm was roaring in his breast and he was dying to share the great news with his friends, that really great news which he simply had to get out of his system. But no one was around to hear it.

For about half an hour, he paced about restlessly under the tin roof of the station adda, his whip under his arm. His mind was on many things, good things that lay in the future. The news that a new constitution was to be implemented had brought him to the doorstep of a new world. He had switched on all the lights in his brain to carefully study the implications of the new law that was going to become operational in India on the first of April. The worried words of the Marwari about a change in the law governing interest or usury rang in his ears. A wave of happiness was coursing through his entire body. Quite a few times, he laughed under his thick moustache and hurled a few words of abuse at the Marwaris. 'The new constitution is going to be like boiling hot water is to bugs who suck the blood of the poor,' he said to himself.

He was very happy. A delightful cool settled over his heart when he thought of how the new constitution would send these white mice (he always called them by that name) scurrying back into their holes for all times to come.

When the bald-headed Nathoo ambled into the adda some time later, his turban tucked under his arm, Ustad Mangu shook his hand vigorously and said in a loud voice, 'Give me your hand, I have great news for you that would not only bring you immense joy but might even make hair grow back on your bald skull.'

Then, thoroughly enjoying himself, he went into a detailed description of the changes the new constitution was going to bring. 'You just wait and see. Things are going to happen. You have my word, this Russian king is bound to do something big.' And as he talked, he continued to slap Ganju's bald head, and with some force as well.

Ustad Mangu had heard many stories about the socialist system the Soviets had set up. There were many things he liked about their new laws and many of the new things they were doing, which was what had made him link the king of Russia with the India Act or the new constitution. He was convinced that the changes being brought in on 1 April were a direct result of the influence of the Russian king.

For the past several years, the Red Shirt movement in Peshawar and other cities had been much in the news. To Ustad Mangu, this movement was all tied up with the 'king of Russia' and, naturally, with the new constitution. Then there were the frequent reports of bomb blasts in various Indian cities. Whenever Ustad Mangu heard that so many had been caught somewhere for possessing explosives or so many were going to be tried for treason, he interpreted it all to his great delight as preparation for the new constitution.

One day he had two barristers at the back of his tonga. They were vigorously criticizing the new constitution. He listened to them in silence. One of them was saying, 'It is Section II of the Act that I still can't make sense of. It relates to the federation of India. No such federation exists in the world. From a political angle too, such a federation would be utterly wrong. In fact, one can say that this is going to be no federation.'

Since most of this conversation was being carried on in English, Ustad Mangu had only been able to follow the last bit. He came to the conclusion that these two barristers were opposed to the new constitution and did not want their country to be free. 'Toady wretches,' he muttered with contempt. Whenever he called someone a 'toady wretch' under his breath, he felt elated that he had applied the words correctly and that he could tell a good man from a toady.

Three days after this incident, he picked up three students from Government College who wanted to be taken to Mozang. He listened to them carefully as they talked.

'The new constitution has raised my hopes. If so and so becomes a member of the assembly, I will certainly be able to get a job in a government office.'

'Oh! There are going to be many openings and, in that confusion, we will be able to lay our hands on something.'

'Yes, yes, why not!'

'And there's bound to be a reduction in the number of all those unemployed graduates who have nowhere to go.'

This conversation was most thrilling as far as Ustad Mangu was concerned. The new constitution now appeared to him to be something bright and full of promise. The only thing he could compare the new constitution with was the splendid brass and gilt fittings he had purchased after careful examination a couple of years ago for his tonga from Choudhry Khuda Bux. When the fittings were new, the nickel-headed nails would shimmer and where brass had been worked into the fittings it shone like gold. It was essential that the new constitution should shine and glow.

By 1 April, Ustad Mangu had heard a great deal about the new constitution, both for and against. However, nothing could change the concept of the new constitution that he had formed in his mind. He was confident that come 1 April, everything would become clear. He was sure that what the new constitution would usher in would soothe his heart.

At last, the thirty-one days of March drew to a close. There were still a few silent night hours left before the dawn of 1 April and the weather was unusually cool, the breeze quite fresh. Ustad Mangu rose early, went to the stable, set up his tonga and took to the road. He was extraordinarily happy today because he was going to witness the coming in of the new constitution.

In the cold morning fog, he went round the broad and narrow streets of the city but everything looked old, like the sky. His eyes wanted to see things taking on a new colour but, except for the new plume made of colourful feathers that rested on his horse's head, everything looked old. He had bought this new plume from Chaudhry Khuda Bux for fourteen annas and a half to celebrate the new constitution.

The road lay black under his horse's hooves. The lampposts that stood on the sides at regular intervals looked the same. The shop signs had not changed. The way people moved about, the sound made by the tiny bells tied around his horse's neck were not new either. Nothing was new, but Ustad Mangu was not disappointed.

Perhaps it was too early in the morning. All the shops were still closed. This he found consoling. It also occurred to him that the courts did not start work until nine, so how could the new constitution be at work just yet.

He was in front of Government College when the tower clock imperiously struck nine. The students walking out through the main entrance were smartly dressed, but somehow their clothes looked shabby to Ustad Mangu. He wanted to see something startling and dramatic.

He turned his tonga left towards Anarkali. Half the shops were already open. There were crowds of people at sweetmeat stalls, and general traders were busy with their customers, their wares displayed invitingly in their windows. Overhead, on the power lines perched several pigeons, quarrelling with each other. But none of this held any interest whatsoever for Ustad Mangu. He wanted to see the new constitution as clearly as he could see his horse.

Ustad Mangu was one of those people who cannot stand the suspense of waiting. When his first child was to be born he had spent the last four or five months in a state of great agitation. While he was sure that the child would come to be born one day, he found it hard to keep waiting. He wanted to take a look at his child, just once. It could then take its time getting born. It was because of this desire that he could not overcome that he had pressed his sick wife's belly and put his ear to it in an attempt to find out something about the baby, but he had had no luck.

One day he had screamed at his wife in exasperation, 'What's the matter with you! All day long you lie in bed as if you were dead. Why don't you get up and walk about to gain some strength? If you keep lying there like a flat piece of wood, do you think you will be able to give birth?'

Ustad Mangu was temperamentally impatient. He wanted to see every cause have an effect, and he was always curious about it. Once his wife, Gangawati, watching his impatient antics, had said to him, 'You haven't even begun digging the well and already you're dying to have a drink.'

This morning he was not as impatient as he normally should have been. He had come out early to take a look at the new constitution with his own eyes, in the same way he used to wait for hours to catch a glimpse of Gandhiji and Pandit Jawaharlal Nehru being taken out in a procession.

Great leaders, in Ustad Mangu's view, were those who were profusely garlanded when taken out in public. Anyone bedecked in garlands of marigolds was a great man in Ustad Mangu's book. And if because of the milling crowds a couple of near-clashes took place, the leader's stature grew in Ustad Mangu's eyes. He wanted to measure the new constitution by the same yardstick.

From Anarkali he turned towards the Mall, driving his tonga slowly on its shiny surface. In front of an auto showroom, he found a fare bound for the cantonment. They settled the price and were soon on their way. Ustad Mangu whipped his horse into action and said to himself, 'This is just as well. One might find out something about the new constitution in the cantonment.'

He dropped his passenger at his destination, lit a cigarette, which he placed between the last two fingers of his left hand, and eased himself into a cushion in the rear of the tonga. When Ustad Mangu was not looking for a new fare, or when he wanted to think about some past incident, he would move into the rear seat of the tonga, with the reins of his horse wound around his left hand. On such occasions his horse, after neighing a little, would begin to move forward at a gentle pace, glad to be spared the daily grind of cantering ahead.

Ustad Mangu was trying to work out if the present system of allotting tonga number plates would change with the new law, when he felt someone calling out to him. When he turned to look, he found a gora standing under a lamppost at the far end of the road, beckoning to him.

As already noted, Ustad Mangu had intense hatred for the British. When he saw that his new customer was a gora, feelings of hatred rose in his heart. His first instinct was to pay no attention to him and just leave him where he was. But then he felt that it would be foolish to give the man's money a miss. The fourteen annas and a half he had spent on the plume should be recovered from these people, he decided.

He neatly turned around his tonga on the empty road, flicked his whip and was at the lamppost in no time. Without moving from his comfortable perch, he asked in a leisurely manner, 'Sahib Bahadur, where do you want to be taken?'

He had spoken these words with undisguised irony. When he had called him 'Sahib Bahadur', his upper lip, covered by his moustache, had moved lower, while a thin line that ran from his nostril to his lower chin had trembled and deepened, as if someone had run a sharp knife across a brown slab of shisham wood. His entire face was laughing, but inside his chest roared a fire ready to consume the gora.

The gora, who was trying to draw on a cigarette by standing close to the lamppost to protect himself from the breeze, turned and moved towards the tonga. He was about to place his foot on the foothold when his eyes met Ustad Mangu's and it seemed as if two loaded guns had fired at each other and their discharge had met in mid-air and risen towards the sky in a ball of fire.

Ustad Mangu freed his left hand of the reins that he had wrapped around it and glared at the gora standing in front of him, as if he would eat every bit of him alive. The gora, meanwhile, was busy dusting his blue trousers of something that couldn't be seen, or perhaps he was trying to protect this part of his body from Ustad Mangu's assault.

'Do you want to go or are you again going to make trouble?' the gora asked.

'It is the same man,' Ustad Mangu said to himself. He was quite sure it was the same fellow with whom he had clashed the year before. That uncalled for argument had happened because the gora was sozzled. Ustad Mangu had borne the insults hurled at him in silence. He could have smashed the man into little bits, but he had remained passive because he knew that in such quarrels it was tongawalas mostly who suffered the wrath of the law.

'Where do you want to go?' Ustad Mangu asked, thinking about the previous year's argument and the new constitution of 1 April. His tone was sharp like the stroke of a whip.

'Hira Mandi,' the gora answered.

'The fare would be five rupees,' Ustad Mangu's moustache trembled.

'Five rupees! Five rupees! Are you . . . ?' the gora screamed in disbelief.

'Yes, yes, five rupees,' Ustad Mangu said, clenching his big right fist tightly. 'Are you interested or will you keep making idle talk?'

The gora, remembering their last encounter, had decided not to be awed by the barrel-chested Ustad Mangu. He felt that the man's skull was again itching for punishment. This encouraging thought made him advance towards the tonga. With his swagger stick, he motioned Ustad Mangu to get down. The polished cane touched Ustad Mangu's thigh two or three times. Ustad Mangu, standing up, looked down at the short-statured gora as if the sheer weight of a single glance would grind him down. Then his fist rose like an arrow leaving a bow and landed heavily on the gora's chin. He pushed the man aside, got down from his tonga and began to hit him all over his body.

The astonished gora made several efforts to save himself from the heavy blows raining down on him, but when he noticed that his assailant was in a rage bordering on madness and flames were shooting forth from his eyes, he began to scream. His screams only made Ustad Mangu work his arms faster. He was thrashing the gora to his heart's content while shouting, 'The same cockiness even on 1 April! Well, sonny boy, it is our Raj now.'

A crowd gathered. Two policemen appeared from somewhere and with great difficulty managed to rescue the Englishman. There stood Ustad Mangu, one policeman to his left and one to his right, his broad chest heaving because he was breathless. Foaming at the mouth, with his smiling eyes he was looking at the astonished crowd and saying in a breathless voice, 'Those days are gone, friends, when they ruled the roost. There is a new constitution now, fellows, a new constitution.'

The poor gora with his disfigured face was looking foolishly, sometimes at Ustad Mangu, other times at the crowd.

Ustad Mangu was taken by police constables to the station. All along the way, and even inside the station, he kept screaming, 'New constitution, new constitution!' but nobody paid any attention to him.

'New constitution, new constitution! What rubbish are you talking? It's the same old constitution.'

And he was locked up.

Translated by Khalid Hasan

Khushia

K HUSHIA WAS THINKING.
He had just got himself a paan laced with black tobacco from the
shop across the road. He was sitting in his usual place, the cemented
plinth by the roadside that served as a showroom for tyres and motor
spares during the day. Evenings, it was his. He was masticating his black-
tobacco-laced paan slowly and he was thinking of what had happened just
half an hour earlier.

He had gone to the fifth street in Khetwari because around the corner lived his new girl, Kanta, who had come from Mangalore. Someone
had told him that she was planning to move and he had gone to check it
out. He had knocked at her door and she had asked who it was. 'It is I,
Khushia,' he had answered. She had opened the door and what he had
seen had nearly thrown him. She was naked, or nearly naked because all
she had covering her was a skimpy towel which was simply not adequate
because whatever women keep covered normally was there in full view.

'Khushia, what brings you here . . . I was about to take a bath . . . sit
down . . . you should have ordered some tea from the shop across the road
before you came in . . . that blasted boy Rama who used to work for me

has run off.' Khushia, who had never seen a woman naked or even half naked, was confused. He did not know how to react or what to say. His eyes wanted to be elsewhere rather than on Kanta's body.

But all he could manage to mutter was, 'Why don't you go and take your bath?' And then, 'If you were not quite dressed, why did you answer the door? You could just have said you were not ready and I would have come another time . . . But go and take your bath.'

Kanta smiled, 'When you said it was Khushia, I asked myself what harm there was in letting you in. After all, I thought, it is Khushia, our own Khushia . . .'

He sat there thinking of the smile on her face as she had spoken to him. The sensation was almost physical, electrifying his mind and body. He could see her standing in front of him naked like a wax figurine. Her body was beautiful. For the first time, Khushia had realized that women who rent out their bodies could be beautiful also. This was like a revelation. But what had thrown him was her standing in front of him without the least sense of shame or self-consciousness. Why?

But then had she not answered that question herself when she said that she had let him in because, after all, he was 'Khushia, our own Khushia.'

Both Kanta and Khushia were in the same line of work, she being the goods that he hawked. In that sense, he was her 'own' but did that justify her standing in front of him without her clothes? Khushia could not figure it out.

He could still see her as she had stood there. Her skin was taut like skin over a drum and her body did not seem to be aware of itself. His probing eyes had gone over her rich brown figure several times, but there had been no reaction from her. She had just stood there like an emotionless statuette. She should have reacted to his gaze. After all, there was a man staring at her, and men's eyes could penetrate through a woman's clothes, but she had shown not the least nervousness. He also remembered that her eyes had a washed and laundered look. Whatever it was, he said to himself again, she should have felt some sense of selfconsciousness, given some sign that her modesty had been outraged. Her face should have turned red with embarrassment. It is true she was a prostitute but did prostitutes stand undressed in front of men as she had done?

He had been in this business for ten years and he knew all the secrets of this profession and the women who worked it. He knew, for instance, that at the end of the street the girl who lived with a man she said was her brother, and who used to play a song from the movie *Achoot Kanya* on her broken harmonium, was in love with the actor Ashok Kumar. Many boys had taken her to bed on the promise that they would introduce her to Ashok. He also knew that the Punjabi girl who lived in Dadar wore a jacket and trousers because a customer had once told her about Marlene Dietrich, the star of the movie *Morocco,* who was said to wear trousers because her legs were so beautiful that they needed to be protected. They were said to be insured for a lot of money. She had seen that movie many times. The trousers sat tightly over her buttocks but it didn't matter. Then there was the girl from Daccan who lived in Mizgaon and who ensnared handsome college students because she wanted to have a good-looking baby, though she knew it was unlikely to happen as she was infertile. There was also the dark one from Madras with diamond earrings who wasted most of what she earned on lotions and bleaching creams that promised to turn dark skin into fair, though in her heart of hearts she knew it would never happen and she was wasting her money.

All these women for whom he worked he knew inside out but what he did not know was that one day one of them, Kanta Kumari, a name he found difficult to remember, would stand in front of him naked, an experience he had never had before. Beads of perspiration appeared on his brow. His pride had been hurt. When he thought of Kanta's bare body, he felt a deep sense of insult. He was speaking to himself. 'It is an insult, is it not! Here is a girl who is practically naked and she stands bang in front of me and says, "Come in, after all, you are Khushia, our own Khushia." As if I was not a man but that stupid cat which is always sprawled on her bed.'

As he sat there thinking, he became convinced that he had been insulted. He was a man and he expected women, whether housewives or the other kind, to treat him like a man, a male. He expected them to maintain the distance laid down by nature between man and woman. He had gone to Kanta's house to find out if she was really moving and, if so, where. It was a business call. When he knocked at her door, he had had no idea what she might be doing. He had thought maybe she was lying in bed with a bandage around her head to fight a headache or de-licing her cat or removing the hair from her armpits with that foulsmelling powder he could not stand. She could even be playing a game of cards with herself.

She lived alone. It could not have even remotely occurred to him that Kanta, the girl whom he had always seen properly dressed, would open the door and stand there in front of him in her birthday suit. She was naked because that skimpy towel could hardly cover anything. But what had she really felt when she had let him in? As for himself, he had the strange feeling that the inside of a banana had suddenly dropped down in front of him leaving the peel in his hands. Her words kept ringing in his ears. 'When you said it was Khushia, I said to myself that there was no harm in letting you in. After all, I said to myself, it is Khushia, our own Khushia.'

'The bitch was smiling,' he kept murmuring. It was a smile as naked as she was. He could not help thinking of her body, which was like smoothly polished wood. He suddenly remembered this woman from his childhood who used to say to him, 'Khushia, my son, go get me a bucket of water.' And when he returned with it, she would say from behind a makeshift curtain, 'Come, place it next to me. I cannot see because I have soaped my face.' He would lift the curtain from a corner and place the bucket next to her. He would see a naked woman with her entire body soaped, but it would mean nothing. He was only a child then and women did not hide themselves from children when they were naked.

But now he was a man, a twenty-eight-year-old man. How could a woman, even an old woman, bare herself in front of him? What did Kanta think he was? Was he not equipped with everything that a young man is supposed to be equipped with? While it was true that her bare body had startled him, he had looked at her stealthily. He could not help noticing that, despite the daily use to which her body was subjected, everything was where it should be, and in good shape too. She charged ten rupees for a throw and that was not much considering what she had on offer. The other day, the bank clerk who had gone back because she would not bring down the price by two rupees was surely an ass. He recalled experiencing a strange tautening of the body. He wanted to stretch out his arms and release the tension until his bones began to rattle. Why had this wheat-coloured girl from Mangalore not seen him as a male? Instead, she had let him gaze at her nakedness because to her he was Khushia, just Khushia.

He got up, spat on the road and jumped into the tram that he always took to get home.

Once there, he took a bath, put on fresh clothes, stepped into the neighbourhood barber shop, looked at himself in the mirror, combed his hair and, on second thought, sat down for a shave, his second that day. The barber said to him, 'Brother Khushia, have you forgotten? I shaved you only this morning.' Khushia ran his hand over his face and replied, 'Your razor was not sharp enough.'

After the shave, he rubbed his face with a bit of talcum powder and crossed the road to a taxi stand. 'Chi chi,' he said – the standard Bombay call for hailing a taxi. The driver opened the door for him, 'Where sahib?' he asked. Khushia was pleased at being called sahib. 'I will let you know. Go towards Pasera House first via Lemington Road, understand,' he replied in a friendly voice. The driver switched on his meter and took off. At the end of Lemington Road, Khushia asked him to turn left.

The taxi turned left and before the driver could change gears, Khushia had told him to stop. He then stepped out, walked across to a paan shop, exchanged a few words with a man who was standing there and after helping himself to a paan came back with the fellow he had talked to. They both got into the taxi. 'Go straight,' Khushia told the driver. The taxi drove for quite a while with Khushia doing the navigation. They went through brightly lit bazaars and, in the end, turned into an ill-lit street where some people had already settled in for the night on makeshift beds. Some were getting their heads massaged and looked contented. Khushia paid no attention to them. 'Stop here,' he told the driver as they went past a wooden hut. In a low voice, Khushia told the man he had picked up from the paan shop that he would wait for him in the car. The man got out without a word and went into the hut.

Khushia reclined into the seat and put one leg on top of the other. Then he pulled out a bidi from his pocket and lit it, but he took only a couple of drags before chucking it out of the window. He was restless. His heart was beating fast and for a moment he thought the driver had not killed the engine in order to increase the fare. 'How much extra do you think you will make by idling that engine?' he asked sharply.

The driver turned, 'Seth, the engine is not idling. It is switched off.'

As he realized his mistake, Khushia felt even more restless. He now began to bite his lips. Then he put on the black, boatshaped cap that lay tucked under his arm. He shook the driver by his shoulder. 'Look, a girl will soon come and get into the car. The moment she does so, drive off. And don't think anything odd is happening. Everything is perfectly all right.'

The door of the hut opened and two people walked out, the man Khushia had picked up and Kanta, who was wearing a bright-coloured sari.

Khushia sank further into his seat. It was quite dark in the car. The man opened the car door and gently pushed Kanta in. Then he banged the door shut. 'Khushia! You!' Kanta screamed. 'Yes, I, but you have already been paid, haven't you!' Then he told the driver to get moving.

The engine coughed and came to life. The car lurched forward and if

Kanta said something it could not be heard. The man who had brought Kanta could be seen standing on the road, looking somewhat bewildered. The taxi soon disappeared into the night.

No one ever saw Khushia at his customary hangout again.

Translated by Khalid Hasan

Babu Gopi Nath

I THINK IT was in 1940 that I first met Babu Gopi Nath. I was the editor of a weekly magazine in Bombay. One day, while I was busy writing something, Abdul Rahim Sando burst into my office, followed by a short, nondescript man. Greeting me in his typical style, Sando introduced his friend. 'Manto Sahib, meet Babu Gopi Nath.'

I rose and shook hands with him. Sando was in his element. 'Babu Gopi Nath, you are shaking hands with India's number one writer.' He had a talent for coining words which, though not to be found in any dictionary, somehow always managed to express his meaning. 'When he writes,' Sando continued, 'it is *dharan takhta*. A master of establishing *kuntinutely* among people and things. So Manto Sahib, what was the joke you unleashed the other day? "Miss Khurshid has bought a car. Verily, God is the great carmaker." Well, Babu Gopi Nath, if that's not the "anti" of pantipo, then what is, I ask you!'

Abdul Rahim Sando was an original. Most of the words he used in ordinary conversation were strictly of his own authorship. After this introduction, he looked at Babu Gopi Nath, who appeared to be impressed.

'This is Babu Gopi Nath, from Lahore, but now of Bombay, accompanied by a *pigeonette* from Kashmir.'

Babu Gopi Nath smiled.

Abdul Rahim Sando continued, 'If you are looking for the world's number one innocent, this is your man. Everyone cheats him out of his money by saying nice things to him. Look at me. All I do is talk and he rewards me with two packets of Polson's smuggled butter every day. Manto sahib, he is a genuine *antifloojustice* fellow, if ever there was one. We are expecting you at Babu Gopi Nath's flat this evening.'

Babu Gopi Nath, whose mind seemed to be elsewhere, now joined the conversation. 'Manto sahib, I insist that you come.' Then he looked at Sando. 'Sando, is Manto sahib . . . well, fond of . . . you know what?'

Abdul Rahim Sando laughed. 'Of course, he is fond of that and of many other things as well. Is it all settled then? May I add that I have also started drinking because it can now be done free of cost.'

Sando wrote out the address and at six o'clock I presented myself at the flat. It was nice and clean. Three rooms, good furniture, all in order. Besides Sando and Babu Gopi Nath, there were four others – two men and two women – to whom I was presently introduced by Sando.

There was Ghaffar Sain, a typical Punjabi villager in a loose tehmad, wearing a huge necklace of beads and coloured stones. 'He is Babu Gopi Nath's legal adviser, you know what I mean?' Sando said. 'In Punjab, every lunatic is a man of God. Our friend here is either already a man of God or about to be admitted to that divine order. He has accompanied Babu Gopi Nath from Lahore, because he had run out of suckers in that city. Here, he drinks Scotch whisky, smokes Craven A cigarettes and prays for the good of Babu Gopi Nath's soul.'

Ghaffar Sain heard this colourful description in silence, a smile playing on his lips.

The other man was called Ghulam Ali, tall and athletic with a pock-marked face. About him Sando provided the following information: 'He is my *shagird*, my true apprentice. A famous singing girl of Lahore fell in love with him. She brought all manner of *kuntiniutees* in play to ensnare him, but the only response she received from Ghulam Ali was: "Women are not my cup of tea." Ran into Babu Gopi Nath at a Lahore shrine and has never left his side since. He receives a tin of Craven A cigarettes daily and all the food he can eat.'

Ghulam Ali smiled good-naturedly.

I looked at the women. One of them was young, fair and round-faced, the Kashmiri *pigeonette* Sando had mentioned. She had short hair, which first appeared to be cropped, but was not. Her eyes were large and bright and her expression suggested that she was raw and inexperienced. Sando introduced her.

'Zeenat Begum, called Zeno, a love-name given by Babu sahib. This apple, plucked from Kashmir, was brought to Lahore by one of the city's most formidable madams. Babu Gopi Nath's private intelligence sources relayed the news of this arrival to him and, overnight, he decamped with her. There was litigation and for about two months the city police had a ball, thanks to Babu Gopi Nath's generosity. Naturally, Babu Gopi Nath won the suit. And so here she is. Dharan takhta.'

The other woman, who was quietly smoking, was dark and red-eyed. Babu Gopi Nath looked at her. 'Sando, and this one?' Sando slapped her thigh and declaimed, 'Ladies and gentlemen, this is mutton tippoti, fulful booti, Mrs Abdul Rahim Sando, alias Sardar Begum. Fell in love with me in 1936 and, inside of two years, I was done for – dharan takhta. I had to run away from Lahore. However, Babu Gopi Nath sent for her the other day to keep me out of harm's way. Her daily rations consist of one tin of Craven A cigarettes and two rupees eight annas every evening for her morphine shot. She may be dark, but, by God, she is a tit-for-tat lady.'

'What rubbish you talk,' Sardar said. She sounded like the hardened professional woman she was.

Having finished with the introductions, Sando began a lecture high-lighting my greatness. 'Cut it out, Sando,' I said. 'Let's talk of something else.'

Sando shouted, 'Boy, whisky and soda. Babu Gopi Nath, out with the cash.'

Babu Gopi Nath reached in his pocket, pulled out a thick bundle of money, peeled off a bill and gave it to Sando. Sando stared at it reverently, raised his eyes to heaven and said, 'Dear God of the universe, bring unto me the day when I put my hand in my pocket and fish out a thick wad of money like this. Meanwhile, I am asking Ghulam Ali to run to the store and return post-haste with two bottles of Johnny Walker Still-GoingStrong.'

The whisky arrived and we began to drink, with Sando continuing to monopolize the conversation. He downed his glass in one go. 'Dharan takhta,' he shouted, 'Manto sahib, this is what I call honest-to-goodness whisky, inscribing "Long Live Revolution" as it blazes its way through the gullet into the stomach. Long live Babu Gopi Nath.'

Babu Gopi Nath did not say much, occasionally nodding to express agreement with Sando's opinions. I had a feeling that the man had no views of his own. His superstitious nature was evident from the presence of Ghaffar Sain, his legal adviser, in Sando's words. What it really meant was that Babu Gopi Nath was a born devotee of real and fake holy men. I learnt during the conversation that most of his time in Lahore was spent in the company of fakirs, mendicants, sadhus and the like.

'What are you thinking?' I asked him.

'Nothing, nothing at all.' Then he smiled, glanced at Zeenat amorously. 'Just thinking about these beautiful creatures. What else do people like us think about?'

Sando explained, 'Manto sahib, Babu Gopi Nath is a great man. There is hardly a singing girl or a courtesan worth the name in Lahore he has not had a *kuntinutely* with.'

'Manto sahib, one no longer has the fire of youth in one's loins,' Babu Gopi Nath said modestly.

Then followed a long discussion about the leading families of courtesans and singing girls of Lahore. Family trees were traced, genealogy analysed, not to speak of how much Babu Gopi Nath had paid for the ritual deflowering of which woman in what year. These exchanges remained confined to Sando, Sardar, Ghulam Ali and Ghaffar Sain. The jargon of Lahore's kothas was freely employed, not all of it comprehensible to me, though the general drift of the conversation was clear.

Zeenat never said a word. Off and on, she smiled. It was quite clear that she was not interested in these things. She drank a rather diluted glass of whisky, and I noticed that she smoked without appearing to enjoy it. Strangely enough, she smoked the most. I could find no visible indication that she was in love with Babu Gopi Nath, but it was obvious that he was with her. However, one could sense a tension between the two, despite their physical closeness.

At about eight o'clock, Sardar left to get her morphine shot. Ghaffar Sain, three drinks ahead, lay on the floor, rosary in hand. Ghulam Ali was sent out to get some food. Sando had got tired of talking. Babu Gopi Nath, now quite tipsy, looked at Zeenat longingly and said, 'Manto sahib, what do you think of my Zeenat?'

I did not know how to answer that, so I said, 'She is nice.' Babu Gopi Nath was pleased. 'Manto sahib, she is a lovely girl and so simple. She has no interest in ornaments and things like that. Many times I have offered to buy her a house of her own and you know what her answer has been? "What will I do with a house? Who do I have in the world?"'

He asked suddenly, 'What does a motor car cost, Manto sahib?'

'I've no idea.'

'I don't believe it, Manto sahib, I'm sure you know. You must help me buy Zeno a car. I've come to the conclusion that one must have a car in Bombay.'

Zeenat's face was devoid of expression.

Babu Gopi Nath was quite drunk now and getting more sentimental by the minute. 'Manto sahib, you are a man of learning. I am nothing but an ass. Please let me know if I can be of some service to you. It was only by accident that Sando brought up your name yesterday. I immediately sent for a taxi and asked him to take me to meet you. If I have shown you any discourtesy, you must forgive me. I am nothing but a sinner, a man full of faults. Should I get you some more whisky?'

'No, we've all had much too much to drink,' I said.

He became even more sentimental. 'You must drink some more, Manto sahib!' He produced his bundle of money, but before he could peel some

off, I thrust it back into his pocket. 'You gave a hundred rupees to Ghulam Ali earlier, didn't you?' I asked.

The fact was that I had begun to feel sorry for Babu Gopi Nath. He
was surrounded by so many leeches and he was such a simpleton. Babu
Gopi Nath smiled. 'Manto sahib, whatever is left of those hundred rupees
will slip through Ghulam Ali's pocket.'

The words were hardly out of his mouth, when Ghulam Ali entered
the room with the doleful announcement that some scoundrel had picked
his pocket on the street. Babu Gopi Nath looked at me, smiled, and gave
another hundred rupees to Ghulam Ali. 'Get some food quickly.'

After five or six meetings, I got to know a great deal more about Babu
Gopi Nath's personality. First of all, my initial view that he was a fool and
a sucker had turned out to be wrong. He was perfectly aware of the fact
that Sando, Ghulam Ali and Sardar, his inseparable companions, were all
selfish opportunists. He let them ride roughshod over him, accepted their
curses and scorn, but never got angry.

Once he said to me, 'Manto sahib, in my entire life, I have never
rejected advice. Whenever someone offers it to me, I accept it with gratitude. Perhaps they consider me a fool, but I value their wisdom. Look
at it like this. They have the wisdom to see that I am the sort of man who
can be made a fool of. The fact is that I have spent most of my life in the
company of fakirs, holy men, courtesans and singing girls. I love them. I
just couldn't do without them. I have decided that when my money runs
out, I would like to settle down at a shrine. There are only two places
where my heart finds peace: prostitutes' kothas and saints' shrines. It's
only a matter of time before I shall be unable to afford the former, because

my money is running out, but there are thousands of saints' shrines in India. I will go to one.'

'Why do you like kothas and shrines?' I asked.

'Because both establishments are an illusion. What better refuge can there be for someone who wants to deceive himself?'

'You are fond of singing girls. Do you understand music?' I asked.

'Not at all. It doesn't matter in the least. I can spend an entire evening listening to the most flat-voiced woman in the world and still feel happy. It is the little things which go with these evenings that I love. She sings, I flash a hundred-rupee bill in front of her. She moves languorously towards me and, instead of letting her take it from my hand, I stick it in my sock. She bends and gently pulls it out. It's the sort of nonsense that people like us enjoy. Everybody knows, of course, that in a kotha parents prostitute their daughters and in shrines men prostitute their God.'

I learnt that Babu Gopi Nath was the son of a miserly moneylender and had inherited ten lakh rupees, which he had been frittering away ever since. He had come to Bombay with fifty thousand rupees, and though those were inexpensive times his daily outgoings were heavy.

As promised, he bought a car for Zeno – a Fiat – for three thousand rupees. A chauffeur was also employed (an unreliable ruffian) but they were the sort of people Babu Gopi Nath felt happy with.

Our meetings had become more frequent. Babu Gopi Nath interested me. In turn, he treated me with great respect and devotion.

One evening, I found among Babu Gopi Nath's regulars a man I had known for a long time – Moham mad Shafiq Toosi. Widely regarded as a singer and a wit, Shafiq had another unusual side to his character. He was the known lover of the most famous singing girls of the time. It was not so commonly known, however, that he had had affairs, one after the other with three sisters, belonging to one of the most famous singing families of Patiala.

Even less known was the fact that their mother, when she was young, had been his mistress. His first wife, who died a few years after their marriage, he did not care for, because she was too housewifely and did not act like a woman of pleasure. He had no use for housewives. He was about forty and, though he had gone through scores of famous courtesans and singing girls, he was not known to have spent a penny of his own on them. He was one of nature's gigolos.

Courtesans had always found him irresistible. When I walked into the flat, I found him engrossed in conversation with Zeenat. I couldn't understand who had introduced him to Babu Gopi Nath. I knew that Sando was a friend of his, but they had not been on speaking terms for some time. In the end, it turned out that the two had made up and it was actually Sando who had brought him here today.

Babu Gopi Nath sat in a corner, smoking his hookah. He never smoked cigarettes. Shafiq was telling stories, most of them ribald and all of them about courtesans and singing girls. Zeenat looked uninterested, but Sardar was all ears. 'Welcome, welcome,' Shafiq said to me, 'I did not know you too were a wayfarer of this valley.'

Sando shouted, 'Welcome to the angel of death. Dharan takhta.'

One could not fail to notice that Mohammad Shafiq Toosi and Zeenat were exchanging what could only be described as amorous glances. This troubled me. I had become quite fond of Zeenat, who had begun to call me Manto bhai.

I didn't like the way Shafiq was ogling Zeenat. After some time, he left with Sando. I am afraid I was a bit harsh with Zeenat, because I expressed strong disapproval of the goings-on between Shafiq and her. She burst into tears and ran into the next room, followed by Babu Gopi Nath. A few minutes later, he came out and said, 'Manto sahib, come with me.'

Zeenat was sitting on her bed. When she saw us, she covered her face with both hands and lay down. Babu Gopi Nath was very sombre. 'Manto sahib, I love this woman. She has been with me for two years, and I swear by the saint Hazrat Ghaus Azam Jilani that she has never given me cause for complaint. Her other sisters, I mean women of her calling, have robbed me without compunction over the years, but she is a girl without greed or love of money. Sometimes, I go away for weeks, maybe to be with another woman, without leaving her any money. You know what she does? She pawns her ornaments to manage until I return.

'Manto sahib, as I told you once, I don't have long to go. My money has almost run out. I don't want her life to go to waste after I am gone. So often have I said to her, "Zeno, look at the other women and learn something from them. Today, I have money, tomorrow, I'll be a beggar. Women can't do with just one rich lover in their lives; they need several. If you don't find a rich patron after I leave, your life will be ruined. You act like a housewife, confined at home all day. That won't do."

'But Manto sahib, this woman is hopeless. I consulted Ghaffar Sain in Lahore and he advised me to take her to Bombay. He knows two famous actresses here who used to be singing girls in Lahore. I sent for Sardar from Lahore to teach Zeno a few tricks of the trade. Ghaffar Sain is also very capable in these matters.

'Nobody knows me in Bombay. She was afraid she would bring me dishonour, but I said to her, "Don't be silly. Bombay is a big city, full of millionaires. I have bought you a car. Why don't you find yourself a rich man who could look after you?"

'Manto sahib, I swear on God that it is my sincere wish that Zeno should stand on her own feet. I am prepared to put ten thousand rupees in a bank for her, but I know that within ten days that woman Sardar will rob her of the last penny. Manto sahib, you should try to persuade her to become worldly-wise. Since she has had the car, Sardar takes her out for a drive every evening to the Apollo Bandar beach, which is frequented by fashionable people. But there has been no success so far. Sando brought Mohammad Shafiq Toosi this evening, as you saw. What is your opinion about him?'

I decided to offer no opinion, but Babu Gopi Nath said, 'He appears to be rich, and he is good-looking. Zeno, did you like him?'

Zeno said nothing.

I simply could not believe what he was telling me: that he had brought Zeenat to Bombay so that she could become the mistress of a rich man, or, at least, learn to live off rich men. But that's the way it was. Had he wanted to get rid of her, it would have been the easiest thing in the world, but his intentions were exactly what he said they were. He had tried to get her into films, Bombay being India's movie capital. For her sake, he had entertained men who claimed to be film directors, but were no such thing. He even had had a phone installed in the flat. None of these things had produced the man he was looking for.

Mohammad Shafiq Toosi, a regular visitor for a month or so, suddenly disappeared one day. True to style, he had used the opportunity to seduce Zeenat. Babu Gopi Nath said to me, 'Manto sahib, it is so sad. Shafiq sahib was all show and no substance. Not only did he do nothing to help Zeno, but he cheated her out of many valuables and two hundred rupees. Now I am told he is having an affair with a girl called Almas.'

This was true. Almas was the youngest daughter of the famous courtesan Nazir Jan of Patiala. She was the fourth sister he had seduced in a row. Zeno's money had been spent on her, but like all his liaisons this too had turned out to be short-lived. It was later rumoured that Almas had tried to poison herself after being abandoned.

However, Zeenat had not given up on Mohammad Shafiq Toosi. She often phoned me, asking me to find Toosi and bring him to her. One day I accidentally ran into him at the radio station. When I gave him Zeenat's message, he said, 'This is not the first one. I have had several. The truth is that while Zeenat is a nice woman, she is too nice for my taste. Women who behave like wives are of no interest to me.'

Disappointed in Toosi, Zeenat resumed her visits to the beach in the company of Sardar. After two weeks of effort, Sardar was able to get hold of two men who appeared to be just the kind of gentlemen of leisure being sought. One of them, who owned a silk mill, even gave four hundred rupees to Zeenat and promised to marry her, but that was the last she heard from him.

One day, while on an errand on Hornsby Road, I saw Zeenat's parked car, with Mohammad Yasin, owner of the Nagina Hotel, occupying the back seat. 'Where did you get this car?' I asked.

'Do you know who it belongs to?'

'I do.'

'Then you can put two and two together.' He winked meaningfully.

A couple of days later, Babu Gopi Nath told me the story. Sardar had met someone at the beach and they had decided to go to Nagina Hotel to spend the evening. There was a quarrel and the man had walked out, which is how Yasin, the hotel's owner, had come into the picture.

Zeenat's affair with Yasin appeared to be progressing well. He had bought her some expensive gifts, and Babu Gopi Nath was mentally prepared to return to Lahore, because he was certain Yasin was the man Zeno could be entrusted to. Unfortunately, things did not work out that way.

A mother and daughter had recently moved into Nagina Hotel and Yasin was quick to see that Muriel, the daughter, was looking for someone to while away the time with. So, while Zeenat sat in the hotel all day long, waiting for him, the two of them could be seen driving around Bombay in Zeenat's car. Babu Gopi Nath was hurt.

'What sort of men are these, Manto sahib?' he asked me. 'I mean if one has had one's fill of a woman, one just says so honestly. I no longer understand Zeenat. She knows what is going on, but she wouldn't even tell him that if he must carry on with that Christian chhokri then at least he should have the decency not to use her car. What am I to do, Manto sahib? She is such a wonderful girl, but she is so naive. She has to learn how to survive in this world.'

The affair with Yasin finally ended, but it seemed to have left no outward effect on Zeenat. One day I phoned the flat and learnt that Babu Gopi Nath had returned to Lahore, along with Ghulam Ali and Ghaffar Sain. His money had run out, but he still had some property left, which he was planning to sell before returning to Bombay.

Sardar needed her morphine and Sando his Polson's butter. They had therefore decided to turn the flat into a whorehouse. Two or three men were roped in every day to receive Zeenat's sexual favours. She had been told to cooperate until Babu Gopi Nath's return. The daily takings were around a hundred rupees or so, half of them Zeenat's.

'You do realize what you are doing to yourself?' I said to her one day.

'I don't know, Manto bhai,' she answered innocently. 'I merely do what these people tell me.'

I wanted to say that she was a fool and the two of them would not even hesitate to auction her off, if it came to that. However, I said nothing. She was a woman without ambition and unbelievably naive. She simply had no idea of her own value or what life was all about. If she was being made to sell her body, she could at least have done so with some intelligence and style, but she was simply not interested in anything, drinking, smoking, eating, or even the sofa on which she was to be found lying most of the time, and the telephone which she was so fond of using.

A month later, Babu Gopi Nath returned from Lahore. He went to the flat, but found some other people living there. It turned out that, on the advice of Sando and Sardar, Zeenat had rented the top portion of a bungalow in the Bandara area. When Babu Gopi Nath came to see me, I told him of the new arrangement, but I said nothing about the establishment Sando and Sardar were running, thanks to Zeenat.

Babu Gopi Nath had come back with ten thousand rupees this time. Ghaffar Sain and Ghulam Ali had been left in Lahore. When we met, he insisted that I should come with him to Zeenat's place. He had left a taxi waiting on the street.

It took us an hour to get to Bandara. As we were driving up Pali Hill, we saw Sando. 'Sando, Sando,' Babu Gopi Nath shouted. 'Dharan takhta,' Sando exclaimed when he saw who it was.

Babu Gopi Nath wanted him to get into the taxi, but Sando wouldn't. 'There is something I have to tell you,' he said.

I stayed in the taxi. The two of them talked for some time, then Babu Gopi Nath came back and told the driver to return to town.

He looked happy. As we were approaching Dawar, he said, 'Manto sahib, Zeno is about to be married.'

'To whom?' I asked, somewhat surprised.

'A rich landlord from Hyderabad, Sindh. May God keep both of them happy. The timing is perfect. The money I have can be used to buy Zeno her dowry.'

I was a bit sceptical about the story. I was sure it was another of Sando and Sardar's tricks to cheat Babu Gopi Nath. However, it all turned out to be true. The man was a rich Sindhi landlord who had been introduced to Zeno through the good offices of a Sindhi music teacher who had failed to teach her how to sing.

One day he had brought Ghulam Hussain — for that was the landlord's name — to Zeenat's place and she had received him with her usual hospitality. She had even sung for him at his insistence Ghalib's ghazal *'Nukta cheen hai gham-e-dil usko sunai na bana.'* Ghulam Hussain was smitten. The music teacher mentioned this to Zeenat, and Sardar and Sando joined hands to firm things up and a date for marriage was set.

One thing had led to another and now they were going to get married.

Babu Gopi Nath was ecstatic. He had managed to meet Ghulam Hussain, having had himself introduced as Sando's friend. He told me later, 'Manto sahib, he is handsome and he is intelligent. Before leaving Lahore, I went and prayed at the shrine of Data Ganj Baksh for Zeno and my prayer has been answered. May Bhagwan keep both of them happy.'

Babu Gopi Nath made all the wedding arrangements. Four thousand rupees was spent on ornaments and clothes and five thousand was to be given in cash to Zeenat.

The wedding guests from Zeenat's side were myself, Mohammad Shafiq Toosi, and Mohammad Yasin, proprietor of the Nagina Hotel. After the ceremony, Sando whispered, 'Dharan takhta.'

Ghulam Hussain was a handsome man. He was dressed in a blue suit and was graciously acknowledging the congratulations being offered to him. Babu Gopi Nath looked like a little bird in his presence.

There was a wedding dinner, with Babu Gopi Nath very much the host. At one point, he said to me, 'Manto sahib, you must see how lovely Zeno looks in her bridal dress.'

I went into the next room. There sat Zeenat, dressed in expensive, silver-embroidered red silk. She was lightly made up, but was wearing too much lipstick. She greeted me by bowing her head slightly. She did look lovely, I thought. However, when I looked in the other corner, I found a bed profusely bedecked with flowers. I just could not contain my laughter. 'What is this farce?' I asked her. 'You are making fun of me, Manto bhai,' Zeno said, tears welling up in her eyes.

I was still wondering how to react, when Babu Gopi Nath came in. Lovingly, he dried Zeno's tears with his handkerchief and said to me in a heartbroken voice, 'Manto sahib, I had always considered you a wise and sensitive man. Before making such fun of Zeno, you should at least have weighed your words.'

I suddenly had the feeling that the devotion he had always shown me had suffered a setback, but before I could apologize to him, he placed his hand affectionately over Zeenat's head and said, 'May God keep you happy.'

When he left the room, his eyes were wet and there was a look of disillusionment on his face.

Translated by Khalid Hasan

The Room with the Bright Light

H E STOOD quietly by a lamppost off the Qaiser Gardens, thinking how desolate everything looked. A few tongas waited for customers who were nowhere in evidence.

A few years ago, this used to be such a gay place, full of bright, happy, carefree men and women, but everything seemed to have gone to seed. The area was now full of louts and vagabonds with nowhere to go. The bazaar still had its crowds, but it had lost its colour. The shops and buildings looked derelict and unwashed, staring at each other like empty-eyed widows.

He stood there wondering what had turned the once fashionable Qaiser Gardens into a slum. Where had all the life and excitement gone? It reminded him of a woman who had been scrubbed clean of all her makeup.

He remembered that many years ago when he had moved to Bombay from Calcutta to take up a job, he had tried vainly for weeks to find a room in this area. There was nothing going.

How times had changed. Judging by the kind of people in the streets, just anybody could rent a place here now – weavers, cobblers, grocers.

He looked around again. What used to be film company offices were now bed-sitters with cooking stoves, and where the elegant people of the city used to gather in the evenings were now washermen's backyards.

It was nothing short of a revolution, but a revolution which had brought decay. In between, he had left the city, but knew through newspaper reports and friends who had stayed back what had happened to Qaiser Gardens in his absence.

There had been riots, accompanied by massacres and rapes. The violence Qaiser Gardens had witnessed had left its ugly mark on everything. The once splendid commercial buildings and residential houses looked sordid and unclean.

He was told that during the riots women had been stripped naked and their breasts chopped off. Was it then surprising that everything looked naked and ravaged?

He was here this evening to meet a friend who had promised to find him a place to live.

Qaiser Gardens used to have some of the city's best restaurants and hotels. And if one was inclined, the best girls in Bombay could be obtained through the good offices of the city's high-class pimps who used to hang out here.

He recalled those good times. He thought nostalgically of the women, the drinking, the elegant hotel rooms. Because of the war, it was almost impossible to obtain Scotch whisky, but he had never had to spend a dry evening. Any amount of expensive Scotch was yours for the asking, as long as you were able to pay for it.

He looked at his watch. It was going on five. The shadows of the February evening had begun to lengthen. He cursed his friend who had kept him waiting. He was about to slip into a roadside place for a cup of tea when a shabbily dressed man came up to him.

'Do you want something?' he asked the stranger.

'Yes,' he replied in a conspiratorial voice.

He took him for a refugee who had fallen on bad times and wanted some money. 'What do you want?' he asked.

'I don't want anything.' He paused, then drew closer and said, 'Do you need something?'

'What?'

'A girl, for instance?'

'Where is she?'

His tone was none too encouraging for the stranger, who began to walk away. 'It seems you are not really interested.'

He stopped him. 'How do you know? What you can provide is something men are always in need of, even on the gallows. So look, my friend, if it is not too far, I am prepared to come with you. You see, I was waiting for someone who hasn't turned up.'

The man whispered, 'It is close, very close, I assure you.'

'Where?'

'That building across from us.'

'You mean that one?' he asked.

'Yes.'

'Should I come with you?'

'Yes, but please walk behind me.' They crossed the road. It was a run-down building with the plaster peeling off the walls and rubbish heaps littering the entrance.

They went through a courtyard and then through a dark corridor. It seemed that construction had been abandoned at some point before completion. The bricks in the walls were unplastered and there were piles of lime mixed with cement on the floor.

The man began to ascend a flight of dilapidated stairs. 'Please wait here. I'll be back in a minute,' he said.

He looked up and saw a bright light at the end of the landing.

He waited for a couple of minutes and then began to climb the stairs. When he reached the landing, he heard the man who had brought him screaming, 'Are you going to get up or not?'

A woman's voice answered, 'Just let me sleep.'

The man screamed again, 'You heard me, are you getting up or not? Or you know what I'll do to you.'

The woman's voice again: 'You can kill me but I won't get up. For God's sake, have mercy on me.'

The man changed his tone. 'Darling, don't be obstinate. How are we going to make a living if you don't get up?'

'Living be damned. I'll starve to death, but for God's sake, don't drag me out of bed. I'm sleepy,' answered the woman.

The man began to roar with anger, 'So you're not going to leave your bed, you bitch, you filthy bitch!'

The woman shouted back, 'I won't, I won't, I won't!'

The man changed his tone again. 'Don't shout like that. The whole world can hear you. Come on now, get up. We could make thirty, even forty rupees.'

The woman began to whimper, 'I beg of you, don't make me go. You know how many days and nights I have gone without sleep. Have pity on me, please.'

'It won't be long,' the man said, 'just a couple of hours and then you can sleep as long as you like. Look, don't make me use other methods to persuade you.'

There was a brief silence. He crossed the landing on tiptoe and peeped into the room where the very bright light was coming from. It was not much of a room. There were a few empty cooking pots on the floor and a woman stretched out in the middle with the man he had come with crouching over her. He was pressing her legs and saying, 'Be a good girl now. I promise you, we'll be back in two hours and then you can sleep to your heart's content.'

He saw the woman suddenly get up like a firecracker which has been shown a match. 'All right,' she said, 'I'll come.'

He was suddenly afraid and ran down the stairs. He wanted to put as much distance between this place and himself as he could, between himself and this city.

He thought of the woman who wanted to sleep. Who was she? Why was she being treated with such inhumanity?

And who was that man? Why was the room so unremittingly bright? Did they both live there? Why did they live there?

His eyes were still partly blinded by the dazzling light bulb in that terrible room upstairs. He couldn't see very well. Couldn't they have hung a softer light in the room? Why was it so nakedly, pitilessly bright?

There was a noise in the dark and a movement. All he could see were two silhouettes, one of them obviously that of the man whom he had followed to this awful place.

'Take a look,' he said.

'I have,' he replied.

'Is she all right?'

'She is all right.'

'That will be forty rupees.'

'All right.'

'Can I have the money?'

He could no longer think clearly. He put his hand in his pocket, pulled out a fistful of bank notes and handed them over. 'Count them,' he said.

'There's fifty there.'

'Keep it.'

'Thank you.'

He had an urge to pick up a big stone and smash his head. 'Please take her, but be nice to her and bring her back in a couple of hours.'

'OK.'

He walked out of the building with the woman, and found a tonga waiting outside. He jumped quickly in the front. The woman took the back seat.

The tonga began to move. He asked him to stop in front of a ramshackle, empty hotel. They went in. He took his first look at the woman. Her eyes were red and swollen. She looked so tired that he was afraid she would fall to the floor in a heap.

'Raise your head,' he said to her.

'What?' She was startled.

'Nothing, all I said was raise your head.'

She looked up. Her eyes were like empty holes topped up with ground chilli.

'What is your name?' he asked.

'Never mind.' Her tone was like acid.

'Where are you from?'

'What does it matter?'

'Why are you so unfriendly?'

The woman was now wide awake. She stared at him with her blood-red eyes and said, 'You finish your business because I have to go.'

'Where?'

'Where you picked me up from,' she answered indifferently.

'You are free to go.'

'Why don't you finish your business? Why are you trying to ridicule me?'

'I'm not trying to ridicule you. I feel sorry for you,' he said in a sympathetic voice.

'I want no sympathizers. You do whatever you brought me here for and then let me go,' she almost screamed.

He tried to put his hand on her shoulder, but she shook it off rudely.

'Leave me alone. I haven't slept for days. I've been awake ever since I came to that place.'

'You can sleep here.'

'I didn't come here to sleep. This isn't my home.'

'Is that room your home?'

This seemed to infuriate her even more.

'Cut out the rubbish. I have no home. You do your job or take me back. You can have your money returned by that '

'All right, I'll take you back,' he said.

And he took her back to that big building and left her there. The next day, sitting in a desolate hotel in Qaiser Park, he told the story of that woman to a friend, who was greatly moved by it. Expressing sorrow, he asked, 'Was she young?'

'I don't know,' he replied. 'The fact is that I didn't really look at her. I only had this savage desire to pick up a rock and smash the head of the man who had brought me there.'

His friend said, 'That would have been a most worthy deed.'

He did not stay with his friend for very long in that hotel. He felt greatly depressed by the events of the day before. They finished their tea and left.

He quietly walked to the tonga stand, his eyes searching for that procurer, who was nowhere to be found. It was now six o'clock and the big building was right across, just a few yards from him. He began to walk towards it and, once there, went in.

There were people walking in. Quite calmly, taking steps through the dark, he came to the stairway and noticed a light at the top. He looked up and began to climb very quietly. For a while, he stood at the landing. A bright light was coming out of the room, but there was no sound, not even a stir. He approached the wide open doors and, standing aside, peeped in. The first thing he saw was a bulb whose light dazzled his eyes. He abruptly moved aside and turned towards the dark to get the dazzle out of his eyes.

Then he advanced towards the doors but in a way that his eyes should not meet that blinding light. He looked in. On the bit of floor he could see, there was a woman lying on a mat. He looked at her carefully. She was asleep, her face covered with her dupatta. Her bosom rose and fell with her rhythmic breathing. He moved deeper into the room and screamed but he quickly stifled it. Next to that woman, on the bare floor, lay a man, his head smashed into a pulp. A bloodied brick lay close by. He saw all this in one rapid sequence, then he leapt towards the stairs but lost his foothold and fell down. Without caring for his injuries, while trying to keep his sanity intact, he managed to get home with great difficulty. All night, he kept seeing terrifying dreams.

Translated by Khalid Hasan

I'm No Good For You!

A HEATED DISCUSSION about Chaudhry Ghulam Abba's latest speech was in full swing in the Tea House. The atmosphere inside was cosy and as warm as the tea. We were in agreement about one thing: We should grab Kashmir no matter what and Dogra rule must end immediately.

They were all *mujahideen*, God's valiant soldiers, who didn't know the first thing about fighting but were ready to jump into the battlefield at any moment. The consensus was that if we launched a surprise attack, Kashmir would be in our hands in a blink.

Well, I was among those mujahideen. My problem, though, is that I'm a Kashmiri right down to the hilt, and no less a Kashmiri than Pandit Jawaharlal Nehru, which makes it my greatest weakness. I just chimed along with the other mujahideen. It was decided that the minute war broke out we would join and fight at the very front.

Although Haneef showed great enthusiasm, I sensed that he was feeling rather melancholy, but I couldn't figure out the reason for his downcast mood.

Everyone left after the tea, only Haneef and I stayed on. By now the

Tea House had become nearly empty with only two boys chatting over their breakfast in a far corner.

I had met Haneef a while back. He was about ten years younger than me. He had finished his BA and was undecided whether to opt for an MA in English or in Urdu. Sometimes he got it into his head to stop his studies altogether and set out to travel.

I looked at him closely. He was picking up the used matchsticks from the ashtray and nervously breaking them into small bits. As I've already mentioned, he was feeling rather blue. It appeared to be a good opportunity to ask him about it. 'Why are you feeling so glum?'

He lifted his head, tossed the broken pieces to one side, and replied, 'Oh, no particular reason.'

I lit up. 'What do you mean 'no particular reason'? That's no answer. There's always a reason for everything. Perhaps you're reminiscing about some old event.'

He nodded. 'Yes.'

'And that event has something to do with Kashmir?'

He started. 'How did you know that?'

I smiled. 'I'm a Sherlock Holmes. My good man, weren't we just now talking about Kashmir? When you agreed that you were thinking, and thinking about some past event, I immediately guessed that this event must have to do with Kashmir. It's got to be. So, did you fall in love there?'

'Love . . . I don't know . . . God knows what it was. Anyway, something did happen and the memory of it still haunts me.'

I was eager to hear his story. 'If you don't mind, tell me about that *something*.'

He asked me for a cigarette and lit it. 'Manto Sahib,' he said, 'it isn't an especially interesting incident. But if you promise to listen quietly without interrupting, I'll tell you everything, down to the last detail, about what transpired three years ago. I'm not a storyteller, all the same I'll try.'

I promised not to interrupt. Actually he wanted to narrate his story by going into the depths of his heart and mind.

After a pause he began, 'Manto Sahib, it happened two years ago, when Partition wasn't even in our imagination. It was summer time. I was feeling down, God knows why. I guess all unattached, single men feel gloomy in the summer. Anyway, one day I decided to go to Kashmir. I packed a few essentials and went to the lorry stand. I bought a ticket and boarded. When the lorry arrived at Kad, I changed my mind. What is there in Srinagar, I thought. I've already seen it many times. I'll get out at the next stop, Batut. It's a salubrious place. Tuberculosis patients frequently go there and leave cured. So I got off at Batut and stayed in a hotel, a rather bare-bones one, but all right. I was quite taken with Batut. I went climbing on the slopes every morning, ate a breakfast of toast and pure butter on my return from the hike, and then, lying down, read some book or other.

'I was spending my days pleasurably in the salubrious environment of the place. I'd become friends with all the shopkeepers in the area around the hotel, especially Sardar Lahna Singh who was a tailor. I would spend hours at his shop. He was a fanatic for love stories. His sewing machines would keep whirring and he'd be absorbed in those stories.

'He knew every last thing about Batut. Who was having an affair with whom, who'd had a tiff, which girls had just started to put on airs – you name it. His pocket was always full of such gossip.

'In the evenings, the two of us went for a stroll on the downward slopes, all the way to the Banihal Pass, and then walked back up slowly. There was a cluster of mud dwellings to the right of the first bend in the road if you were coming from the hotel and headed towards the slopes. One day I asked Sardarji whether those quarters were meant to be lived in. I asked because they had caught my fancy. Yes, they were for living in, he told me. 'A railway babu from Sargodha is staying there these days. His wife is ill.'

'She must have tuberculosis,' I concluded at once. God knows why I'm so scared of this disease. From that day on I never passed by those quarters without covering my nose and mouth with a kerchief. I don't want to prolong the story. In short, eventually, I became friends with Kundan Lal, the railway babu. I soon realized he wasn't at all concerned about his wife's condition. He was simply going through the motions of being a caring husband. He visited her occasionally and lived in a sepa-rate dwelling, which he disinfected with phenyl three times a day. It was his wife's younger sister Sumitri, hardly fourteen years old, who took care of her with unflinching devotion.

'I first saw Sumitri by the Maggu stream. A big pile of dirty laundry lay by her side and she was perhaps washing a shalwar when I passed by. The sound of my footsteps startled her. She quickly joined her hands and said namaste to me. I returned her greeting and asked, 'You know me?' 'Yes,' she said in her shrill voice, 'you're Babuji's friend.' What stood before me, I felt, was not Sumitri, but suffering itself, moulded into her form. I felt like talking to her, to help her with her washing, to lessen her burdens just a little, but such informality seemed out of place at our very first meeting.

'The second time I met her, again by the very same stream, she was rubbing soap into some clothes when I said namaste and sat down on top of a bed of fallen apples. She felt somewhat nervous, but her trepidation disappeared once we started talking. She became so friendly that she started telling me all about the affairs of her household.

'It'd been five years since her elder sister got married to Babuji, she told me. During the first year of their marriage, Babuji treated her sister well, but when he was suspended from his job for allegedly taking bribes, he wanted to sell her jewellery and gamble with it, hoping it would double the amount. Her sister wouldn't agree, so he started beating and abusing her. He would shut her up in a small dark room all day long without food for months. Finally, when she couldn't take it anymore, she handed him the jewellery. He disappeared with it and didn't show his face for six months, during which time she was reduced to starvation. Had she wanted to, she could have gone back to her parents. Her father was quite wealthy; he even loved her a lot. But she didn't think it was proper to go back. She ended up contracting tuberculosis. When Kundan Lal finally reappeared six months later, he found his wife bedridden. He had been reinstated. When asked where he'd been all this time, he hedged and fudged.

'Sumitri's sister didn't ask him about her jewellery. She was happy that God had heard her entreaties and sent her husband back to her. Her health improved a little, but a month later her condition deteriorated sharply. It was only then that her parents somehow learned about her illness. They immediately came over and forced Kundan Lal to bring her to the mountain right away and said they would bear the expenses. Kundad Lal thought, why not, let's have some recreation. He brought Sumitri along for his amusement and landed in Batut.

'Once here, he took absolutely no notice of his wife. He stayed out the whole day playing cards. Sumitri prepared the special diet for her sister. Every month Kundan Lal wrote to his in-laws that the expenses were mounting, and every month they added extra to the amount they sent.

'I don't wish to let this story drag on. I was now seeing Sumitri practically every day. The area by the stream where she washed clothes was pleasantly cool, just like the water of the stream. The shade under the apple trees was heavenly, and I wished I could sit there all day long, picking up the lovely round apples and tossing them into the clear water. The reason for this rather crude lyricism that has crept into my account is that I'd fallen in love with Sumitri and somehow sensed that she had accepted it. So one day, overwhelmed by a sudden surge of emotion, I clasped her to my bosom and kissed her on the lips with my eyes closed. Birds were twittering on the branches of the apple trees and the stream was humming gently.

'She was pretty, though a bit skinny. But if you thought deeply, you'd have felt that this is how she had to be. If she had been a bit fleshy, she wouldn't have looked so delicate. She had the eyes of a gazelle, which nature had lined with a dark eye shadow. She was short but infinitely pleasing, and her long, thick, dark hair reached down to her waist. A virgin, blossoming youth. Manto sahib, I was lost in her love.

'As she was expressing her love for me, I told her what had been sticking like a thorn in my heart for some time. 'Look, Sumitri,' I said, 'I'm Muslim and you're Hindu. What would be the end of this love? I'm not a libertine or rake that I could take advantage of you and be on my way. I want to make you my mate for life.' She threw her arms around my neck and told me firmly, 'Haneef, I'll convert.'

'The weight on my heart lifted and I felt light. We decided that as soon as her sister got well she would leave with me. But it was not in her sister's fate to get well. Kundan Lal had told me plainly that he was waiting for his wife to die. In a matter of speaking, what he said had a ring of truth to it, though thinking such a thought and then blaming yourself for thinking it didn't seem right. Reality was staring us in the face. The disease being what it is, there was no way to escape from it.

'Sumitri's sister's condition worsened by the day. However, Kundan Lal couldn't care less. With more money coming from his in-laws and expenses reduced, or being purposely reduced, he had started going to the Dak Bangla to booze it up, and had even started coming on to Sumitri.

'My blood boiled, Manto Sahib, when I heard about that. Had I not lacked the courage, I'd have thrashed him black and blue with my shoes right there in the middle of the street. I hugged Sumitri to my chest, wiped away her tears and started to talk of love.

'As I passed by their quarters one morning on my walk, I had the uncanny feeling that Sumitri's sister was no longer in this world. I halted and called out to Kundan Lal. I was right. The poor woman had passed away at eleven o'clock the night before.

'He asked me to stay there a while so he could go and make arrangements for her last rites. He went out. As I stood there I was reminded of Sumitri. Where was she? The room with her sister's corpse was deathly quiet. I walked over to the adjoining quarters and peeked in. Sumitri was curled up on the bed like a bundle. I went in and shook her shoulder. 'Sumitri! Sumitri!' I called her name. She didn't respond. Just then I spotted her shalwar stained with big splotches of blood. I shook her again. Again she didn't answer. I asked her tenderly, lovingly, 'What's the matter, Sumitri?' She burst into tears. I sat down beside her. 'What's the matter, Sumitri?' She said through her sobs, 'Go, Haneef, go!' 'But why?' I asked. 'I know your sister has died. But please don't kill yourself crying.' She choked on her words as she said, 'She's dead, but I can't grieve over her. I've died myself.' I didn't understand. 'Why must you die? You have yet to become my life-mate, remember?' At this she started to cry bitterly. 'Go, Haneef, go! I'm no good for you anymore. Last night . . . last night Babuji finished me off. I screamed. Jiji screamed from her quarters. She had guessed everything. The shock killed her. Oh, how I wish I hadn't screamed. She couldn't have saved me. Go, Haneef, go!' She got up from the bed, grabbed my hand like someone possessed and dragged me out of the room. She quickly went back in and bolted the door. That son-of-a-bitch Kundan Lal returned after some time with four or five men in tow. I would have stoned him to death then and there had he been alone, I swear.

'This, then, this is my story. . . Sumitri's story. Those three words of hers, 'Go, Haneef, go!' never leave my ears. They're filled with such pain, such anguish.'

Tears had appeared in Haneef's eyes.

'Well, what happened, happened,' I said. 'You could still have married her. . .'

He lowered his eyes, uttered a coarse invective directed at himself, and said, 'Call it my weakness. Man turns out to be such a coward when it comes to that. God's curse upon him.'

Translated by Muhammad Umar Memon

Empty Bottles, Empty Cans

WHY SINGLES are so taken with empty bottles and cans continues to amaze me even now. By singles I mean people generally not interested in getting married – ever.

Granted, this breed tends to be eccentric and fosters idiosyncrasies; however, what throws me off is their exaggerated fondness for empty bottles and cans. Often they also keep birds and animals. I can understand their need for companionship, but empty bottles and cans? In heaven's name, what possible companionship can these inanimate objects offer?

Call it the result of transgressing nature if you wish to find a reason for such strange habits and eccentricities, but you can't explain it as easily in psychological terms. Indeed it's hugely difficult.

I have a relative, about fifty now, who is fond of keeping pigeons and dogs as pets. There's nothing odd about that. His affliction is this: Every day he goes to the bazaar to buy cream, which he boils down to clarified butter. *This* is what he uses to cook his food. He believes this is how pure ghee is distilled.

He also keeps a reserve pot of water especially for his personal use. It's always covered with a piece of thin, gauzy fabric to prevent insects from getting in while still allowing the continuous passage of fresh air. Before going to the toilet, he takes off all his clothes, wraps a small towel around himself and slips on his wooden clogs. Now, if you want to understand the psychology behind the clarified butter, the thin, gauzy fabric over the mouth of the water pot, the towel and the wooden clogs – be my guest.

I have a friend – a single. He appears to be quite normal. He works as a reader at the high court. His affliction: He smells foul odours everywhere all the time. So, as a consequence, his kerchief is never far from his nose. He's fond of keeping rabbits.

There's another single. He drops down to offer *namaz* whenever and wherever the opportunity presents itself. But he's perfectly sane. He has a profound understanding of world politics. He's an expert in training parrots to speak.

And this wealthy old major in the military – he's fond of collecting hookahs. *Gurguris, pechwans*, you name it; he's got quite a collection. Although he owns several houses, a rented room in a hotel is where he lives. Pheasants are his passion.

And this retired Colonel Sahib, he lives in a spacious bungalow with his dozen or so dogs, big and small. He keeps a collection of whiskies, of all types and brands. He drinks four glasses every evening with one or another of his favourite canines and treats the dog to some as well.

All the singles I've mentioned so far are, without exception, fond of empty bottles and cans. Whenever my kinsman, the one who distils pure ghee from cream, spots an empty bottle anywhere in the house, he washes it thoroughly and puts it in his cupboard, thinking that it might come in handy some day. The high court reader, who smells foul odours everywhere, all the time, collects only bottles and cans that he has made absolutely sure will never smell bad. The fellow who is ready to pray anywhere and any time keeps dozens of bottles to wash himself after going to the toilet, and tin cans to use for ablutions. He thinks that these items are both inexpensive and clean. The major, who is given to stockpiling hookahs, collects empty bottles and cans for the sole purpose of selling them to scrap merchants. The retired colonel is only fond of collecting empty bottles of whisky. If you happen to visit him, you will see these whisky bottles neatly arranged inside several glass cabinets in a small, tidy room. No matter how antiquated the brand, you can be sure to find it in his rare collection. Just as some people are fond of collecting stamps and coins, he has a passion – or rather obsession – for collecting empty whisky bottles and displaying them.

The Colonel Sahib has no relatives. If he does, I'm certainly not aware of it. Even though he's alone in the world, he doesn't suffer from loneliness at all. He's happy with his dozen or so dogs and he cares as much for them as an affectionate father for his children. He spends his entire day with his pets, and whatever free time he has is spent rearranging his darling bottles in their cabinets.

Now, you might say, well, all right, empty bottles make sense, but why have you tacked on empty cans along with them? Why in the world would it be necessary for a bachelor to be interested not just in empty bottles but also in empty cans? And whether bottles or cans – why should they be empty? Why not full?

Haven't I already told you that I wonder about that too? This and similar questions often assail my mind. Yet I'm unable to come up with an answer, no matter how hard I try.

Empty bottles and cans represent a void. The only logical connection between them and celibate men is perhaps that the latter's life is characterized by a gaping emptiness. This doesn't help, for it begs the question: Do such men try to fill one void with another? A person can at least say that dogs, cats, rabbits and monkeys fill the emptiness of a man's life to some degree. They can amuse with their funny antics and airs, and even respond to love. But what possible enjoyment can empty bottles and cans afford?

It's possible that the following might offer you an answer to these questions.

Ten years ago, when I went to Bombay, a film produced by a famous studio had been running for twenty weeks. The heroine was an experienced actress, but the hero was a complete novice and looked very young in the advertisements. After reading great things about his acting skills in the newspapers, I decided to go see the film. It was quite all right. The story was interesting enough and, considering that the hero was appearing before the camera for the first time in his life, his acting was okay.

It is generally difficult to guess the true age of an actor or actress on the screen. Thanks to the wonders of make-up, a young man can look years older, an old man like a strapping youth. But this newcomer was in fact quite young, vibrant and very agile, like a college student. Although not exactly handsome, every limb on his firm body was well proportioned and finely shaped.

In the years that followed I saw many more films with the same actor. He had become more mature in his work. The raw, boyish softness of his features had gelled into the firmness that comes with age and experience. He was now among the finest film stars in Bombay.

Scandals are nothing new in the film world. Every day brings the news that some actor has become amorously involved with some actress or other, or that actress X has ditched her lover for director Y. No actor or actress is immune from a romantic affair at some time or other. However, the life of this new actor was entirely free of any such entanglements. This fact, though, was not talked about much in the newspapers. No one ever mentioned, even in passing, that Ram Saroop's life was absolutely free of any kind of gossip in spite of his close involvement with the film world.

To tell you the truth, I'd never given much thought to these matters because I had absolutely no interest in the personal lives of film people. Watch a film, form an opinion of it, that was the extent of my involvement. However, when I met Ram Saroop, I learned many interesting things about him. This meeting took place nearly eight years after I saw his first film.

During his early days in the film industry he lived in a village quite far from his Bombay. With his increasing involvement in motion pictures, he was obliged to move into a modest flat in the Shivaji Park neighbourhood near the sea. This flat was where I met him. It had four rooms, including the kitchen. The family that lived here comprised eight members: Ram Saroop himself, his servant who doubled as the cook, three dogs, two monkeys and one cat. Ram Saroop and the servant were both bachelors; the dogs and the cat were also without mates of the opposite sex; the monkeys were the exception but they stayed in their separate wire mesh cages most of the time.

Ram Saroop loved his six animals dearly. He also treated his servant kindly, which had little, if anything, to do with emotion. He had set a routine, and performed tasks at fixed times with the cold regularity of a machine, as if automatically. It almost seemed as though Ram Saroop had jotted down the set of rules and regulations governing his life and handed them over to his servant, who had then memorized them.

If Ram Saroop took off his clothes and slipped into a pair of shorts, the servant immediately placed a few bottles of soda and some flasks of ice on the glass-topped teapoy. This meant that the sahib would now drink rum and play with his dogs. If the phone rang in the meantime, he was supposed to say that the sahib was not home.

An empty bottle of rum or can of cigarettes was never to be trashed or sold. It was put away carefully in the sahib's room, which was already crowded with piles of empty bottles and cans.

If a woman came to the door, she would be turned away with the excuse that the sahib had spent the night shooting a film and was asleep. If she showed up in the evening she was told that the sahib was out on a shoot.

The ambience of Ram Saroop's place wasn't very different from that of any bachelor who lives alone. It lacked the decor and tidiness beholden to a woman's delicate touch. Yes, it was neat and clean, but in a coarse sort of way. The first time I entered, the feeling that I'd stepped into the part of a zoo where tigers and cheetahs and such are kept overwhelmed me; it exuded the same animal odour.

One of the rooms was a bedroom, another a sitting room, and the third was where the empty bottles and cans were kept – all the rum bottles and cigarette cans that Ram Saroop had emptied himself. They were just sitting around haphazardly without any particular order, bottles and cans, one on top of the other, face up or face down. Some stood in a line in one corner, while others were just heaped up in another, coated with dust, giving off the pungent odours of stale tobacco and equally stale rum blended together.

I must say I was bowled over when I first saw this room, crowded as it was with numberless bottles and cans – all empty.

'What's going on?' I asked Ram Saroop.

'Whatever do you mean?'

'I mean this junk?'

'It just kind of piled up,' was all he could say.

'It would take seven or eight years to collect so much junk' – I thought out loud.

I was mistaken. As I later found out, it had taken ten. When he moved over to Shivaji Park he had hauled along the bottles and cans that had accumulated in his old house. Once, I asked him, 'Saroop, why don't you sell these? In the first place, they shouldn't have been allowed to get out of hand, but now that they have, and you can get a good price on account of the war, you'd better get rid of this junk.'

His only answer: 'Drop it, yaar! It's just too much bother.'

This sort of gave the impression that he really had no interest in empty bottles and cans, but his servant let me in on the fact that Ram Saroop raised hell if even a single bottle or can was moved from its place.

Ram Saroop had no interest in women. We had become close friends. Several times I asked him casually, 'So my friend, when are you getting married?' and each time I was given the same type of answer: 'Whatever for?'

Yes, indeed, whatever for – really? I thought. *Will he shut her up in his*

junk room? Or play with her in his shorts as he sipped his rum? While I did
bring up the subject of marriage with him now and then, try as hard as I
could in my imagination, I couldn't picture him with a woman.

Our association was now several years old. During this time the
rumour went round several times that he had fallen in love with some
actress named Sheela. I absolutely didn't believe in the veracity of the
story. For one thing, it wasn't something one could expect from Ram
Saroop; for another, Sheela wasn't quite the woman any sane young man
would lose his heart to. She always looked lifeless, as though she was
suffering from tuberculosis. She did look tolerable in her first few movies, but eventually lost whatever panache she might have had, morphing
into a totally insipid, bland character, now consigned to appear only in
third-class movies.

I asked him just one about this Sheela woman. He replied with a smile,
'Do you think she's the only woman left for me?' About this time his
dearest dog Stalin caught pneumonia. Ram Saroop had it treated in the
best way he knew, but the poor animal's days were numbered. Its death
pained him deeply. His eyes remained teary for quite some time. Then
one day he gave away his other dogs to a friend. I thought it was due to
the terrible shock of Stalin's death, otherwise he would never have parted
with them. However, it surprised me a bit when, not long afterwards, he
also got rid of the monkeys. Must be because he didn't want to go through
another harrowing experience in the future, I concluded. Now he only
played with his cat Nargis, as usual, in his shorts while sipping rum. The
cat loved him equally in return because she had no competition; she alone
was the recipient of his affections.

Soon, his living quarters no longer smelled of tigers and cheetahs and reflected a noticeable order and taste in their decor. His face, too, now assumed a slightly fresher look. However, all this happened so slowly that it was difficult to determine the exact moment of the onset of the change.

Time rolled on. His new film was released. I observed a marked freshness in his acting. When I congratulated him, he smiled and said, 'Come, have some whisky?'

'Whisky?' I asked, surprised. Didn't he always drink rum . . . only rum?

His earlier smile shrank somewhat on his lips as he answered, 'I'm tired of drinking rum.'

No further questioning was necessary.

A week later when I went to see him, he was drinking as usual, not rum but whisky, not in his shorts but in a kurta-pyjama. We played cards and drank for a long time. After a while I noticed his tongue and palate were having difficulty accepting the taste of the new drink, for with every sip he made a face as if he was drinking something foreign. I said to him, 'Looks as if you haven't got used to whisky yet, have you?'

'Oh, I will. Give it some time,' he said smiling.

Ram Saroop's flat was on the second floor. As I was passing by one day I saw great big piles of empty bottles and cans near the garage being loaded on to a couple of rickety carts by a few junk dealers. I was aghast; this treasure could only have belonged to Ram Saroop. I felt a tingle of indescribable pain to see it being hauled away. I ran up to his flat and rang the bell. The door opened, but when I tried to step inside his servant uncharacteristically stopped me, saying, 'Sahib was out on a shoot last night. He's sleeping now.'

I left in surprise and anger, muttering something under my breath.

That very evening Ram Saroop came to my house with Sheela in tow, draped in a new crisp Banarasi sari. 'Meet my wife,' Ram Saroop said, pointing at Sheela.

Had I not already downed four pegs of whisky I would certainly have been knocked out. Both of them sat for a short while and then left. For a long time afterwards I kept ruminating: *What did Sheela remind me of? A papery, beige sari over a sparse, thin body, puffed out here, shrunk there?* Suddenly the image of an empty bottle floated before my eyes, an empty bottle wrapped in paper.

Sheela was a woman – totally empty, but it was possible that one void had filled another.

Translated by Muhammad Umar Memon

It Happened in 1919

'IT HAPPENED IN 1919. The whole of Punjab was up in arms against the Rowlatt Act. Sir Michael O'Dwyer had banned Gandhiji's entry into the province under the Defence of India rules. He had been stopped at Pulwal, taken into custody and sent to Bombay. I believe if the British had not made this blunder, the Jallianwala Bagh incident would not have added a bloody page to the black history of their rule in India.'

I was on a train and the man sitting next to me had begun talking to me, just like that. I hadn't interrupted him and so he had gone on.

'Gandhiji was loved and respected by the people, Muslims, Hindus and Sikhs alike. When news of the arrest reached Lahore, the entire city went on strike. Amritsar, where the story I am going to narrate happened, followed suit.

'It is said that by the evening of 9 April, the deputy commissioner had received orders for the expulsion from Amritsar of the two leaders, Dr Satyapal and Dr Kitchlew, but was unwilling to implement them because, in his view, there was no likelihood of a breach of the peace. Protest meetings were being organized and no one was in favour of using violent methods.

'I was a witness to a procession taken out to celebrate a Hindu festival, and I can assure you it was the most peaceful thing I ever saw. It faithfully kept to the route marked out by the officials, but this Sir Michael was half-mad. They said he refused to follow the deputy commissioner's advice because he was convinced that Kitchlew and Satyapal were in Amritsar waiting for a signal from Gandhiji before proceeding to topple the government. In his view the protest meetings and processions were all part of this grand conspiracy.

'The news of the expulsion of the two leaders spread like wildfire through the city, creating an atmosphere of uncertainty and fear. One could sense that disaster was about to strike. But, my friend, I can tell you that there was also a great deal of enthusiasm among the people. All businesses were closed. The city was quiet like a graveyard and there was a feeling of impending doom in the air.

'After the first shock of the expulsions had died down, thousands of people gathered spontaneously to go in a procession to the deputy commissioner and call for the withdrawal of the orders. But, my friend, believe me, the times were out of joint. That this extremely reasonable request would be even heard was out of the question. Sir Michael was like a pharaoh and we were not surprised when he declared the gathering itself unlawful.

'Amritsar, which was one of the greatest centres of the liberation struggle and which still proudly carries the wound of Jallianwala Bagh, is now of course changed but that is another story. Some people say that what happened in that great city in 1947 was also the fault of the British. But if you want my opinion, we ourselves are responsible for the bloodshed there in 1947. But that's another matter. . .

'The deputy commissioner's house was in the Civil Lines. In fact, all senior officers and the big toadies of the Raj lived in that exclusive area. If you know your Amritsar, you will recall that bridge which links the city with the Civil Lines. You cross the bridge from the city and you are on the Mall, that earthly paradise created by the British rulers.

'The protest procession began to move towards the Civil Lines. When I reached Hall Gate, word went round that British mounted troops were on guard at the bridge, but the crowd was undeterred and kept moving. I was also among them. We were all unarmed. I mean there wasn't even a stick on any of us. The whole idea was to get to the deputy commissioner's house and protest to him about the expulsion of the two leaders and demand their release. All peacefully.

'When the crowd reached the bridge, the tommies opened fire, causing utter pandemonium. People began to run in all directions. There were no more than twenty to twenty-five soldiers, but they were armed and they were firing. I have never seen anything like it. Some were wounded by gunshots; others were trampled.

'I stood well away from the fray at the edge of a big open gutter and someone pushed me into it. When the firing stopped, I crawled out. The crowd had dispersed. Many of the injured were lying on the road and the tommies on the bridge were having a good laugh. I'm not sure what my state of mind at the time was, but I think it couldn't have been normal. In fact, I think I fainted when I fell in. It was only later that I was able to reconstruct the events.

'I could hear angry chants in the distance. I began to walk. Going past the shrine of Zahra Pir, I was in Hall Gate in no time, where I found about thirty or forty boys throwing stones at the big clock which sits on top of the gate. They finally shattered its protective glass and the pieces fell on the road.

'"Let's go and smash the queen's statue," someone shouted.

'"No, let's set fire to the police headquarters."

'"And all the banks too."

'"What would be the point of that? Let's go to the bridge and fight the tommy soldiers," suggested another.

'I recognized the author of the last proposal. He was Thaila kanjar – kanjar, because he was the son of a prostitute – otherwise Mohammad Tufail. He was quite notorious in Amritsar. He had got into the habit of drinking and gambling while still a boy. He had two sisters, Shamshad and Almas, who were considered the city's most beautiful singing and dancing girls.

'Shamshad was an accomplished singer and big landlords and the like used to travel from great distances to hear her perform. The sisters were not exactly enamoured of the doings of their brother, Thaila, and it was said that they had practically disowned him. However, through one excuse or the other, he was always able to get enough money from them to live in style. He liked to dress and eat well and drink to his heart's content. He was a great storyteller, but unlike other people of his type he was never vulgar. He was tall, athletic and quite handsome, come to think of it.

'However, the boys did not show much enthusiasm for his suggestion of taking on the tommies. Instead, they began to move towards the queen's statue. Thaila was not the kind to give up so easily. He said to them, "Why are you wasting your energy? Why don't you follow me?

We'll go and kill those tommies who have shot and killed so many innocent people. I swear by God, if we're together, we can wring their necks with our bare hands."

'Some were already well on their way to the queen's statue, but there were still some stragglers who began to follow Thaila in the direction of the bridge where the tommies stood guard. I thought the whole thing was suicidal and I had no desire to be part of it. I even shouted at Thaila, "Don't do it, yaar, why are you bent upon getting yourself killed?"

'He laughed. "Thaila just wants to demonstrate that he's not afraid of their bullets," he said cavalierly. Then he told the few who were willing to follow him, "Those among you who are afraid can leave now."

'No one left, which is understandable in such situations. Thaila started to walk briskly, setting the pace for his companions. There seemed to be no question of turning back now.

'The distance between Hall Gate and the bridge is negligible, maybe less than a hundred yards. The approach to the bridge was being guarded by two mounted tommies. I heard the sound of fire as Thaila closed in, shouting revolutionary slogans. I thought he'd been hit, but no, he was still moving forward with great resolution. Some of the boys began to run in different directions. He turned and shouted, "Don't run away . . . Let's go get them."

'I heard more gunfire. Thaila's back was momentarily towards the tommies, since he was trying to infuse some life into his retreating entourage. I saw him veer towards the soldiers and there were big red spots of blood on his silk shirt. He had been hit, but he kept advancing, like a wounded lion. There was more gunfire and he staggered, but then he regained his footing and leapt at the mounted tommy, bringing him down to the ground.

'The other tommy became panic-stricken and began to fire his revolver recklessly. What happened afterwards is not clear, because I fainted.

'When I came to, I found myself home. Some men who knew me had picked me up and brought me back. I heard from them that angry crowds had ransacked the town. The queen's statue had been smashed and the town hall and three of the city bands had been set on fire. Five or six Europeans had been killed and the crowd had gone on a rampage.

'The British officers were not bothered by the looting, but by the fact that European blood had been shed. And as you know, it was avenged at Jallianwala Bagh. The deputy commissioner handed the city over to General Dyer, so on 12 April the general marched through the streets at the head of columns of armed soldiers. Dozens of innocent people were arrested. On 13 April a protest meeting was organized in Jallianwala Bagh which General Dyer "dispersed" by ordering his Gurkha and Sikh soldiers to open fire on the unarmed crowed.

'However, I was telling you about Thaila and what I saw with my own eyes. Only God is without blemish and Thaila was, let's not forget, the son of a prostitute and he used to practise every evil in the book. But he was brave. I tell you he had already been hit when he exhorted his companions not to run away but to move forward. He was so intoxicated with enthusiasm at the time that he did not realize he had been hit. He was shot twice more, once in the back and then in the chest. They pumped his young body full of molten lead.

'I didn't see it, but I'm told that when Thaila's bullet-ridden body was pulled away both his hands were dug into the tommy's throat. They just couldn't get his grip to loosen. The tommy had of course been well and truly dispatched to hell.

'Thaila's bullet-torn body was handed over to his family the next day. It seemed the other tommy had emptied the entire magazine of his revolver into him. He must have been dead by then, but the devil had nevertheless gone on.

'It is said that when Thaila's body was brought to his mohalla it was a shattering scene. It's true he wasn't exactly the apple of his family's eye, but when they saw his minced-up remains, there wasn't a dry eye to be seen anywhere. His sisters, Shamshad and Almas, fainted.

'My friend, I have heard that in the French Revolution, it was a prostitute who was the first to fall. Mohammad Tufail was also a prostitute's son, so whether it was the first bullet of the revolution which hit him or the tenth or the fiftieth, nobody really bothered to find out because socially he did not matter. I have a feeling that when they finally make a list of those who died in this bloodbath in Punjab, Thaila kanjar's name won't be included. As a matter of fact, I don't think anyone would even bother about a list.

'Those were terrible days. The monster they call martial law held the city in its grip. Thaila was buried amid great hurry and confusion, as if his death was a grave crime which his family should obliterate from the record. What can I say except that Thaila died and Thaila was buried.'

My companion stopped speaking. The train was moving at breakneck speed. Suddenly I felt as if the clickety-clack of its powerful wheels was intoning the words 'Thaila died, Thaila buried . . . Thaila died, Thaila buried . . . Thaila died, Thaila buried.' There was no dividing line between his death and his burial. He had died and in the next instant he had been buried. 'You were going to say something,' I said to my companion.

'Yes,' he replied, 'yes . . . there is a sad part of the story which I haven't yet come to.'

'And what's that?'

'As I have already told you, he had two sisters, Shamshad and Almas, both very beautiful. Shamshad was tall, with fine features, big eyes, and she was a superb thumri singer. They say she had taken music lessons from the great Khan Sahib Fateh Ali Khan. Almas, the other one, was unmusical, but she was a fantastic dancer. When she danced it seemed as if every cell of her body was undulating with the music. Oh! They say there was a magic in her eyes which nobody could resist . . .

'Well, my friend, it is said that someone who was trying to make his number with the British told them about Thaila's sisters and how beautiful and gifted they were. So it was decided that to avenge the death of that English woman what was the name of that witch? Miss Sherwood I think . . . the two girls should be summoned for an evening of pleasure. You know what I mean.'

'Yes.'

'These are delicate matters, but I would say that when it comes to something like this, even dancing girls and prostitutes are like our sisters and mothers. But I tell you, our people have no concept of national honour. So, you can guess what happened.

'The police received orders from the powers that be and an inspector personally went to the house of the girls and said that the sahib log had expressed a desire to be entertained by them.

'And to think that the earth on the grave of their brother was still fresh. He hadn't even been dead two days and there were these orders: come and dance in our imperial presence. No greater torture could have been devised! Do you think that it even occurred to those who issued these orders that even women like Shamshad and Almas could have a sense of honour? What do you think?'

But he was speaking more to himself than to me. Nevertheless, I ventured, 'Yes, surely they too have a sense of honour.'

'Quite right. After all, Thaila was their brother. He hadn't lost his life in a gambling brawl or a fit of drunkenness. He had volunteered to drink the cup of martyrdom like a valiant national hero.

'Yes, it's true he was born of a prostitute, but a prostitute is also a mother and Shamshad and Almas were his sisters first and dancing girls later. They had fainted when they had brought Thaila's bullet-ridden body home, and it was heart-breaking to hear them bewail the martyrdom of their brother.'

'Did they go?' I asked.

My companion answered after a pause, 'Yes, yes, they went all right. They were dressed to kill.' There was a note of bitterness in his voice.

'They went to their hosts of the evening and they looked stunning. They say it was quite an orgy. The two sisters displayed their art with fascinating skill. In their silks and brocades they looked like the fairy queens of Mt Caucasus. There was much drinking and merrymaking and they danced and sang all night.

'And it is said that at two in the morning the guest of honour indicated that the party was over.'

'The party was over, the party was over' the wheels intoned as the train ran headlong along the tracks. I cleared my mind of this intrusion and asked my companion, 'What happened then?'

Taking his eyes away from the passing phantasmagoria of trees and power lines, he said in a determined voice, 'They tore off their silks and brocades and stood there naked and they said . . . look at us . . . we are Thaila's sisters . . . that martyr whose beautiful body you peppered with your bullets because inside that body dwelt a spirit which was in love with this land yes, we are his beautiful sisters come, burn our fragrant bodies with the red-hot irons of your lust but before you do that, allow us to spit in your faces once.' He fell silent as if he did not wish to say any more.

'What happened then?'

Tears welled up in his eyes. 'They . . . they were shot dead.'

I did not say anything. The train stopped. He sent for a porter and asked him to pick up his bags. As he was about to leave, I said to him, 'I have a feeling that the story you have just told me has a false ending.'

He was startled. 'How do you know?'

'Because there was indescribable agony in your voice when you reached the end.'

He swallowed. 'Yes, those bitches . . .' he paused, 'they dishonoured their martyred brother's name.'

He stepped onto the platform and was gone.

Translated by Khalid Hasan

The Woman in the Red Raincoat

THIS DATES BACK to the time when both East and West Punjab were being ravaged by bloody communal riots between Hindus and Muslims. It had been raining hard for many days and the fire which men had been unable to put out had been extinguished by nature. However, there was no let-up in the murderous attacks on the innocent, nor was the honour of young women safe. Gangs of young men were still on the prowl and abductions of helpless and terrified girls were common.

On the face of it, murder, arson and looting are really not so difficult to commit as some people think. However, my friend 'S' had not found the going so easy.

But before I tell you his story, let me introduce 'S.' He's a man of ordinary looks and build and is as much interested in getting something for nothing as most of us are. But he isn't cruel by nature. It is another matter that he became the perpetrator of a strange tragedy, though he did not quite realize at the time what was happening.

He was just an ordinary student when we were in school, fond of games, but not very sporting. He was always the first to get into a fight when an argument developed during a game. Although he never quite played fair, he was an honest fighter.

He was interested in painting, but he had to leave college after only one year. Next we knew, he had opened a bicycle shop in the city.

When the riots began, his was one of the first shops to be burnt down. Having nothing else to do, he joined the roaming bands of looters and arsonists, nothing extraordinary at the time. It was really more by way of entertainment and diversion than out of a feeling of communal revenge, I would say. Those were strange times. This is his story and it is in his own words.

'It was really pouring down. It seemed as if the skies would burst. In my entire life, I had never seen such rain. I was at home, sitting on my balcony, smoking a cigarette. In front of me lay a large pile of goods I had looted from various shops and houses with the rest of the gang. However, I was not interested in them. They had burnt down my shop but, believe me, it did not really seem to matter, mainly because I had seen so much looting and destruction that nothing made any sense any longer. The noise of the rain was difficult to ignore but, strangely enough, all I was conscious of was a dry and barren silence. There was a stench in the air. Even my cigarette smelt unpleasant. I'm not sure I was thinking even. I was in a kind of daze. Very difficult to explain. Suddenly a shiver ran down my spine and a powerful desire to run out and pick up a girl took hold of me. The rain had become even heavier. I got up, put on my raincoat and, fortifying myself with a fresh tin of cigarettes from the pile of loot, went out in the rain.

'The roads were dark and deserted. Not even soldiers – a common sight in those days – were around. I kept walking about aimlessly for hours. There were many dead bodies lying on the streets, but they seemed to have no effect on me. After some time, I found myself in the Civil Lines area. The roads were without any sign of life. Suddenly I heard the sound of an approaching car. I turned. It was a small Austin being driven at breakneck speed. I don't know what came over me, but I placed myself in the middle of the road and began to wave frantically for the driver to stop.

'The car did not slow down. However, I was not going to move. When it was only a few yards away, it suddenly swerved to the left. In trying to run after it, I fell down, but got up immediately. I hadn't hurt myself. The car braked, then skidded and went off the road. It finally came to a stop, resting against a tree. I began to move towards it. The door was thrown open and a woman in a red raincoat jumped out. I couldn't see her face, but her shimmering raincoat was visible in the murky light. A wave of heat gripped my body.

'When she saw me moving towards her, she broke into a run. However, I caught up with her after a few yards. "Help me," she screamed as my arms enveloped her tightly, more her slippery raincoat than her, come to think of it.

'"Are you a Englishwoman?" I asked her in English, realizing too late that I should have said 'an', not 'a'.

'"No," she replied.

'I hated Englishwomen, so I said to her, "Then it's all right."

'She began to scream in Urdu, "You're going to kill me. You're going to kill me."

'I said nothing. I was only trying to guess her age and what she looked like. The hood of her raincoat covered her face. When I tried to remove it, she put both her hands in front of her face. I didn't force her. Instead, I walked towards the car, opened the rear door and pushed her in. I started the car and the engine caught. I put it in reverse and it responded. I steered it carefully back on to the road and took off.

'I switched off the engine when we were in front of my house. My first thought was to take her to the balcony, but I changed my mind, not being sure if she would willingly walk up all those stairs. I shouted for the houseboy. "Open the living room door," I told him. After he had done that, I pushed her into the room. In the dark, I caught hold of her and gently pushed her onto the sofa.

'"Don't kill me. Don't kill me please," she began to scream.

'It sounded funny. In a mock-heroic voice I said, "I won't kill you. I won't kill you, darling."

'She began to cry. I sent the servant, who was still hanging around, out of the house. I pulled out a box of matches from my pocket, but the rain had made it damp. There hadn't been any power for weeks. I had a torch upstairs but I didn't really want to bother. "I'm not exactly going to take pictures that I should need a light," I said to myself. I took off my raincoat and threw it on the floor. "Let me take yours," I suggested to her.

'I fumbled for her on the sofa but she wasn't there. However, I wasn't worried. She had to be in the room somewhere. Methodically, I began to comb the place and in a few minutes I found her. In fact, we had a near collision on the floor. I touched her on the throat by accident. She screamed. "Stop that," I said. "I'm not going to kill you."

'I ignored her sobbing and began to unbutton her raincoat, which was made of some plastic material and was very slippery. She kept wailing and trying to struggle free, but I managed to get her free of that silly coat of hers. I realized that she was wearing a sari underneath. I touched her knee and it felt solid. A violent electric current went through my entire body. But I didn't want to rush things.

'I tried to calm her down. "Darling, I didn't bring you here to murder you. Don't be afraid. You are safer here than you would be outside. If you want to leave, you are free to do so. However, I would suggest that as long as these riots last, you should stay here with me. You're an educated girl. Out there, people have become like wild beasts. I don't want you to fall into the hands of those savages."

'"You won't kill me?" she sobbed.

'"No sir," I said.

'She burst out laughing because I had called her sir. However, her laughter encouraged me. "Darling, my English is rather weak," I said with a laugh.

'She did not speak for some time. Then she said, "If you don't want to kill me, why have you brought me here?"

'It was an awkward question. I couldn't think of an answer, but I heard myself saying, "Of course I don't want to kill you for the simple reason that I don't like killing people. So why have I brought you here? Well, I suppose because I'm lonely."

'"But you have your live-in servant."

'"He is only a servant. He doesn't matter."

'She fell silent. I began to experience a sense of guilt, so I got up and said, "Let's forget about it. If you want to leave, I won't stop you."

'I caught hold of her hand, then I thought of her knee which I had touched. Violently, I pressed her against my chest. I could feel her warm breath under my chin. I put my lips on hers. She began to tremble. "Don't be afraid, darling. I won't kill you," I whispered.

'"Please let me go," she said in a tremulous voice.

'I gently pulled my arms away, but then on an impulse I lifted her off the ground. The flesh on her hips was extremely soft, I noticed. I also found that she was carrying a small handbag. I laid her down on the sofa and took her bag away. "Believe me, if it contains valuables, they will be quite safe. In fact, if you like, there are things I can give you," I told her by way of reassurance.

'"I don't need anything," she said.

'"But there is something I need," I replied.

'"What?" she asked.

'"You," I answered.

'She didn't say anything. I began to rub her knee. She offered no resistance. Feeling that she might think I was taking advantage of her helplessness, I said, "I don't want to force you. If you don't want it, you can leave, really."

'I was about to get up, when she grabbed my hand and put it on her breast. Her heart was beating violently. I became excited. "Darling," I whispered, taking her into my arms again.

'We began to kiss each other with reckless abandon. She kept cooing "darling" and God knows what nonsense I myself spoke during that mad interlude.

'"You should take those things off," I suggested.

'"Why don't you take them off yourself?" she answered in an emotional voice.

'I began to caress her. "Who are you?" she asked.

'I was in no mood to tell her, so I said, "I am yours, darling."

'"You're a naughty boy," she said coquettishly, while pressing me close to her. I was now trying to take off her blouse, but she said to me, "Please don't make me naked."

'"What does it matter? It's dark," I said.

'"No, no!"

'She lifted my hands and began to kiss them. "No, please no. I just feel shy."

'"Forget about the blouse," I said. "It's all going to be fine."

'There was a silence, which she broke. "You're not annoyed, are you?"

'"No, why should I be? You don't want to take off your blouse, so that's fine, but . . ." I couldn't complete the sentence, but then with some effort, I said, "But anyway something should happen. I mean, take off your sari."

'"I am afraid." Her throat seemed to have gone dry.

'"Who are you afraid of?" I asked flirtatiously.

'"I am afraid," she replied and began to weep.

'"There is nothing to be afraid of," I said in a consoling voice.

'"I won't hurt you, but if you are really afraid, then let's forget about it. You stay here for a few days and, when you begin to feel at home and are not afraid of me any longer, then we'll see."

'"No, no," she said, putting her head on my thighs. I began to comb her hair with my fingers. After some time, she calmed down, then suddenly she pulled me to her with such force that I was taken aback. She was also trembling violently.

'There was a knock at the door and streaks of light began to filter into the dark room from outside.

'It was the servant. "I have brought a lantern. Would you please take it?"

'"All right," I answered.

'"No, no," she said in a terrified, muffled voice.

'"Look, what's the harm? I will lower the wick and place it in a corner," I said.

'I went to the door, brought the lantern in and placed it in a corner of the room. Since my eyes were not yet accustomed to the light, for a few seconds I could see nothing. Meanwhile, she had moved into the farthest corner.

'"Come on now," I said, "we can sit in the light and chat for a few minutes. Whenever you wish, I will put the lantern out."

'Picking up the lantern, I took a few steps towards her. She had covered her face with her sari. "You're a strange girl," I said, "after all, I'm like your bridegroom."

'Suddenly there was a loud explosion outside. She rushed forward and fell into my arms. "It's only a bomb," I said. "Don't be afraid. It's nothing these days."

'"My eyes were now beginning to get used to the light. Her face began to come into focus. I had a feeling that I had seen it before, but I still couldn't see it clearly.

'I put my hands on her shoulders and pulled her closer. God, I can't explain to you what I saw. It was the face of an old woman, deeply painted and yet lined with creases. Because of the rain, her make-up had become patchy. Her hair was coloured, but you could see the roots, which were white. She had a band of plastic flowers across her forehead. I stared at her in a state bordering on shock. Then I put the lantern down and said, "You may leave if you wish."

'She wanted to say something, but when she saw me picking up her raincoat and handbag, she decided not to. Without looking at her, I handed her things to her. She stood for a few minutes staring at her feet, then opened the door and walked out.'

After my friend had finished his story, I asked him, 'Did you know who that woman was?'

'No,' he answered.

'She was the famous artist Miss "M,"' I told him.

'Miss "M,"' he screamed, 'the woman whose paintings I used to try to copy at school?'

'Yes. She was the principal of the art college and she used to teach her women students how to paint still lifes. She hated men.'

'Where is she now?' he asked suddenly.

'In heaven,' I replied.

'What do you mean?' he asked.

'That night when you let her out of your house, she died in a car accident. You are her murderer. In fact, you are the murderer of two women. One, who is known as a great artist, and the other who was born from the body of the first woman in your living room that night and whom you alone know.'

My friend said nothing.

Translated by Khalid Hasan

The Last Salute

THIS BATTLE for Kashmir was nothing like any other battle. It had confused Subedar Rub Nawaz so much that he couldn't think clearly. He felt as though he had turned into a rifle, but one whose trigger was jammed.

He had fought on so many fronts in the last Great War and knew how to kill and be killed. All the high- and low-ranking officers regarded him with admiration and respected his wits, daring and pluck. The platoon commanders always assigned him the most hazardous duty and he never failed to live up to their expectations. But this battle . . . it was so strange. He had joined it with great fervour and passion, obsessed with the single thought – annihilate the enemy at any cost. But when he confronted the enemy, he saw familiar faces. Some had once been his friends, his bosom buddies in fact. They had fought alongside him against the enemies of the Allied forces, but now they seemed to have become sworn enemies hell-bent on killing him.

Sometimes it all seemed like images in a dream: the declaration of the last Great War, enlistment, the usual physical tests, target practice, being packed off to the front and moved from one theatre of war to another, and, finally, the war's end. And close upon its heels the creation of Pakistan, followed immediately by the Kashmir war – so many events occurring in dizzying succession. Could it be that all this was done to confound people, to prevent them from taking the time to grasp it all? Why else would all these momentous events occur so rapidly that it made your head spin?

Subedar Rub Nawaz understood one thing: They were fighting to win Kashmir. Why did they need to win Kashmir? Its annexation was vital for the survival of Pakistan. But as he took aim to shoot and a familiar face appeared on the opposite side, he forgot for a moment why they were fighting, why he had lifted his gun and aimed. At such times he had to remind himself repeatedly that he was no longer fighting for wages, a parcel of land or medals, but for his country. But this was his country before too, wasn't it? He belonged to this same region that had now been included in Pakistan. Now he had to fight the very person who, not long ago, had been his countryman – why even his next-door neighbour, and their two families had been bonded for generations. All of a sudden that man's country had become an alien piece of land where he had never set foot before, whose water he had never tasted. He had been given a gun and ordered, 'Go fight for this land where you still haven't set up your home, acquired a taste for its water or gotten used to the feel of its air. Go fight Pakistan – where you've lived so many years of your life.'

Rub Nawaz's thoughts drifted off to the Muslim soldiers who had been forced to abandon their homes and property to come here. Whatever they owned had been taken away. And what had they found here? Nothing, except guns, of the same weight and calibre, even the same make.

Whereas before they had fought together against a common enemy, whom they had merely imagined to be their enemy for the sake of their stomachs and rewards and recognition, now they had themselves split into two groups. They were no longer Indian soldiers, but Indian and Pakistani soldiers. The thought that there were still Muslim soldiers back in India flummoxed his mind, and when he thought about Kashmir his mind became even more muddled. It just refused to think further. Were Pakistanis fighting for Kashmir or for Kashmiri Muslims? If the latter, why not also fight for the Muslims of Hyderabad and Junagarh? And if this was purely a war for Islam, why weren't other Muslim countries fighting alongside of them?

After thinking long and hard, Rub Nawaz concluded that these matters were far too subtle for the intelligence of an ordinary soldier, who needed to be a little thick in the head if he wanted to be a good soldier. It was best not to think about them. There were times, though, when his disposition got the better of him and he did pursue these thoughts furtively only to have a hearty laugh about his lapse.

The battle for control of the road that led from Muzaffarabad to Kiran had been raging along the banks of the Kishan Ganga for some time. It was a strange battle. At night, rather than the sound of bullets, a crescendo of abuses, each one smuttier than the last, rose from the neighbouring hills.

One evening, as Subedar Rub Nawaz was getting his platoon ready for a surprise assault, a barrage of obscenities shot up from a trench below their position. Initially he freaked out. It seemed as if a gang of afreets were jitterbugging and laughing raucously. 'Pig's ass,' he muttered. 'What the hell's going on?'

One member of his platoon responded with filthy abuse and said to Rub Nawaz, 'Subedar Sahib, the motherfuckers are swearing at us.'

At first, when he heard the provocative insults, Rub Nawaz thought of throwing himself headlong into the fray, but decided to hold back. His men couldn't stay quiet for very long. Soon they had had enough and began returning the enemy's noxious abuse with their own equally hideous invectives at the top of their lungs. It was a peculiar battle for Subedar Rub Nawaz. He tried a few times to restrain his men, but the profanities got so vicious it wasn't possible to hold back. Naturally the enemy couldn't be seen at night, but it also couldn't be spotted in the daylight because of the cover of thick vegetation. Only their foul abuse rose from the foothills, crashed against the rocks and melted into thin air. Rub Nawaz felt that his men's counter-abuses probably weren't making it all the way down to the valley but were simply evaporating overhead. This rattled his nerves and in a huff he ordered them to attack.

He noticed something rather peculiar about the hills. Some were densely covered with trees and vegetation on the upward slope and entirely barren on the downward, while others were the reverse, with tall, sturdy pines on the downward side. The needles on these pines were so damp that the boots of the soldiers lost all traction so his men kept slipping again and again.

On the hill occupied by the Subedar's contingent, the slope provided no cover as it was completely without trees or brush. It was obvious the attack would be quite hazardous, but his men, chomping at the bit to get even for the blistering obscenities hurled at them, were more than willing to go for it anyway. As it turned out, they were successful. Their losses included two men dead and four wounded. The enemy lost three men and the rest took to their heels, leaving their provisions behind.

The Subedar and his men were terribly disappointed that they were unable to capture even a single enemy soldier alive whom they would have treated to their choicest profanities for as long as they liked. However, they did succeed in capturing a major enemy fortification. Rub Nawaz immediately relayed the outcome of the attack to his platoon commander, Major Aslam, over the wireless and received his commendation.

Almost every hill had a pond at the top, including the one they had captured. This one was quite a bit larger than the others and had crystal-clear water. Everyone took a dip despite the frigid weather. Their teeth chattered, but they didn't care. They were still splashing when the sound of a gunshot rang through the valley. They all immediately dropped flat on the ground, completely naked. A little while later Subedar Rub Nawaz scanned the downward slope with his binoculars, but failed to spot the enemy hideout. As he was looking, another gunshot rang out. He saw smoke rising from a relatively low hill just beyond the bottom of the slope. Without delay he ordered his troops to open fire.

A volley of bullets rained down and was returned from the other side. Subedar Rub Nawaz tried to study the enemy position through his binoculars. Most likely they were huddled behind a pile of large stones but this provided scanty cover. He was sure they couldn't remain there much longer. The second any of them decided to make a move, they would come within range of his men's guns.

Firing continued for a while. Eventually he ordered his men to save their ammunition and shoot only when the enemy made a move and was exposed. Just then he noticed his naked body and muttered under his breath, 'Goddamn it . . . Without clothes, a man looks like an animal!'

Now and then the enemy fired a random bullet that was returned just as sporadically from this side. This silly game continued for two whole days. The weather had suddenly turned brutally cold, so cold that it froze your blood even in the daytime. Subedar Rub Nawaz got round after round of tea going to stay warm. The kettle was kept at a boil all the time, but they never took their eyes off the enemy. When one soldier had to move, another took the binoculars and kept watch.

A bone-piercing wind was gusting. When the soldier on the lookout said there was some surreptitious movement behind the stone fortification, Subedar Rub Nawaz took the binoculars himself and peered through them. He didn't detect any movement. Suddenly a call tore through the air, its echo ricocheting for a long time against the rocks in the clump of neighbouring hills. He couldn't make out what it was saying. He fired a shot in exchange. Once the echo of his fire had died out, the same voice rose again. Clearly, it was calling him. 'You pig's ass!' he shouted back. 'What do you want?'

'Don't call me bad names, brother,' the enemy shouted. Apparently he wasn't too far away.

Rub Nawaz looked at his men and repeated 'brother . . .' just as surprised as he was pissed off. Then he cupped his hands around his mouth and yelled, 'No brothers here, only your mottha's, fuckers.'

'Rub Nawaz,' a wounded voice rose quickly from the other side.

Rub Nawaz trembled.

The pained voice kept crashing against the hills, repeating 'Rub Nawaz

. . . Rub Nawaz' like a refrain, each with a different cadence, before it evaporated into the freezing air.

Rub Nawaz came around after a long time. 'Who might that be?' he said to himself, and then muttered, 'Pig's ass!'

He knew that the bulk of the Tithwal front was made up of troops from the old 6/9 Regiment; he had been one of them too. But the voice – whom did it belong to? Many people had been his close friends, and there were others he bore enmity towards on account of some personal matters, but who was this person who had taken his abuse to heart and was calling loudly to him? He brought the binoculars to his eyes and peered through them again. He couldn't see anyone in the sparse, swaying vegetation on the hill. He cupped his hands around his mouth again and blared, 'Who is it? This is Rub Nawaz . . . Rub Nawaz.'

And this 'Rub Nawaz' also kept bouncing off the rocks. 'Pig's ass!' he muttered again.

Instantly a voice boomed, 'It's me . . . it's Ram Singh.'

Rub Nawaz jumped, as if he wanted to leap over to the other side right away. 'Ram Singh,' he first said to himself, and then he screamed at the top of his voice, 'Ram Singh! Hey you, Ram Singha . . . Pig's ass!'

Before 'pig's ass' had time to crash against the hills and disappear altogether, Ram Singh's cracking voice shot up, 'You, potter's ass!'

Rub Nawaz fumed. With commanding presence, he looked at his troops and muttered, 'He's talking shit, pig's ass.' And then he retorted to Ram Singh, '*Oaye, Baba Tal ke karah parshad – Oaye, khinzeer ke jhatke!*'

Ram Singh started to laugh uncontrollably, and so did Rub Nawaz. The hills tossed their exchange playfully back and forth. Subedar Rub Nawaz's men were dead silent.

When the hysterical bout of laughter subsided, Ram Singh's voice rose. 'Look, yaar, we'd like to drink some tea.'

'So drink. Have fun.'

'How can we have fun?' Ram Singh shouted. 'All our stuff is over there.'

'Over where?' Rub Nawaz asked.

'Over there, where your bullets can make us into mincemeat.'

Rub Nawaz laughed. 'So what do you want, pig's ass?'

'Just let us retrieve it.'

'All right, go get it.' Rub Nawaz looked at his men.

Ram Singh's anxious voice came back. 'You'll fire on us, potter's ass.'

An irritated Rub Nawaz shot back, 'Damn you, you lousy turtle, stop raving!'

Ram Singh let out a big laugh. 'Swear that you won't fire.'

'Swear by what?'

'By anyone, doesn't matter.'

'Okay, send someone out to grab your stuff,' Rub Nawaz said grinning.

Silence pervaded the atmosphere for a few moments. Rub Nawaz's man, who had the binoculars trained on the enemy, gave him a look and was about to fire when Rub Nawaz stopped him emphatically: 'No! Don't!'

He snatched the binoculars from the man's hand and squinted into them. He saw a man slithering out from behind the pile of stones and advancing gingerly on tiptoe. He walked like this for some distance and then suddenly took off at a gallop, disappearing quickly into the bushes. A couple of minutes later he emerged carrying some stuff in his hands. He stopped for a moment before bolting towards the makeshift fortification and slipping into the precarious safety of that buffer. The second he disappeared from sight, Rub Nawaz pulled the trigger of his gun. His loud laughter and the bullet's ping rose almost simultaneously, reverberating in the valley for a while, followed by Ram Singh's 'Thank you!'

'Don't mention it,' Rub Nawaz acknowledged. Then, looking at his men, he said, 'What do you say, shall we have a round?'

A few rounds of gunfire were exchanged playfully and then a hush fell over the landscape for some time. Rub Nawaz looked through the binoculars again and spotted a cloud of smoke curling up from the hill. 'So have you fixed your tea, Ram Singha?' he shouted.

'Not yet, potter's ass,' came the answer.

Rub Nawaz was a potter by caste. His blood boiled whenever anyone even vaguely hinted at his origins. Only with Ram Singh was it different. Rub Nawaz didn't let it get on his nerves with him because Ram Singh was a special chum of his. They had grown up in the same village and were born only a few days apart. Not just their fathers, even their grandfathers had enjoyed close, friendly ties. Rub Nawaz and Ram Singh had gone to the same primary school and enlisted in the army on the same day. In the last Great War they had fought side by side on several fronts.

Feeling embarrassed before his men, Rub Nawaz mumbled, 'Pig's ass, he never gets it up.' And then he hollered at Ram Singh, 'Don't go shooting off your mouth, you lice-infested donkey.'

Ram Singh's loud laugh shot through the air. Rub Nawaz had his gun aimed in the direction of the enemy and let it go off playfully. A scream tore through the air. He quickly peered into the binoculars and saw a man rise and hobble out from behind the stone bulwark, doubled over.

Holding his stomach, the man crumbled to the ground after going a short distance. It was Ram Singh.

'Ram Singh!' Rub Nawaz screamed and jumped to his feet. Immediately, three or four shots were fired from the other side. One bullet brushed past his right arm. He quickly threw himself on the ground facedown. His men started firing back but failed to hit the enemy, so he ordered them to attack. Three lost their lives within seconds but the rest kept advancing and, with great difficulty, finally managed to capture the other hill.

Ram Singh was lying on the rocky ground in a pool of blood, groaning. He had been hit in the stomach. A gleam appeared in his eyes when he saw Rub Nawaz. Smiling he said, 'You potter's ass, you did this . . . Whatever for?'

Rub Nawaz felt as if he was the one who had been shot in the stomach and was now writhing in agony. He smiled, bent over Ram Singh and started to unfasten his belt. 'Pig's ass, who asked you to stand up?'

As his belt was loosened, Ram Singh cried out from the intensity of the pain. Rub Nawaz examined the wound. It was very nasty. Ram Singh pressed Rub Nawaz's hand and mumbled in a feeble voice, 'I only got up to show myself to you and you fired, you son of a gun.'

'I fired just for the heck of it. I swear to God, the One and Only One,' Rub Nawaz said in a choking voice. 'I knew you, always an ass, were getting up . . . I'm so sorry.'

Ram Singh had lost a lot of blood. It had taken a few hours for Rub Nawaz and his men to get over here, long enough for Ram Singh to lose a whole bucket's worth of blood. Rub Nawaz was amazed that Ram Singh was still alive. He didn't expect him to last long. Moving him was out of the question. He got on the wireless and requested his platoon commander to dispatch a medic immediately; his friend Ram Singh had been wounded badly.

Rub Nawaz knew it would be impossible for the medic to arrive in time and that it was a matter of minutes before Ram Singh's life ebbed away. After sending the message he smiled and said to Ram Singh, 'The medic is on his way. Don't worry.'

In a sinking voice, Ram Singh's voice said pensively, 'Why would I worry . . . But tell me, how many of my men have you killed.'

'Only one.'

'And yours?' Ram Singh inquired still more feebly.

'Six,' Rub Nawaz lied, giving his men a meaningful look.

'Six . . . six,' Ram Singh counted in his heart. 'My men lost their spirit when I was wounded. But I told them to fight on, risking their lives . . . Six, yes.' Then his mind drifted off into a hazy past. 'Rub Nawaz . . . you remember those days, don't you?'

And he went down memory lane, talking about their childhood, their village, the stories of their schooldays and of their time in the 6/9 Jat Regiment, the jokes about their commanding officers and their affairs with strange women in foreign lands. Somewhere along the way he remembered something interesting and let out a big laugh, which sent a wave of excruciating pain through his body, but he paid no attention to it and said, still laughing, 'You, pig's balls, you remember that madam?'

'Which one?'

'The one in Italy. We used to call her . . . What was it now? Some woman she was, a real man-eater . . .'

Rub Nawaz remembered her right away. 'Yes, yes, that . . . Madame

Moneyto Finito, "no money, no action." But now and then she let you have a ride for less, that daughter of Mussolini.'

Ram Singh laughed loudly, some clotted blood gushing from his wound as a result. Rub Nawaz's makeshift bandage had slipped off. He secured it in place and admonished Ram Singh, 'Don't talk.'

Ram Singh was running a high fever and this made his brain work faster. Although he had no strength left, he was babbling on and on, stopping briefly now and then as if to check how much petrol was left in his tank. Soon afterward he lapsed into a delirium punctuated by moments of perfect lucidity. During one lucid moment, he asked Rub Nawaz, 'Yaar, tell me honestly, do you people really want Kashmir?'

Rub Nawaz replied in all earnestness, 'Yes, Ram Singha, we do.'

'No, no, I can't believe it. You've been taken for a ride.'

'No, it's you who's been taken for a ride,' Rub Nawaz said emphatically to convince him. 'I swear by Panchtan Pak.'

'No, yaar, don't swear.' Ram Singh grabbed his hand as he said, 'Maybe you're right.' But it was evident from his tone that he didn't believe Rub Nawaz.

Major Aslam, the platoon commander, arrived with some of his soldiers a little before sundown, but there was no medic. Floating between semi-consciousness and the throes of death, Ram Singh was babbling about something, but his voice was so weak and broken that it was difficult to make out his words. Major Aslam had also been part of the 6/9 Jat Regiment and knew Ram Singh quite well. He had Rub Nawaz tell him the details about what had transpired and then he called out, 'Ram Singh! Ram Singh!'

Ram Singh opened his eyes and came to attention still lying on the ground. He raised his arm with great difficulty and saluted. For a moment he looked at the major closely and then his rigid arm fell limply to his side. He started to murmur in visible irritation, 'O Ram Singha, you pig's balls, you forgot this is a war . . . a war . . .'

He couldn't finish. His slowly closing eyes looked at Rub Nawaz with bewilderment and then he turned cold.

Translated by Muhammad Umar Memon

archipelago books
is a not-for-profit literary press devoted to
promoting cross-cultural exchange through innovative
classic and contemporary international literature
www.archipelagobooks.org